The THREE KINGDOMS

VOLUME 1

The Sacred Oath

LUO GUANZHONG

Translated by YU SUMEI

Edited by RONALD C. IVERSON

TUTTLE Publishing

Tokyo | Rutland, Vermont | Singapore

Published by Tuttle Publishing, an imprint of Periplus Editions (HK) Ltd.

www.tuttlepublishing.com

Library of Congress Cataloging-in-Publication Data

Luo, Guanzhong, approximately 1330-approximately 1400.
  [San kuo chih yen i. Selections. English]
  The Three Kingdoms. Volume 1, The Sacred Oath, an epic Chinese tale of loyalty and war in a dynamic new translation / Lo Kuan-Chung ; translated by Yu Sumei ; edited by Ronald C. Iverson.
     414 pages ; 21 cm
   ISBN 978-0-8048-4393-5 (paperback) -- ISBN 978-1-4629-1437-1 (ebook) 1. China--History--Three Kingdoms, 220-265--Fiction. 2. Historical fiction. 3. Epic fiction. I. Yu, Sumei, translator. II. Iverson, Ronald C., editor. III. Title. IV. Title: Sacred Oath.
  PL2690.S3E543 2014
  895.13'46--dc23

                          2014015275

ISBN 978-0-8048-4393-5

Distributed by

North America,
Latin America & Europe
Tuttle Publishing
364 Innovation Drive
North Clarendon,
VT 05759-9436 U.S.A.
Tel: 1 (802) 773-8930
Fax: 1 (802) 773-6993
info@tuttlepublishing.com
www.tuttlepublishing.com

Asia Pacific
Berkeley Books Pte. Ltd.
3 Kallang Sector #04-01
Singapore 349278
Tel: (65) 6741-2178
Fax: (65) 6741-2179
inquiries@periplus.com.sg
www.tuttlepublishing.com

Japan
Tuttle Publishing
Yaekari Building 3rd Floor
5-4-12 Osaki Shinagawa-ku
Tokyo 141 0032
Tel: (81) 3 5437-0171
Fax: (81) 3 5437-0755
sales@tuttle.co.jp
www.tuttle.co.jp

25 24 23 22   11 10 9 8 7   2208TP
Printed in Singapore

Dedication

To my son, Winston, and my daughter, Aimee, who, from a toddler's age to adulthood, were thrilled with my telling and retelling of the stories from this great book.

With sincere gratitude to Yu Sumei for accepting the challenge to work with me to create a new translation of this classic literature with the goal of turning it into an exciting novel. My belief is that it is not just what you say but how you say it. My appreciation to Yu Sumei's daughter who typed out each page. They worked diligently for two years to produce a uniquely compelling version of this epic work, complete with footnotes for clarification of certain events and words in the text. My gratitude extends to a friend, Shen Li who was instrumental in recommending and introducing me to Yu Sumei.

And certainly a note of gratitude to Cheryl Banks for her suggestions as to improving the look of the book, as well as her many hours of help in preparing this text for printing which ultimately led to its publication.

No dedication would be complete without the mention of my many Chinese and American friends who encouraged me to continue this new translation and share it with the world. May readers enjoy the journey as much or beyond what we have experienced in the production of this classic, which will live in perpetuity.

Ronald C. Iverson

Contents

List of Main Characters

Cai Mao—brother-in-law of Liu Biao

Cao Cao (Cao Meng-de, A.D. 155–220)—prime minister to Emperor Xian, controls the real power of the state; later created Duke of Wei, Prince of Wei and posthumously, Emperor Wu of Wei Dynasty

Cao Hong—cousin of Cao Cao and senior officer under him

Cao Pi (A.D. 187–226)—second son of Cao Cao, later first emperor (Emperor Wen) of Wei Dynasty, which he established in A.D. 220

Cao Ren—cousin of Cao Cao and senior officer under him

Cao Rui—son of Cao Pi, later Emperor Ming of Wei

Cao Shuang—son of Cao Zhen, enemy of Sima Yi

Cao Zhen—senior officer of Wei

Cao Zhi (Cao Zi-jian, A.D. 192–232)—favorite son of Cao Cao and a famed poet

Chen Deng—advisor to Lu Bu but later plots his destruction

Chen Gong—chief advisor to Lu Bu

Chen Lin—notable scholar, first served as advisor to Yuan Shao but later surrendered to Cao Cao

Chen Wu—senior officer of Wu

Cheng Pu—senior officer of Wu

Cheng Yu—advisor to Cao Cao

Deng Ai—commander of the forces of Wei after Sima Yi

Dian Wei—bodyguard to Cao Cao

Diao Chan (Sable Cicada)—singing girl at Wang Yun's house, who helps her master destroy Dong Zhuo; concubine of Lu Bu

Ding Feng—senior officer of Wu

Dong Cheng—general of Han and relative to the imperial house, who receives the secret edict from Emperor Xian to assassinate Cao Cao

Dong Zhuo—governor of Hedong, later establishes himself as prime minister of Han; set up Emperor Xian in place of his brother, Emperor Shao, in order to build his own power

Emperor Shao (Liu Bian)—son of Emperor Ling and Empress He, deposed and murdered by Dong Zhuo

Emperor Xian (Liu Xie)—brother of Emperor Shao, a puppet ruler controlled by his ministers; deposed by Cao Pi in A.D. 220 (r. A.D. 189–220)

Empress Dowager He—mother of Emperor Shao, sister of He Jin; murdered by Dong Zhuo

Fa Zheng—Liu Zhang's official who helped Liu Bei acquire the rule of Shu

Feng Ji—advisor to Yuan Shao, enemy of Tian Feng

Gan Ning (Gan Xin-ba)—senior officer of Wu, famed for his bravery

Gao Shun—officer under Lu Bu

Gongsun Zan—patron of Liu Bei and one of the seventeen lords who join forces to wage war on Dong Zhuo; commits suicide after being destroyed by Yuan Shao

Guan Lu, famous sage

Guan Ping—adopted son of Guan Yu, killed by Sun Quan

Guan Xing—elder son of Guan Yu

Guan Yu (Guan Yun-chang, A.D. ?–219)—sworn brother of Liu Bei and Zhang Fei, Lord of Hanshou, famed for his valor and rectitude; respected greatly by Cao Cao

Guo Jia (Guo Feng-xiao)—trusted advisor to Cao Cao

Guo Si—fellow rebel with Li Jue after the downfall of Dong Zhuo

Guo Tu—advisor to Yuan Shao and later to his eldest son Yuan Tan

Han Dang—senior officer of Wu

Han Sui—warrior from the northwest, sworn brother of Ma Teng

He Jin—brother of Empress Dowager He and commander of Han forces; murdered by eunuchs

Hua Tuo—famous physician who cures Zhou Tai and Guan Yu; killed by Cao Cao

Hua Xin—senior official under Cao Cao and Cao Pi, notorious for his cruelty toward Empress Fu

Huang Gai (Huang Gong-fu)—senior officer of Wu, whose false defection to Cao Cao plays a key role in the Battle of the Red Cliff

Huang Zhong (Huang Han-sheng)—veteran warrior, joins Liu Bei after the latter's seisure of Changsha

Huang Zu—commanding officer under Liu Biao

Ji Ling—commanding officer under Yuan Shu

Ji Ping—physician of Han court, killed by Cao Cao after failing to poison him

Jia Xu—resourceful strategist, advisor first to Li Jue and Guo Si, then to Zhang Xiu, and finally to Cao Cao

Jian Yong—advisor to Liu Bei

Jiang Gan—official under Cao Cao, an old friend of Zhou Yu's

Jiang Wei (Jiang Bo-yue)—successor to Zhuge Liang as commander-in-chief of Shu forces

Kan Ze—senior advisor of Wu, who delivers Huang Gai's false letter of defection to Cao Cao

Kong Rong—notable Han scholar, descendant of Confucius, Prefect of Beihai; later killed by Cao Cao for his outspokenness

Kuai Yue—advisor to Liu Biao

Lady Cai—second wife of Liu Biao, sister of Cai Mao

Lady Gan—wife of Liu Bei, mother of Liu Shan (A Dou)

Lady Liu—wife of Yuan Shao and mother of Yuan Shang

Lady Mi—wife of Liu Bei, sister of Mi Zhu and Mi Fang

Lady Sun—wife of Liu Bei and sister of Sun Quan

Li Dian—officer under Cao Cao

Li Jue—chief rebel after the downfall of Dong Zhuo

Liao Hua—officer of Shu under Guan Yu

Lin Tong—officer of Wu

Liu Bei (Liu Xuan-de, A.D. 161–223)—descendant of the imperial house, sworn brother of Guan Yu and Zhang Fei, later Prince of Hangzhong and first ruler of the kingdom of Shu

Liu Biao (Liu Jin-sheng, A.D. 142–208)—Prefect of Jingzhou, who gives shelter to Liu Bei and leaves in his care his two sons, Liu Qi and Liu Zong

Liu Qi—elder son of Liu Biao; hated by his stepmother Lady Cai

Liu Shan (A Dou, A.D. 207–271)—eldest son of Liu Bei, second ruler of Shu (r. A.D. 223–263)

Liu Ye—senior advisor to Cao Cao

Liu Zhang—Governor of Yizhou, later overthrown by his kinsman Liu Bei

Liu Zong—younger son of Liu Biao; killed with his mother, Lady Cai, by Cao Cao

Lu Bu (Lu Feng-xian)—valiant warrior, adopted son first of Ding Yuan and later of Dong Zhuo, both of whom die at his hands; killed by Cao Cao

Lu Meng (Lu Zi-ming)—senior officer of Wu; succeeds Lu Su as commander-in-chief of forces

Lu Shang—chief counselor to King Wen of Zhou and his son King Wu, who founded the Zhou Dynasty

Lu Su (Lu Zi-jing)—chief advisor of Wu, successor to Zhou Yu as commander-in-chief; advocates alliance with Liu Bei against Cao Cao

Lu Xun (Lu Bo-yan)—son-in-law of Sun Ce; succeeds Lu Meng as commander-in-chief of Wu forces to foil Liu Bei's attack

Lu Zhi—Han general who commands an imperial force in the suppression of the Yellow Turban Uprising

Ma Chao (Ma Meng-qi)—son of Ma Teng, later one of Liu Bei's Five Tiger Generals

Ma Dai—cousin of Ma Chao, officer of Shu

Ma Liang—advisor to Liu Bei, brother of Ma Su

Ma Su (Ma You-chang)—advisor to Liu Bei, younger brother of Ma Liang; put to death after the fall of Jieting

Ma Teng—Han general, loyal to the House of Han; killed by Cao Cao

Man Chong—advisor to Cao Cao, who persuades Xu Huang to submit to Cao Cao

Meng Da—good friend of Fa Zheng and Zhang Song; assists Liu Bei in conquering Shu

Mi Fang—brother of Lady Mi and Mi Zhu, who fails to rescue Guan Yu and is later killed by Liu Bei

Mi Zhu—brother of Lady Mi and Mi Fang, loyal follower of Liu Bei

Pan Zhang—senior officer under Sun Quan

Pang De—formerly serves under Ma Chao but later joins Cao Cao; killed by Guan Yu

Pang Tong (Pang Shi-yuan, or Phoenix Fledgeling)—chief strategist in the Battle of the Red Cliff and later advisor to Liu Bei

Shen Pei—advisor to Yuan Shao, and later his youngest son Yuan Shang

Sima Yan—grandson of Sima Yi; first emperor of Jin Dynasty after forcing the abdication of Cao Huan, last emperor of Wei Dynasty

Sima Yi (Sima Zhong-da)—advisor to Cao Cao, father of Sima Zhao, who later overthrows Wei Dynasty and establishes Jin Dynasty

Sima Zhao—son of Sima Yi, father of Sima

Sun Ce (Sun Bo-fu, A.D. 175–200)—eldest son of Sun Jian, brother of Sun Quan; enlarges the territory he inherits from his father east of the Yangtze River; later assassinated

Sun Jian (Sun Wen-tai, A.D. 155–191)—founder of Wu and father of Sun Ce and Sun Quan; killed by Liu Biao's men

Sun Qian—senior counselor to Liu Bei

Sun Quan (Sun Zhong-mou, A.D. 182–252)—second son of Sun Jian and brother of Sun Ce; succeeds them to be ruler of the land of Wu and later Emperor of Wu (r. A.D. 229–252)

Taishi Ci—valiant warrior of Wu

Tao Qian—Prefect of Xuzhou, who yields his district to Liu Bei

Tian Feng—advisor to Yuan Shao

Wang Ping—officer of Shu

Wang Yun—senior official of the Han court, who instigates the "chain" scheme to destroy Dong Zhuo, but is later killed by Li Jue and Guo Si

Wei Yan (Wei Wen-chang)—senior officer under Liu Bei, later commander of Hanzhong; distrusted by Zhuge Liang

Wen Chou—general under Yuan Shao, slain by Guan Yu

Xiahou Ba—son of Xiahou Yuan, cousin of Xiahou Dun

Xiahou Dun—senior officer in the service of Cao Cao

Xiahou Yuan—senior officer in the service of Cao Cao; later killed by Huang Zhong

Xu Chu—bodyguard of Cao Cao

Xu Huang—senior officer in the service of Cao Cao

Xu Sheng—senior officer of Wu

Xu You—advisor first to Yuan Shao and later to Cao Cao; killed by Xu Chu

Xun You—advisor to Cao Cao, nephew of Xun Yu

Xun Yu (Xun Wen-ruo)—senior advisor to Cao Cao

Yan Liang—general under Yuan Shao, slain by Guan Yu

Yang Feng—officer under Li Jue, but later leaves him to serve Emperor Xian; killed by Liu Bei

Yi Ji—advisor to Liu Biao first, but later joins Liu Bei, to whom he exposes Cai Mao's plot to harm him

Yu Fan—advisor to Sun Quan

Yu Jin—senior officer under Cao Cao

Yuan Shang—youngest son of Yuan Shao

Yuan Shao (Yuan Ben-chu, A.D. ?–202)—born into a family of high-ranking officials of Han; leader of a confederacy army against Dong Zhuo; rules four northern districts but is later destroyed by Cao Cao

Yuan Shu (Yuan Gong-lu, A.D. ?–199)—brother of Yuan Shao, assumes the title of emperor at Shouchun but is soon destroyed by Cao Cao

Yuan Tan—eldest son of Yuan Shao

Yue Jin—senior officer under Cao Cao

Zhang Ba—officer under Lu Bu

Zhang Bao—son of Zhang Fei

Zhang Fei (Zhang Yi-de, A.D. ?–221)—sworn brother of Liu Bei and Guan Yu; courageous warrior, fiery-tempered after drinking

Zhang He—senior officer under Yuan Shao but later joins Cao Cao

Zhang Liao (Zhang Wen-yuan)—formerly served under Lu Bu but later surrendered to Cao Cao; friend of Guan Yu

Zhang Lu—ruler of Hanzhong; later defeated by Cao Cao

Zhang Song—official of Shu, but secretly persuades Liu Bei to kill his old master and take his land

Zhang Xiu—one of the feudal lords

Zhang Zhao—chief counselor to Sun Quan

Zhao Yun (Zhao Zi-long)—warrior of unusual strength and resourcefulness; loyal follower of Liu Bei

Zhong Hui—commander of Wei

Zhong Yao—senior official of Wei

Zhou Tai—senior officer under Sun Quan

Zhou Yu (Zhou Gong-jin)—commander-in-chief of the forces of Wu, who directs the Battle of the Red Cliff against Cao Cao; rival of Zhuge Liang

Zhu Jun—Han general

Zhuge Jin—elder brother of Zhuge Liang, advisor to Sun Quan

Zhuge Ke—officer of Wu, son of Zhuge Jin

Zhuge Liang (Kongming, or Sleeping Dragon, A.D. 181–234)—hermit of Nangyang, later chief counselor to Liu Bei; his ingenious policy of uniting Wu to oppose Wei leads to the emergence of the balance of power among the three kingdoms of Wei, Shu, and Wu; his wisdom and military skill enable Liu Bei to set up his own rule

Zhuge Zhan—son of Zhuge Liang

The Immortal by the River

Waves upon waves the Yangtze River rushes on its eastbound way,
Its white crests wash away all the heroes, gallant and brave.
Right or wrong, triumph or defeat, all is forgotten in the blink of an eye.
What remains only are the hills, so green,
And the glow of the sunsets, so red.

On the river banks come the white-haired fisherman and woodsman.
Enough have they witnessed spring wind and autumn moon.
Over a jar of wine, they rejoice at their happy meeting.
And so many great events of past and present
Serve as but food for their talk and laughter.

Yang Shen (1488–1559)

———————◄o►———————

Three Heroes Swear Brotherhood
at a Feast in the Peach Garden
The Sworn Brothers Render Good Services
in Fighting Against the Rebels

———————◄o►———————

U nity succeeds division and division follows unity. One is bound to
be replaced by the other after a long span of time. This is the way
with things in the world. At the end of the Zhou Dynasty* the empire was divided into seven competing principalities, warring against one
another till finally they were united by Qin.† When Qin had fulfilled its
destiny, there arose Chu‡ and Han§ to contend for the reign, and ultimately it was Han that united the country.

The rise of the fortunes of the Hans began when Liu Bang, later its first
emperor, slew the white serpent and staged an uprising against Qin. After seven years of fighting he succeeded in gaining control of the whole
empire and the Han Dynasty ruled the land for more than two centuries.
Then their power weakened and the empire was lost for a brief period of
time to a usurper. Later, it was Emperor Guang Wu¶ that restored the line
of Han—which continued for another century or more until the reign of
Emperor Xian, when the empire was divided into three parts, known to
history as The Three Kingdoms.**

In fact, the trouble started in the reigns of the two previous emperors,

---

*   841–256 B.C.

†   221–206 B.C.

‡   Headed by Xiang Yu (232–202 B.C.) who, though more powerful in military strength, was
     defeated by his rival Liu Bang of Han.

§   Headed by Liu Bang (256–195 B.C.) who established Han Dynasty, composed of West Han
     (206 B.C.–A.D. 8) and East Han (A.D. 25–220).

¶   Guang Wu (6 B.C.–A.D. 57), founder of East Han Dynasty, who restored the rule of Han
     after destroying the usurper Wang Mang (45 B.C.–A.D. 23).

**   Referring to the three kingdoms of Wei, Shu (Han), and Wu, reigning from A.D. 220–280.

Huan and Ling. The former prohibited many upright men from holding office, but trusted the palace eunuchs. When Emperor Ling inherited the throne, he was aided by General Dou Wu and Grand Tutor Chen Fan. Disgusted with the way the eunuchs meddled in state affairs, these two men planned their destruction. Unfortunately, the secret leaked out and they fell victims instead. From that time the eunuchs became even more powerful.

The signs of impending trouble were many. On the day of the full moon in the fourth month of the second year of the period of Jian Ning, Emperor Ling went to Wende Hall. As he drew near his seat, a strong gust of wind arose in the corner of the hall, and from the roof beams flew down a monstrous green serpent that coiled itself up on his seat. The Emperor fell in a swoon and his attendants hastily bore him to the palace, while all the officials in the hall fled away. In a moment, the serpent disappeared. However, there followed a mighty storm with torrential rain, thunder, and hail, lasting till midnight and destroying countless houses. During February two years later, an earthquake erupted in the capital Luoyang, while along the coast heavy flooding claimed the lives of all those who lived near the sea. Another evil omen was recorded seven years later when the reigning title was changed to Guang He: certain hens suddenly developed male characteristics. At the new moon of the sixth month that year, a long column of black vapor descended into Wende Hall, while in the following month a pale-colored rainbow was seen in the Jade Chamber. Far from the capital in the district of Wuyuan, mountains collapsed and riverbanks cracked.

Such were some of the evil omens. The Emperor, greatly upset by these signs of the displeasure of Heaven, issued an edict asking his ministers for an explanation of the calamities and aberrations. Cai Yong, one of the ministers, presented a memorial in which he stated that the sight of the pale-colored rainbow in the palace and the change of fowls' sexes were brought about by feminine interference in state affairs. The Emperor sighed when he read this. But, as he rose to change clothes, one of the chief eunuchs, from his place behind the throne, spied the document and later told his fellows of its contents. Before long a charge was trumped up against Cai Yong, who was driven from the court and forced to retire to the country. With this victory the eunuchs grew bolder. Ten of them, rivals in wickedness and associates in evil deeds, formed a powerful party known as The Ten. Their head, Zhang Rang, won such trust from his master that the Emperor even addressed him as Father. So the rule of the state deteriorated from day to day until the land was ripe for rebellion and swarmed with brigands.

At this time there lived in Julu three brothers of a certain Zhang family named Jue, Bao, and Liang. Zhang Jue was a scholar who had failed in a court exam for the selection of officials. One day, while collecting medicinal herbs in the mountains, he met an old man with very bright eyes and a fresh complexion who had a cane in his hand to help him in walking. Beckoning Zhang Jue into a cave, the old man gave him three volumes of the Book of Heaven and said, "This book is the Way of Peace. Now that you have got it, you must act in the name of Heaven and rescue mankind. If you should have evil thoughts, you will surely suffer a terrible punishment."

Zhang Jue knelt down as he took the book and asked the old man his name.

"I am the Immortal of the Southern Land of Glory," said the old man as he disappeared into thin air.

For days and nights Zhang Jue studied the book eagerly and strove to practice what it taught. Before long he could summon the wind and command the rain and came to be known as the Mystic of the Way of Peace.

In the first month of the reign of Zhong Ping a serious epidemic swept the land. Zhang Jue, calling himself the Wise and Good Master, distributed charmed remedies to cure people. At the same time he developed a following of more than five hundred disciples, all of whom had been taught to write and recite charms. They were sent to various parts of the country to spread his ideas. Later, as his disciples increased, Zhang Jue began to organize them into units, the larger ones with 10,000 or more members and the smaller ones with about 6–7,000 members. Each unit had its own chief who was given the title of General. They spread the rumor that the blue heavens were dead and the yellow ones were to be established. They said that a new cycle was beginning which would bring universal good fortune, and told people to chalk on their gates the two characters of *Jia Zi*, meaning the first year of a cycle. And all at once every household in eight regions, including Qingzhou and Youzhou in northern China had a memorial tablet made bearing the name of the Wise and Good Master Zhang Jue.

As his ambition for empire grew, Zhang Jue sent Ma Yuan-yi, one of his trusted supporters, to take gifts to the eunuch Feng Xu in order to plant allies in the palace. To his brothers Zhang Jue said: "The most difficult thing is to gain the popular support. Now that the people are already on our side, it'll be a great pity if we don't take this opportunity and establish our own empire."

So they began to make preparations. Many yellow flags were made in secret and a day was chosen to strike the first blow. They also sent the information by dispatch to Feng Xu through a disciple called Tang Zhou. However, Tang Zhou went straight to a government office and reported their plot. The Emperor summoned General He Jin and bade him look into it. He Jin immediately sent troops to capture Ma Yuan-yi and put him to death. Feng Xu and his accomplices were thrown into prison.

When the news reached the Zhang family, they decided to set forth at once. Assuming the grandiose titles of General of Heaven, General of Earth, and General of Mankind, they called their followers together and declared: "The good fortunes of the Han will soon run out and the Wise Man has emerged. You people should submit yourselves to the will of Heaven and join in a righteous cause. Only thus can you gain final peace."

Support was not lacking. As many as half a million people from every side bound their heads with a yellow turban and took part in the rebellion led by Zhang Jue. Soon, his strength became so great that the official troops fled at the mere whisper of his coming.

Back in the capital, General He Jin presented an urgent memorial to the Emperor, calling for all-out preparations against the rebels. An edict was issued immediately, asking every officer to exert himself in fighting against the rebels. In the meantime, three generals leading veteran soldiers were ordered to join forces in suppressing the rebels from three different directions.

At this time, however, Zhang Jue's army was marching toward Youzhou, whose prefect was Liu Yan, a descendant of the imperial house through a certain prince. On hearing of the approach of the rebels, he called in his chief officer Zou Jing for counsel.

"They are many but we are few, sir," said the officer. "You must enlist more men at once to oppose them."

The prefect saw this was true so he had notices put out, asking for volunteers to fight against the rebels. One of these notices was posted up in the district of Zhuo,* which caught the attention of a great man in that place. This man was not very studious but he was generous and kind. Being a man of few words, he controlled his feelings well, always maintaining a calm exterior. He was not reconciled to his fate but had always cherished high aspirations. Therefore, he liked nothing better than cultivating the friendship of men of substance. In appearance, he was tall of stature. He had exceptionally long ears, the lobes touching his shoulders so that his eyes could see his own ears. His arms were long, too, with his hands hanging down below his knees. He had a jade-like complexion and rich, red lips. His name was Liu Bei—or more commonly, Liu Xuan-de—

---

* A place near modern Beijing.

a descendant of Prince Jing of Zhongshan named Liu Sheng, whose father was Emperor Jing in West Han. Many years before, the prince's son had been governor of that very district, but had lost his rank for failing to present enough gold in court offerings. Therefore, this branch of the imperial house was left to survive in this place.

Liu Bei's grandfather was Liu Xiong and his father, Liu Hong. Noted for his devotion to his parents and austerity of lifestyle, Liu Hong had been promoted to the rank of an official, but unfortunately he had died when Liu Bei was still very young. The widow and orphan were left alone and as a lad, Liu Bei won a reputation for filial piety. At this time the family had sunk deep into poverty and he had to make a living by selling straw sandals and weaving mats. The family house was in a village near the city of Zhuo. To the southeast of their house stood a huge mulberry tree of great height, and seen from afar, its luxuriant foliage resembled the shape of a chariot. A soothsayer once predicted that a man of distinction would come forth from this family. As a child, Liu Bei and the other village boys often played beneath this tree and he would say, "When I'm emperor, I'll ride a chariot with such a canopy." Struck by the uniqueness of his words, his uncle recognized that he was no ordinary boy and saw to it that the family did not fall into a state of want.

When he was fifteen, his mother sent him traveling to different places for his education. For a time he served Zheng Xuan and Lu Zhi as masters and became friends with Gongsun Zan. He was already twenty-eight when the outbreak of the rebellion called for soldiers.

That day, after reading the notice, he sighed deeply. Suddenly a rasping voice behind him cried: "Noble sir, why do you only sigh but not do something for your country?" Turning around, he saw a man even taller than himself, with a bullet head like a leopard's, large round eyes, a pointed chin, and a bristling mustache. He had a thunderous voice and an imposing manner as powerful as a galloping steed. Impressed by the man's unusual appearance, Liu Bei asked him who he was.

"Zhang Fei is my name and I am usually called Yi-de," replied the man. "My family had always lived in this part of the country. We have a farm and some land here. I work as a wine seller and a butcher as well. I like to get acquainted with worthy men. Just now I heard you sigh as you read the notice, so I took the liberty to inquire."

To this Liu Bei said, "I am related to the imperial family. My name is Liu Bei. The country is now in great danger and I wish I could help wipe out these rebels and bring peace to the people. But as I am incapable of taking any action, I can only sigh."

"I am not without means," said Fei. "Suppose you and I called together some local men of courage to serve in the cause against the rebels. What do you say to that?"

This was really happy news to Liu Bei and the two went to the village inn to discuss the matter over drinks. After they had been drinking for some time they saw a big fellow pushing a cart to the gate of the inn. Then he came in and sat down by a table.

"Waiter, bring me wine quickly," he shouted. "I'm in a hurry to go to the city to offer myself to the army."

Liu Bei looked over the newcomer and noted his very tall stature, his long beard, his dark brown face, and his rich red lips. He had eyes like those of a phoenix and fine bushy eyebrows like sleeping silkworms. His whole appearance was dignified and awe-inspiring. Presently, Liu Bei went over to invite him to sit with them and asked him his name.

"My name is Guan Yu," he said, "I am also known as Yun-chang. I am a native of Xieliang, east of the river, but I have been a fugitive on the run for more than five years because I killed a ruffian. When I heard they needed soldiers to fight against the rebels here, I decided to offer myself to the army."

Guan Yu was overjoyed when Liu Bei told him of his intention. Then the three of them went together to Zhang Fei's farm to talk over their grand project.

"There is a peach garden at the back of my farm," said Zhang Fei. "The flowers are in full bloom at the moment. Let us institute a sacrificial offering and swear brotherhood and unity of hearts and mind before Heaven and Earth. Only thus can we embark upon our great mission."

"That is just what we think," agreed the other two.

So the next day, an altar was set up in the garden and sacrifices including a black ox, a white horse, and other things were prepared. Beneath the smoke of the burning incense, they knelt down and declared a solemn oath.

"We three, Liu Bei, Guan Yu, and Zhang Fei, though of different families, swear brotherhood and mutual help to one end. From now on, we will aid each other in difficulty and rescue each other in danger. We will serve the country and protect the people. We ask not the same day of birth but we are willing to die at the same time. May Heaven, the all-powerful, and Earth, the ever bountiful, read our hearts! If we break our oath or betray each other's trust, may Heaven and man smite us!"

After they had made the oath, they asked each other's ages. As Liu Bei was the oldest of the three, he became the respected eldest brother. Next came Guan Yu and Zhang Fei was the youngest of the trio. This solemn ceremony performed, they had more meat and wine prepared for a huge feast to which they invited over three hundred young men in the village. All of them drank to their hearts' content in the garden.

The following day weapons were mustered. But there were no horses for them to ride. Just as they were grieving over this, news came of the arrival of two horse dealers who were seeking shelter in the house. They had a group of attendants and a drove of horses with them.

"That surely is a blessing from Heaven!" cried Liu Bei. And the three brothers went forth to welcome the guests, who turned out to be big merchants from Zhongshan. Every year they went northwards to buy horses. They were now on their way home because of the rebellion. Liu Bei invited the two to the house and entertained them with food and drinks. Then he told them about the plan to defeat the rebels and protect the people. The two merchants were so pleased to hear it that they gave them 50 fine steeds, 500 taels of gold and silver, and 1,000 *jin** of steel to be used for the forging of arms.

After the merchants had taken their leave, Liu Bei immediately called in good armorers to make weapons for the three of them. They made Liu Bei double swords and Zhang Fei an eighteen-foot long steel spear. For Guan Yu they made a special sword called "Blue Dragon and Half Moon" or "Cold Beauty" with a long handle and a curved blade, weighing more than eighty catties. Each, too, had a helmet and full armor made to match. When all these were ready they led the troops, now five hundred strong, to the city to see Zou Jing, who presented them to Prefect Liu Yan. The three of them paid their respects to the prefect and told him their names. When Liu Bei mentioned his ancestry, Prefect Liu was very pleased and immediately accepted him as a relative.

Several days later, a messenger came with the news that a rebel army of 50,000 men was marching toward the city. Zou Jing and the three brothers were ordered to oppose them with 500 soldiers. Liu Bei and the others gladly undertook to lead the vanguard. At the foot of the Daxing Mountains they saw the rebels, who all wore their hair flying about their shoulders and had yellow turbans wrapped around their foreheads.

When the two armies had drawn up opposite each other, Liu Bei, with his two brothers, one on each side, rode to the front, and flashing his whip, began to hurl reproaches at the rebels and called upon them to surrender. Furious, the rebel leader sent out his chief officer to begin the battle. Zhang Fei at once rode forward, his long spear poised to strike. One thrust and the man rolled off his horse, pierced through the heart. At this

---

* One *jin* equals half a kilogram.

the leader himself whipped up his steed and rode forth, his sword raised high, ready to slay Zhang Fei. Immediately, out rushed Guan Yu, swinging his heavy weapon. At the sight of this the rebel leader was seized with fear and before he could collect his wits, the great sword fell, cutting him down from his horse.

Of this day, a poet wrote the following words:

> *Two heroes new to war's alarms,*
> *Ride boldly forth to try their arms.*
> *Their valiant deeds three kingdoms tell*
> *And poets sing how these befell.*

Seeing that their chief was slain, the rebels threw down their weapons and fled. The regular soldiers dashed in among them. Many thousands surrendered and the victory was complete. Liu Bei and his army returned to town in great triumph. The prefect himself came out to welcome the returning warriors and distribute rewards among officers and men. Thus this part of the rebellion was broken up.

However, the next day, a letter came from the Prefect of Qingzhou, saying that the city, besieged by rebel forces, was near falling and help was urgently needed. When Liu Yan consulted Liu Bei on the matter, the latter said, "I will go and rescue them." So Liu Yan told Zou Jing to take 5,000 soldiers and set out for Qingzhou with Liu Bei and his two brothers. Seeing the army approaching, the rebels at once sent out part of their forces to oppose them. Being smaller in number, Liu Bei's army could not prevail and had to retreat some thirty *li*,* where they made a camp.

"They are many but we are few," said Liu Bei to his two brothers. "We can only win by a superior strategy."

So he prepared an ambush. He told his two brothers to take a thousand men each and hide behind the hills right and left. At the sound of the gongs they were to move out to aid the main army.

The following day, Liu Bei and Zou Jing advanced with the remaining 3,000 soldiers amid the sound of the beating drums. When the rebels came forward to fight, Liu Bei suddenly retreated. Thinking this was their chance, the rebels pressed forward. But as soon as they were led over the hills, the gongs sounded and the two armies that had been lying in ambush rushed out from the flanks, and the main army also turned around to face the rebels. Attacked on three sides, the rebels lost heavily and were driven to the gate of the city, where they were further attacked by local forces, for the prefect also led out his soldiers to assist in the battle. The

---

* One *li* equals half a kilometer.

rebels were comprehensively defeated and many were slain. So the siege of Qingzhou was lifted at last.

> *Tho' fierce as tigers soldiers be,*
> *Battles are won by strategy.*
> *A hero comes; he gains renown,*
> *Already destined for a crown.*

After the celebrations in honor of the victory were over, Zou Jing proposed to return home, but Liu Bei preferred to go to the aid of his old master Lu Zhi, then struggling with a large number of rebels led by Zhang Jue. So they separated and the three brothers with their troops made their way to Guangzong. When they got there they were taken to see Lu Zhi in his camp. The general received them with great warmth when he learned about the reason of their coming, and asked them to remain with him in the camp while he deployed troops.

The rebel forces were then three times greater in number than the imperial army (150,000 against 50,000). So far they had been drawn up against each other in the place, with no significant victory on either side. "I am surrounding the rebels here," said Lu Zhi to Liu Bei, "but Zhang Jue's two brothers, Liang and Bao, are opposing Huangfu Song and Zhu Jun at Yingchuan. I will give you a thousand more men, and with these you can go and find out what is happening there so that we can settle on a date for joint action."

So Liu Bei and his men set out at once on a quick march to Yingchuan. At that time the imperial troops led by Huangfu Song and Zhu Jun were attacking with success and the rebels had withdrawn to Changshe, where they pitched camp by the thick grass. Seeing this, Huangfu Song decided to attack them by fire. So he ordered every soldier to prepare a bundle of dry grass and lie in ambush. That night a strong wind suddenly rose and just after midnight a blaze was started and the rebels were attacked. Fed by the strong wind, the flames went high into the sky. The rebels were thrown into utter confusion. There was no time for them to saddle horses or don armor and they fled in all directions. The battle continued till dawn. Zhang Liang and Zhang Bao, with what was left of their men managed to find a way of escape. Suddenly, however, a troop of soldiers with red banners confronted them and blocked their way. The leader was a man of medium stature with small eyes and a long beard whose name was Cao Cao, or more commonly, Cao Meng-de. He was from Qiaojun in Peiguo* holding the rank of an officer in the imperial army. His father

---

* A place in modern Anhui in East China.

was Cao Song, who had changed his family name from Xiahou to Cao because he was adopted by the eunuch Cao Teng. When Cao Cao was a child, he was also given the affectionate names of Ah-man and Ji-li.

As a young man Cao Cao had been fond of hunting and traveling, and delighted in songs and dances. He was resourceful and full of guile. Dissatisfied with the young man's idleness, his uncle used to get angry with him and told his father Cao Song of his misbehavior. As a result, he would be reproached by his father.

But the youth was equal to the occasion. One day, seeing his uncle coming, he dropped to the ground, pretending to be seized by a fit. Alarmed, the uncle ran to tell the young man's father, but when the latter hurried to Cao Cao's side, he found the youth in perfect health.

"Your uncle said you were in a fit. Are you better now?"

"I never have such illness," answered Cao Cao. "But I have lost my uncle's affection so he always speaks evil of me." From then on, whatever the uncle might say of his faults, his father paid no attention. So the young man grew up self-willed and uncontrolled.

At that time a certain man called Qiao Xuan said to Cao Cao: "Rebellion is at hand and only a man of the greatest ability can restore tranquillity to the land. That man is you."

Another person from Nanyang said this of him: "The House of Han is about to fall. He who can bring peace back to the people is none other than this man."

To inquire about his future, Cao Cao went to see a wise man in Runan. "What manner of man am I?" he asked. The seer made no reply. When Cao Cao put the question again, he replied, "You are capable enough to rule the world but wicked enough to bring trouble to it." Hearing this Cao Cao was extremely pleased.

At twenty he was recommended to be an official and he began his career in a district near Luoyang. As soon as he arrived at his post, he had clubs of various sorts hung up at the four gates of the city. Any breach of the law would be met with severe punishment, whatever the rank of the offender. One night, an uncle of a powerful eunuch was found walking in the street with a sword and was arrested. In due course the man was beaten. After that, no one dared to defy the law and Cao Cao's name began to spread. Later he became a magistrate.

At the outbreak of the rebellion he was created an officer and was given command of 5,000 soldiers to help fight at Yingchuan. He just happened to come across the newly defeated rebels, whom he cut to pieces. Many thousands were slain and countless banners, drums, and horses were captured. However, the two rebel leaders put up a desperate struggle and managed to get away. After an interview with Huangfu Song and Zhu Jun, Cao Cao went in pursuit of the rebels again.

We return now to Liu Bei and his two sworn brothers. On arriving at Yingchuan, they heard the din of battle and saw flames rising high toward the sky. They hastened to the spot but were too late for the fighting. So they went to see the two generals to inform them of Lu Zhi's intention.

"Zhang Liang and Zhang Bao have little strength left," said the two generals, "but they will surely make for Guangzong to join Zhang Jue. You'd better hurry back to help Lu Zhi."

The three brothers retraced their steps. Halfway on their journey they saw a group of soldiers escorting a prisoner in a cage-cart. When they drew near, they found to their great surprise that the prisoner was none other than Lu Zhi. Hastily dismounting, Liu Bei asked him what had happened. Lu Zhi explained, "I had surrounded Zhang Jue's troops and was on the verge of smashing them when he employed some of his supernatural tricks and I was prevented from winning an immediate victory. The Emperor sent down a eunuch to investigate my failure and that official demanded a bribe. I told him that the army did not even have enough grain to feed itself and asked him where, in the circumstance, I could find extra money for him. In resentment he reported to the Emperor that I was hiding behind my ramparts and would not give battle, and accused me of disheartening my men. Infuriated, the Emperor gave orders that I was to be taken to the capital to answer the charge and my army was to be commanded by a man called Dong Zhuo."

This story put Zhang Fei into a rage. He held up his long spear and was about to slay the escorting soldiers to free Lu Zhi when his eldest brother checked him.

"The government will take the proper course," he said. "You mustn't act too rashly." Then the soldiers took Lu Zhi away.

It was pointless to continue their journey. So Guan Yu proposed to go back to their hometown. Liu Bei agreed and they retook the road toward the north. They had not been two days on the road when they heard the thunder of battle behind some hills. Hastening to the top of a mound they saw the imperial soldiers suffering great loss and chasing after them were a whole army of Yellow Turbans, swarming from all around the place. On their banners were the words "General of Heaven" written in big characters.

"That's Zhang Jue," said Liu Bei. "Let's attack him, quick!" And they galloped down with their men to join in the battle.

Zhang Jue had defeated Dong Zhuo and was following up his victory, in hot pursuit of his retreating enemy, but the three brothers charged into his army, throwing his ranks into great confusion and driving him back some fifty *li* or more. The three of them rescued Dong Zhuo and returned with him to his camp.

"What offices do you hold now?" asked Dong Zhuo, when he had leisure to speak to the three brothers.

"None," replied Liu Bei. Dong Zhuo was contemptuous of them and brushed them aside with disrespect. Liu Bei retired quietly to the outside but Zhang Fei was furious.

"We've just rescued this wretch in a bloody fight," he cried, "and now he's so rude to us! Nothing but his death can slake my anger!"

So saying he took his sword and was all set to dash into the tent and slay the insulter.

> As it was in old times so it is now,
> True heroes may not to snobs be known.
> A blessing it'll be if Zhang Fei the bold
> Could slay all the ungrateful in the world.

Whether Dong Zhuo would be slain or not will be told in the next chapter.

CHAPTER TWO

Zhang Fei Thrashes the Inspector in Wrath
He Jin Plots to Kill the Eunuchs in Secret

——◄◦►——

Now this Dong Zhuo, also known as Dong Zhong-ying, was from Lintao in northwest China. An arrogant man by nature, he held the official rank of Prefect of Hedong. But that day his disrespectful manner toward the three brothers had angered Zhang Fei so much that he wanted to kill him.

"Remember he's a government official," said Liu Bei and Guan Yu, checking him hastily. "We've no right to slay him."

"It's bitter to take orders from such a wretch—I'd rather slay him," roared Zhang Fei. "You can stay here if you want but I'll seek some other place."

"We three are one in life and death, there is no parting for us," said Liu Bei. "We'll all go, then."

This put Zhang Fei in a better mood, and they decided to go back to Zhu Jun's place. They set out and lost no time in traveling till they came to Zhu Jun, who received them well and accepted their aid in attacking Zhang Bao.

At this time Cao Cao had joined Huangfu Song in fighting against Zhang Liang and a fierce battle was fought at Quyang. In the meantime, Zhu Jun was ready to attack Zhang Bao who had mustered an army of about 80–90,000 men positioned behind some hills. Liu Bei was made to be leader of the vanguard to confront the rebels. When the two armies were drawn facing each other, a subordinate officer from the rebels' side came out to offer battle. Liu Bei ordered Zhang Fei to smite him. Zhang Fei rode out at full speed, his spear ready to strike. After a few bouts he pierced his opponent, who fell from his horse. At this Liu Bei led his army to press forward. But just then, Zhang Bao, while still mounted, loosened his hair, held up his sword and uttered incantations. All of a sudden the wind began to howl and the thunder to roll. A dense black cloud from the sky settled upon the ground and an innumerable number of horsemen and footmen seemed to rush out of the cloud, charging at the imperial troops. Liu Bei immediately turned back but the soldiers were already scared and they returned defeated.

Liu Bei reported the matter to Zhu Jun, who said, "So he uses black magic. Tomorrow I will prepare the blood of slaughtered hogs, goats, and dogs as a counter magic.* Tell the soldiers to hide themselves at the hilltops, and when they see the enemies approach, sprinkle this blood over them. Then the black magic will lose its power."

Following Zhu Jun's order, Liu Bei gave his two brothers a thousand men each and told them to get ready a plentiful supply of the blood of hogs, goats, and dogs and all kinds of filthy things and hide themselves on the high ground behind some hills. The next day, when the rebels with fluttering banners and beating drums came out to challenge, Liu Bei rode forth to meet them. While the two armies were fighting, again Zhang Bao resorted to black magic and again there were high winds and loud thunder. Sand and stones were swept up and flew through the air. Black masses of vapor filled the sky and numerous troops descended from on high. Liu Bei turned, as before, to flee and Zhang Bao followed in hot pursuit. But just as the rebels were passing through the hills, trumpets sounded and the ambushed soldiers threw down filth and showered blood. Then the masses of troops in the air fluttered to the ground, revealing themselves as paper men and straw horses. At once the wind abated, the thunder ceased to roll, the sand sank, and the stones lay still on the ground.

Seeing that his magic had been countered, Zhang Bao quickly turned to retreat. But, attacked on the flanks by Guan Yu and Zhang Fei and in the rear by Liu Bei and Zhu Jun, his army was completely routed. Liu Bei, seeing from afar the banner bearing the title of "General of Earth", galloped toward it at full speed. Scared, Zhang Bao picked a side path and fled. Then Liu Bei shot an arrow, wounding Zhang Bao in the left arm. However, he still managed to get away into the city of Yangcheng, where he fortified himself and would not come out to fight.

Zhu Jun laid a siege outside the city. At the same time he sent out scouts to get news of Huangfu Song. The scouts returned with the following report: "Huangfu Song had won great victories and was given the command of Dong Zhuo's army by the Emperor because Dong Zhuo had suffered many defeats. When Huangfu Song arrived at Guangzong, Zhang Jue had already died and his brother Zhang Liang had added Jiao's army to his own in a vain attempt to confront the imperial troops. Huangfu Song had won seven successive victories and Zhang Liang was slain at

---

* Superstition has it that the blood of animals and filth can render black magic ineffective.

Quyang. Beside this, Zhang Jue had been exhumed, the corpse beheaded and the head, after exposure, had been sent to the capital. For these services Huangfu Song had been promoted to the rank of General of Carriage and Cavalry and now ruled the prefecture of Jizhou. Then he presented a memorial to the Emperor concerning the case of Lu Zhi, who was restored to his former rank after the Emperor learned that he had committed no crime but had rendered good service. Cao Cao, too, had received advancement for his services and would soon return from the front and go to his new post at Jinan."

After hearing these reports, Zhu Jun pressed even harder on the city of Yangcheng, putting the rebels in a desperate situation. Then one of Zhang Bao's officers killed the rebel leader and brought his head as a token of submission. So Zhu Jun was able to wipe out rebellion in that part of the country and a report was sent to the Emperor to announce the victory.

However, the embers still smoldered. Three remaining members of the Yellow Turban rebellion—Zhao Hong, Han Zhong, and Sun Zhong—again gathered an army of tens of thousands of men. They burned and looted as they went, calling themselves avengers of Zhang Jue. Zhu Jun was commanded to lead his victorious troops to destroy them.

So he at once set out toward Wancheng, which had fallen into the hands of the rebels. When he arrived, the rebels sent Han Zhong to oppose him. Zhu Jun asked Liu Bei and his two brothers to attack the city from the southwest. Han Zhong immediately rushed to the scene with the best of his men to confront them. Meanwhile, the general himself led 2,000 armored horsemen to attack it from the opposite direction. Afraid that the city might be lost, the rebels abandoned the southwest and turned back. Liu Bei pressed hotly in their rear, defeating them completely. The rebels took refuge behind the high walls of the city, which was surrounded on all sides by the imperial forces. Famine soon followed and in desperation the rebel leader sent out a messenger to offer surrender, but the offer was turned down by the general.

Liu Bei asked, "In the past, Emperor Gao-zu, founder of the Han Dynasty, welcomed and accepted those who surrendered, so he was able to rule the land. Why do you reject Han Zhong, sir?"

"The situations are different," replied Zhu Jun. "In those days disorder was everywhere and the people had no fixed lord. Therefore, submission was welcomed and those who surrendered were rewarded so as to encourage people to come over. Now the empire is united and the Yellow Turbans are the only malcontents. To allow brigands to plunder and rob when successful and to let them surrender when unsuccessful is to encourage brigandage. This is not a good policy."

"It is well not to let them surrender," said Liu Bei. "But the city is enclosed on all sides like an iron barrel. As their submission is refused, they will be desperate in their fight. A myriad of such men cannot be withstood. But in the city they are several times that number, all doomed to die. It is better to withdraw from the east and the south and only attack the west and the north. They will surely give up the place and flee, without much desire to fight. We can capture them then."

The general saw that the advice was good and followed it. He withdrew the troops from the east and the south and only attacked from the west and the north. As predicted by Liu Bei, the rebels gave up the city and ran out, led by their leader. The general and the three brothers fell upon them as they fled and Han Zhong was shot to death by an arrow. The rest of them scattered in all directions, still pursued by the imperial troops. But just then the other two rebel leaders came with large reinforcements and as they appeared very strong, Zhu Jun decided to retreat temporarily. And Wancheng was recaptured by the rebels.

Zhu Jun encamped ten *li* from the city and was preparing to attack again when there arrived a body of horsemen and footmen from the east. Riding in front was a young officer with a broad open face and a lithe yet powerfully-built body. His name was Sun Jian, also known as Sun Wentai. He was a native of Wu in Southeast China and a descendant of Sun Wu, a famous military strategist during the period of Spring and Autumn.[*] When he was only seventeen, he was once with his father on the Qiantang River[†] and saw a gang of pirates dividing their booty on the river bank after plundering some merchants.

"I can capture these pirates," he said to his father. So, gripping his sword he jumped boldly ashore. There he cried out to this side and that as if calling his men to come quickly. This made the pirates believe that the soldiers were on them and he even succeeded in killing one of the pirates. In this way he became known throughout the region and was recommended to be an officer. Later, in collaboration with the local officials, he mobilized a thousand warriors and helped quell a rebellion headed by a man who called himself Emperor Yangming. Both the rebel leader and his son were killed by him. For this he was commended in a memorial to the throne and received a further promotion.

When he heard about the Yellow Turban rebellion, he gathered together over 1,500 men made up of local youths, merchants, and veteran soldiers to aid in the fighting. Now he had reached the battlefront.

---

[*]   776–476 B.C.

[†]   A river in Hangzhou in East China.

Zhu Jun welcomed him very warmly and asked him to attack the south gate. Liu Bei and Zhu Jun himself were to attack the north and west gates respectively, leaving the east gate free to give the rebels a false impression of an escape route. Sun Jian was the first to mount the wall and killed more than twenty rebels single-handedly. The other rebels ran away but Zhao Hong, their leader, rushed over on horseback to fight with Sun Jian, his spear at the ready. Sun Jian leaped down the wall, snatched the spear, and with it pierced the rebel who fell down from his horse. Then mounting the horse, Sun Jian rode hither and thither, slaying as he went.

The other rebel leader, Sun Zhong, led his men to escape by the north gate, where they were met by Liu Bei. By then the rebels had lost their heart to fight and only wanted to get away. Liu Bei drew his bow, fitted an arrow to it, and shot Sun Zhong down from his horse. The main army led by Zhu Jun came up, and after tremendous slaughter, the others surrendered. Thus peace was restored to the region around Nanyang.

Zhu Jun led his army to the capital. He was promoted to the rank of General of Carriage and Cavalry and given the governorship of Henan. He did not forget those who had helped him, though. In a memorial to the Emperor he mentioned the merits of Sun Jian and Liu Bei. As he had influential friends, Sun Jian was appointed chief military officer in another region, and soon left for his post. But Liu Bei waited in vain for days on end and the three brothers became very sad.

One day while walking aimlessly in the street, they saw the carriage of a court official by the name of Zhang Jun. Liu Bei went up to him and told of his services to the country. Greatly surprised at this neglect of our heroes, Zhang Jun spoke to the Emperor about it at court.

"The Yellow Turbans rebelled because the ten eunuchs sold offices and bartered ranks," he said. "There was employment only for their friends and punishment only for their foes. This led to rebellions across the land. Now it would be better to execute the eunuchs and expose their heads. Then inform the nation of the execution and assure the worthy that they will be well rewarded. Naturally tranquillity will ensue throughout the land."

But the eunuchs accused the minister of insulting the Emperor. And he was thrust out by guards at the Emperor's order.

However, the eunuchs took counsel together and they realized that the incident had been caused by complaints from those who had rendered services against the rebels but had received no reward. So they decided to have a list of unimportant people prepared for preferment and wait until later to seek vengeance upon them. Among them was Liu Bei, who then received the post of magistrate of a small place called Anxi and was ordered to get there within a certain date. Liu Bei disbanded his men and sent them back to their villages, retaining only a score or so as escort. Then he set out immediately with his two brothers and the escort for Anxi.

Liu Bei had been in the place for only one month and was able to reform the people there by his intelligent and incorruptible rule. The three brothers lived in perfect harmony, eating at the same table and sleeping on the same couch. But when Liu Bei was in the company of others, the two younger brothers would stand in attendance without betraying any sign of fatigue, even if it were for a whole day.

Four months later, however, there came an order from above that the number of military officers holding civil posts should be reduced, and Liu Bei began to fear that he would be among those thrown out. Just at that time an inspecting official arrived and Liu Bei went outside the city wall to welcome him. But to his courteous salute, the official made no return save a wave of his whip as he sat on his horse. The two younger brothers were furious, but worse was to follow.

When the inspector got to his lodging, he took his seat on the dais, leaving Liu Bei standing in attendance below.

It was only after a long time that he addressed Liu Bei.

"What was your origin, Magistrate Liu?" he asked.

"I am a descendant of Prince Jing of Zhongshan. Since my first fight with the Yellow Turban rebels at my hometown I have been in some thirty big and small battles and have gained some trifling merit. My reward was this office," replied Liu Bei.

"You lie about your descent and your statement about your services is false," roared the inspector. "Now the Emperor has ordered the reduction of your sort of corrupt officials."

Liu Bei dared not retort but withdrew. On returning to his office, he took counsel with his subordinates.

"This intimidating attitude only means he wants a bribe," they said.

"I have never taken even the smallest thing from the people. Where am I to find a bribe for him?"

The next day the inspector had the minor officials before him and forced them to bear witness that their magistrate had oppressed the people. Liu Bei went time after time to rebut this charge but the doorkeepers drove him away and he could not enter.

Now Zhang Fei had been drowning his sorrow in wine. Calling for his horse he rode out past the lodging of the inspector, and at the gate saw a small crowd of white-haired men weeping bitterly.

"Why are you crying?" he asked them.

"The inspector is forcing the minor officials to bear false witness against Magistrate Liu. We came to beg him for mercy but he would not let us in. Instead, he sent the doorkeepers to drive us away and beat us," they replied.

This provoked the irascible man to fury. His eyes opened so wide that they became circles; he ground his teeth; in a moment he was off his steed, had forced his way past the scared doorkeepers into the house, and was in the rear hall. There he saw the inspector sitting on high with the official underlings paying homage at his feet.

"You wicked oppressor of the people!" roared Zhang Fei. "Do you know me?" But before he could reply, Zhang Fei had seized him by the hair and dragged him out of the house to the hitching post in front of the town office. Lashing the inspector firmly to the post, he broke off a switch from a willow tree and started thrashing his legs very hard. Soon a dozen or so switches were broken in the beating but his anger was still not appeased.

At this time Liu Bei was sitting in his office, contemplating his own sorrow. The noise in front reached his ear and he asked his attendants what the matter was. They told him that General Zhang had bound somebody to a post in front of the office and was thrashing him hard. Liu Bei at once went outside and was surprised to see who the victim was. He asked Zhang Fei the reason.

"If we don't beat this sort of corrupt official to death now, what may we expect?" demanded Zhang Fei.

"Noble sir, save me!" cried the inspector.

Now Liu Bei was by nature a kind and benevolent soul. So he told his brother to stop. Then Guan Yu came up and said, "You've rendered magnificent services to the country, brother, but all you got is this petty post of a magistrate. Today you're even insulted by this fellow. A thorn bush is no place for a phoenix, I think. Let's slay this fellow, give up the post, and go back home. We'll wait until we can develop a bigger scheme."

Guan Yu's words helped Liu Bei make up his mind. Hanging his official seal about the neck of the inspector, he said sternly: "You oppress people so much that you deserve to be killed. I now spare your life for the time being. If you injure people again, I will surely take your life. Now I return you the seal. We are leaving for good."

The inspector went to the prefect and complained, and orders were issued for the arrest of the three brothers, but they got away to Daizhou and sought refuge with Liu Hui who sheltered them after learning about Liu Bei's noble birth.

Back in the capital, The Ten had by this time all the power they wanted. They took counsel together and decided to put to death all those that dared disobey them. From officers who had helped put down the Yellow Turban rebels they demanded presents, and if anyone refused to do so, he would be removed from office. Huangfu Song and Zhu Jun both fell victims to these intrigues, while on the other hand the eunuchs received the highest honors. Some of them were given the rank of General of Carriage and thirteen others were ennobled. The state's affairs went from bad to worse and cries of discontent rose all around. Consequently, rebellions broke out in Changsha led by a man called Ou Xing, and also in Yuyang led by two Zhangs, one of whom called himself "Emperor" and the other "Supreme General." Messages asking for aid came like snowflakes but the eunuchs suppressed them all.

One day the Emperor was having a feast in the back garden with the ten eunuchs when Liu Tao, a senior official, suddenly appeared before him showing great distress. The Emperor asked him why he was crying.

"Your Majesty, how can you be still feasting with these people when the empire is at its last gasp?"

"All is well," said the Emperor. "Where is the danger?"

Liu Tao replied: "Robbers swarm on all sides and plunder towns and cities. All this is the fault of the ten eunuchs. They sell offices and bully the people. And they deceive Your Majesty and hide the truth from you. Virtuous officials have all left their services and misfortune is before our very eyes."

At this the eunuchs pulled off their hats and threw themselves at their master's feet. "His Excellency disapproves of us," they said, "and we will not be able to live. Pray spare our lives and let us go home. We will hand over our property to help bear military expenses." And they burst into tears.

The Emperor turned angrily to Liu Tao and said, "You also have servants in your home; why is it that you cannot bear with mine?" He called the guards to take him out and put him to death. Liu Tao cried out, "My death does not matter, but alas, what a great pity it is that the Hans, after ruling for four centuries, are falling fast!"

The guards hustled him out and were about to carry out the Emperor's order when another senior official came up and stopped them, "Halt! Wait till I have spoken with His Majesty." They found that the speaker was Minister Chen Dan.

Chen Dan went straight into the palace to see the Emperor and asked, "For what fault is Minister Liu to be put to death?"

"He has vilified those close to me and insulted me," said the Emperor.

"All the nation hates those ten eunuchs so much that they would eat their flesh, but you respect them as if they were your parents. They have rendered no services, yet they are made nobles. Moreover, Feng Xu and others collaborated with the Yellow Turban rebels and meant to create internal disorder. If Your Majesty does not look into the matter now, the empire will be ruined."

"There was no proof against Feng Xu," said the Emperor. "And there must be some faithful ones among The Ten."

The minister beat his forehead on the steps of the throne while continuing in his remonstrance. Then the Emperor grew angry and ordered his removal and imprisonment with Liu Tao. That night the eunuchs had them both murdered in prison.

Later, they forged an edict in the name of the Emperor, appointing Sun Jian, Prefect of Changsha, with orders to suppress the rebellion there. In less than fifty days Sun Jian reported victory and the district of Jiangxia became peaceful again. For this he was made a noble. In the meantime, Liu Yao was made Prefect of Youzhou and ordered to suppress the two Zhangs in Yuyang.

The Prefect of Daizhou wrote a letter to Liu Yu to recommend Liu Bei, who was consequently given the command of an army to destroy the Zhangs in their very base. After several days of fighting Liu Bei succeeded in blunting the edge of the rebels' spirit. One of the Zhangs was cruel and his men turned against him. He was slain by one of his own officers, who took both his army and his head to Liu Bei. Seeing that all was lost, the other Zhang hanged himself.

As Yuyang was restored to the control of the government, Liu Bei's great services were reported to the throne. Soon he received a full pardon for whipping the inspector and he was restored as an official. Later, his former superior Gongsun Zan stated his previous good services and he was made an officer of a higher rank and sent to Pingyuan as magistrate. This place was quite prosperous and Liu Bei recovered something of his old manner before the days of adversity. Liu Yu, too, received a promotion for his part in suppressing the rebels.

Let us now return to the throne. In the fourth month of the sixth year of the reign Zhong Ping (A.D. 189), the Emperor became seriously ill and He Jin, the Empress' brother, was summoned into the palace to arrange for the future. Now, He Jin came from a humble family of butchers, but was given a powerful position in court because his sister was at first a concubine of rank to the Emperor and, after she bore him a son, was made Empress. Later a beautiful girl named Wang became the Emperor's favorite and she bore him another son, named Xie. Out of jealousy, the Empress poisoned the girl and the baby was left in the care of Empress Dowager Dong, who was the mother of the Emperor and wife of Liu Chang, Prince of Jiedu. In the past, because Emperor Huan had no son of his own he had adopted the son of the prince, who succeeded to the throne as Emperor Ling. After his accession, he had his own mother brought into the palace to live and conferred upon her the title of Empress Dowager.

The Empress Dowager had often tried to persuade her son to name Xie as heir apparent, and in fact the Emperor himself was in favor of the boy. When he fell seriously ill, one of the eunuchs called Jian Shuo said, "If Prince Xie is to succeed, He Jin must die." The Emperor saw this was true, so he commanded He Jin to come to him. But at the gate of the palace, he was warned of the eunuchs' plot to kill him, and he hurried back to his own house, where he called many of the court officials to his side to consider how to put all the eunuchs to death.

One of them stood out and said: "The influence of the eunuchs dates back half a century and has spread like a creeping weed in all directions. How can we hope to destroy it thoroughly? If there should be any leakage of the plot, your clan will be exterminated. Please consider this carefully."

He Jin looked at the speaker and found that it was Cao Cao. He Jin was very angry and cried, "What do inferiors like you know of the ways of the state?"

In the midst of their indecision, the minister who had warned him at the palace gate came and said: "The Emperor is no more. Jian Shuo has reached an agreement with The Ten not to announce the death. They have forged an edict to command you to go into the palace so as to destroy you. Furthermore, they want to make Prince Xie the new Emperor to avoid future trouble." He had hardly finished speaking when the edict arrived, urging He Jin to go to the palace to discuss the succession.

"The matter for the moment is to set up the rightful heir first," said Cao Cao. "Then deal with the eunuchs."

"Who dares to join me?" asked He Jin.

At once there stepped forward a man who said: "Give me 5,000 veteran soldiers and we will force our way into the palace, set up the new heir, slay all the eunuchs, and sweep clean the government so as to restore peace to the land." The energetic speaker was Yuan Shao, son of a high-ranking minister and a senior officer in the imperial army.

He Jin mustered 5,000 palace guards for Yuan Shao to command, while he himself went into the palace, followed by some thirty other ministers.

And before the very coffin of the late Emperor, they installed Prince Bian on the throne.

After the ceremony was over and all the officials had paid their respects to the new ruler, Yuan Shao went in to arrest Jian Shuo. The terrified man escaped into the palace garden and hid among the flowers, where he was discovered and murdered by one of his colleagues. All his guards surrendered. Yuan Shao thought this was the most opportune moment to destroy The Ten and advised He Jin to take immediate actions against them. But they had already scented the danger and they went to Empress Dowager He for help.

They said to her: "It was Jian Shuo who plotted against your brother, the General. None of us had anything to do with it. Now the General has taken Yuan Shao's advice and wishes to kill every one of us. Please have pity on us."

"Do not worry," she said, "I will protect you."

Then she sent for her brother and said to him in private, "You and I are of lowly origin. We owe our good fortunes to the eunuchs. Now that the treacherous Jian Shuo is dead, why do you listen to other people's words and want to kill them all?"

He Jin obeyed and came out to explain to his party, "Jian Shuo was the one who plotted against me and his family should be exterminated. But it's not necessary to kill the rest of them."

"If you do not destroy them, root and branch," said Yuan Shao, "they will surely harm you."

"I have decided," said He Jin coldly. "Say no more." Then all the other officials withdrew.

The next day He Jin was promoted to an even higher rank and all those who helped him received new offices.

Meanwhile Empress Dowager Dong became worried. Summoning the ten eunuchs to a council, she said: "I was the one who first brought her forward. Now that her son is on the throne and all the officials are on her side, her influence is enormous. What should I do?"

"Your Highness, you can administer the state affairs by sitting behind the curtain in court. You should create Prince Xie head of a fief and give your brother, Dong Zhong, a high rank and place him at the command of the army and also put all of us in important positions. That will help you achieve everything."

The Empress Dowager was very glad to hear this. The next day in court she did just as she was advised, creating Prince Xie as Prince of Chenliu and her brother Dong Chong as a general of a very high rank, and allowing the ten eunuchs to participate in running state affairs.

When Empress Dowager He saw this she gave a banquet to which she invited her rival. In the middle of the feast, she rose and offered her guest a cup of wine, saying, "Both of us are women. It is not suitable for us to meddle in state affairs. In the old days, Empress Dowager Lu's* whole clan were put to death because she had tried to seize supreme power. Now we ought to content ourselves with living in the palace and leave the state affairs to the ministers. That would be best for the country and I hope you will act accordingly."

Empress Dowager Dong flared up. "You poisoned Lady Wang out of jealousy. Now you think you can say such nonsense to me because your son sits in the throne and your brother is powerful. In fact I can have your brother beheaded as easily as I turn my hand."

Now it was Empress Dowager He's turn to become angry. "I tried to persuade you with well-intended words—why are you so unreasonable?"

"You low-born daughter of a butcher, what do you know of state affairs?" retorted the other lady.

And the quarrel went on and on until at last the eunuchs managed to persuade them to retire to their separate palaces. However, that very night Empress Dowager He summoned her brother into the palace and told him about what had happened. He Jin then sought counsel with the principal ministers.

The next morning a petition was presented in court which said that the late Emperor's mother, being originally the consort of a "frontier" prince, was not fit to live long in the palace, but should be resettled in Hejian without delay. As the late Emperor's mother was being escorted out of the capital, her brother's house was surrounded by imperial guards and his seal of office demanded. Knowing this was the end, he committed suicide in his private chamber. The soldiers only left when his family started wailing over his death.

When they saw that Empress Dowager Dong's line was destroyed, two of the ten eunuchs bribed He Jin's brother, He Miao, and his mother with expensive gifts, asking them to speak on their behalf with the Empress Dowager He now and again. So once more The Ten won favor in court.

Two months later He Jin sent his men to murder Empress Dowager Dong in her residence in Hejian. Her remains were brought back to the capital and buried in the imperial graveyard. He Jin feigned illness and did not attend the funeral.

Yuan Shao went to see him and said: "The eunuchs are spreading the rumor that you caused the death of the late Empress Dowager, and that

---

* Consort of Liu Bang, first emperor of West Han.

you are aiming for the throne. If you don't take this opportunity to put them out of the way, they'll become a real menace to you." He also reminded him of how in the past Dou Wu had missed his chance and was later murdered by the eunuchs because the secret had not been kept. Then he said: "Now the officers under the command of you and your brother are all valiant fighters. If you can make them exert themselves, you are sure to succeed. This is a heaven-sent opportunity. Don't miss it."

But He Jin only replied, "Let me think it over."

His servants secretly told this to the eunuchs, who went to see his brother and gave him more gifts. Corrupted by these offerings, He Miao went to the palace to speak to his sister. He said, "Our brother is responsible for assisting the new emperor in ruling the country, yet he does not exercise mercy and benevolence, but thinks only of slaughter. Now he intends to kill The Ten without cause. I think this will only lead to trouble." His sister agreed.

After a while, He Jin also went in to see his sister and tell her about his plan to put the eunuchs to death. She objected: "It's the practice of the Hans for the eunuchs to look after palace affairs. The late Emperor had died only recently and yet you want to kill his old servants. This is not the way to show respect for the crown." Being a man of indecision, He Jin murmured assent and withdrew.

"What about it?" Yuan Shao came forward to ask.

"Her Highness will not consent," He replied. "What can we do then?"

"Call in warriors from all sides and ask them to lead their forces to the capital to slay the eunuchs. This is imperative. She cannot but consent."

"Excellent!" said He Jin.

And he was about to send out orders all around when Chen Lin, an important adviser objected: "No, this won't do. As the saying goes, 'Cover the eyes while trying to capture the swallows.' It is only cheating oneself. A small thing like a swallow cannot be fooled, let alone the machinery of state. Backed by the imperial house and the army, you had enormous power—to put the eunuchs to death would be as easy as lighting up a furnace to burn a hair. But you should act promptly and decisively. Then all the people will be on your side. If you summon forces from outside to enter the capital and gather many ambitious men together, each with his own schemes, you will be putting your weapons in the hands of others and placing yourself in their power. Nothing but failure can come of it, nothing but confusion."

"The view of a coward!" said He Jin with a sneer.

Then one of those beside him suddenly clapped his hands and laughed. "It is as easy as turning over one's hand. Why so much talk?"

The speaker was Cao Cao.

To get rid of wicked men from your king's side,
Then seek counsel from the wise men of the state.

What Cao Cao said to them will be told in the next chapter.

CHAPTER THREE

Dong Zhuo Silences Ding Yuan at Wenming Gardens
Li Su Bribes Lu Bu with Lavish Gifts

Cao Cao said to He Jin: "The evil of the eunuchs has a long history. It arises because the ruler has given them improper power and favor. To deal with it, we need only execute the prime culprits. And a jailer would be enough to do the job. So why busy yourself summoning troops from the provinces? But if you want to kill them all, you would not be able to maintain the secret and the plan will fail."

"Are you also harboring some scheme of your own, Meng-de?" asked the angry He Jin.

Cao Cao withdrew and said to himself, "He Jin will be the man to throw the empire into confusion."

Then He Jin immediately sent envoys bearing secret letters to various provinces.

One of the men who received this secret message was our old acquaintance Dong Zhuo. He had at first failed in his attempt to destroy the Yellow Turbans and would have been punished if not for the protection of The Ten, whom he had bribed. Later he had also managed to associate with high-ranking officials in court and was promoted to become commander of some 200,000 men in the west. But he was treacherous and disloyal at heart. He rejoiced greatly when he received the summons to go to the capital and lost no time to obey it. Leaving behind his son-in-law Niu Fu to guard Shanxi, he set out for Luoyang with some of his trusted subordinates.

Li Ru, another son-in-law and an advisor, said: "Although we are acting according to a formal edict, our actions are not without ambiguity. It would be well to send up a petition stating our aims plainly. Then we can proceed with our grand scheme." Dong Zhuo agreed. So a memorial was composed which read something like this:

*I, your humble servant, hear that the continual rebellions owe
their origin to the ten eunuchs, who disregard all recognized
precepts. Now, to stop the boiling of a pot, the best way is to put
out the fire; to cut out an abscess, though painful, is better than
to keep it nourished. I will undertake a military advance on the
capital to eliminate The Evil Ten for the benefit of the empire and
the people.*

When He Jin received this, he showed it to the other court officials.
One of the ministers admonished him: "Dong Zhuo is as vicious as a
wolf. If you allow him into the capital, he'll surely harm you."

"You are too suspicious; therefore, unequal to great schemes," sneered
He Jin.

Lu Zhi also tried to warn him. "I know Dong Zhuo very well. He appears kind but actually he is cruel at heart. Let him in and disaster is
bound to follow. It would be better to stop him to avoid trouble."

But He Jin would not listen and both of them gave up their posts and
retired. So did more than half of the court officials. He Jin sent his men to
welcome Dong Zhuo to Mianchi. However, Dong Zhuo took no action.

By then the news had traveled fast. The eunuchs knew that He Jin was
directing a move against them and recognized that if they did not strike
first, their families would be wiped out. So they arranged to have fifty
swordsmen hidden behind a palace gate and then went in to see the Empress Dowager.

They said: "The Great General has issued an edict in the name of the
Emperor to call up armies from all around to destroy us. Please save
us."

"Go to the Great General's house and confess your faults." she said.

"If we do, we would be cut to mincemeat. Please summon him in and
tell him to cease. If he does not, we will die in your presence."

So she gave orders for He Jin to enter the palace. And he readily prepared to obey. But just as he was leaving, Chen Lin advised him not to,
saying that the eunuchs were certainly behind the order and warned him
of the danger of going.

"It is the Empress Dowager who wants to see me, how can there be any
danger?" retorted He Jin.

"The plot is no longer a secret," Yuan Shao said, "and you still want to
go to the palace?"

"First get the eunuchs out, then go in," suggested Cao Cao.

"How childish you are!" laughed He Jin. "I have all the power in the
world, what can The Ten do to me?"

"If you must go, we will get a band of guards to go with you, in case anything happens," said Yuan Shao finally.

So Yuan Shao and Cao Cao each choose five hundred veteran soldiers. Placed at their command was Yuan Shao's brother, Yuan Shu, who, clad in full armor, drew up his men outside Qingsuo Gate, while the other two went as the general's escort. When they came near the palace, a eunuch came to announce the Empress Dowager's words: "The orders are to admit the Great General and none other." So the escort was detained outside the palace.

He Jin walked on proudly. When he got to Jiade Gate, he was met by the two chief eunuchs, Zhang Rang and Duan Gui—to his great alarm, they came to his sides, holding him trapped in between. Then Zhang Rang began rebuking him harshly.

"What crime had Empress Dowager Dong committed that you should have her poisoned to death? And when she, mother of the empire, was buried, you even dared feign sickness and did not attend the funeral. You and your followers were but lowly butchers and hucksters. It is we who recommended you to the Emperor and raised you to the dignity and wealth you now have. And this is your gratitude! You only want to slaughter us. You called us sordid and dirty, who is the clean one?"

He Jin was panic-stricken and looked about for a way to escape, but the gates were all closed. Then the assassins appeared, and did their bloody work.

> *Closing the days of the Hans, and the years of their rule were near spent,*
> *Stupid and tactless was He Jin, yet stood he highest in office;*
> *Many were those who advised him, but he was deaf as he heard not;*
> *Therefore he fell a victim under the sharp swords of the eunuchs.*

So He Jin was killed.

Meanwhile, Yuan Shao had been waiting for him to come out for a long time. Impatient at the delay, he called out through the gate: "Your carriage is waiting, General!" In response, the head of the murdered man was flung over the wall. A decree was then proclaimed that He Jin had contemplated treachery and had therefore been slain, but all his followers would be given pardon. Yuan Shao shouted angrily, "The eunuchs have murdered the Great General. Let all those who want to slay this wicked party come and help me!"

Then one of He Jin's officers set fire to a palace gate. Yuan Shu and his men burst into the palace and began slaying eunuchs regardless of their age or rank. At the same time, Yuan Shao and Cao Cao also broke in. Four of the notorious Ten were driven to the Blue Flower Lodge, where they were cruelly killed. Everywhere in the palace, flames of fire went high into the sky. Another four eunuchs led by Zhang Rang carried off the Empress Dowager, the new Emperor, and the Prince of Chenliu toward the North Palace.

Now Lu Zhi did not leave the capital after his resignation. Hearing of the trouble in the palace, he donned his armor, took his spear, and stood waiting by the side of a building, ready to fight. Then he saw in the distance the eunuch Duan Gui hurrying the Empress Dowager along. "You treacherous rebel, how dare you abduct the Empress!" he shouted. Duan Gui fled at once. The Empress leaped out of a window but was rescued in time by Lu Zhi and was taken to a place of safety.

At this time, He Jin's brother He Miao came out of the inner palace, sword in hand. "He was also in the plot to slay his brother," cried an officer. "He shall die with the others!"

"Let's kill the plotter against his own brother," cried the others in unison. He Miao tried to escape but was hemmed in on all sides. He was slain mercilessly.

Yuan Shao then ordered his soldiers to go and seek out all the families of The Ten, sparing none. In that slaughter many beardless men were killed by mistake.

In the meantime, Cao Cao was busy putting out the fire in the palace. Then he asked the Empress Dowager to assume responsibility for state affairs for the time being. A search party was also sent out at his order to chase Zhang Rang and others and to look for the young Emperor.

The two chief eunuchs, Zhang Rang and Duan Gui, had hustled away the Emperor and the Prince of Chenliu. Breaking through the fire and smoke, they rushed all the way to Beimang Hills. At about the second *geng*,* or the second watch, they heard an uproar behind them and saw the soldiers chasing them. Riding in front was an officer from Henan called Ming Gong who shouted, "Stop, you wicked rebels!" Zhang Rang, seeing that the end had come, drowned himself in a river.

The two boys, ignorant of the meaning of all this, dared not utter a cry, but crept in among the rank grass by the river bank. The soldiers scattered in all directions to look for them but failed to find them. Four hours later they were still hiding among the dew-wet grass, feeling very hungry. They wept in each other's arms quietly lest anyone should hear them.

---

* Unit of measuring time in ancient China. A night was divided into five *gengs*, each covering for about two hours. The third *geng*, or the third watch, was roughly midnight.

"This is no place to stay long," said the Prince, "We must find some way out."

So they knotted their clothes together and managed to crawl up the bank. They found themselves in a thicket of brambles and they could not see any path in the dark. Just as they were feeling desperate, hundreds of thousands of fireflies emerged out of nowhere and circled in the air in front of the Emperor, lighting up the path ahead.

"God is helping us," said the Prince.

So they followed the fireflies and gradually found a road. They walked for about two hours and their feet became so sore that they could go no further. Seeing a heap of straw by a hill, they crept over to it and lay down to rest.

Close to the heap of straw was a farmhouse, whose owner dreamed of two bright red suns dropping behind his dwelling in the night. Alarmed, he hastily threw a coat upon his shoulders and went out to investigate. Then he saw a bright red light shooting up from a heap of straw behind his house. He hastened forward and found two boys lying by its side.

"Whose children are you?" he asked.

The Emperor was too frightened to reply but the Prince, pointing to his brother, said, "This is the Emperor. There has been a rebellion against the ten eunuchs at the palace and we have fled here. I am his brother, Prince of Chenliu."

The owner of the house was greatly surprised. He immediately knelt down and said, "My name is Cui Yi. My brother was a minister under the late Emperor. I was disgusted with the behavior of the eunuchs, so I retired here."

Then he helped them into the house and on his knees served them with food and drinks.

Meanwhile, Ming Gong had overtaken and caught Duan Gui.

"Where is the Emperor?" he bellowed.

"He got lost on the way. I do not know where he is," answered Duan Gui.

Ming Gong slew him and hung the bleeding head on his horse's neck. Then he sent his men searching in all directions for the Emperor while he rode off by himself on the same quest. Presently he came to the farm. Cui Yi, seeing what hung on his horse's neck, questioned him and, satisfied with his story, led him to the Emperor. The meeting was emotional—all were moved to tears.

"The state cannot be without its ruler, not even for one day," said Ming Gong. "Pray return to the capital, Your Majesty."

At the farm they had but one sorry nag and this they saddled for the

Emperor, while the Prince was taken on Ming Gong's charger. Thus they left the farm. Soon, however, they fell in with a big search party of officials and hundreds of soldiers. Among them was Yuan Shao. Tears were shed freely as the ministers met their Emperor. One of them was sent at once to the capital to expose the head of Duan Gui. Placing the Emperor and the Prince on better horses and guarding them carefully, they then began their journey back to Luoyang.

The Emperor and his men had not proceeded far when they saw coming toward them a large body of soldiers, their banners covering up the sun, their dust rising up to the sky. All the officials turned pale and the Emperor was greatly alarmed. Yuan Shao rode out and asked who they were. From under the shade of an embroidered banner rode out an officer, shouting in a harsh voice: "Where is the Emperor?" His Majesty trembled in fright, unable to respond, but the Prince of Chenliu rode forth to the front and demanded angrily, "Who are you?"

The man replied, "My name is Dong Zhuo. I am governor of Xiliang."

"Have you come to protect the Emperor or to harm him?" asked the Prince.

"I have come specially to protect," answered Dong Zhuo.

"If so, the Emperor is here. Why do you not dismount?" said the Prince.

Dong Zhuo hastily got down from his horse and knelt on the left side of the road. Then the Prince spoke graciously to placate him, carrying himself very well in his speech. Dong Zhuo was very much impressed and in his heart rose the desire to set aside the Emperor in favor of the Prince. They returned to the palace that same day and there was an emotional meeting with the Empress Dowager. Then they checked the things in the palace to see if everything was all right. To their great dismay, they found the imperial jade seal, the hereditary seal for the Emperor, was missing.

Dong Zhuo camped outside the capital, but every day he was seen playing the tyrant in the streets with an escort of armored soldiers so that the common people were in a constant state of trepidation. He also went in and out of the palace regardless of any rules of propriety. His unscrupulous behavior angered an officer called Bao Xin, who went first to see Yuan Shao and then Wang Yun, warning them of Dong Zhuo's ambition and urging them to take measures to get rid of him. But both of them were undecided, so Bao Xin left the capital with his army to go to Taishan.

By this time Dong Zhuo had gained control of all the soldiers of the former He brothers. He spoke to Li Ru in private about his intention to depose the present Emperor in favor of the Prince of Chenliu.

Li Ru said, "The empire is really without a ruler. There can be no better time than this to carry out your plan. Any delay will spoil it. Tomorrow, assemble the officials at Wenming Gardens and address them on the subject. Put all opponents to death and your absolute power is established."

Dong Zhuo was very pleased to hear these words. So the next day he invited all the high-ranking officials and generals to a huge banquet. As all of them were terrified of him, no one dared stay behind. He himself rode up at leisure, the last to arrive, and took his seat without taking off his sword. When the wine had gone round several times, he stopped the service and the music. Then he began to speak.

"I have something to say—listen quietly, all of you."

All turned toward him.

He said, "The Emperor is lord of all and if he lacks dignity in manner, he is not fit to inherit the throne. The present Emperor is a weakling, inferior to the Prince of Chenliu in intelligence and love of learning. The Prince is in every way fitted for the throne. So I want to depose the Emperor and set up the Prince of Chenliu in his place. What do you say?"

The assembly was stupefied. None of them dared utter a word of dissent at first. Then suddenly one guest rose from his seat and, pushing his table to the side, he came forth and cried out: "No! No! Who do you think you are that you dare utter such nonsense? The Emperor is the son of the lawful consort and has done no wrong. How can you talk about deposing him? Do you want to usurp the throne?"

The speaker was Ding Yuan, governor of Jingzhou.

Dong Zhuo glared at him. "There is life for those who are with me and death for those against," he roared.

He drew his sword and made for the dissenter. But the watchful Li Ru had noticed standing behind Ding Yuan a particularly powerful and dangerous-looking young man, who was then glowering at Dong Zhou, his long and heavy halberd in his hand. So he hastily interposed, saying, "But this is the banquet hall and state affairs should be left outside. These matters can be fully discussed in the meeting hall at a later date."

The other guests persuaded Ding Yuan to leave, and after his departure, Dong Zhuo asked: "Is what I said just and reasonable?"

"No, sir," said Lu Zhi. "In ancient times, Emperor Tai Jia* of the Shang Dynasty broke the law and his chief minister Yi Yin imprisoned him in Tong Palace till he reformed. There was also the case of Prince Chang† in

---

* 1750 B.C.

† 74 B.C.

our dynasty. He had not been on the throne for a month when he had committed 3,000 or more wrongs. Therefore Huo Guang, the regent, declared his faults in the ancestral temple and deposed him. Our present Emperor is young but he is intelligent and kind. He has not committed a single fault. You, sir, are a mere governor of a frontier region and have had no experience in state administration. Neither have you the great ability of Yi and Huo. How can you pretend to be an authority on matters like enthronement and dethronement? As sages say, 'With Yi Yin's good intentions, such an act is justified; otherwise it is usurpation.'"

Dong Zhuo was furious. He drew his sword to slay the bold speaker but two other officials remonstrated with him. "Minister Lu is a cynosure of the whole country. If you kill him now, you will offend all the people."

Dong Zhuo stayed his hand.

Then another minister, Wang Yun, said: "An important question like this is not to be decided after a drinking party. Let it be put off till another time." So all the officials dispersed.

As Dong Zhuo stood by the garden gate with his hand on his sword watching them depart, he noticed a warrior galloping around on a fiery steed just outside the garden. He asked Li Ru if he knew the young man.

"That is Lu Bu, also called Feng-xian. He is the adopted son of Ding Yuan. You must keep out of his way, my lord," said Li Lu.

So Dong Zhuo went inside to avoid being seen by Lu Bu. But next day report came to him that Ding Yuan had come out of the city with his army and was challenging him to a battle. The angry Dong Zhuo went forth to accept the challenge, accompanied by Li Ru, and the two armies were drawn up in proper array.

Lu Bu was a conspicuous figure in the forefront. His hair was arranged under a handsome headdress of gold and he had donned his armor and breastplate. Over his shoulders was draped a beautifully embroidered fighting robe and around his waist was a fine belt with a lion's head clasp. With his halberd set to strike at any moment he rode forth beside his adopted father.

Ding Yuan, pointing his finger at Dong Zhuo, began to revile the latter.

"Unfortunate enough was our empire when it was dominated by the eunuchs and the people were driven into extreme poverty. Now you, entitled to no merit at all, dare to talk about deposing the rightful Emperor and setting up another. This is to desire rebellion and no less."

Dong Zhuo had not yet been able to reply when Lu Bu rode straight at him. He fled in haste and Ding Yuan's army came on. He suffered a great loss and had to retreat about thirty *li* to set up another camp. Here he called in his subordinates for counsel.

"This Lu Bu is a marvel," he said. "If only he could be on my side I would defy the world."

At this one of his officers came forward and said, "Don't worry, my lord, Lu Bu and I come from the same village and I know him well. He's valiant but not resourceful and he puts profits before morals. I promise to persuade him to come over willingly."

Dong Zhuo was delighted and gazed admiringly at the speaker who was Li Su, an officer in his army. "What arguments will you use with him?"

"You have a fine horse, the Red Hare, one of the best ever bred. I must have this steed, and gold and pearls to win his heart. Then I will go and persuade him. He will certainly abandon Ding Yuan's service for yours."

Dong Zhuo sought advice from Li Ru. "What do you think of this?"

"One cannot begrudge a horse to win an empire," was the reply.

So Dong Zhuo gave the corrupter of morals what he demanded—the Red Hare, a thousand taels of gold, ten strings of beautiful pearls, and a jeweled belt, and these accompanied Li Su on his visit to his fellow villager. He reached the camp and said to the guards, "Please tell General Lu that a very old friend has come to visit him."

He was admitted into the camp.

"My worthy brother, have you been well since we last met?"

"How long it is since we last saw each other!" replied Lu Bu, bowing in return. "And where are you now?"

"I am an officer in the Tiger Company. When I learned you were a strong supporter of the throne I could not say how I rejoiced. I have come now to present to you a really fine horse, a thousand *li* a day horse. It can cross rivers and climb hills as if it were on level ground. It is called the Red Hare. Surely it will be a fitting aid to your valor."

Lu Bu told his men to lead the horse out for him to see. Truly enough, it was a fine steed, all its hair being of a uniform color of glowing charcoal, not a single one of another color. It measured ten feet from head to tail and eight feet from hoof to neck. When it neighed, it had the appearance of riding up into the air or down into the sea. Later, a poet wrote the following in praise of the steed:

> *The fine steed gallops a thousand* li *a day, kicking off dust as it goes;*
> *It crosses rivers and climbs hills, dispersing the purple mist;*
>
> *Now he breaks the rein and shakes the jade bridle;*
> *Like a fiery dragon, he descends from the highest heaven.*

Lu Bu was delighted with the horse and said, "Thank you for giving me such a fine horse. But what can I hope to offer in return?"

"I came here out of a sense of loyalty to my friend, not for repayment."

Then wine was brought in and they drank. After they had been drinking for some time, Li Su said, "I have seen very little of you but I am constantly meeting your honorable father."

"You are drunk," said Lu Bu. "My father has been dead for years. How can you meet him?"

Li Su laughed. "Oh, no. I mean Minister Ding Yuan, the man of the day."

Lu Bu started. "Yes, I am with him but only because I can do no better," he explained.

"My worthy brother, you have talents to rule the air and control the seas. Who in the world does not admire you? Ranks and riches are yours for the taking. And you say you can do no better than remain a subordinate!"

"If only I could find the right master to serve!" sighed Lu Bu.

Li Su smiled and said, "The clever bird chooses the best branch on which to perch and the wise official selects the worthy master to serve. If you don't seize the chance when it comes, you will only repent when it's too late."

"Now you are in the government. Who do you think is the most worthy of all?" Lu Bu asked.

"None of the officials can be compared with Dong Zhuo. He is the one who respects the wise and reveres the scholarly; he is discriminating in his rewards and punishments. I am sure he is destined for a great cause."

"I wish I could serve him but there is no way, I fear," replied Lu Bu.

Then Li Su produced the gold, the pearls, and the jade belt, laying them out before his host.

"What does this mean?" asked Lu Bu in surprise.

"Send away the attendants," said Li Su. After they were gone, he continued, "These gifts are from Dong Zhuo, who has long admired you for your valor. The Red Hare is also from him."

"He is so kind to me. What can I do in return?"

"If an untalented person like me can be an officer in his army, think what great honor awaits you if you serve under him."

"But I am afraid I can offer him no service worth mentioning to grant an audience with him."

"There is an easy service for you to perform—only you will not do it."

For a long time Lu Bu sat thinking in silence. In the end he said, "I would slay Ding Yuan and bring over his soldiers to your side. What do you say to that?"

"If you would do that, there could be no greater service. But make haste. There should be no delay."

Lu Bu promised his friend that he would submit to Dong Zhuo the next day. Then Li Su left to report his success.

That very night, Lu Bu entered his adopted father's tent. The unsuspecting man was reading by the candlelight. Seeing who came in he asked, "My son, why do you come here?"

"I am a man of dignity," said Lu Bu, "do you think I am willing to be a son of yours?"

"Why this sudden change of heart, Feng-xian?"

The young man stepped forward and, with one single swing of his sword, cut off his protector's head. Then he shouted, "Ding Yuan was an unjust man and I have slain him. Let those who are with me stay; the others may leave!" A majority of the soldiers ran away.

The next day, holding the head of the murdered man, Lu Bu went to see his friend Li Su, who introduced him to his master. Dong Zhuo was very pleased to see him and treated him with wine. He even bowed to the younger man, saying, "I welcome your coming to me, General, just like parched grass welcomes dew."

Lu Bu made him take his seat and then knelt before him. "If you do not dislike me, sir, please let me bow to you as my adopted father," he said.

Dong Zhuo rewarded him with gold armor and silken robes. Then they all had a hearty drink before they separated.

From then on Dong Zhuo's power and influence increased rapidly. He made himself the supreme commander of the army and gave high military ranks to his brother and Lu Bu, both of whom were also created members of the nobility. To strengthen his place in the empire, Li Ru advised him to carry out the plan to depose the young Emperor.

So Dong Zhuo prepared a banquet in the palace at which all the important officials were expected to be present. He also ordered Lu Bu to post a thousand and more guards around the place as a military back-up. On the day of the banquet, the Emperor's tutor Yuan Wei and all the officials came. After several rounds of wine, Dong Zhuo rose from his seat, his hand on his sword, saying: "The Emperor being weak and irresolute is unfit for the duties of high office. I will do as Yi Yin and Huo Guang did in the past and reduce the present Emperor to the status of Prince of Hongnong, and I will place on the throne the present Prince of Chenliu. Those who dare to object will have to die!"

All the officials were silenced by an intense fear, except Yuan Shao, who stepped forward and said: "The Emperor has not been on the throne for long. He is innocent of any fault, yet you want to set him aside for another. What is it if this is not treason?"

"The empire is in my hands," cried the infuriated Dong Zhuo, "and I choose to do this today. Who dares to say no? Do you think my sword lacks an edge?"

"If your sword is sharp, mine is never blunt," retorted Yuan Shao as his sword flashed out of its sheath.

The two men stood glowering at each other in the banquet hall.

> *Daring to speak up against the tyrant, Ding Yuan was murdered;*
> *Confronting the usurper, Yuan Shao puts his life in danger.*

Whether Yuan Shao would be killed or not will be told in the next chapter.

CHAPTER FOUR

Prince of Chenliu Sits in the Throne to Replace the Deposed Emperor
Cao Cao Presents Dong Zhuo a Sword in an Attempt to Kill Him

Dong Zhuo was on the point of slaying Yuan Shao, but his advisor Li Ru checked him, saying, "You must not kill rashly while the business hangs in the balance." Then Yuan Shao, sword in hand, left the assembly. He hung up the symbol of his office at the east gate and went to Jizhou.

Dong Zhuo said to Yuan Wei, "Your nephew was impudent but I pardoned him for your sake. What do you think of my proposal?"

"What you said is right," was the reply.

"If anyone opposes the great scheme he will be dealt with by military law," said Dong Zhuo.

After the banquet Dong Zhuo asked two of his subordinates what they thought of Yuan Shao's departure. One of them said, "He left in a state of great anger. If you press him too hard, he will surely rebel. The Yuan family have been noted for their kindness to the people for four generations, and their protégés and dependents are everywhere. If he assembles bold spirits and disciples, all the valiant warriors will rise in arms and the vast area east of Huashan Mountains will be lost. It would be better if you pardon him and make him head of a prefecture. He will be glad to be forgiven and will do no harm."

As the other one was also of the same opinion, Dong Zhuo followed this advice. An envoy was sent that day to announce the appointment of Yuan Shao as Prefect of Bohai.

On the first day of the ninth month, the Emperor was asked to be present at Jiade Hall to meet all his officials and generals. There, Dong Zhuo, sword in hand, addressed the assembly. "The Emperor is weak and unintelligent, and not fit to be the ruler of the empire. Now, all of you, listen to the document I have prepared."

Li Ru read as follows: "The dutiful Emperor Ling too soon left his subjects. And all the people of the land looked up to his inheritor, but upon the present Emperor Heaven has conferred small gifts: in dignity and deportment he is deficient and in mourning he is remiss. His faults being apparent, he is inadequate for the throne. The Empress Dowager is improper in instruction and inefficient in administration. The sudden death of the late Emperor's mother has caused many to wonder. How can the doctrine of The Three Guides* and the rule of Heaven and Earth be injured? Now Prince Xie of Chenliu is sage and virtuous in every way. He conforms to all the rules of propriety. In mourning he is sincere and in speech he is always correct. His fine reputation spreads throughout the empire. He is well-fitted for the great duty of continuing the rule of Han to infinity.

"Therefore the Emperor is deposed and created Prince of Hongnong and the Empress Dowager retires from the administration.

"Pray accept Prince of Chenliu as the new Emperor in compliance with the will of Heaven and the desires of men, so as to fulfill the hopes of all the people."

This having been read, Dong Zhuo ordered the attendants to lead the Emperor down from the throne, remove his imperial seal, and cause him to kneel facing the north as befitting his new status of a prince waiting to be commanded by his master. Moreover, he bade the mother take off her dress of ceremony and await the imperial command.

Both victims wailed bitterly, and every official present was deeply affected. One of them put his anger in words, saying, "Shameless Dong Zhuo, how dare you plot this insult against the will of Heaven? I will give my life to stop it!" So saying he threw his ivory baton† at the conspirators. It was Minister Ding Guan and he was immediately taken and put to death at the vicious man's order. But before he was executed he never ceased rebuking the oppressor nor was he frightened at death.

> *The rebel Dong conceived the foul design,*
> *To thrust the King aside and wrong Han's line.*
> *With indifference the courtiers stood, save one*
> *Ding Guan who dared to cry that wrong was done.*

---

* Feudal code of behavior that requires officials to obey their king, sons to obey their father, and wives to obey their husbands.

† An official carries this in his hands at court for writing things on.

Then the Emperor designate was asked to take the seat of the throne to receive respects from his officials. After this the deposed Emperor, his mother, and his wife were removed to a separate building. The entrance gates were locked and no official could enter without permission. It was pitiful! There was the young Emperor, having reigned less than six months, already deposed and another put in his place. The new Emperor was his younger brother Xie, then only nine years old. He was known in history as Emperor Xian of the East Han Dynasty. The reign title was changed to Chu Ping.

As prime minister, Dong Zhuo was arrogant beyond all reason. When he bowed before the throne he did not declare his name; when he went to court he did not hasten; and when he entered the audience hall he did not take off his boots or sword. Never had anyone been as powerful as he.

His chief advisor constantly urged him to employ men of reputation so as to gain public esteem. So when someone recommended Cai Yong as a man of talent, Dong Zhuo summoned him, but to his fury, Cai Yong refused to come. Then Dong Zhuo sent a message to him, threatening to kill his whole clan unless he did as he was told to do. Cai Yong had to give in and appeared before him. Dong Zhuo was very gracious to him and promoted him three times in one month. He became a high-ranking official and seemed to be much favored by the tyrant.

Meanwhile the deposed Emperor, his mother, and wife were imprisoned in their lodging and found their daily supplies of food and clothing gradually diminishing. The former ruler wept incessantly. One day he chanced to see a pair of swallows flying about in the courtyard, which moved him to verse.

> *Green in the mist grows the tender grass,*
> *Graceful and gentle do the swallows dance.*
> *Clear is the water in the rippling stream*
> *Which travelers praise when they softly pass.*
> *With lingering gaze the roofs I see,*
> *Of the palace that once sheltered me.*
> *May someone with a noble mind*
> *Help me vent the grievance in my heart.*

The spy, sent by Dong Zhuo occasionally to the place for news of the prisoners, got hold of this poem and showed it to his master.

"So he shows his resentment by writing poems, eh! A good excuse to put them all out of the way," he said.

Li Ru went with ten armed men to commit the foul deed. The three were in one of the upper rooms when they arrived. The deposed Emperor shuddered with fright when the maid announced the visitor's name.

Presently Li Ru entered and offered a cup of poisoned wine to the Emperor. The Emperor asked him what it meant.

Li Ru said, "Spring is the season of harmony and the prime minister Dong sends you the wine of longevity."

"If so, you drink it first," said the Empress Dowager.

"You will not drink?" cried Li Ru furiously. He called his men to place the dagger and the roll of white cloth before her.

"Take these if not the cup," he bellowed.

Then Lady Tang, the Emperor's wife, knelt down and pleaded, "Let me drink the wine for my lord. Please spare the mother and son."

"Who do you think you are that can die for a prince?" he shouted.

Then he presented the cup to the mother once more and pressed her to drink. She railed against her brother, the unresourceful He Jin, for bringing in the wicked Dong Zhuo and causing all this trouble.

Li Ru approached the Emperor and pressed hard.

"Let me bid farewell to my mother," he entreated, and weeping heart-brokenly, he sang the following lines:

> Oh, Heaven and Earth change places, the sun and the moon leave their courses,
> I, deprived of my empire, am driven to the farthest confines.
> Oppressed by a vicious minister, my life nears its end,
> Everything fails me and in vain my tears fall.

Lady Tang also sang:

> Heaven is to be rent asunder, Earth to fall away,
> I, having served an emperor, would grieve if I followed him not.
> We are fated to part for the quick and the dead do not cross in their ways,
> Alas, I am left alone with grief in my heart.

When they had sung these lines they fell weeping into each other's arms.

"The prime minister is expecting my report," shouted Li Ru, "and you delay too long. Do you think there is any hope of succor?"

The Empress Dowager burst into another fit. "The vicious Dong Zhuo forces us, mother and son, to die. Heaven will not permit it! And all of you who help him to do this evil will surely suffer extermination of your whole clans!"

Li Ru became more angry. He laid his brutal hands on her and pushed her down the stairs. Then he ordered the soldiers to strangle Lady Tang and poured the wine of death down the throat of the poor young Emperor. Then he reported the bloody deed to his master, who ordered him to bury the victims outside the city.

After this Dong Zhuo's behavior was more atrocious than ever. He spent nights in the palace, defiled the maids there, and even slept on the imperial couch. Once he led his soldiers out of the city, and came to a place called Yangcheng where the villagers, men and women, were assembled for an annual festival in the second month of the lunar year. Dong Zhuo ordered his soldiers to surround the place and begin killing and plundering. All the men were killed and all the women taken prisoners. They took away booty by the cart load, and they hung their victims' heads under the carts. The procession returned to the city and fabricated a story that they had obtained a major victory over some rebels. They burned the heads beneath the city walls and the women and booty were shared out among the soldiers.

An officer named Wu Fu was disgusted at this ferocity and sought a chance to slay the tyrant. He constantly wore a breastplate underneath his court dress and carried a concealed sharp dagger. One day when Dong Zhuo came to court Wu Fu met him on the steps and tried to stab him. But Dong Zhuo was a very powerful man and held him off till Lu Bu came to his help. Wu Fu was struck down at once.

"Who told you to rebel?" asked Dong Zhuo.

Wu Fu glared at him and cried, "You are not my lord, I am not your minister: where is the rebellion? Your crimes fill the heavens and every man would slay you. I am sorry I cannot tear you apart to appease the wrath of the whole land."

Dong Zhuo ordered him to be taken out and hacked to pieces. He only ceased cursing as he ceased to live.

> *Men praise Wu Fu, that loyal servant of the latter days of Han.*
> *His valor was high as the Heavens, in all ages unequaled;*
> *In court itself would he slay the tyrant, so great is his fame!*
> *Throughout all time will men call him a hero.*

Dong Zhuo's misuse of power had also reached Yuan Shao in Bohai. He sent a secret letter to Wang Yun in which he mentioned that he had assembled an army and would sweep clean the royal habitation. He urged Wang Yun to find an opportunity to destroy the wicked man.

One day while waiting in attendance at court he noticed that all the officials of long service were present. So he said to his colleagues, "It is my birthday today. Would you like to come to a little party at my house this evening?"

"Certainly," they said. "We'll come to wish you long life."

That evening a banquet was given in the inner hall and his friends gathered there. When the wine had made a few rounds, the host suddenly covered his face with his sleeves and wept bitterly.

All the guests were aghast. "Why do you cry, sir, and on your birthday, too?" they asked in surprise.

"This isn't my birthday," he replied. "But I wanted to call you together and I was afraid lest Dong Zhuo should suspect, so I used that as an excuse. This villain insults the Emperor and dominates the court so that the state is in imminent danger. I think of the days when our illustrious founder destroyed Qin and annihilated Chu to establish the empire. Who could have foreseen this day when it should be lost to Dong Zhuo. That is why I weep."

Then they all wept with him.

Seated among them, however, was Cao Cao who did not join in the weeping but clapped his hands and laughed. "If all the officials weep from dawn to night and from night to dawn, will the tears kill Dong Zhuo?" he demanded.

His host turned on him angrily. "Your forebears also benefited from the bounty of the Hans—do you feel no gratitude? You can still laugh?"

"I laughed because none of you can think of a way to kill him. Incapable as I am, I will cut off his head and hang it at the city gate to avenge the nation."

The host left his seat and went over to Cao Cao's. "What good idea do you have, Meng-de?"

"These days I have bowed my head to Dong Zhuo," replied Cao Cao. "In fact, I have been waiting for a chance to destroy him. Now he trusts me greatly and I can often approach him. I hear you have a seven-treasure dagger which I would like to borrow and I will take it with me to go to his house and kill him even though I may die for it."

"What good fortune for the whole country if you are willing to do that!" exclaimed his host. And he himself filled a goblet with wine for his guest, who held it in hand and swore an oath. Then the precious dagger was brought out and given to Cao Cao, who hid it under his robe. Then he finished his wine, took leave of the others, and left. Before long they all dispersed.

The following day, Cao Cao, with the dagger girded on, came to Dong Zhuo's house. "Where is the minister?" he asked.

"In the small chamber, "answered the attendants.

Cao Cao went in and found him seated on a couch. Lu Bu was standing at his side.

"Why are you so late, Meng-de?" asked Dong Zhuo.

"My horse is too weak to go fast."

Dong Zhuo turned to his adopted son and said, "Some good horses have come in from Xiliang. You go and pick one out for Meng-de." And the young man left.

He's doomed to die, thought Cao Cao. He thought to strike then but, knowing how powerful Dong Zhuo was, he wanted to make sure of his blow. Now Dong Zhuo was very fat and he could not remain sitting for long, so he rolled over and lay facing inwards.

"Now's the time," thought Cao Cao, and he at once took the dagger in his hand. But just as he was to deal the fatal blow, Dong Zhuo happened to look up and in the big mirror he saw Cao Cao drawing a dagger behind him.

"What are you doing, Meng-de?" he asked, turning suddenly.

Cao Cao, in a panic, dropped on his knees and said, "I have a choice sword here which I want to present to Your Benevolent Lordship." At that moment Lu Bu was already outside the chamber with the horse.

Dong Zhuo took it and found that it was over a foot long, inlaid with seven treasures and had a very sharp edge—a fine sword indeed. He handed the weapon to Lu Bu and Cao Cao took off the sheath, which he also gave to the young man.

Then they went out to look at the horse. Cao Cao thanked the minister and said that he would like to try riding it. So Dong Zhuo told his men to bring him saddle and bridle. Cao Cao led the horse out of the house, leaped into the saddle and urged his horse to gallop away at full speed toward the southeast.

Lu Bu said, "It seemed to me Cao Cao was going to stab you just now. Only when he was exposed did he present the sword."

"I suspected him too," said Dong Zhuo. Just then Li Ru came in and they told him about it.

"He has no family here but lives quite alone by himself," said Li Ru. "Send for him now. If he comes without any suspicion then the sword was meant as a gift, but if he makes excuses he intended assassination. And you can arrest him."

So Dong Zhuo sent four prison warders to call Cao Cao. They were gone for a long time and then came back with the news that he had not returned to his lodging but had ridden in haste out of the east gate. When he was questioned by the gate wardens he said that he was on an urgent mission for the minister and gone off at full speed.

"He was afraid that he might be found out so he fled. There is no doubt that he meant to stab you," said Li Ru.

"And I trusted him so much," cried Dong Zhuo in a rage.

"There must be accomplices—when we catch him we will know," said Li Ru.

Dispatches and images of the fugitive were sent out everywhere with orders to arrest him on sight. A large reward of money and a promise of promotion to noble status were offered to whoever caught Cao Cao, while anyone who sheltered him would be held to share his guilt.

Cao Cao escaped outside the city and fled toward his hometown. Unfortunately, while he was passing through Zhongmou, he was recognized by the guards at the gate and made a prisoner. They took him to the magistrate. Cao Cao declared that he was a merchant and his surname was Huangfu. The magistrate looked at him closely but did not speak for a long time—he seemed to be lost in thought.

Then he said, "When I was seeking a post in the capital I knew you as Cao Cao. How can you conceal your identity?"

He ordered the guards to keep him in prison until the next day when he would be sent to the capital and the reward claimed. However, late that night, the magistrate sent a trusty servant to bring the prisoner into his private chamber for interrogation.

"They say the prime minister treated you well. Why did you want to bring trouble to yourself?" asked the magistrate.

"How can swallows and sparrows understand the aspirations of the wild goose? I am your prisoner and you will give me over to Dong Zhuo for a reward. Why so many questions?"

The magistrate sent away his attendants and said to the prisoner, "Do not despise me. I am not a mere hireling, only I have not yet found the rightful lord to serve."

"My ancestors all served under the Hans and enjoyed their bounty. I would be no different from a beast if I did not desire to dedicate myself to the empire. I had submitted to Dong Zhuo's tyranny in the hope that I might find an opportunity to slay him so as to remove this evil for the people. I have failed this time. Such is the will of Heaven."

"And where are you going?"

"Home to my village. I will issue a call, urging all the lords to come up with arms and join their forces in destroying the tyrant. This is what I intend to do," said Cao Cao.

At this, the magistrate himself loosened the cord that bound the prisoner's hands, helped him to a seat and bowed to him, saying, "You are truly a man of loyalty and justice, sir."

Cao Cao in his turn also bowed to the magistrate and asked him his name.

"My name is Chen Gong. My aged mother and family are in another place in the east. Your loyalty to the country and your sense of justice have moved me deeply. I will abandon my office and escape with you," said the magistrate.

Cao Cao was delighted with this turn of events. Then the magistrate prepared some money for the journey and asked his new friend to change his clothes. Carrying a sword each on their backs, they left for Cao Cao's home village. Three days later, they reached Chenggao toward the evening. Cao Cao, pointing with his horsewhip to somewhere deep in the woods, said: "There lives my uncle, Lu Bo-she, a sworn brother of my father's. Shall we go and ask news of my family and seek shelter for the night?"

"Very good," agreed Chen Gong.

So they rode up to the farmhouse and dismounted at the gate. Then they went in to see the host.

"I hear they have sent stringent orders everywhere to arrest you. Your father has gone into hiding in Chenliu. How did you manage to come here?" asked the uncle.

Cao Cao told him what had happened and said, "If not for the magistrate, I would have been hacked to pieces by now."

Lu Bo-she bowed low to the magistrate and said, "Thank you so much for saving my nephew and the Cao family. Without your help the entire household would be exterminated. But rest at ease now. You can spend the night in my humble cottage."

He then rose and went to the inner chamber. After a long while, he came out and said to the former magistrate: "There is no good wine in the house. I'm going to get some for you in the West Village." And he hastily mounted his donkey and rode away.

The two fugitives sat for a long time. Suddenly they heard the sound of the sharpening of a knife coming from the back of the house.

Cao Cao said, "He's not my real uncle. I begin to doubt his reasons for going off. Let's go inside and listen."

So they quietly stepped into the back of the cottage. Soon they heard someone inside saying, "Bind first, then kill, eh?"

"As I thought," said Cao Cao, "unless we strike first we will be taken."

They burst into the room, swords in hand, and slew everyone they saw, male and female, eight persons in all. After this they searched the house. When they came to the kitchen they found a pig bound ready to be slaughtered.

"You are too suspicious," said the former magistrate. "We have killed honest folk."

They at once mounted and rode away in a great hurry. But presently they met their host coming home with two vessels of wine hanging down from the saddle and fruit and vegetables in his hands.

"Why are you leaving so soon?" asked the old man.

"Condemned people dare not linger," said Cao Cao.

"But I have told my folk to kill a pig. Why do you refuse to spend just one night here? Please ride back with me."

Cao Cao paid no attention but urged his horse forward. Suddenly, however, he drew his sword and rode after the old man.

"Who is that coming along?" he called out to his uncle.

The old man turned back to look and at the same instant Cao Cao cut him down from his donkey.

His companion was shocked. "You were wrong enough before," he cried. "What now is this?"

"When he got home and saw his family killed, do you think he would let the matter drop? If he should raise an alarm and chase after us, we would certainly be in danger."

"To kill deliberately is very wrong," said Chen Gong.

"I would rather betray the world than let the world betray me," was Cao Cao's reply.

Chen Gong could say nothing. They rode on in silence for several *li* by the moonlight and then knocked on the door of a village inn for shelter.

After feeding the horses, Cao Cao went to sleep first but his companion sat thinking.

"I took him for a true man and left all to follow him, but he is actually as vicious as a wolf. If I spare him today, he will surely be the cause of trouble later." And he drew his sword, intending to kill Cao Cao.

> *With a heart full of vice he is not a true man,*
> *In no way does he differ from his foe Dong Zhuo.*

The fate of Cao Cao will be told in the next chapter.

CHAPTER FIVE

Many Lords Respond to Cao Cao's Call Against Dong Zhuo
The Three Brothers Fight with Lu Bu in the Battle at Tigertrap Pass

A t the end of the last chapter Chen Gong was about to slay Cao Cao. But the memory of why he had decided to throw in his lot with his companion's stayed his hand. He put the sword back into the sheath and, without waiting for daybreak, rode off toward his own home-town in the east. Cao Cao awoke at daybreak and missed his companion. He thought to himself, "He thinks me brutal because of a couple of egoistic phrases I used and so he has gone. I must also push on and not linger here."

So he traveled as quickly as possible toward home. When he saw his father he related to him what had happened and said that he wanted to dispose of all their property and enlist soldiers with the money.

"Our possessions are but small," said his father, "and not enough to do anything with. However, there's a scholar here by the name of Wei Hong, careless of wealth but careful of virtue, whose family is very rich. With his help we might hope for success."

Following his father's advice, Cao Cao invited the rich man to a feast at his home. At the feast, Cao Cao said to his guest, "The Hans have no lord of their own and Dong Zhuo is really a tyrant. He disregards the Emperor and persecutes the people, who gnash their teeth in hatred. I would restore the Hans but my means are insufficient. You are a man of loyalty and justice, sir, may I appeal to you for help?"

To this, his guest replied: "I have for so long desired this but so far have not found a man fit to undertake the task. Now that you, Meng-de, have so noble a desire, I am willing to devote my property to your cause."

This was really joyful news for Cao Cao. So the call to arms was prepared and sent far and near. Then he established a corp of volunteers and set up a large, white banner inscribed with the words "Loyalty and Justice." The response was rapid and volunteers came like rain drops in number.

Two of these volunteers were Yue Jin and Li Dian, who were both appointed to Cao Cao's personal staff. Another man called Xiahou Dun was descended from a notable general's family and had been trained from his boyhood to use the spear and the club. When only fourteen he had been attached to a certain master-in-arms. One day when someone spoke disrespectfully of his master, he killed the man and had to live in exile for some years. On hearing of Cao Cao's actions he came to give service, accompanied by his cousin Xiahou Yuan, each bringing a thousand or so valiant young men. In fact, these two were Cao Cao's cousins, since his father was originally of the Xiahou family and had become a member of the Cao family only by adoption.

Several days later, two young men from the Cao family, Cao Ren and Cao Hong, also came to assist, each accompanied by a thousand soldiers. As the two Cao brothers were accomplished horsemen and trained in the use of arms, they were asked to drill the troops in the village ground. Clothing, armor, flags, and banners were purchased with the money donated by the generous Wei Hong. Numerous people from all sides also poured in to give grain to the army.

When Yuan Shao received the call to arms, he left his prefecture of Bohai with all his advisors and officers as well as 30,000 soldiers to form an alliance with Cao Cao. Then Cao Cao issued a denunciation of Dong Zhuo, which ran as follows:

> *We, Cao Cao and associates, moved by a high sense of justice, now proclaim to the world: The arch-devil Dong Zhuo defies Heaven and Earth. He has destroyed the empire and slain the Emperor. He pollutes the palace and persecutes the people. Being cruel, vicious, and greedy, he has committed heinous crime upon crime. Now we have received a secret edict from the new Emperor to mobilize soldiers of justice. We vow to cleanse the empire and wipe out all the malicious elements. We hope you will raise a voluntary army. Let us join our forces in an effort to avenge the public wrong, maintain the dynasty, and succor the people. Respond immediately when you receive this."*

Soon, response came from seventeen lords of various regions, including Yuan Shao, Yuan Shu, Gongsun Zan, Bao Xin, and Sun Jian. All of them led their subordinates, civil and military, and an armed force of about 30,000 soldiers on a journey to the capital Luoyang.

Now Gongsun Zan, Prefect of Beiping,* was on his way to the capital with his force of 15,000 veteran soldiers. While passing through the city of Pingyuan he saw among the mulberry trees in the distance a yellow banner under which rode a small group of people. When they drew near, he found the leader was Liu Bei.

"Why are you here, my good brother?" asked the general.

"I am magistrate of this district. It was on your recommendation that I got this post. I hear that you and your army are passing through, so I have come specially to invite you to take a rest inside the city."

"Who are these two?" asked the general, pointing to Liu Bei's two brothers.

"They are Guan Yu and Zhang Fei, my sworn brothers," answered Liu Bei.

"Were they the people who fought with you against the Yellow Turban rebels?"

"Yes. I owe all my successes to their efforts," said Liu Bei.

"And what offices do they fill?"

"Guan Yu is a mounted archer and Zhang Fei, a foot archer."

"How sad to waste the talents of real heroes like this!" sighed the general. Then he continued, "Now Dong Zhuo is stirring up trouble and all the lords in the country are uniting to destroy him. I suggest you abandon this petty office and join us in our fight against Dong Zhuo for the restoration of the House of Han. What do you think of this?"

"I would like to go with you," said Liu Bei.

"If you'd let me kill that fellow at that time, you wouldn't have the trouble today," said Zhang Fei.

"Well, what's the use of talking about that? Let's just pack and go," said Guan Yu.

So the three brothers, with a few horsemen as their escort, followed Gongsun Zan to the capital, where they were received by Cao Cao. One after another all the other lords also came and set up their camps which extended over 200 *li* and more. When all had arrived, Cao Cao, as the organizer, prepared sacrificial bullocks and horses and invited all the lords to a great assembly to discuss their plan of attack.

Prefect Wang Kuang of Henei said: "We have assembled here to uphold justice. We must first elect a leader and bind ourselves to obedience to him. Then can we start the battle against our enemy."

Cao Cao continued, "For four generations the Yuan family have held highest offices in the government and their former subordinates are eve-

---

* An old town in modern Hebei in north China.

rywhere. As a descendant of notable ministers of Han, Yuan Shao is a suitable man to be our leader."

Yuan Shao again and again declined this honor. But all those present said, "It must be you. There is no one else." Finally he agreed.

The next day, a three-storied altar was erected and all around it were planted banners inscribed with the five characters meaning east, south, west, north, and center. They also set up white yaks' tails and golden axes as well as emblems of military authority and the commander's seal on the altar. Clad in a ceremonial robe and girt with a sword, he stepped onto it like a true hero. There he lit the incense and bowed reverently several times. Then he read out the oath:

> Misfortune has befallen the House of Han and the imperial
> authority has suffered. The wicked minister Dong Zhuo takes
> advantage of this to start trouble. He brought disasters to the
> Emperor and tyrannized over the common folk. We, Shao, and his
> confederates, have assembled military forces to rescue the country
> from calamity. All of us who join the alliance pledge to exert
> ourselves and act in unison for the success of our cause. There
> must never be any departure from our aim. Should anyone fail to
> observe this pledge, may he lose his life and leave nothing for
> posterity. Almighty Heaven and Earth and the enlightened spirits
> of our ancestors, please be our witnesses!

The reading finished, he smeared the blood of the sacrifice upon his lips. Moved by the strong fervor of his speech, all the listeners shed tears.

Then he descended from the altar and was led to his tent, where he took the seat of the commander-in-chief while the others arranged themselves on both sides according to rank and age.

After serving wine for several rounds, Cao Cao said, "Now that we've chosen our own leader we must obey him in every move and join our efforts in protecting the empire. There must be no feeling of rivalry or superiority among us."

Yuan Shao said, "Unworthy as I am, yet as elected leader I will reward every merit and punish every offense. A state has its criminal laws and an army its precepts. All of us must obey these and not break them."

"Your orders will be strictly observed," promised everyone.

Then Yuan Shao appointed his brother Yuan Shu to be in charge of army provision and ordered him to keep all the camps well-supplied.

He continued, "But the need for the moment is a van leader who will go to Sishui Pass to provoke a battle and the others must take up key positions to support him."

"I will lead the van," volunteered Sun Jian, Prefect of Changsha.

"You are valiant and fierce, equal to this service," said the commander.

The army under Sun Jian set out and presently came to Sishui Pass. The officer there dispatched a swift rider to Dong Zhuo's house in the capital to report the urgency of the situation.

Ever since Dong Zhuo had secured his dominant position he had indulged himself in excessive eating and drinking. When Li Ru, his chief advisor, got the urgent news, he went straight to his master. On hearing this, Dong Zhuo was much alarmed and immediately called a great council.

Lu Bu stood up and said, "Don't worry, father. I look upon all the lords outside the pass as mere stubble and with the men of our fierce army I will put every one of them to death and hang their heads at the gates of the capital."

"With you in my service I can sit back and relax." Dong Zhuo was greatly relieved.

He had hardly finished his speech when someone behind Lu Bu cried out, "A butcher's knife to kill a chicken! There is no need for the young master to go. I will cut off their heads as easily as I would take a thing out of my pocket."

Dong Zhuo looked up and his eyes rested upon a stalwart man of fierce mien, lithe and supple. He had a tiger's body and a wolf's waist. His head was like a leopard's and his shoulders like an ape's. His name was Hua Xiong. Dong Zhuo was overjoyed at his bold words and at once gave him high rank and command over 50,000 horse and foot soldiers. Without delay, Hua Xiong led the men on a quick march toward Sishui Pass together with three other commanding officers.

Among the lords serving Yuan Shao was Bao Xin, who was jealous lest the chosen van leader, Sun Jian, should win the honor of the victory of the first battle. Determined to meet the foe first, he secretly dispatched his brother Bao Zhong with 3,000 horse and foot soldiers to get to the pass by a back road. As soon as this small force reached their destination they offered battle. Hua Xiong, at the head of five hundred mail-clad horsemen, swept down from the pass to meet them. Frightened, Bao Zhong hastened to turn back but it was too late. Hua Xiong raised his arm and the great sword fell, cutting his victim down from his horse. Many of his men were captured. The poor man's head was sent to Dong Zhuo as proof of the victory and Hua Xiong was duly promoted to an even higher rank.

Soon Sun Jian also approached the pass. He had four subordinate officers with him: Cheng Pu, whose weapon was an iron-spined spear; Huang

Gai, who wielded an iron whip; Han Dang, a swordsman; and Zu Mao, who fought with double swords. Sun Jian himself donned fine silver armor and wore a red turban wrapped around his head. He carried across his body his sword of ancient ingot iron and rode a dappled horse with flowing mane. He advanced to the pass and shouted up at its defenders: "Surrender, you lackeys of Dong Zhuo!"

Down from the pass came Hu Zhen with 5,000 men to respond to the challenge. Cheng Pu with the snaky lance rode out to fight against him. After only a few bouts, Hu Zhen was killed by a thrust through his throat. Then Sun Jian led his army to push forward, but from the pass rained down showers of stones that proved too much for the assailants and they retired into their camp at Liangdong. A messenger was sent to announce the victory to Yuan Shao and also to ask Yuan Shu for immediate supplies of grain.

But some of his advisors said to Yuan Shu, "Sun Jian is a very tiger. If he should take the capital and destroy Dong Zhuo, it would be like driving out a wolf to bring in a tiger. Do not send him grain and his army will fall apart." Yuan Shu listened to this and sent no grain or forage. Soon, chaos emerged among the hungry soldiers under Sun Jian and spies reported the news to the pass defenders, who decided upon a speedy attack on Sun Jian from the front and rear. They hoped to capture him in this way.

Hua Xiong gave his soldiers a large meal and told them to be ready to set out when darkness fell. That night the moon was bright and the wind cool. By midnight his troops had reached Sun Jian's camp. Then they beat drums and shouted loudly as they pressed forward. Sun Jian hastily put on his fighting gear and rode out. He ran straight into Hua Xiong and the two immediately engaged in battle. After they had exchanged a few passes, another army came up from the rear and set fire to whatever would burn. Sun Jian's men were thrown into great confusion and fled like rats. A general melee ensued and soon only Zu Mao was at his chief's side. The two of them broke through the enemy's encirclement and fled. Hua Xiong came in hot pursuit. Sun Jian took his bow and let fly two arrows in quick succession but both missed. When he fitted a third arrow to the string he drew the bow so fiercely that it snapped. He had to give it up and rode off at full speed.

Zu Mao said, "My lord, the red turban around your forehead is a mark that the enemy recognizes easily. Take it off and let me wear it."

So they exchanged their headpieces and parted. The pursuers went only after the wearer of the red turban. So Sun Jian was able to escape through a bypath. Zu Mao, hotly pursued, tore off the headpiece and hung it on the post of a half-burned house. Then he dashed into the thick woods to hide. Seeing the turban from a distance, Hua Xiong's men dared not approach it but instead encircled from every side and shot at it with arrows. Before long the deception was discovered and they went up to seize the turban.

This was the moment Zu Mao was waiting for. He rushed out of the woods and swinging his double swords, dashed at Hua Xiong. But his enemy was too powerful for him. With a loud yell, Hua Xiong cut him down from his horse. The killing continued till daybreak and it was only then that the victor led his men back to the pass.

Sun Jian's three other chief officers finally joined him. They collected the remaining soldiers and encamped again. He was much grieved at the loss of the faithful Zu Mao.

When news of the disaster was reported to Yuan Shao he was greatly alarmed and called all the lords to a council. All came, with Gongsun Zan being the last to arrive. Yuan Shao invited them to sit inside his tent and said: "First it was General Bao's brother who disobeyed the orders and rashly went to attack the enemy. He ended up getting himself slain and with him many of our soldiers. Now General Sun has also been defeated. Our fighting spirit has suffered from these two losses. What do you think we should do?"

Everyone was silent. Lifting his eyes, Yuan Shao looked from one to another till he came to Gongsun Zan and noted the three unusual-looking men behind his seat. All three were smiling cynically.

"Who are those men behind you?" he asked.

Gongsun Zan asked Liu Bei to come forth and said, "This is Liu Bei, Magistrate of Pingyuan and an old friend of mine. We used to live under the same roof."

"He must be the Liu Bei who defeated the Yellow Turban rebels," said Cao Cao.

"Yes, he is," replied Gongsun Zan. And he asked Liu Bei to pay his respects to the assembly, to whom he then related in full detail Liu Bei's services and his origin of birth.

"He should be seated since he is of the Han line," said Yuan Shao and he bade Liu Bei sit down.

Liu Bei thanked him modestly.

Yuan Shao said, "This consideration is not for your fame or your office. I respect you as a scion of the imperial family."

So Liu Bei took his seat at the end of the long line of lords while his two brothers stood behind him with folded arms.

Suddenly a scout came in to say that Hua Xiong and his mail-clad horsemen had left the pass and were already outside their camp. They were flaunting Sun Jian's red turban on the end of a bamboo pole and hurling insults at people inside the stockade, challenging them to fight.

"Who dares to go out and fight?" asked the commander.

"I will," answered Yu She, a veteran officer under Yuan Shu.

So he went out and almost immediately a messenger came back to say that he had been killed by Hua Xiong in the third bout. Fear began to lay its cold hand on the assembly. Then another lord said, "I have a brave warrior among my men. Pan Feng is his name and he can slay this Hua Xiong." So Pang Feng was ordered to meet the foe. With his great ax in hand he mounted and rode forth. But soon came the sorrowful news that he, too, had fallen. All those present turned pale at this.

"What a pity my two able officers, Yan Liang and Wen Chou, are not here! If but one of them was present, how could Hua Xiong defy us?"

He had hardly finished his speech when from the lower end someone cried out, "I will go and take his head! I will lay it before you here!"

All turned to look at the speaker. He was very tall of stature with a long beard. He had eyes like those of a phoenix and bushy eyebrows like sleeping silkworms. His face was a swarthy red and his voice deep and resonant, like the sound of a great bell.

"Who is this man?" asked the commander.

Gongsun Zan told him that it was Guan Yu, sworn brother of Liu Bei.

"And what office does he hold?"

"He is a mounted archer in the service of Liu Bei."

"An insult to us all!" roared Yuan Shu from his seat. "Do you think we have no valiant officers of our own? How dare an archer speak thus before us ? Drive him out!"

But Cao Cao quickly intervened. "Don't be angry. Since he talks big he must be valiant. Let him go and if he fails, you can punish him then."

"Hua Xiong will laugh at us if we send a mere archer to fight with him," said the commander.

"He doesn't look a common person. How can the enemy know he is but a bowman?" said Cao Cao.

"If I fail you can behead me," persisted Guan Yu.

Cao Cao bade the attendants bring some hot wine and offered a stirrup cup to Guan Yu as he went out to fight.

"Wait until I come back to drink it," he said.

Sword in hand, he went out and vaulted onto his horse. Then loud shouts and the fierce beating of drums could be heard as if the sky was falling and the earth sinking, mountains trembling and hills tearing asunder. All those inside the tent were gripped with fear. When they were about to send someone out to inquire, there came the gentle tinkle of a

horse bell—then Guan Yu threw at their feet the head of Hua Xiong.
The wine was still warm! This heroic deed was celebrated in verse:

> *The most brilliant deed shook the world far and wide,*
> *At the gate of the camp was heard the rolling of the battle drums.*
> *Guan Yu set aside the wine cup till his valor was displayed,*
> *And the wine was still warm when the enemy was slain.*

Cao Cao was greatly pleased at this success. Just then Zhang Fei
stepped forth from behind Liu Bei and shouted, "My brother has slain
Hua Xiong. Why don't we just break through the pass and seize Dong
Zhuo? There could be no better time than this!"

Again arose the voice of the peevish Yuan Shu, "We high officials are
modest and yielding. Here are the petty followers of a small magistrate
daring to flaunt their prowess before us! Expel them from the tent, I say!'

But again Cao Cao interposed, "Should we consider the status of him
who has done a great service?"

"If you hold a mere magistrate in such honor then I will simply withdraw," answered Yuan Shu.

"We cannot allow our great cause to suffer just for one word," said Cao
Cao.

He told Gongsun Zan to take his three companions back to their own
camp. Then the other lords also dispersed. That night Cao Cao secretly
sent meat and wine to soothe the three brothers.

In the meantime, Hua Xiong's men had returned to the pass and related to one of the other commanding officers the story of the defeat. He
immediately wrote to his master to ask for emergency aid. Dong Zhuo
called in his trusted advisors for counsel. Li Ru summed up the situation:
"We have lost our senior officer Hua Xiong and the enemy has therefore
become very strong. Yuan Shao is head of this confederacy and his uncle, Yuan Wei, is holding a high office in the government. If those inside
the capital collaborate with those outside, we will suffer. Therefore, we
must first remove the ones in the city. Then I suggest your lordship
should place yourself at the head of your army and lead it to wipe out all
the rebels."

Dong Zhuo agreed and at once ordered two of his followers, called Li
Jue and Guo Si, to take five hundred soldiers to surround the residence of
Yuan Wei. They killed everyone in the household, no matter whether old
or young, and even hung the head of the old official outside the gate as a
trophy. Then Dong Zhuo commanded 200,000 soldiers to advance in two
armies. The first 50,000 men were under Li Jue and Guo Si, who were to
hold Sishui Pass and not to fight. The main body under Dong Zhuo him-

self went to Tigertrap Pass, which is about fifty *li* from the capital.

As soon as they arrived there, Lu Bu was ordered to take 30,000 men and make a stockade outside of Tigertrap Pass. The major force with Dong Zhuo occupied the fortress.

News of this deployment of Dong Zhuo's soon reached the confederate lords and a meeting was again convened in Yuan Shao's camp. Cao Cao said, "The occupation of Tigertrap Pass will cut our force in two. We must use half of our armies to oppose them." This being generally accepted, eight of the lords, including Gongsun Zan and Bao Xin, marched toward Tigertrap Pass to oppose the enemy. Cao Cao and his men acted as a reserve force to render help where needed.

Of the eight, Wang Kuang, Prefect of Henei, was the first to arrive with his army. Lu Bu rushed forth to give battle with 3,000 mailed horsemen.

When Wang Kuang had arranged his army, horse and foot, in battle array, he took his position under the great banner and looked over at his foe. There he saw Lu Bu, a conspicuous figure in the front. On his head was a triple curved headdress of ruddy gold. He wore a robe of Xichuan silk embroidered with flowers; over that, breast and back mail adorned with a gaping animal's head, joined by rings at the sides and girt to his waist with a belt fastened by a beautiful lion's head clasp. His bow and arrows were slung over his shoulders and he carried a halberd. He was seated on his snorting steed, the Red Hare. Indeed he was a man among men, as his steed was a horse among horses.

"Who dares to go and fight with him?" asked the prefect, turning to those behind him.

In response, a skilled warrior spurred to the front, his spear set ready for battle. The two met, but before the fifth bout, he fell under a thrust of the halberd and Lu Bu dashed forward. The prefect's men could not hold and scattered in all directions. Lu Bu went to and fro, slaying whoever was in his way. He was quite irresistible.

Fortunately, two other prefects with their troops came to the rescue and Lu Bu retreated. All three having lost many men, withdrew thirty *li* and made a stockade. And before long the remaining five lords also arrived and joined them. They held a council.

"This Lu Bu is invincible," they said.

But even as they sat there anxious and uncertain, news came that Lu Bu had returned to challenge them to a battle. All the eight lords mounted and their forces spread out in eight lines on high hills. They saw in the distance under fluttering banners Lu Bu and his army charging forward to break their battle array.

Mu Shun, an officer from Shangdang, rode out but, to the horror of the others, he fell at first contact with Lu Bu. Then Wu An-guo from Beihai rushed out, swinging his iron mace. Lu Bu, whirling his halberd, rode forth to meet him. After about a dozen bouts a blow from the halberd broke Wu's wrist, and he fled, giving up his weapon. Then all eight armies came up to his rescue and Lu Bu withdrew.

The lords also retired to camp for another council. Cao Cao said, "Lu Bu's prowess has no match. Let's consult all the lords for a good plan. If only he could be captured, then Dong Zhuo would be easily destroyed."

However, while the council was still in progress, again Lu Bu came forth to challenge them and again they went out to oppose him. This time Gongsun Zan, flinging his mace, went to meet the enemy himself, but had to flee after a few bouts. Lu Bu followed at topmost speed on the Red Hare. As his horse was as swift as the wind and could ride a thousand *li* a day, Lu Bu gained rapidly upon his fleeing opponent, with his weapon poised, ready to pierce Gongsun Zan's heart from behind. Just at that moment, from the confederate side a warrior with round, glaring eyes and a bristling mustach dashed in, his long, snaky spear raised high to strike.

"Halt, you menial servant with three surnames!" he roared. "I, Zhang Fei, am here, waiting for you!"

Seeing his new opponent, Lu Bu gave up his pursuit of Gongsun Zan and turned around to fight with Zhang Fei. They were equally matched and neither could gain any advantage over the other after an exchange of about three score of bouts. At this point, Guan Yu urged his horse forward and, whirling his weighty moon-shaped sword, he attacked Lu Bu from the other side. The three steeds stood like the letter T and their riders fought to the thirtieth bout, yet Lu Bu still held his ground.

Then Liu Bei went to his brothers' aid, drawing out his double swords and urging his horse to cut in at an angle. The three of them circled around Lu Bu and attacked him, one after another, like a revolving lantern during New Year. All the spectators from the eight confederate forces gazed aghast at such a battle. But gradually Lu Bu's defense began to flag and he looked for a chance to retreat. As Liu Bei was the weakest in strength of the three brothers, Lu Bu feigned a fierce thrust in the face of Liu Bei, who dodged to one side to avoid him. Lu Bu immediately dashed through this temporary opening, his trident lowered to force a way out of the encirclement.

The three brothers, however, would not allow him to escape. They whipped their steeds and pressed hard upon him.

The men of the eight armies cheered in a thunderous roar and all rushed forward, chasing after Lu Bu and his troops as he made for Tigertrap Pass. And first among the pursuers were the three heroic brothers, who followed him to the very gate of the pass. Looking up, they saw an immense umbrella of blue gauze, its lace fluttering in the west wind.

"That must be Dong Zhuo!" cried Zhang Fei. "What's the use of pursuing Lu Bu? Better seize the chief villain and so eradicate the evil by plucking up its roots."

And Zhang Fei whipped up his steed toward the pass to seize the wicked minister.

> *To quell rebellion seize the leader if you can;*
> *A wondrous service waits a wondrous man.*

The result of this battle will be told in the next chapter.

CHAPTER SIX

Burning the Capital, Dong Zhuo Commits Atrocities

Hiding the Emperor's Seal, Sun Jian Breaks His Faith

Zhang Fei galloped to the pass but there showered a rain of arrows and stones from on top, which prevented him from entering and he returned. The eight lords all joined in felicitations to the three heroes for their remarkable services and the victory of the battle was sent to Yuan Shao, who then ordered Sun Jian to advance.

Sun Jian, together with two of his trusted subordinates, went over to Yuan Shu's camp. Tracing figures on the ground with his staff, Sun Jian said, "I bear no personal grudge against Dong Zhuo, yet I have thrown myself into this life-and-death battle regardless of my own safety and exposed my own person to the enemy's fierce attacks. And why? That I might help eliminate an evil in the country and for the private advantage of your family. But you, giving heed to some slanderous tongues around you, deliberately withheld the supplies of grain, and so I suffered defeat. How can you explain that, General?"

Yuan Shu, feeling guilty and afraid, had no word to reply. To placate Sun Jian, he ordered the death of the slanderers.

Then suddenly a messenger came with the news that Sun Jian had a visitor from the pass waiting for him in his camp. So Sun Jian took his leave and returned to his own camp, where he found the visitor was a favorite officer of Dong Zhuo's, named Li Jue.

"What do you want?" he asked.

"You are the one person that the prime minister truly admires," said Li Jue, "so he sends me here to arrange a matrimonial alliance between your family and his. He wishes that his daughter may marry your son."

Sun Jian was enraged at this. "What nonsense!" he rebuked, "Dong Zhuo acts against the will of Heaven and subverts the throne. I wish I could uproot his nine generations to appease the nation! Do you think I will ever consent to having an alliance with such a family? I am not going to kill you now. But go back quickly and yield the pass at once and I may spare your life. If you delay you will be killed without mercy."

Li Jue threw his hands over his head and scurried off like a rat. He returned to his master and told him of Sun Jian's rudeness. Dong Zhuo, very angry, asked Li Ru how to reply to this.

As always, Li Ru gave an appraisal of the general situation. He said that as Lu Bu's late defeat had somewhat blunted the edge of the army's desire for battle it would be better to return to Luoyang first and then remove the Emperor to Chang'an* so as to respond to what street boys had been singing recently:

> *A Han in the west, a Han in the east;*
> *The deer will be safe in Chang'an, poor beast.*

Li Ru continued to explain the street rhyme: "I think 'a Han in the west' refers to the founder of the dynasty, who became ruler in the western city of Chang'an, which became the capital for twelve emperors; while 'a Han in the east' refers to Emperor Guangwu, who ruled from the eastern city of Luoyang, which has also been the capital of twelve emperors. It is the will of Heaven for us to return. If you move back to Chang'an, sir, there will be no need for anxiety."

Dong Zhuo was exceedingly pleased and said, "I would not have seen it in this light if you had not explained it to me." So he set out at once for the capital, taking Lu Bu with him.

Back at Luoyang, he called all the officials and generals together in the palace.

"After two centuries of rule here in Luoyang," he declared, "the fortune of Han has been exhausted. I perceive that the aura of rule has actually migrated to Chang'an. So I intend to move the court there. All of you had better pack up for the journey."

Three high-ranking officials voiced their opposition to the move, saying that the city of Chang'an had been burned down during a previous rebellion and that it would not be right to abandon the imperial tombs and ancestral temples. They also argued that the move would alarm the people so greatly that it would be difficult to pacify them again. But Dong Zhuo paid no heed to any of them and that day all three were stripped of their official ranks and reduced to common folk. Two other officials again tried to dissuade him but were ruthlessly put to death. Thus Dong

---

* Modern Xian.

Zhuo had silenced all objectors to the scheme. An order was issued for the journey to begin the next day.

But before he set out, he did not forget to rob the people of Luoyang of their property and to destroy the city completely. Several thousand rich families were labeled "rebels" and put to death outside the city, their money confiscated. Millions of people were driven from their homes and forced to make the journey. Countless innocent folks died on the way, some falling into ditches and others killed by soldiers. In order to get more gold and jewelry, he even ordered Lu Bu to desecrate the tombs of former emperors and their consorts for the treasures buried within. However, worse was still to come. His most atrocious act was his final order to burn the whole city, houses, palaces, and temples and the capital became nothing but a patch of scorched earth.

Having committed all the atrocities, Dong Zhuo and his stooges left for the new capital, taking with them the Emperor and his household, followed by an extremely long procession of thousands of carts filled with gold and silver, pearls and silk, and all kinds of treasures.

The city of Luoyang being thus abandoned, the commander at Sishui Pass surrendered and Sun Jian at once entered with his army. Liu Bei and his two brothers took Tigertrap Pass and all the other lords also advanced with their armies.

Meanwhile, Sun Jian headed toward the deserted capital in haste. Even from a distance he could see the city lit up in flames and a dense smoke curling over the ground. No living thing, not a fowl or a dog or a human being, could be found for miles and miles around. Sun Jian ordered his men to extinguish the fire and then asked the lords to camp on the barren fields.

Cao Cao went to see Yuan Shao and said, "Dong Zhuo is now on his way to Chang'an. We ought to seize this opportunity to pursue and attack without loss of time. Why do you take no action?"

"The armies are all exhausted. There is nothing to gain by advancing," answered Yuan Shao.

Cao Cao argued, "The whole country is greatly upset by Dong Zhuo's atrocities of burning down the palaces and abducting the Emperor. No one knows which way to turn. This is the Heaven-sent moment to destroy him. With one decisive battle we can rule the world. Why are you so hesitant and do not advance?"

But all the lords disagreed with him. Exasperated, he cried out, "You cowards! I have nothing more to say to you!" He left the city that very night with his trusted subordinates and army in pursuit of Dong Zhuo.

Now Dong Zhuo and his cavalcade had reached Yingyang on their way to the newly-chosen capital and the prefect of the city went out to welcome them. Li Ru warned his master of the danger of their being pursued.

"Tell the prefect to lay an ambush beside some hills outside the city," he said. "If the pursuers come, do not fight with them, but let them proceed. Wait until our army beats them off, then storm out to prevent them from escaping. That will teach the others not to follow us."

So everything was arranged as Li Ru had planned. With a company of veteran soldiers, Lu Bu was placed at the rear, ready to fight any pursuers. Soon they saw Cao Cao and his troops coming. Lu Bu laughed. "It's just as Li Ru has predicted." And he set out his men in fighting order.

Cao Cao rode forth and cried out, "You rebels, where are you taking the Emperor and the people?"

Lu Bu replied, "Traitor and coward, what nonsense are you talking!"

Then from Cao Cao's side Xiahou Dun came forth to fight against Lu Bu. They had exchanged only a few bouts when another army led by Li Jue came up from the left. Cao Cao hurriedly ordered Xiahou Yuan to oppose him. But almost at once shouts came from the right and still another army led by Guo Si emerged. Cao Ren was sent in a hurry to confront him. The onrush of the three armed forces, however, proved too much to withstand. Very soon, Xiahou Dun could not ward off Lu Bu's attack and had to flee back to his own army. Lu Bu led his mail-clad veterans and pressed forward, defeating Cao Cao's men completely. The beaten men turned back toward Yingyang.

At about nine in the evening they got to the foot of a barren hill. The moon was shining brightly, making it almost as light as day. Here they collected together what remained of their army and were about to bury the boilers to prepare a meal when all of a sudden there arose loud shouting on all sides—out came the men waiting in ambush.

Cao Cao, thrown into a flurry, mounted and fled as fast as he could. Unfortunately he ran right into the waiting prefect. He turned and dashed off in another direction but the prefect drew an arrow to his bow and shot him in the shoulder. With the arrow still in the wound, Cao Cao escaped for his life, galloping past the hillside. Two soldiers lying in ambush saw him approaching and suddenly both of them struck his horse with their spears. The horse fell, throwing down Cao Cao, who was seized and made prisoner.

At this critical moment, an officer riding at full speed came to his rescue. Whirling his sword, he killed both his captors and then dismounting, helped Cao Cao up. It was his cousin Cao Hong.

"I'm doomed," said Cao Cao. "Go and save yourself at once, good brother."

"Mount my horse quickly. I will go on foot," said his cousin.

"What if those rogues come up?" asked Cao Cao.

"The world can do without me, but not without you," was the reply.

"If I live, I owe you my life," said Cao Cao.

So he mounted. His cousin took off his breastplate and followed the horse on foot, dragging along his heavy sword. They went in this way for several hours, when there appeared before them a broad stream, and behind them the shouts of the pursuers came nearer and nearer.

"This is my fate," sighed Cao Cao. "I'm really doomed to die here."

Cao Hong at once helped him down from his horse. Then taking off his fighting robe, he carried Cao Cao on his back and waded across the river. No sooner had they gained the other bank, the pursuers also came up to the river, from where they shot arrows at them.

By daybreak they had walked another thirty *li* or more. Too exhausted to proceed any further, they took a short rest under a slope. All at once loud shouting was heard and a band of horses and men appeared. It was the Prefect of Yingyang, who had forded the river upstream to chase them. It seemed impossible for Cao Cao to escape this time but just at that moment he saw the Xiahou brothers galloping along with some dozens of horsemen.

"Do not harm my lord!" cried Xiahou Dun to the prefect, who at once rushed at him. After a few exchanges the prefect was pierced to death and his men driven off. Before long, Cao Cao's other officers arrived. Feelings of sadness and joy were expressed at the reunion. Then they gathered together the remaining five hundred men and returned to their base in Henei.

Dong Zhuo and his followers went their way to Chang'an.

Back in Luoyang all the lords had encamped. Sun Jian, after extinguishing the fire in the palace, camped within the city walls, his tent being set up on the ground of the former Jianzhang Hall of the palace. He ordered his men to clear away the debris and close the tombs that had been robbed by Dong Zhuo and bar the gates to the mausoleum. On the site of the Royal Temple he put up three rooms to serve as the temporary shrine of worship. Here, he invited the lords to replace the sacred tablets and a ceremony was held, with the offer of sacrifices and solemn prayers.

When all the others had left, Sun Jian returned to his own camp. That night, the moon and the stars vied with each other in brightness. So he sat in the open air looking up at the sky, his hand on his sword. There, he noticed a mist spreading over the Emperor's star.*

---

* In ancient China people believed that the conditions and movements of the stars were

"The Emperor's star is dulled," he sighed. "No wonder the empire is in such great trouble." And he lamented over the recent calamity the country and the people had been through.

Then a soldier, pointing to a well in the south, said: "There are colored lights rising from there."

Sun Jian told his men to light torches and descend into the well to investigate. Soon, they brought up the corpse of a woman not in the least decayed, although the body had been in there many days. She was dressed in palace clothing and from her neck hung an embroidered bag. When they opened it they found a red box with a golden lock. Unlocking the box, they saw a jade seal, square in shape, one inch each way. On it were delicately engraved five intertwining dragons. One corner had been broken off and repaired with gold. There were eight characters in the style of seal writing, which could be interpreted as follows: "I have received the command from Heaven, may longevity and prosperity be always with me."

Sun Jian showed this to Cheng Pu, who at once recognized it as the hereditary seal of the Emperor.

He said, "This seal has a history. In past days a man called Bian He saw a phoenix sitting on a certain stone at the foot of Jing Hill. He took the stone and offered it at court. Duke Wen of Chu split open the stone and found a piece of jade inside. Early in the Qin Dynasty it was cut into a seal and Minister Li Si engraved these eight characters. Two years later, when the first Emperor of Qin Dynasty was sailing on Dongting Lake, there suddenly arose a terrible storm. The seal was thrown overboard as a propitiatory offering, and the storm immediately ceased. Ten years later, when the Emperor was in Huayin, a man waiting by the roadside handed a seal to one of the attendants and said, 'Give this back to Zulong,'* and then disappeared. Thus the seal was returned to Qin. The next year the Emperor died.

"Later, Ziying presented this seal to the founder of the Han Dynasty. During Wang Mang's usurpation† the Empress Dowager struck two of the rebels with the seal and broke off a corner, which was repaired with gold. Emperor Guangwu got possession of it at Yiyang and it has been regularly bequeathed to later emperors. I heard that during the trouble in the palace when The Ten hurried off the Emperor to Beimong it was found missing on His Majesty's return. Now Heaven has sent it to you,

---

related to important men and events on earth.
*   Another name for the first Emperor of Qin.
†   A.D. 8–23

my lord. You will certainly come to the imperial dignity. But you must not remain here. Return to the east at once where you can make plans for the accomplishment of the great design."

"That's just what I think," said Sun Jian. "Tomorrow I will make an excuse that I'm unwell and get away."

The soldiers were told to keep the discovery a secret. But who could have guessed that one among them was from the same village as Yuan Shao? He thought this might be a chance for him to get promoted, so he stole out of the camp and betrayed his master. He received a handsome reward and Yuan Shao kept him in his own camp. The next day Sun Jian came to take leave, saying that he was rather unwell and had to return to Changsha.

Yuan Shao laughed and said, "I know what you are suffering from; it is called the Hereditary Seal illness."

This was a shock to Sun Jian. He turned pale and asked, "What do you mean?"

Yuan Shao said, "We've raised the armies to destroy evils for the empire. The seal is imperial property. Since you have got hold of it you should openly hand it over to me as leader of the armed forces. After Dong Zhuo is slain it'll be handed over to the Emperor. What do you mean by concealing it and going away?"

"How could the seal get into my hands?" asked Sun Jian.

"Where is the thing you got out of the well in Jianzhang Hall?"

"I do not have it; why harass me like this?"

"Give it to me quickly or it will be worse for you."

Sun Jian, pointing to the sky, vowed: "If I have this seal and am hiding it, may my end be unhappy and my death violent."

The other lords all said, "After a vow like this, he cannot have it."

Then Yuan Shao called out his informant. "When you pulled that thing out of the well, was this man there?" he asked.

Sun Jian burst into anger and sprang forward to kill the man. Yuan Shao also drew his sword and said, "You touch that soldier and it is an insult to me."

In a moment, on both sides swords flew from their scabbards. But the confusion was checked by the efforts of the others and Sun Jian left the assembly. Soon, he broke up his camp and left the city of Luoyang. Yuan Shao was furious. He wrote a letter to Liu Biao, Governor of Jingzhou, and sent a reliable servant to deliver it to him at once. In the letter he told the governor to stop Sun Jian and force him to surrender the seal.

The following day news came of Cao Cao's return after his disastrous defeat at Yingyang. Yuan Shao sent people to welcome him to his camp.

All the lords gathered together and wine was prepared to console him. At the assembly, Cao Cao said, sadly: "It was for the sake of ridding the country of the evil Dong Zhuo that I called upon you to support me. Since you had come for a noble cause I had hoped that Benchu* could lead his Henei force to approach Menjin while the others from Suanzao could hold Chenggao, take possession of Ao Granary, and seize Huanyuan and Taigu, so that the crucial vantage points would be in our hands. In the meantime, Gonglu† could lead his Nanyang force to enter the Wu Pass, in order that the three cities near Chang'an would be under our military threat. It would be better for all of us to fortify our positions and not fight. In this way, the enemy would be kept in apprehension of our military strength. And we could take full advantage of this to show the world that justice would prevail over rebellion. Then victory would be ours at once. But now you hesitate in taking any immediate action, thus failing to meet the expectations of the people. I cannot but feel ashamed."

Yuan Shao and the others could find no words to reply and presently the guests dispersed. Cao Cao saw that the others all had their own schemes. He realized that nothing could be accomplished, so he led his men off to Yangzhou.

Gongsun Zan said to the three brothers: "This Yuan Shao is incapable of action. If things continue in this way, disaster will come. We'd better go our way, too." So they broke camp and went north. At Pingyuan the general parted with the three brothers and placed Liu Bei in command of the town while he himself went to his own position to refresh his men.

Among the remaining lords one of them was the Prefect of Yanzhou, who wished to borrow grain from the Prefect of Dongjun. Being refused, he attacked the other's camp, killed the prefect, and took over all his men. Yuan Shao saw that the confederacy had collapsed, and he, too, struck camp and left Luoyang for Guandong.

Now the Governor of Jingzhou, named Liu Biao, was a scion of the imperial house. As a young man, he had made friends with many famous persons and he and his companions were known as The Fine Eight. He also had three trusty subordinates who helped him in the administration of his district. They were Kuai Liang, Kuai Yue, and Cai Mao.

After he received Yuan Shao's letter detailing the fault of Sun Jian, he sent Kuai Yue and Cai Mao with 10,000 soldiers to stop Sun Jian on the way. When Sun Jian drew near, the waiting Kuai Yue arranged his troops in fighting order and rode to the front.

---

*   Yuan Shao's familiar name.
†   Yuan Shu's familiar name.

"Why are you barring my way with armed men?" asked Sun Jian.

"Why do you, a minister of Han, try to hide the Emperor's seal? Leave it with me at once and I will let you go," said Kuai Yue.

Sun Jian angrily ordered Huang Gai out, while on the other side came Cai Mao to oppose him. The two of them had exchanged only a few bouts before Huang Gai dealt his opponent a blow right on the breastplate with his iron whip. Cai Mao turned his steed and fled. Following this victory, Sun Jian pushed on with his army and managed to get through. However, from behind the hills came the sound of gongs and drums and there was Liu Biao in person with a large army. Sun Jian bowed to him while still mounted and asked: "Why do you resort to force against your neighboring prefecture based on a mere letter from Yuan Shao?"

"You have concealed the Hereditary Seal of the empire. Do you want to rebel?" replied Liu Biao.

"If I have it, may I die under swords and arrows."

"If you want me to believe you, let me search your luggage."

"Do you think you are so powerful that you can humiliate me like this?" said Sun Jian angrily.

They were about to engage in battle when Liu Biao retreated. Sun Jian urged his steed to press on, but all at once the men waiting in ambush emerged from behind the hills on both sides and worse still, Kuai Yue and Cai Mao also came up from the rear, leaving Sun Jian trapped on all sides.

What does it advantage a man to hold the imperial seal
If its possession leads to nothing but strife?

How Sun Jian broke through the encirclement will be told in the next chapter.

CHAPTER SEVEN

Yuan Shao Fights with Gongsun Zan at River Pan
Sun Jian Crosses the River to Attack Liu Biao

At the close of the last chapter Sun Jian was surrounded by Liu Biao's army. Fortunately, his three best officers battled desperately to rescue him so he eventually fought his way through and returned to the east, although more than half of his men were lost. From then on he and Liu Biao became sworn enemies.

At that time Yuan Shao was stationed in Henei but there were not enough provisions for his army. When Han Fu, Prefect of Jizhou, learned about this, he sent grain to help him.

Feng Ji, one of Yuan Shao's advisors, said to him: "A powerful man like you is capable of ruling the world. Why do you have to depend on another for food? Jizhou is rich and well-supplied. Why not seize it, General?"

"I don't have an effective plan," replied Yuan Shao.

"You can send a letter to Gongsun Zan in secret, asking him to attack Jizhou and promising him your support. He'll surely do as you suggest. Han Fu, lacking resourcefulness, is certain to invite you to take over the administration of his prefecture and you can get it without having to lift a finger."

Yuan Shao was very pleased to hear this. So the letter was sent at once. When Gongsun Zan learned about Yuan Shao's proposal of a joint attack and division of the territory of Jizhou, he, too, was pleased. Very soon he led his army on a march to attack Jizhou. In the meantime, Yuan Shao sent a secret message of warning to Han Fu, who sought advice from two of his advisors.

One of them said: "Gongsun Zan has under his command the veteran soldiers of Yan and Dai regions as well as the help of the three brothers, Liu, Guan, and Zhang. It won't be possible for us to stand against him. But Yuan Shao is superior to others in wisdom and valor, and has many able and famous warriors under him. If you invite him to assist you in administering the prefecture, he will certainly treat you well. Then you don't have to fear Gongsun Zan."

The prefect agreed and immediately sent a message to Yuan Shao. But Geng Wu, a faithful subordinate of his, remonstrated with him and said: "Yuan Shao is a needy man with a hungry army and as dependent on us for life as an infant is on its mother. Stop the flow of milk and the baby dies. Why should you hand the administration of the district over to him? It's nothing less than letting a tiger into the sheepfold."

Han Fu replied, "I used to be a subordinate under the Yuan family and I know I'm not as capable as Yuan Shao. The ancients practiced yielding to the sage. Why are you all so jealous?"

Geng Wu sighed, "Jizhou is lost!"

When the news got out, a large number of his men left their posts and the city. However, Geng Wu and another man hid themselves outside the city to await the arrival of Yuan Shao.

They did not have to wait for long. Several days later, Yuan Shao appeared with his army. The two men rushed forward in an attempt to assassinate him but were both instantly killed by Yan Liang and Wen Chou, Yuan Shao's two best fighters.

After he entered the prefecture, Yuan Shao's first act was to confer on Han Fu a high-sounding title, but the administration was entrusted to four of his own close advisors, thus depriving Han Fu of all power. Full of chagrin Han Fu abandoned all, even his family, and took refuge with the Prefect of Chenliu.

Hearing of Yuan Shao's possession of Jizhou, Gongsun Zan sent his younger brother Yue to see his ally and demand his share of the district. The brother was sent back to request Gongsun Zan himself to come but on his way home he was killed by assassins, who loudly proclaimed that they worked for Prime Minister Dong. Those of his followers who escaped carried the news to their late master's brother.

Gongsun Zan was very angry and said, "He prevailed on me to attack Han Fu while he took advantage and occupied the city. Now he even sent his men to murder my brother and lied about who they belonged to. How could I not avenge this wrong?"

Then he assembled all his force for the attack. Yuan Shao, too, sent out his men. The two armies met on opposite sides of a bridge on the Pan River, Yuan Shao's men to the east and Gongsun Zan's to the west. Taking his position on the bridge, Gongsun Zan cried to his enemy: "You faithless scoundrel, how dare you betray me?"

Yuan Shao rode to his end of the bridge and, pointing at his foe, replied: "Han Fu yielded the place to me because he was unequal to the task of ruling. What concern is it of yours?"

Gongsun Zan said, "Formerly we thought you were loyal and public-spirited and we elected you chief of the confederacy. But what you have done proves that you are cruel and base, wolf-hearted and currish in behavior. How can you look the world in the face?"

"Who will capture him?" cried the outraged Yuan Shao.

At once Wen Chou rode up the bridge with his spear set and the two engaged. After half a score or so bouts Gongsun Zan was unable to resist and drew off. His opponent came on. Gongsun Zan took refuge within his own army but Wen Chou cut into the central line and rode this way and that, slaying right and left. Four valiant warriors under Gongsun Zan came forward to offer joint battle but one of them fell at the first exchange with Wen Chou and the other three fled. Then he chased the general all the way till he was out of the protection of his own army and was running toward a valley. Wen Chou spurred his horse on, crying hoarsely, "Down! Dismount and surrender!"

Gongsun Zan was then in a pitiful condition, his bow and arrows all lost, his helmet fallen off and his hair disheveled as he rode desperately in and out between the sloping hills. Then his steed stumbled and he was thrown rolling over and over to the foot of a slope.

Wen Chou at once raised his spear for the deadly thrust but all of a sudden there flew out from the grassy mound on the left a young warrior. With his spear poised to attack he rode directly at Wen Chou and Gongsun Zan crawled up the slope to look on.

The new warrior was a youth of commanding presence, tall in height, with bushy eyebrows and big eyes, a broad face and a heavy jowl. The two of them exchanged some three score of bouts and yet neither had the advantage over the other. Then Gongsun Zan's rescue force came up and Wen Chou turned and rode away. The youth did not pursue.

Gongsun Zan hurried down the slope and asked the young man who he was.

He bowed low and replied, "I am from Zhending in Changshan. My name is Zhao Yun or Zhao Zi-long. I first served Yuan Shao, but when I saw that he was disloyal to the throne and indifferent to the welfare of the people I left him and I was on my way to offer my service to you. I did not expect to meet you here in this place, though."

The general was very pleased and the two went together to the camp, where they at once busied themselves with preparations for a new battle.

The next day Gongsun Zan divided his army into two portions, like the wings of a bird. He had more than 5,000 cavalrymen, nearly all mounted on white horses. During his earlier battles against Qiang tribesmen he had always placed white horses in the van of his army and had won the nickname of "General of the White Horse." The tribesmen held him so much in fear that they fled as soon as the white horses appeared. That was why he had so many horses of this color.

On Yuan Shao's side Yan Liang and Wen Chou were leaders of the van. Each had a thousand archers and crossbowmen who were also divided into two groups, those on the left to shoot at Gongsun Zan's right flank, and those on the right to shoot at his left flank. In the center was Qu Yi with 800 archers and 15,000 foot soldiers, while Yuan Shao took command of the reserve force in the rear.

For this battle Zhao Yun was put in command of a company in the rear, as his new master had acquired him only recently and did not feel assured of his faithfulness; a senior officer called Yan Gang was placed in the front to lead the van. Gongsun Zan himself commanded the center as he took his position on the bridge beside a standard on which was displayed the word "Commander" in red embroidery and gold outline.

For two hours the drums rolled but Yuan Shao's army made no move. Qu Yi ordered his bowmen to hide under their shields and wait until the roar of explosions to shoot. Amid loud beating of drums and shouts, Yan Gang made straight for Qu Yi, but seeing the approach of the enemy, Qu Yi and his men seemed to be rooted to the ground and did not stir at all. They waited until Yan Gang had got very close and then, as the sound of a bomb rent the air, the whole company, eight hundred bowmen in all, let fly their arrows in a cloud.

Yan Gang hastened to turn back but Qu Yi rode furiously toward him, whirled his sword and cut him down. This put Gongsun Zan's army in utter confusion. The two wings that should have come to the rescue were kept back by the bowmen under Yan Liang and Wen Chou and Yuan Shao's army advanced right up to the bridge. At the head was Qu Yi, who rode forward, killed the standard bearer, and hacked down the embroidered banner. Seeing this, Gongsun Zan turned his steed and galloped away.

Qu Yi led his men to press forward. However, when he reached the rear he was stopped by Zhao Yun, who rode directly at him with his spear, ready to strike. After a few passes, Qu Yi was laid in the dust. Then Zhao Yun dashed into Yuan Shao's army all by himself, plunging this way and that, as if there were no antagonists around. At this, Gongsun Zan turned and came again into the fight and this time it was Yuan Shao's army that suffered heavy losses.

From the scouts sent to find out the battle's progress, Yuan Shao had heard the good news of Qu Yi's success in slaying the van leader, felling the standard, and his pursuit of the defeated enemy. So he took no further precautions but rode out with Tian Feng to enjoy his victory.

"Ha ha!" he laughed. "The poor fool, what an imbecile he is!"

But even as he spoke he saw in front of him the redoubtable Zhao Yun. The archers hastened to prepare their bows, but before they could shoot, Zhao Yun had pierced several of them to death, and the rest fled. Gongsun Zan's army then gathered around and closed in Yuan Shao.

"Take refuge in this empty building here, sir," said Tian Feng to his master.

But Yuan Shao threw his helmet to the ground and cried, "I would rather face death in battle than seek safety behind a wall!"

This bold speech gave new courage to his men, who fought desperately together, thus preventing Zhao Yun from cutting in. Soon, Yuan Shao was reinforced by the arrival of two of his forces, the main body and Yan Liang's men, so that Zhao Yun could only just get his master safe out of the encirclement and back to the bridge. But Yuan Shao urged his men to press on and again they fought their way across the bridge, causing multitudes of their adversaries to drown in the Pan River.

Riding at the head of his advancing army was Yuan Shao himself, who relentlessly pursued his opponents. But soon a great shouting was heard behind some hills, from where suddenly emerged an armed force led by Liu Bei and his two brothers. They had been informed about the struggle between their protector and Yuan Shao and had come specially to help.

Now the three riders, each with his own powerful weapon, flew straight at Yuan Shao, who was so terrified that his sword fell from his hand and he fled for his life. His followers put up a desperate fight and eventually rescued him from across the bridge. And Gongsun Zan also called back his men and returned to camp.

When the details of the battle were explained, Gongsun Zan said to Liu Bei: "If you had not come to our aid, we would have been in very bad shape indeed."

Then he introduced Zhao Yun to Liu Bei and a warm affection immediately sprang up between the two, so that from the very first, Liu Bei wanted to have Zhao Yun in his service.

After losing that battle, Yuan Shao strengthened his defense and would not come out to fight, so the two armies lay inactive for over a month. In the meantime, news of the fighting was reported to Dong Zhuo in Chang'an.

His advisor Li Ru said to him: "Both Yuan Shao and Gongsun Zan can be regarded as the true warriors of today. They are now struggling against each other at the Pan River. I think it feasible for you, sir, to send an envoy to make peace between them in the name of the Emperor—they will support you out of gratitude for your intervention."

"Good idea," said Dong Zhuo. So the next day he forged an edict and sent two high-ranking officials on the mission.

When the two arrived in Hebei, Yuan Shao went a hundred *li* from his camp to welcome them and received the edict with the greatest respect. Then they went to see Gongsun Zan and made known their errand. Consequently Gongsun Zan wrote to his adversary proposing a reconciliation. The two emissaries returned to the capital to report their task complete. Soon, Gongsun Zan withdrew his army and went back to Beiping. He also presented a memorial recommending Liu Bei to be governor of Pingyuan.

The farewell between Liu Bei and Zhao Yun was affecting. With tears in their eyes they held each other's hand and could not bear to take leave of one another.

Zhao Yun said with a sigh, "I used to think Gongsun Zan a noble soul but I was quite mistaken. From what he has done I can see that he is no different from Yuan Shao."

"You just submit to him for the time being. We will certainly meet again," replied Liu Bei. And both wept as they separated.

Now Yuan Shu, hearing of his brother's annexation of Jizhou, sent an envoy to beg a thousand horses. The request was refused and enmity developed between the two brothers. Later he tried to borrow grain from Liu Biao in Jingzhou, but once again his request was turned down. In resentment Yuan Shu wrote to Sun Jian in an attempt to get him to attack Liu Biao. The letter ran like this:

> "When Liu Biao stopped you on your way home it was at the instigation of my brother. Now these two are plotting to fall on your district. Therefore you should at once strike at Liu Biao and I will get my brother for you. Then both your resentments can be appeased. You will get Jingzhou and I will have Jizhou. Please do not miss this good opportunity!"

"I cannot bear Liu Biao," said Sun Jian as he finished reading the letter. "He certainly did bar my way home and I may have to wait many years for my revenge if I let slip this chance."

So he called in his three most trusted subordinates for a council.

"You cannot trust Yuan Shu—he is very deceitful," said Cheng Pu.

"I want my own revenge," said Sun Jian. "Do you think I care for help from Yuan Shu?"

He first dispatched Huang Gai to prepare a fleet of warships to carry arms and provision. Some large ones were set aside for taking horses on board. And a date was chosen for the action.

News of these maneuvers came to Liu Biao who, greatly alarmed, hastily summoned his advisors and officers for a council.

"Do not worry, sir," said Kuai Liang. "You can put Huang Zu at the head of the Jiangxia troops to confront the enemy in advance. And you will lead the men of Jingzhou and Xiangyang to support him. Sun Jian has to cross the Yangtze River to fight us. How can he expect to fight well after such a journey?"

Liu Biao took the advice. So Huang Zu was commanded to make the necessary preparations. In the meantime, a great army was assembled as a reinforcement.

Here it should be mentioned that Sun Jian had four sons from his wife Lady Wu. The two eldest sons were called Sun Ce and Sun Quan. Lady Wu's younger sister was his second wife, who also bore him a son and a daughter. Besides, he had adopted a son from the Yu family. And he had a younger brother named Sun Jing.

As Sun Jian was leaving on the expedition, his brother led all his sons to kneel before his steed and tried to dissuade him from going. He said, "At present the emperor is weak and Dong Zhuo has become the real ruler. The whole country is torn apart as every lord is scrambling for territory to establish his own kingdom. Our district has just enjoyed some peace and it is not proper to begin a war because of a minor grudge. Please consider this, brother."

"Say no more, brother," replied Sun Jian. "I desire to make my strength felt everywhere in the country. How can I not revenge my injuries?"

"If you must go, father, let me accompany you," said the eldest son Sun Ce.

Sun Jian agreed and the father and son embarked. Their first target for attack was Fancheng.

Now Huang Zu had placed along the riverbank archers and crossbowmen, who were commanded to shoot whenever they saw the ships approaching. On his side, Sun Jian ordered his men to remain under cover in the ships, which sailed to and fro to induce the enemy to shoot. For three days the ships sailed near the shore dozens of times, and each time they were met by a flight of arrows until at last their opponents had no more arrows left. Then Sun Jian told his men to pull out the arrows on the ships and collected them all. As a fair wind was blowing, they shot them back at their enemy. Unable to resist, those on the shore had to retreat. Sun Jian's army then landed and two divisions under the command of Cheng Pu and Huang Gai set out directly for Huang Zu's camp along two different routes. Behind them marched Han Dang with the main body. Attacked by the three forces, Huang Zu was completely routed. He gave up and escaped to the city of Dengcheng.

Leaving the fleet under the care of Huang Gai, Sun Jian himself led the pursuing army. The two opposing forces drew up in the open country outside the city. Sun Jian rode out to the front under the standard. His son, clad in full armor and spear in hand, placed himself beside him.

Huang Zu rode out with two of his officers, named Zhang Hu and Chen Sheng. Flourishing his whip, he abused his enemy: "You rebels from the east, how dare you invade the land of a scion of the ruling Han house!"

He ordered Zhang Hu to challenge for battle. From Sun Jian's side came Han Dang to accept. The two exchanged two score of bouts. Then, seeing his friend losing strength, Chen Sheng flew to his aid. When he saw this, Sun Ce laid aside his spear, reached for his bow and shot Chen Sheng in the face, who fell from his horse. Distracted by his fall, Zhang Hu could no longer defend himself and Han Dang, with a slash of his sword, clove his skull in two. Then Cheng Pu galloped up to take Huang Zu, who threw off his helmet, slipped from his steed, and ran for life amid common soldiers. Sun Jian led on the attack and drove his enemy to the Han River, where he ordered Huang Gai to advance.

Huang Zu assembled his defeated men and went back to tell Liu Biao that they were no match for Sun Jian. The advisor Kuai Liang was again called in for counsel.

"Our army has just suffered defeat and the soldiers will have no heart for fighting," said Kuai Liang. "All we can do at the moment is to fortify our position and avoid direct confrontation with them. At the same time we must send a message to Yuan Shao to seek his help. Then we can extricate ourselves from the predicament."

"An unwise move indeed!" said Cai Mao. "The enemy is right at the city gates—are we going to fold our hands and wait to be slain? Unworthy as I am, I would rather fight it out."

So he was placed in command of more than 10,000 men and went out of the city to draw up his battle line at a hill. The invading army advanced triumphantly. When Cai Mao approached, Sun Jian looked at him and said: "This is Liu Biao's brother-in-law—who will capture him for me?"

Cheng Pu set his iron spear and rode out to oppose him. After a few bouts, Cai Mao turned to flee. The Sun forces smote him until corpses filled the countryside and he took refuge inside the city of Xiangyang.

Kuai Liang said, "Cai Mao should be put to death by military law. This defeat was due to his obstinacy." But Liu Biao was unwilling to punish the brother of his newly-wedded wife.

Meanwhile, Sun Jian had surrounded the city of Xiangyang and assaulted the four walls daily. One day a fierce wind blew up suddenly, breaking the pole of the banner bearing the word "Commander."

"This is not an auspicious sign," said Han Dang. "Let us withdraw for the time being."

"I have won every battle and the city will be mine in no time. Should I return because the wind has broken a flagstaff?" replied Sun Jian.

So he ignored the advice and attacked the city even more vigorously.

Within the city, Kuai Liang told his master that while studying the night sky, he had noticed a great star on the point of falling. He calculated that it meant their enemy Sun Jian was about to perish. He advised Liu Biao to write to Yuan Shao to seek assistance.

The letter was written. But who would undertake to fight his way through with the letter? One officer named Lu Gong, a warrior of great strength, offered himself for the dangerous task.

Before he went, Kuai Liang said to him: "If you dare to undertake this task, do as I tell you. Take five hundred men with you—choose good bowmen. Dash through the enemy's formation and make for the hills at once. You will be pursued, of course, but send one hundred men up the hill to prepare large stones and another hundred, all archers, to lie in ambush in the woods. When the pursuers come, do not just run away aimlessly but follow a devious way up the hill until you have deceived them to the place where the ambushed men are lying in wait. Then roll down the stones and let fly the arrows. If you succeed, fire off a series of bombs as a signal and we will come to help. If you are not pursued, send no signal but get away as fast as possible. The moon is dim tonight. You can start at dusk."

Lu Gong, having received these instructions, prepared his force to carry them out. When dusk fell, they quietly opened the east gate and hastened out. Sun Jian was in his tent when he heard shouting. He at once mounted and rode out to find the cause, escorted by some thirty riders.

When he was told about the movement of the enemy, Sun Jian, together with his escort, followed in hot pursuit immediately, without waiting for his other officers. By that time, Lu Gong's men had already been lying in ambush up on the hill and down in the woods. As Sun Jian was riding on a better steed, he was soon ahead of his escort and close to his enemy.

"Halt!" he shouted.

Lu Gong turned back as if to fight. But they had only exchanged a single pass when he retreated, taking a tortuous route up the hill. Sun Jian followed but soon lost sight of his foe. He was about to climb up the hill when suddenly there came the loud clanging of a gong. All at once, showers of stones fell down from the hill and clouds of arrows shot out from the thick woods, crushing his head and covering his body with wounds. Both he and his steed were killed. At the time of his death he was only thirty-seven years of age.

His escort, too, was overpowered and every one of them slain. Then, Lu Gong let off a series of bombs to signal his victory. At this sign, three forces led by Huang Zu, Kuai Liang, and Cai Mao came out and fell upon their enemies, throwing them into utmost confusion.

Hearing the thunder of noise, Huang Gai led his men from the ships to join in the battle. Soon he came face to face with Huang Zu, and captured him after a brief fight.

Cheng Pu had now taken the son of Sun Jian in his care. While looking desperately for a way out, he came across Lu Gong. He at once put his horse at full speed and the two engaged in battle. After a few bouts he pierced the killer of Sun Jian to death.

Meanwhile, the two contending forces fought a fierce battle till daybreak, when each withdrew its troops.

Liu Biao withdrew into the city and Sun Ce returned to the Han River. Only then did he learn about his father's tragic death and that his body had been carried inside the city. He uttered a great cry and the whole army joined him with wailing and tears.

"How can I return home while my father's body lies in there?" cried Sun Ce.

Huang Gai said, "We have taken Huang Zu prisoner. If only someone can go inside the city to negotiate peace and tell them that we will free Huang Zu in exchange for our lord's body."

He had barely finished speaking when a man called Huan Jie stood up and expressed his willingness to go as an envoy, saying that he was an old acquaintance of Liu Biao's. Presently he went into the city to negotiate peace with the prefect.

Liu Biao told him that Sun Jian's body was already laid in a coffin and ready to be delivered as soon as Huang Zu returned.

"Let us both cease fighting and never again invade each other's territory," he continued.

Huan Jie bowed to him in gratitude and was ready to leave. Suddenly, Kuai Liang cried: "No! No! I have thought of a scheme to wipe out their entire army. Please execute Huan Jie first, then carry out my plan."

> *Pursuing his enemy, Sun Jian dies;*
> *Seeking peace, Huan Jie's life is again threatened.*

The fate of the envoy will be told in the next chapter.

CHAPTER EIGHT

Wang Yun Cleverly Employs the "Chain" Scheme
Dong Zhuo Raises Havoc at Fengyi Pavilion

At the end of the previous chapter, Kuai Liang was about to disclose his scheme to destroy the enemy. This is what he said: "Sun Jian is dead and his sons are all young. They are at their weakest now. If you seize this moment to launch a speedy attack, the district will be yours in no time. But if you return the body and make peace, you give them time to grow stronger again and they will pose hidden danger to our city."

"But how can I leave Huang Zu in their hands?" said the prefect.

"Why not sacrifice this blundering man for a district?" answered Kuai Liang.

"But he is my dear friend and it is wrong to abandon him."

So the envoy was allowed to go back to his own camp with the understanding that Sun Jian's remains would be returned in exchange for the prisoner.

Sun Ce, the eldest son of Sun Jian, freed the prisoner and brought back the coffin—then the fighting ceased. When he returned home, he buried his father in Qua. Then he applied himself to the task of ruling well. He welcomed men of wisdom and valor and treated them with modesty and respect so that gradually they came to his service from all sides.

By then the news of Sun Jian's death had also reached Dong Zhuo in the capital.

"A dangerous enemy of mine has been removed," he said in exultation.

Then he asked which sons of Sun Jian remained and when people told him that the eldest was but seventeen, he dismissed all anxiety from his mind.

From that time onward he became even more arrogant and domineering. He used the highly honored title "Shang Wu"* for himself and went

---

* A title of great honor used by Emperor Wu during the Zhou Dynasty to address his chief minister, Lu Shang, to show that he respected the latter as if he were his senior.

about aping the Emperor's state. He created his younger brother a Lord and Commander of the Left Division of the Imperial Army. A nephew of his was placed head of the palace guards and everyone of his clan, young or old, was ennobled. At some distance from the capital he employed a quarter of a million people to build a palace the size of a city, an exact replica of Chang'an, with its thick and high walls, its granaries, and its treasures. Here, he accumulated supplies sufficient for twenty years. He selected eight hundred of the most beautiful maidens and young men to be in his service in the new palace. The stores of wealth in every form were incalculable. All his family found quarters in this magnificent palace named Meiwu.

Dong Zhuo visited his palace at intervals of a month or so and every visit was like an imperial trip, with booths by the roadside to entertain the officials and courtiers who attended him to Hengmen Gate and saw him depart.

On one occasion he spread a great feast for all those assembled to witness his departure and while it was in progress there arrived several hundred rebels from the north who had voluntarily surrendered. The tyrant had them brought before him as he sat at his table and meted out to them wanton cruelties. The hands of this one was lopped off; the feet of that; one had his eyes gouged out; another lost his tongue. Some were boiled to death. Shrieks of agony arose to the very heavens and the courtiers trembled with terror, but the author of the misery ate and drank, chatted and smiled, as if nothing was going on.

Another day Dong Zhuo was presiding at a great gathering of officials who were seated in two long rows. After the wine had gone up and down several times Lu Bu entered and whispered a few words in his master's ear. Dong Zhuo smiled and said: "So that is how it is! Take Zhang Wen outside." The others all turned pale. In a little time a serving man brought the head of their fellow guest on a red dish and showed it to the tyrant. They nearly died with fright.

"Do not fear," said Dong Zhuo smiling. "He was plotting with Yuan Shu to assassinate me. A letter sent to him fell by mistake into the hands of my son, so I had him put to death. But you have done no wrong. There is no need to fear."

The officials dispersed quickly. One of them, Wang Yun, who had witnessed all this, returned to his home greatly distressed. Late that night he took his staff and went strolling under the bright moonlight in his back garden. Standing near one of the creeper trellises he gazed up at the sky and tears rolled down his cheeks. Suddenly he heard a rustle in the peony pavilion and someone sighing deeply. Approaching quietly he saw there one of the household singing girls named Diaochan, or Sable Cicada.

This maiden was brought up at his house and taught to sing and dance. She was then just maturing into womanhood, a pretty and clever girl whom Wang Yun regarded more as a daughter than a dependent.

After listening for some time he suddenly called out, "What mischief are you up to there, Cicada?"

The maiden dropped on her knees in terror. "I dare not do anything wrong," she said.

"Then what are you sighing about out here in the darkness?" asked her master.

"Please, sir, let me speak from the bottom of my heart," she pleaded.

"Tell me the whole truth—do not conceal anything."

And the girl said, "I have received bountiful kindness from you, sir. I have been taught to sing and dance and been treated so kindly that were I torn to pieces for Your Lordship's sake, I would not be able to repay a thousandth part. I have noticed lately that your brows have been knit in distress and I know it is on account of state troubles. But I dared not ask. This evening you seemed more upset than ever and I felt miserable, too. But I did not know I would be seen. If I could be of any use I would not shrink from a myriad deaths."

A sudden idea came to Wang Yun and he struck the ground with his staff. "Who would have imagined that the fate of the Hans lies in your hands? Come with me!"

The girl followed him into the house. Then he ordered all the waiting women and girls out, placed Sable Cicada on a chair and knelt before her. She was frightened and threw herself on the ground, asking in terror what it all meant.

Wang Yun said, "Oh, please sympathize with the people of Han!" and tears streamed down his cheeks.

"As I said just now: use me in any way, I will never shrink," said the girl.

Still kneeling, Wang Yun said, "The people are on the brink of destruction, the Emperor and his officials are in jeopardy, and you, you are the only savior. That wretch Dong Zhuo wants to depose the Emperor and not a man among us can find the means to stop him. Now he has an adopted son, a bold warrior it is true, but both the father and the son have a weakness for beauty and I am going to use what I call the 'chain scheme.' I will first propose to marry you to Lu Bu and then, after you are engaged, I will present you to Dong Zhuo. You are to take every opportunity to sow discord between them so as to cause the son to kill his adopted father and thus put an end to the great evil. In so doing you can restore the line of the Hans and the empire may thrive again. All this lies within your power—will you do it?"

"I have promised not to recoil from death itself. You may use my poor self in any way and I will do my best."

"But if the secret gets abroad then we are all lost!"

"Do not worry," she said. "If I do not show gratitude, may I perish be neath myriad swords!"

Wang Yun bowed again in gratitude.

Then he took from the family treasury several big pearls and asked a skilled jeweler to make a fine golden headpiece inlaid with these pearls. It was sent as a present to Lu Bu, who was so delighted that he came to thank the donor in person. When he arrived he was met at the gate by the host himself and conducted into the inner hall, where he found a table full of dainties for his delectation. He was then invited to sit in the seat of honor.

"I am only an officer in the house of the prime minister, but you are an exalted official of the state," he said. "Why do you treat me with such great honor?"

"Because in the whole land there is no warrior your equal. I do not bow to your officer's rank but to your ability."

Lu Bu was much flattered. His host continued to ply him with wine while praising his virtues and those of his adopted father. The young man laughed heartily and drank huge goblets.

Presently most of the attendants were sent away and only a few remained to urge the guest to drink. When he found his guest quite mellow Wang Yun said to the servants, "Tell the child to come in."

Soon appeared two female attendants leading between them the exquisite and fascinating Sable Cicada.

"Who is this?" said Lu Bu, startled into sobriety.

"This is my little girl, Cicada. You won't be annoyed at my familiarity, will you? But you have been so very friendly to me and I feel as if we were close relations. So I have told her to come and see you."

Then he bade the girl present a goblet of wine to the guest and her eyes met those of the warrior.

Feigning intoxication the host said, "My child, beg the general to drink some more wine. Our whole family depends upon him."

Lu Bu asked the girl to sit down. She pretended to wish to retire but Wang Yun said she could remain since the guest was a dear friend. So she took a seat modestly beside her master.

Lu Bu kept his gaze fixed upon the maid while he drank cup after cup of wine.

"I would like to present her to you as a concubine. Would you accept?"

The young man left his seat to thank him. "If this is so, I will be your most humble servant," he said.

"I will choose a propitious day soon and send her to your house."

Lu Bu was overjoyed. He could not keep his eyes off the girl and loving glances also flashed from her watery orbs.

However, the time came for the guest to leave and Wang Yun said: "I would like to ask you to spend the night here but the prime minister might suspect something."

The young man thanked him again and again before he departed. A few days later Wang Yun met Dong Zhuo at court. Seeing that Lu Bu was absent he bowed low to him and said: "I wish that Your Lordship would condescend to come to dine at my humble cottage. Could your noble thoughts bend that way?"

"Should you invite me I would certainly hasten," was the reply.

Wang Yun thanked him. He went home and prepared every delicacy from land and sea for a feast to entertain Dong Zhuo. In the center of the front hall was placed a special seat for the guest of honor. Beautiful embroideries and brocade carpeted the floor and elegant curtains were hung within and without. At noon the next day Dong Zhuo arrived and his host knelt by the gate in full court costume to welcome him. Dong Zhuo stepped out of his chariot, followed by a host of armed guards, who crowded into the hall. Dong Zhuo took his seat at the top, his retinue fell into two lines right and left, while the host knelt humbly again at the lower end. Dong Zhuo bade his people conduct Wang Yun to a place beside himself.

"Your Lordship's abundant virtue is as high as the great mountains; none of the ancient ministers could attain that height."

Dong Zhuo smiled. Then wine was served and the music began. Wang Yun plied his guest with assiduous flattery and studied deference. When it grew late and the wine had done its work the guest was invited to the inner chamber. So he sent away his guards and went inside. Here the host raised a goblet and said, "Since my youth I have understood something of astrology. I have been studying the aspect of the heavens these nights. I find that the days of the Hans are numbered and that Your Lordship's merits are known to all the world. As Shun seceded Yao and Yu* continued the work of Shun in ancient times, Your Lordship's accession to the throne conforms to the will of Heaven and the desire of man."

"How dare I expect this?" said Dong Zhuo.

---

* Legendary kings of China in its earliest days.

"From the days of old, those who are just have replaced those who are unjust; those who lack virtue have fallen before those who possess it. Can one escape fate?"

"If that indeed is the decree of Heaven, you will be held the first in merit," said his guest.

Wang Yun bowed. Then candles were lit and all the attendants were dismissed, save the serving maids to handle the wine. So the evening went on.

Presently the host said, "The music of everyday musicians is too commonplace for your ear, but there happens to be in the house a little maid that might please you."

"Excellent!" said the guest.

Then a curtain was lowered. The melodious tones of reed instruments lingered in the air and maids led forward Cicada, who then danced behind the curtain.

A poem describes her dancing like this:

> *For a palace this maiden was born,*
> *So graceful, so slender, and so shy.*
> *Like a tiny bird flitting at morn*
> *She dances to the music with style.*
> *Fair as a flower that sways in the breeze,*
> *She brings spring to the room warm and sweet.*

Another poem runs as follows:

> *The music calls; the dancer comes, a swallow gliding in,*
> *A dainty little damsel, light as air;*
> *Her beauty captivates the guest yet saddens him within,*
> *For he must soon depart and leave her there.*
> *No amount of money could buy her smile,*
> *No need to deck her form with jewels rare,*
> *But when the dance is over and coy glances come and go,*
> *Then who shall be the chosen of the fair?*

The dance ended, Dong Zhuo bade the maiden be led before him, and she came, bowing low as she approached him. He was much taken with her beauty.

"Who is she?" he asked.

"A singing girl, called Sable Cicada."

"Then can she sing?"

The master told her to sing and she did so to the accompaniment of castanets. Here is a poem to describe her sweet singing:

You stand, a dainty maiden,
Your cherry lips so bright,
Your teeth so pearly white,
Your fragrant breath love-laden;
Yet is your tongue a sword;
Cold death is the reward
Of loving you, oh maiden.

Dong Zhuo was delighted and praised her warmly. She was told to present a goblet of wine to the guest, who took it from her hands and then asked her age.

She replied, "Your unworthy maid is just sixteen."

"A perfect little fairy!" exclaimed Dong Zhuo.

Then Wang Yun rose and said, "If Your Lordship does not despise her, I would like to offer this little maid to you."

"How could I be grateful enough for such a kindness?"

"She would be most fortunate if she could wait on you," said Wang Yun.

Dong Zhuo thanked his host again and again.

Then orders were given to prepare a closed carriage and send Sable Cicada to the prime minister's house.

Soon after that, Dong Zhuo also took his leave and his host accompanied him the whole way.

When he was riding back, Wang Yun saw Lu Bu on horseback, halberd in hand, escorted by two lines of men with red lamps. Seeing Wang Yun he at once reined in, seized him by the sleeve, and said angrily: "You promised Cicada to me and now you have given her to the prime minister—what foolery is this?"

Wang Yun checked him. "This is no place to talk—please come to my house."

Lu Bu followed him to his place, where he was led into the inner hall. After the usual exchange of polite greetings Wang Yun asked, "Why do you blame me, General?"

"Somebody told me that you had sent Cicada to the prime minister's house in a covered carriage. What does it mean?"

"So you have not been told yet! Yesterday, when I was at court, the prime minister told me that he would come to my house today as he needed to talk to me. So naturally I prepared for his coming and while we were at dinner he said, 'I was told that you have a daughter named Sable Cicada and you have promised to give her to my son Feng-xian. I was afraid you might not be serious, so I have come to ask for his sake. Besides, I would like to see her.' I could not say no, so I told her to come out and bow to her father-in-law. Then he said that it was a lucky day and he would take her away with him and marry her to you. Just think, when the prime minister had come himself, could I stop him?"

"Please forgive me," said Lu Bu, "I was confused just now. I owe you an apology."

"The girl has some trousseau, which I will send as soon as she has gone over to your dwelling."

Lu Bu thanked him and went away. The next day he went into Dong Zhuo's house to find out the truth, but could hear nothing. Then he made his way into the private quarters and questioned the maids. They told him that the prime minister had brought home a new girl the night before and was not up yet. Lu Bu was very angry. He crept behind his master's bedroom and peeped.

By this time Cicada had risen and was combing her hair at the window. Looking out she saw a long shadow fall across the pond. She recognized the headdress and, shooting a stealthy glance, saw it was none other than Lu Bu. Then she contracted her eyebrows, simulating the deepest grief, and with her dainty handkerchief she wiped her eyes again and again. Lu Bu stood watching her for a long time. Then he went out.

Soon after, he went inside again. His master was sitting in the central hall. Seeing his henchman Dong Zhuo asked: "Is everything all right outside?"

"Yes," was the reply and he waited while Dong Zhuo took his breakfast. As he stood beside his master he glanced toward the embroidered curtain and saw a female peeping out from behind it, showing half of her face from time to time and throwing amorous glances at him. He felt it was his beloved and his thoughts flew to her. Dong Zhuo noticed his infatuated expression and began to feel suspicious.

"In that case, you may go," he said.

Lu Bu sulkily withdrew.

Dong Zhuo now thought of nothing but his new mistress and for more than a month neglected all affairs, devoting himself entirely to pleasure. Once, he was a little indisposed and Cicada was always at his side, gratifying his every whim. He grew more and more fond of her.

One day Lu Bu went to inquire after his father's health. Dong Zhuo was asleep and Cicada was sitting at the head of his couch. Leaning forward she gazed at the young man, with her hand pointing first at her heart, then at the sleeping old man, and her tears fell. Lu Bu felt heartbroken.

Dong Zhuo drowsily opened his eyes, and, seeing his son's gaze fixed on something behind him, turned over and saw who it was. He angrily rebuked Lu Bu, "How dare you seduce my love?" He told the servants to turn him out and banned him from entering the inner quarters again.

Lu Bu went off in a fury. On his way home he met the advisor Li Ru, and related to him the cause of his anger. The latter hastened to see his master and said: "Sir, you aspire to be ruler of the state, why do you blame Lu Bu for a small offense? If he turns against you, it is all over."

"What can I do then?" asked his master.

"Recall him tomorrow and treat him well. Overwhelm him with gifts and fair words and all will be well."

So Dong Zhuo sent for the young warrior the next day and was very gracious to him.

"I was irritable and confused yesterday owing to my illness. I know I wronged you. Don't take it to heart," he said.

He gave Lu Bu ten catties of gold and twenty rolls of brocade. And so they made up. But although the young warrior's body was with him, his heart flew to his promised bride.

His peace of mind restored, Dong Zhuo went to court and Lu Bu followed him as usual. But seeing him deep in conversation with the Emperor, Lu Bu, armed as always, went out of the palace and rode off to Dong Zhuo's residence. He tied up his steed at the entrance and, halberd in hand, went to the private quarters to seek his love. When he found her, she told him to wait for her beside Fengyi Pavilion and she would join him soon. Taking his halberd with him, he went into the back garden and leaned against the railing of the pavilion to wait for her.

After a long time she appeared, swaying gracefully as she made her way, brushing the drooping willows and parting the dainty flowers. She was exquisite, a perfect little fairy from the Palace of the Moon. Tears were in her eyes as she came up and said: "Though I'm not my master's real daughter, yet he treated me as his own child. The desire of my life was fulfilled when I was betrothed to you. But oh! To think of the wickedness of the prime minister, violating my poor self as he did. I suffered so much. I longed to die, only that I had not told you the truth. So I lived on in shame and humiliation. Now that I have seen you I can end it all. My poor sullied body is no longer fit to serve a hero. I will die before your eyes to prove how true I am!"

So speaking she seized the curving rail as if to jump into the lotus pond. Lu Bu caught her in his strong arms and wept as he held her close.

"I know. I've always known your heart," he sobbed. "Only we never had a chance to talk to each other."

She threw her arms about him. "If I can't be your wife in this life, I will in my next one," she whispered.

"If I can't marry you in this life, I'm no hero," he replied.

"Every day is a year long to me. Oh, please! Have pity on me! Rescue me!"

"I've only stolen away for a brief moment and I'm afraid the old scoundrel will suspect something. I mustn't stay too long," he said.

The girl clung to his robe.

"If you fear the old rascal so much, I will never be able to see the sunlight."

Lu Bu stopped. "Give me a little time to think," he said. And he picked up his halberd to go.

"In the deep seclusion of my chamber I heard stories of your prowess. I thought you were the one man who excelled all others. Little did I expect you of all men to rest content under the dominion of another." And tears welled up in her eyes again.

A wave of shame flooded his face. Leaning his halberd against the railing he turned and clasped the girl to his breast, soothing her with fond words. The lovers held each other close, swaying to and fro with emotion, unable to tear themselves apart.

In the meantime, Dong Zhuo missed his escort and suspicion rose in his heart. Hastily taking leave of the Emperor, he mounted his chariot and returned home. There at the gate stood Lu Bu's well-known steed, but the rider was nowhere to be seen. He questioned the doorkeepers and they told him that the young master was inside. He sent away his attendants and went alone to the inner hall, but Lu Bu was not there. He called Cicada, but she did not reply. The waiting maids told him that she had gone to the garden to look at the flowers.

So he went into the garden and there he saw the lovers in the pavilion in most tender talk. Lu Bu's halberd was leaning on the railing beside him.

A howl of rage escaped Dong Zhuo and startled the lovers. Lu Bu turned, saw who it was, and fled. Dong Zhuo snatched the halberd and chased after him. But the young man was much faster and his master was too fat to catch up with him. So Dong Zhuo hurled the weapon at the runaway. Lu Bu fended it off and it fell to the ground. Dong Zhuo picked it up and ran on. By this time, however, Lu Bu was far ahead. Just as Dong Zhuo was turning at the garden gate he ran full tilt into another man dashing in, and down he went.

> *Surging wrath within him heavenward leaps,*
> *Crashing to earth his obese body in a shapeless heap.*

Who knocked down Dong Zhuo will be told in the next chapter.

CHAPTER NINE

Lu Bu Helps Wang Yun Destroy the Tyrant
Li Jue Seeks Counsel from Jia Xu
on Attacking the Capital

The person who collided with the indignant Dong Zhuo was Li Ru, his most trusted advisor. Li Ru at once helped his master to his feet and led him inside to the library, where they sat down.

"What were you coming about?" asked Dong Zhuo.

"I was coming to see you. When I got to the gate I was told that you had gone into the back garden in a fury to look for your adopted son. Then Lu Bu came running and crying out that you wanted to kill him, and I was coming in as fast as I could to plead for him when I accidentally collided with you. I am very sorry. I deserve death."

"The wretch! How could I bear to see him toy with my fair one? I will be the death of him yet."

"Your Lordship is making a mistake. Remember in the days of the Spring and Autumn, Prince Zhuang of the Kingdom of Chu did not punish the man who took liberties with his queen. His restraint stood him in good stead, for the same man fought desperately to save his life when he was hemmed in by enemy troops. After all, Cicada is only a woman, but Lu Bu is your trustiest warrior and most dreaded commander. If you took this chance to give the girl to him, your kindness would win his undying gratitude. I beg you, sir, to think it over."

Dong Zhuo thought for a long time. Then he said, "What you say is right. I will think it over."

Li Ru felt satisfied. He took leave of his master and went away. Dong Zhuo went to his room and called Cicada.

"What were you doing there with Lu Bu?" he asked.

She began to weep. "I was looking at flowers in the garden when he suddenly came. I was frightened and wanted to get away. He said that there was no need for me to avoid him as he was a son of the family. Then he pursued me right to the pavilion. He had that halberd in his hand all the time. I felt he had evil intentions and would force me to do his will, so I tried to throw myself into the lotus pond, but he caught me in his arms and held me so that I was helpless. Luckily, just at that moment you came and saved my life."

"Suppose I give you to him. What do you say?"

She was so startled that she burst into tears.

"After having been yours, to be given to a mere servant! Never! I would rather die."

And with this she grabbed a sword hanging on the wall to kill herself. Dong Zhuo snatched it from her hand in a hurry, and throwing his arms around her, cried: "I was only joking."

She lay back on his breast, hiding her face and sobbing bitterly. "This is the doing of that Li Ru," she said. "He is much too thick with Lu Bu. So he suggested that, I know. Little does he care for your reputation or my life. Oh! I would like to eat him alive."

"Do you think I could bear to lose you?"

"I know you love me yet I'm afraid this is no place for me to stay for long. That Lu Bu will certainly harm me if I do. I fear him."

"Don't worry. You and I will go to Meiwu tomorrow, and we will be happy together."

She dried her tears and thanked him. The next day Li Ru came again to persuade Dong Zhuo to send the damsel to Lu Bu. "This is a propitious day," he said.

"With he and I standing as though father and son, I cannot very well do that," said Dong Zhuo. "But I will say no more about his faults. You may tell him so and soothe him as well as you can."

"Do not be misled by that woman, sir," said Li Ru.

Dong Zhuo lost his temper. "Are you willing to give your wife to Lu Bu? Say no more about this. Otherwise you will be killed."

Li Ru went outside and, casting his eyes heavenward, he sighed: "We will all die at the hands of that girl!"

A poem was written about this episode:

> *Just introduce a woman,*
> *Conspiracies succeed;*
> *Of soldiers, or their weapons,*
> *There really is no need.*
> *Three times they fought at Hulao Pass,*
> *And in vain doughty deeds were done;*
> *But in a garden summer house,*
> *The victory was won.*

Dong Zhuo gave an order to journey to Meiwu and the whole body of officials assembled again to cheer them on their way. Cicada, from her carriage, saw Lu Bu among the crowd. She at once dropped her eyes and assumed an appearance of deepest melancholy. After her carriage had disappeared in the distance, the disappointed lover reined in his steed on a mound, from where he gazed at the dust raised by the vehicle. Unutterable sadness and hatred filled his heart.

Suddenly a voice behind him said, "Why don't you accompany the prime minister, General, instead of standing here and sighing?"

It was Wang Yun. "I have been confined to the house these days because of illness, so I have not seen you," he continued. "I had to struggle out today to see the prime minister off. This meeting is most fortunate. But why were you sighing?"

"Just on account of that damsel of yours," said Lu Bu.

Feigning great astonishment, Wang Yun said, "So long a time and yet not given to you!"

"The old ruffian has kept her for himself."

"Surely this cannot be true."

Lu Bu related the whole story. Wang Yun listened in silence. Then he looked up and stamped his feet as with irritation and perplexity. After a long time he said, "I did not know he was such a beast."

Taking Lu Bu by the hand he said, "Come to my house and we will talk it over."

So Lu Bu went with him to his house and was led to a secret room. After some refreshments, Lu Bu told him again about his meeting with the girl in the garden, just as it had happened.

"He seems to have violated my girl and stolen your wife. The whole episode will be a source of ridicule to the entire world. But people will not laugh at him. They will laugh at you and me. Alas! I am old and powerless and can do nothing. More is the pity! But you, General, you are a warrior, the greatest hero in the world. Yet you, too, have been put to this shame and exposed to this contempt."

Lu Bu became enraged. Banging the table he shouted and roared.

His host ostentatiously tried to calm him. He said, "I forgot myself. I should not have spoken like that. Do not be so angry, General."

"I swear I will kill the ruffian. In no other way can I wash away my shame."

"No, no! Do not say such a thing," said Wang Yun, putting his hand over the other's mouth. "You will bring trouble to me."

"I'm a warrior. How can I be subdued for long under another man's domination?" said Lu Bu.

"It does need someone greater than the prime minister to curb such talents as yours."

Lu Bu said, "I would not mind killing the old wretch were it not for the relation in which we stand. I fear to provoke the hostile criticism of posterity."

His host smiled. "Your surname is Lu—his is Dong. Where was the paternal feeling when he threw the halberd at you?"

"I nearly made a great mistake if you had not pointed this out to me," said Lu Bu hotly.

Seeing that Lu Bu had made up his mind, Wang Yun continued. "It will be a loyal deed to restore the House of Han, and your glorious name will be recorded in history and handed down to posterity. If you aid Dong Zhuo you will be a traitor and your name will stink for all time."

Lu Bu rose from his seat and bowed to Wang Yun. "I have decided," he said. "Trust me, sir."

"But you may fail and bring great misfortune upon yourself," said Wang Yun.

Lu Bu drew his dagger and, pricking his arm, swore a solemn oath by the blood that flowed.

Wang Yun fell on his knees and thanked him. "Then the line of Han will not be cut off, thanks to your efforts. But this must remain a secret. I will tell you how this is going to be worked out."

Lu Bu promised secrecy and departed.

Wang Yun took two of his colleagues into confidence. One of them said, "The time is favorable. The Emperor has just recovered from his illness and we can dispatch an able emissary to Meiwu who will persuade Dong Zhuo to come here to discuss affairs. At the same time we will obtain a secret decree from the Emperor as authority for Lu Bu to act. Lay an ambush just inside the palace gate to kill Dong Zhuo as he enters. This is the best plan to adopt."

"But who will be bold enough to go?"

"Li Su will be the right person. He comes from the same district as Lu Bu and is very angry with his master for not advancing him. His going will not excite any suspicions."

"Good," said Wang Yun. "Let's see what Lu Bu thinks of it."

When Lu Bu was consulted he told them that this man's persuasive arguments had led him to kill Ding Yuan, his former benefactor. "If he should refuse this mission, I would kill him," he said.

So they sent for Li Su. When he arrived Lu Bu said: "Formerly you talked me into killing Ding Yuan and going over to Dong Zhuo. Now this Dong Zhuo bullied the Emperor and oppressed the people. His iniquities are so many that he is hated by both gods and men. I want you to go to Meiwu and say that you have a decree from the Emperor to summon him to the palace. When he comes he will be put to death. Thus we can restore the House of the Hans and you will have the credit of being a loyal official. Will you undertake this?"

"I have been wishing to slay him, too," said Li Su. "Only I could not find anyone to assist me. Now your intervention is really a heaven-sent opportunity. How can I hesitate?" And he snapped an arrow in two to pledge his allegiance to the scheme.

"If you can succeed, what glorious rank will not be yours!" said Wang Yun.

The next day, Li Su set out for Meiwu with a small escort. When he got there he announced himself as bearer of a decree from the Emperor. He was admitted to Dong Zhuo's presence. After he had made his obeisance the prime minister asked what the decree was.

"His Majesty has recovered and wishes his ministers to meet him in the palace to consider the question of his abdication in your favor. That is what this summons is about."

"What does Wang Yun think of this?"

"He has already begun the construction of an altar for your succession to the throne and only awaits your arrival, sir."

"Last night I dreamed of a dragon coiling round my body," said Dong Zhuo, greatly pleased. "And now I get this happy tiding! I must not neglect this good opportunity."

So he announced his intention of starting for the capital that very day, leaving the palace in the care of Li Jue, Guo Si, and two others with the "Flying Bear" force.

"When I am Emperor you shall be my precursor," he said.

Li Su thanked him, addressing himself as his official.

Dong Zhuo went inside to bid farewell to his aged mother.

"Where are you going, my son?" asked his mother.

"I'm going to receive the throne of Han, and soon you'll be Empress Dowager."

"I've been feeling nervous and spooked these last few days. It's a bad sign."

"Anyone about to become the mother of the head of state must have premonitions," said her son.

And he left her with these words. Just before starting he said to Cicada: "When I'm Emperor, you'll be *Guei-fei*, the first of my ladies." She knew what this really meant but pretended to rejoice at the news and thanked him.

He went out, mounted his carriage, and began his journey to the capital with an imposing escort. Less than halfway the wheel of his carriage broke. He stepped down and mounted a horse. But soon after the horse snorted and neighed, threw up his head and snapped the reins.

Dong Zhuo turned to Li Su and asked what these signs meant.

"They mean that you are going to be the new ruler, which is to cast away everything old and bring forth the new, to mount the jeweled chariot and sit in the golden saddle."

Dong Zhuo believed him. On the second day a violent gale sprang up and the sky became covered with a thick mist. The wily Li Su had an interpretation for this, too. "You are ascending to the dragon seat—there must be red light and lurid vapor to dignify your majestic approach."

Dong Zhuo had no more doubts. When he arrived he found all the officials waiting outside the city gate to welcome him—all but Li Ru, who was ill and unable to leave his chamber. He entered and proceeded to his house in the capital and Lu Bu came to congratulate him.

"When I sit on the throne, you will command the whole army of the Empire, both horse and foot soldiers," he said.

That night Lu Bu did not return to his own lodging but stayed at Dong Zhuo's house. In the suburbs that evening some children at play were singing a little ditty and the words drifted over on the wind.

> *The grass in the meadow looks fresh now and green,*
> *Yet wait but ten days, not a blade will be seen.*

The song sounded ominous but Li Su was again able to provide a happy interpretation. "It only means that the Lius are about to disappear and the Dongs to be exalted."

The next morning, at the first streak of dawn, Dong Zhuo set out to appear in court. On arriving there he found all the officials in court dress lining the road. Li Su walked beside his carriage, sword in hand. When he reached the north gate, all his guards were ordered to remain outside and only the pushers of the carriage, a score or so men, were allowed to proceed further. Then he saw in the distance Wang Yun and the other officials standing at the entrance of the Audience Hall. They were all carrying swords in their hands!

"Why are they all armed?" he asked Li Su.

Li Su did not reply but pushed the carriage straight to the entrance.

Suddenly Wang Yun shouted, "The rebel is here! Where are the executioners?"

At this call, more than a hundred armed guards sprang from both sides and attacked Dong Zhuo with their halberds and spears. He had worn a soft breastplate underneath and the weapons could not penetrate his heart. But he was wounded in the arm and he fell down from his carriage. Feeling desperate, he called loudly, "Where is my son Feng-xian?"

"Here, and with a decree to execute you, the rebel!" said Lu Bu savagely, as he appeared from behind his carriage.

With one thrust of his halberd he pierced his victim's throat. Then Li Su hacked off the head and held it up. Lu Bu, holding his halberd in his left hand, drew the decree from his bosom with his right hand. "The decree was to slay the rebel Dong Zhuo only, but no other."

The whole assembly shouted, "Long live the Emperor!"

The lust for blood awakened, Lu Bu urged the slaughter of Li Ru as he had helped Dong Zhuo to do evil. Li Su volunteered to go in search of him. But just then a shouting was heard at the gate and it was reported that Li Ru's servants had brought him in. Wang Yun ordered his immediate execution in the market place.

Dong Zhuo's head was exposed in a crowded thoroughfare. He was very fat and the guards made torches by sticking splints into his navel. The passers-by pelted the head with stones and kicked the body.

A large force under Lu Bu was sent to confiscate his property and exterminate his clan at Meiwu. Their first captive was Cicada. Then they slew every member of the Dong family, sparing none, not even his aged mother. Many young ladies of good family were hidden in the place. These were set free. Then they searched the whole palace for valuables. The spoils were enormous—stores of wealth of all types had been collected there. However, four of Dong Zhuo's main supporters, including Li Jue and Guo Si, fled to Liangzhou with the "Flying Bear" force.

When they returned to report their success, Wang Yun gave big feasts in celebration. Banquets were also held in the meeting hall to which all the officials were invited. They drank and congratulated each other. While the feasting was in progress, a messenger came in to say that someone was wailing over the corpse exposed in the market place.

"Everybody is glad at Dong Zhuo's execution," said Wang Yun angrily. "Who is this man that dares to lament over him?"

So he gave orders to arrest the mourner. Soon the man was brought in. When they saw him all were startled, for he was none other than the talented Cai Yong.

Wang Yun reproached him angrily, "Dong Zhuo has been put to death and all the land rejoices. Yet you, a Han minister, instead of rejoicing, weep for him. Why?"

Cai Yong admitted guilt. "Unworthy though I am, I know what is right. Am I the man to turn my back on my country and toward Dong Zhuo?

Yet once I experienced his kindness and I could not help mourning for him. I know my crime is grave but I pray you consider the reasons. If you punish me severely but do not kill me, you may still use me to continue the writing of the history of Han. In this way I may have the good fortune of expiating my crime."

All were sorry for him, for he was a man of great talents and they begged that he might be spared. One of them secretly interceded for him, pointing out that he was a rare scholar and it would be wonderful if he could be entrusted with the writing of the annals. He also argued that it was inadvisable to put to death a man renowned for filial piety. But his effort was in vain. Wang Yun was now strong and obdurate.

He said, "In the past, Sima Qian* was spared and employed on the annals, with the result that many slanderous stories have been handed down to later generations. These are trying times of great perplexity and we dare not let a specious fellow like this wield his pen in criticism of the court and a youthful emperor, and abuse us as he will."

Remonstrance and appeal being in vain, the official retired. But he said to his colleagues: "Does Wang Yun have no regard for the future? Worthy men are the mainstay of the state and laws are the precepts of action. To destroy the mainstay and nullify the laws is to hasten destruction."

Meanwhile, ignoring the appeal of the others, Wang Yun ordered Cai Yong to be thrown into prison and there strangled. Officials and men of letters all wept for him. Later, people commented that it was wrong for Cai Yong to lament over the tyrant's death, but it was equally wrong for Wang Yong to kill the scholar.

> *Dong, the cruel dictator,*
> *Tyrannized the state,*
> *Fell and his sole mourner*
> *Shared his direful fate.*
> *But Zhuge Liang the sage*
> *Content to live unknown.*
> *Ne'er would he stain his name*
> *To help a tyrant's reign.*

Now let us follow the story of the four adherents of Dong Zhuo who had fled to Shanxi when their master was slain. There, they offered a petition entreating amnesty. But Wang Yun would not hear of it.

"These four were the chief instruments of Dong Zhuo's evils," he said.

---

* Famous historian in West Han, author of the *Book of History*, written between 104 and 91 B.C.

"Although a general amnesty was proclaimed, these men should be excluded from enjoying its benefit."

The messenger returned to tell the four that there was no hope of pardon, so they decided to flee separately. But the advisor Jia Xu thought differently.

He said, "If you throw away your army and flee singly, you will fall easy victims to any village official who may seize you. Why not cajole the Shanxi people to share your lot and make a sudden attack on the capital, and so avenge the old master? If you succeed, you gain control of the court and the country. If not, there will be time enough to run away."

The plan was adopted and they started spreading the rumor that Wang Yun intended to harry the district. The people there were thrown into a state of terror. Then they went a step further and said, "There is no point in dying for nothing. Revolt and join us." So they succeeded in inciting the people to join them. Together they mustered a huge army, which was divided into four units, and they all set out to raid the capital. On the way they fell in with Niu Fu, a son-in-law of their late chief, with 5,000 soldiers. He had set out to avenge his father-in-law and he became the van leader of the rebel force.

When the news of their rebellion came to Wang Yun he consulted Lu Bu. "Don't worry," Lu Bu assured him. "They are mere rats to me. Never mind how many there are of them."

So Lu Bu and Li Su went to oppose them. The latter was in advance and met Niu Fu. They fought hard but Niu Fu was outmatched and retreated. However, he returned unexpectedly in a night attack. Li Su was quite unprepared and was driven some thirty *li* from his camp, losing many of his men.

When Lu Bu learned about the defeat he raged at his former friend, saying, "You have blunted the fighting spirit of my army." Then he put Li Su to death, exposing his head at the camp gate.

The next day Lu Bu led his own force to engage Niu Fu in battle. But how could the wretch be strong enough to confront the powerful Lu Bu? He was immediately driven off.

That night Niu Fu took a trusted friend of his into confidence. "Lu Bu is too valiant a fighter for us to hope to overcome. I think we'd better desert Li Jue and the others, take our valuables, and leave the army."

His friend agreed and the two traitors packed up and left their camp with several followers. Before long they came to a river. Tempted by greed, his companion slew him and went to see Lu Bu to offer his head. Lu Bu inquired into the matter and when he learned about the truth he put the double traitor to death.

Then he advanced and soon fell in with Li Jue's force. Without giving them time to form in battle array, he led his men in a fierce attack against his enemy; Li Jue, making no stand, retreated a long way. At last he took up a position beside a hill, where he called together the other three.

Li Jue said, "Though he is brave in battle, Lu Bu is no strategist and so not really formidable. I will lead my men to hold the mouth of the gorge and every day I will incite him to attack. And when he comes toward me, General Guo can smite his rear. Both of us will begin our assault at the sound of gongs and withdraw at the sound of drums. While we are thus engaged, you other two will march off on different routes to capture the capital. Such an attack at two points is sure to end in his defeat."

All being of one mind, they prepared themselves to carry out this scheme. As soon as Lu Bu reached the hills, Li Jue came out to attack him. Lu Bu made an angry dash toward the enemy, who withdrew to the hills, from where they shot arrows and hurled stones like rain. Lu Bu's men halted. At this moment a report came with the urgent news that the rear was being attacked by Guo Si. At once Lu Bu wheeled toward his new enemy but immediately the rolling drums gave them the signal to retreat, so Lu Bu could not come to blows with them. As he called in his men the gongs clanged on the other side and his former opponent came forth as if to smite him. But before he could give battle, his rear was again threatened by Guo Si, who in his turn drew off without striking a blow.

Thus Lu Bu was baited till his bosom nearly burst with rage. The same tactics continued for several days. He could neither advance nor retreat; his men had no rest.

In the midst of these distracting maneuvers a messenger rode up in haste to say that the capital was in imminent danger from a double attack. Lu Bu at once ordered a march back to save the capital. At this, both his opponents came to attack him from behind. As he was in a hurry to return to Chang'an, he had no heart to involve himself in serious fighting and his losses were quite heavy.

However, he eventually reached the capital and found the rebels there in enormous numbers and the city besieged. His attack had but little effect and as his temper became more savage many of his men went over to the rebels.

Lu Bu fell into deep melancholy. Several days later, two of Dong Zhuo's adherents still in the capital secretly opened the city gate and the besiegers poured in. Lu Bu exerted himself to the utmost but could not stem the tide. So at the head of a few hundred horsemen he dashed over to Qingsuo Gate and called out to Wang Yun. He told the minister that the situation was desperate and asked him to ride with him to safety.

Wang Yun replied: "If the fortune of the state prevails and tranquillity is restored, my wish is fulfilled; if not, then I will sacrifice myself for it. I will not quail before danger. Pray give my thanks to the noble supporters east of Tong Pass and ask them to remember their country."

Lu Bu urged him again and again, but he would not leave. Soon fires started up all over the city and Lu Bu had to leave, abandoning his family to their fate. He fled to seek protection from Yuan Shu in Nanyang.

Now Li Jue and his fellow rebel leaders gave full license to their ruffians, who robbed and murdered their fill. Many high officials perished in the disaster. In time they penetrated into the inner palace and the courtiers begged the Emperor to ascend the tower of Xuanping Gate to quell the rioting. At the sight of the yellow umbrella Li Jue and Guo Si checked their men and paid their respects to the Emperor. The young ruler leaned over the tower and addressed them: "My generals, why do you enter the capital in this unruly manner without my summons?"

The two rebel leaders looked up and said, "The prime minister has been slain by Wang Yun and we are here to avenge him. We are not rebels, Your Majesty. Let us have Wang Yun and we will withdraw our men."

Wang Yun was actually among the courtiers at the Emperor's side. Hearing this demand he said, "My plan to kill Dong Zhuo was for the benefit of the country, but as this evil has grown out of it, I will go down to these rebels."

Torn by sorrow, the Emperor hesitated. But the faithful minister leaped from the wall, crying, "Wang Yun is here."

The two men drew their swords and asked, "For what crime was Prime Minister Dong slain?"

"His crimes filled the heavens and covered the earth, too numerous to list. The day he died was a day of rejoicing in the whole city as you well know," said Wang Yun.

"And if he was guilty, what have we done not to be forgiven?"

"Seditious rebels, why bandy words? I am ready to die."

And he was slain at the foot of the tower.

> *Moved by the people's sufferings,*
> *Vexed at his prince's grief,*
> *Wang Yun compassed the tyrant's death*
> *That they might find relief.*
> *His courage to all was known,*
> *His loyalty across the land spread,*
> *Dead though he is, his noble soul*
> *Keeps guard at the tower today.*

Having put the loyal minister to death, they proceeded to exterminate his whole family. All the people wept in great sorrow.

But the rebels did not stop here. Li Jue and Guo Si said to each other: "Since we have gone thus far, what could be better than to do away with the Emperor and establish our own rule?" So thinking, they drew their swords and rushed in.

> *The arch-devil was slain when the disaster ended,*
> *But his licentious followers disturbed the Empire's peace again.*

Whether the Emperor would be slain or not will be told in the next chapter.

CHAPTER TEN

Ma Teng Raises an Army to Fight the Rebels
Cao Cao Attacks Xuzhou to Avenge his Father

At the end of the last chapter the two rebel leaders proposed to murder the Emperor, but the other two objected.

"No, the people won't approve of his death now," they said. "It's better to let him stay in power and we can use him as a bait to induce the lords to come. Remove his supporters first, then plan his destruction. Then the land will be ours."

Li Jue and Guo Si agreed, so they ceased the attack.

The Emperor again spoke from the tower: "You have slain Wang Yun. Why do you still remain here?"

The rebel leaders replied, "Your servants desire promotions in rank as a reward for their good service to the imperial house."

"And what ranks do you want?" asked the Emperor.

All four wrote down their wishes and passed them to the Emperor, who had no choice but to accede to their requests. So they were created generals and lords, and were given enormous power in court administration. Even the two traitors that opened the city gate for the rebels were gratified with promotions. Only then did they withdraw their troops outside the capital.

Next, they spent time finding their late master's corpse for burial, but all they could find were a few fragments of skin and bones. So they had his image engraved in fragrant wood. Somehow they managed to lay this out in state and put in place a huge memorial service, with sacrifices and prayers. The body was dressed in robes fit for a prince and laid in a royal coffin. They selected an auspicious day to convey the coffin to Meiwu, where his tomb would stand.

But on the day when Dong Zhuo was to be entombed, a terrific thunderstorm broke out and the ground was heavily flooded. The coffin was riven asunder by thunder and his remains thrown out. They waited for the weather to change for the better so they could bury him a second time, but another thunderstorm disrupted their plan again. Altogether they tried three times to bury him, but three times their plan was thwarted and what was left of his remains was consumed by lightning. Heaven showed its full wrath with the arch villain.

Back in the capital, the real power fell to Li Jue and Guo Si, who cruelly oppressed the common folk. They also placed their own trusted followers in the company of the Emperor to keep a close watch over his every movement, so that he was hampered in whatever he did. The court officials, too, were controlled by these two rebels, who decided who was promoted or demoted. To gain popularity among the people, they especially summoned Zhu Jun to court, making him an important official in the administration of the government.

One day came a report that Ma Teng, Prefect of Xiliang, and Han Sui, Prefect of Bingzhou, with a large armed force, were rapidly approaching the capital with the intention of attacking the rebels.

Now these two generals from the west had laid careful plans. They had sent agents to the capital earlier and had found support in three officials who were to be their local allies in their scheme to destroy the rebels. These three had obtained from the Emperor two secret edicts conferring the rank of general to both of them. Ma Teng was given the title of Conqueror of the West and Han Sui, Warden of the West. With these powers the two joined forces and marched toward the capital.

Hearing of their imminent arrival the four rebel leaders called a general council to discuss how to deal with the situation. The advisor Jia Xu said: "Since the attackers are coming from a long distance, our best tactics is to fortify ourselves and wait till shortage of food works in our favor. In a hundred days their supplies will be consumed and they will have to withdraw. Then we can pursue and capture them."

But this scheme was rejected by two officers called Li Meng and Wang Fang. They said, "This plan is no good. Give us 10,000 men and we will put an end to both of them and offer their heads to you."

"If you fight today you will surely be defeated," said the advisor.

The two officers cried with one voice: "If we fail we are willing to be executed, but if we win you will pay by forfeiting your life."

The advisor then said to his two masters: "Two hundred *li* west of the capital stands a high hill where the passes are narrow and difficult. Send Generals Zhang Ji and Fan Chou to occupy this vantage point and fortify themselves so that they may support Li Meng and Wang Fang when they go out to fight."

This advice was adopted and Li Meng and Wang Fang left happily with 1,500 horse and foot soldiers. They set up their camp some two hundred and eighty *li* from the capital. When the army from the west arrived they led out their men to the attack. Their opponents spread out in battle array and the two leaders, Ma Teng and Han Sui, rode to the front side by side. Pointing to Li Meng and Wang Fang, they abused them, calling them traitors. Then, turning to their own men, they asked, "Who will capture them?"

Hardly were the words spoken when there flew out a youth with a clear, white complexion, shining bright eyes, a lithe body, and strong limbs. He was armed with a long spear and riding an excellent steed. This young warrior was called Ma Chao (or Ma Meng-qi), son of Ma Teng, then only seventeen years of age but already renowned for his valor and skill in fighting.

Wang Fang, despising him on account of his youth, galloped forth to fight him. Before they had exchanged many passes Wang Fang fell to a thrust of the young man's spear. The victor turned to join his own army but Li Meng rode after him to avenge his fallen friend. The young man pretended not to notice his pursuit but his father called out from his position under the banner, "You are followed!" No sooner had he spoken than he saw that his son had taken the pursuer prisoner.

Now Ma Chao had known he was being followed and he had deliberately slowed down, waiting for his enemy to come near. When the pursuer raised his spear to strike, Ma Chao suddenly dodged to one side and the spear was thrust into empty air. As the two horses were very close against each other at that moment, Ma Chao shot out his powerful, long arm and pulled his enemy down from his saddle. Thus the rebels were left without a leader and they fled in all directions. Then the army loyal to the Emperor dashed in pursuit to win a complete victory. They pressed on as far as the pass, where they encamped. Li Meng was decapitated and his head displayed.

When Li Jue and Guo Si learned that both the boastful officers had fallen under the hand of one young man, they realized that Jia Xu was gifted with foresight and that his advice was good. So they followed his scheme and acted on the defensive, refusing all challenges to combat.

Just as Jia Xu had predicted, after a few months the supplies of the loyalists were all exhausted and the two generals began to consider retreat.

At this juncture a household servant of one of their allies in the capital betrayed his master and disclosed the secret alliance between the three officials and the generals. In a rage, the two rebel leaders seized them, together with every member of their household, and beheaded them in the market place. The heads of the three were exposed by the city gate.

Pressed with the shortage of food and the loss of their allies, Ma Teng and Han Sui had no way out but to break camp and withdraw. Then at once the two rebels waiting on the high hill were ordered to give chase. One of them, Zhang Ji, went in pursuit of Ma Teng and the other, Fan Chou, followed Han Sui. The retreating army under Ma Teng was beaten and only by Ma Chao's desperate efforts were the pursuers driven off.

By that time Fan Chou had come close to his opponents. Seeing this, Han Sui halted and addressed his pursuer: "You and I, sir, are from the same place. Why then so unfriendly?"

Fan Chou replied, "I must obey the commands of my chief."

"I am here for the service of the state. Why do you press me so hard?"

At this Fan Chou turned his horse, called in his men, and let Han Sui pass. But little did he know that a nephew of Li Jue's had been a witness of this scene and when he saw the enemy allowed to go free he went back to tell his uncle about it. Li Jue was furious and he would have wreaked vengeance on his former ally if Jia Xu had not checked him. The advisor said that it was dangerous to provoke another war at such an unstable time. He proposed inviting the defaulting officer to a banquet and, while the feast was in progress, executing him for his neglect of duty. Li Jue was very pleased with the idea and so the banquet was prepared and the two unwitting officers came cheerfully.

In the middle of the feast, however, Li Jue suddenly changed his countenance and asked Fan Chou angrily, "Why have you been collaborating with Han Sui? You are turning traitor, eh?"

The poor guest was greatly taken aback and before he could begin to reply assassins rushed out with swords and axes. In a moment it was all over and his head lay beneath the table.

Scared beyond measure, his fellow guest threw himself to the ground.

"I killed him because he was a traitor," said Li Jue, helping him to his feet. "But you are my most trusted friend and there is no need to fear."

Zhang Ji was then given command of the murdered man's troops and returned to his own position in Hongnong.

After the loyalist army from the west was defeated, none of the lords dared attempt a further attack on the newly-established dictators. On the other hand, the advisor Jia Xu never ceased urging his masters to pacify the people and associate with the wise and the valiant. So the government began to show signs of prosperity.

However, a new trouble arose in Qingzhou in the shape of a resurgence of Yellow Turbans. They came in large numbers and plundered wherever they went. Zhu Jun recommended Cao Cao to destroy them, saying that he was the only person who could be entrusted with the task.

"Where is he?" asked Li Jue.

"He is Prefect of Dongjun. He has a large army under his command. If you employ him in this service, the uprising will be put down."

So a decree was prepared in haste and dispatched to Dongjun, commanding Cao Cao to act together with Bao Xin of Jibei in quelling the Yellow Turbans. As soon as he received the court order Cao Cao arranged with Bao Xin to attack the rebels at Shouyang. But Bao Xin made a dash right into their midst and fell victim to his opponents.

Cao Cao was more successful and he chased his enemy as far as Jibei. Many of them surrendered. Then he placed these in the van to induce more of his opponents to yield. This tactic worked very well for him—wherever his army went, the rebels surrendered and joined his force. Within three months or so he had won over more than 300,000 rebel soldiers as well as a million ordinary folk. Of these, the strongest and boldest were organized into a special force called "Soldiers of Qingzhou," while the rest were sent home to their fields. Consequently, Cao Cao's prestige rose from day to day. He reported this success to the capital and as a reward, he was conferred the title of General–Warden of the East.

At his headquarters in Yanzhou, Cao Cao welcomed wise counselors and bold warriors, and many gathered around him. Two Yingzhou men, uncle and nephew, named Xun Yu and Xun You, came to offer their service. After talking with the elder Xun, Cao Cao was so pleased that he called the latter his chief advisor. The nephew was famed throughout the country for his intelligence and ability. He used to be a court official but had abandoned that career and retired to his village.

The elder Xun said to his new master, "There is a certain wise man in this region but I don't know where he is now."

"Who is he?" asked Cao Cao.

"Cheng Yu. He is a native of Dongjun."

"Yes, I have also heard of him," said Cao Cao. After some inquiries it was found that Cheng Yu was away in the hills, engaged in study. However, he came at Cao Cao's invitation.

"I am unworthy of your recommendation for I am ignorant and ill-informed," he said to Xun Yu. "But I know of a native of yours, named Guo Jia. He is a real scholar. Why not ask him to come here?"

"How careless of me!" Xun Yu suddenly remembered. So he told his master of this man, who was at once invited to offer his views about state affairs. In his turn, Guo Jia spoke highly of one Liu Ye, and when he arrived he introduced two further scholars, Man Chong and Lu Qian, who were already known to Cao Cao by their good reputation. These two brought to their new master's notice the name of Mao Jie, who also came at Cao Cao's call. All of them were duly given office.

Then a famous warrior with several hundred soldiers under his command arrived to offer his service. This man was called Yue Jin, an expert horseman and archer, and skilled in every form of military arts. He was made an army inspector.

On another day Xiahou Dun brought a big fellow to present to Cao Cao.

"Who is this man?"

"He is Dian Wei from Chenliu, an extremely brave and strong warrior. He was one of Zhang Miao's men, but quarreled with his tent companions and killed a lot of them with his fists. Then he fled to the mountains, where I found him. I was out shooting and saw him follow a tiger across a stream. I persuaded him to join my troop and now I recommend him to you."

"I see he is no ordinary man," said Cao Cao. "He is so big and tall. He must be very powerful and bold."

"He is. He killed a man once to avenge a friend and carried his head through the whole market place. Hundreds saw him but none dared to come near. The weapon he uses now is a pair of iron spears weighing over a hundred pounds, and he vaults into his saddle with these under his arm."

Cao Cao told Dian Wei to give proof of his skill, so he galloped to and fro, whirling his heavy spears. Then he saw away among the tents a huge banner swaying dangerously in the strong wind and on the point of falling. A crowd of soldiers were vainly struggling to keep it steady. Down he leaped from his horse, shouted to the men to clear out and, with one hand, he held the staff perfectly upright in spite of the ferocious wind.

Cao Cao was much impressed and gave the warrior a post in his army. Besides, he also gave him his own fine robe and a swift steed with a handsome saddle as presents.

Thus Cao Cao encouraged able men to assist him. With wise advisors on the civil side and valiant officers in the army, his powerful reputation began to spread throughout Shandong.

Cao Cao's father, Cao Song, was then living in seclusion with his family at Longye, where he had escaped after the earlier trouble caused by his son's attempt to slay Dong Zhuo. As he became quite successful, Cao Cao sent the Prefect of Taishan to escort his father to Yanzhou. The old man read his son's letter with joy and the family prepared to move. They were forty in all, with a train of about a hundred servants and numerous carts.

On their way they passed through the city of Xuzhou, where the prefect, named Tao Qian, was a sincere and upright man who had long wished to get acquainted with Cao Cao but so far had found no means of effecting such a bond. When he heard that Cao Cao's father and his family were passing through his district he went to welcome them, treated them with great cordiality, and entertained them with feasts for two days; when they finally left he accompanied them as far as the city gate. To make sure that they would arrive safely at their destination he even sent an officer of his, named Zhang Kai, and five hundred soldiers to escort them all the way to Yanzhou.

It was the end of summer, just turning to fall, and rain was frequent. That day they reached a small place where they were stopped by a tremendous storm of rain. The only shelter was an old temple, to which they went. The family occupied the main hall and the escort the two side wings. The soldiers were drenched, angry, and discontented. Zhang Kai called his followers together and said, "We used to belong to the Yellow Turbans and only submitted to Tao Qian because there was no way out. But we have never got any benefit in his service. Now here is the Cao family with no end of gear and we can be rich very easily. Let us make a sudden onslaught at the third watch tonight and slay the whole lot. Then we will take the money and get away to the mountains. What do you say to this?" And they all agreed.

That night the wind continued to roar and the rain pelted down furiously. Cao Song was sitting in his room when he suddenly heard a hubbub outside. His brother Cao De, drawing his sword, went out to find out what was the matter and was at once cut down. Cao Song took one of the concubines by the hand and rushed with her through the passage toward the back of the temple so that they might escape through the wall. But the lady was stout and could not climb over it, so the two hid themselves in an outhouse. However, they were found and slain.

The Prefect of Taishan managed to get away and he fled for his life to Yuan Shao's place. The murderers, after slaying the whole Cao family and setting fire to the old temple, made away with their plunder into Huainan.

> *Cao Cao, whom the ages praise,*
> *Slew the Lus in former days.*
> *Nemesis ne'er turns aside,*
> *Murdered, too, his family died.*

Some of the escort escaped and took the evil tidings to Cao Cao. When he heard the news he fell to the ground with a great cry. His attendants hurriedly helped him up. With set teeth he muttered, "Tao Qian has allowed his men to slay my father. Never can I share the same sky with him. I will sweep Xuzhou off the face of the earth. Only thus can I satisfy my vengeance."

Leaving one small army to guard three counties in the region, he set forth with the remainder on an expedition to destroy Xuzhou and avenge his father. The three most powerful warriors, Xiahou Dun, Yue Jin, and Dian Wei were placed in the van and orders were given to tell soldiers to kill every one of its inhabitant when the city was seized.

Now the Prefect of Jiujiang was a close friend of Tao Qian's. When he learned that Xuzhou was threatened he set out with 5,000 soldiers to his friend's aid. Cao Cao immediately sent Xiahou Dun to destroy him before he got to the city. At this time Chen Gong, the former magistrate who had saved Cao Cao's life, was in Dongjun, and he was also on friendly terms with Tao Qian. Hearing of Cao Cao's design to wipe out the whole population, he came in haste to see his former companion. Knowing the purpose of his visit Cao Cao would have put him off but, as he could not forget the kindness he had once received from him, he had to invite him in.

Chen Gong said, "I was told that you are going to avenge your worthy father's death on the city of Xuzhou and its people. I have come specially to put in a word. Tao Qian is kind and honest, not a man who cares only for his own advantages and forgets morals before profits. Your worthy father died at the hands of Zhang Kai, not Tao Qian. The prefect is innocent. And still more innocent are the people of that city—to slay them would be an evil. Please think over this."

Cao Cao retorted angrily: "You once abandoned me and now you have the impudence to come to see me! Tao Qian slew my whole family and I vow to tear his heart out in revenge. You may speak for his sake but I will not listen."

His intercession having failed, Chen Gong took his leave and went out. Sighing deeply, he said to himself, "Alas! I'm ashamed to go back and face Tao Qian." So he rode off to Chenliu to try his fortune there.

Cao Cao's vengeful army laid waste to whatever place it passed through, slaying the people and desecrating their cemeteries. When Tao Qian heard the terrible tidings he turned toward Heaven and cried bitterly: "I must have been guilty of some sin before Heaven to have brought this calamity to my people!" He hastily called together his subordinates for counsel. One of them, Cao Bao, said, "Now that the enemy is upon us, we cannot sit and await death with folded hands. I for one will help you to make a fight."

So Tao Qian had to lead his army out to meet Cao Cao. From a distance he saw the enemy, all in mourning white, spread out in enormous numbers as if the ground was covered with frost or snow. In the center were two big white flags on which were written the word "Vengeance."

When he had ranged his men, Cao Cao, dressed completely in white, rode out to the front and started hurtling abuses at his foe. Tao Qian also advanced and from beneath his ensign he bowed to Cao Cao and said, "I wished to make friends with you, sir, so I sent Zhang Kai to escort your family. I did not know that his evil heart refused to change. And the tragedy happened. It was really not my fault, as you must recognize."

"You old rascal! You killed my father and now you dare to talk such nonsense to me!" shouted Cao Cao. Then, turning to his men, he asked, "Who will capture him for me?"

At his call Xiahou Dun rode out. The prefect fled to his own army and as Xiahou Dun came on, Cao Bao went to engage him. But just as the two horses met a strong gale suddenly arose, sweeping up dust and pebbles from the ground and throwing the two opposing sides into the utmost confusion. Both drew off.

The prefect retired into the city and said to his men, "The enemy force is too strong for us to counter. I will give myself up and let him wreak his vengeance on me. Thus I may save the people."

He had hardly finished speaking when someone stepped forward and said, "You have long ruled here and the people love you. Strong as the enemy are, they are not necessarily able to break down our walls. Now we must fortify ourselves and not go out and give battle. I will use a little scheme to destroy Cao Cao so that he will die without a burial place."

The bold words startled the assembly and all asked him anxiously what the scheme was.

> *Making overtures for friendship he encounters deadly hate,*
> *But, amid the gravest danger he discovered safety's gate.*

Who the bold speaker was will be told in the next chapter.

CHAPTER ELEVEN

Liu Bei Rescues Kong Rong in Beihai
Lu Bu Defeats Cao Cao at Puyang

I t was Mi Zhu who said he knew how to defeat Cao Cao completely. He came from a wealthy family in Donghai. Once, when returning home in a carriage after trading in Luoyang, he met a beautiful lady who asked him to let her ride with him. He stepped down from his carriage to walk and yielded his place to her. She invited him to share the seat with her. He mounted but sat rigidly upright, never even glancing in her direction. They traveled thus for some miles when she thanked him and alighted. Just before she took her leave she said, "I am the Goddess of Fire from the South. I am on my way to execute a decree of the Supreme God to burn down your dwelling, but your extreme courtesy has so deeply touched me that I now warn you. Go back home quickly and remove all your valuables. I will come tonight."

Then she disappeared. Mi Zhu hastily finished his journey and as soon as he arrived he removed everything from his house. Sure enough, that night a fire started in the kitchen and soon devoured the whole house. After this he devoted most of his wealth to relieving the poor and comforting the afflicted. Later, Tao Qian gave him the office that he now held.

Mi Zhu disclosed his plan. "I will go to Beihai to seek help from Kong Rong. Another one of us should go to Qingzhou on a similar mission, and if the armies of these two places come to assist us, Cao Cao will surely withdraw his forces."

The prefect accepted the plan and wrote the letters to be sent to the two places. Then he asked for a volunteer to go to Qingzhou and a certain Chen Dun offered himself for the errand. Soon, both of them left and the prefect led all the people to hold the city as long as they could.

This Kong Rong was a native of Qufu,* in the old kingdom of Lu, a descendant of the twentieth generation of the great teacher Confucius. He

---

* Birthplace of Confucius in modern Shandong Province.

had been noted as a very intelligent lad, if somewhat precocious. When he was only ten years old he had gone to see the governor of the district, but the doorkeeper would not let him in. Then he said, "Our two families are intimate friends," and he was admitted. When he went in, the governor asked him what relations had existed between the two families. The boy replied, "Of old my ancestor (Confucius) had asked yours (Lao Zi*) concerning ceremonial rites. So our families have known each other for many generations." The governor was surprised at the boy's ready wit.

Presently there came another visitor of high rank, to whom the governor told the story of his youthful guest. "He's a wonder, this boy," he said.

The visitor replied, "It doesn't follow that a clever boy grows up into a clever man."

The lad took him up at once, saying, "By what you say, sir, you were certainly clever as a boy."

The others all laughed. "This boy is going to be a great man one day," they said.

Thus from boyhood he became famous. When he grew up he became an official and was then Prefect of Beihai. Renowned for his hospitality, he used to say: "Let the rooms be full of guests, and the cups be full of wine. That is what I desire." After six years at Beihai he was much loved by the people there.

The day Mi Zhu arrived he was, as usual, seated among his guests and the envoy was ushered in without delay. In reply to a question about the reason for his visit Mi Zhu presented the letter from Tao Qian.

"Cao Cao is pressing hard on the city. Please come and rescue us," he added.

"Your master and I are good friends," said Kong Rong. "And you have come to ask me for help yourself. Of course I will go to your aid. However, I bear no grudge against Cao Cao either, so I will first write to him to try to make peace. If he refuses, then I will set the army in motion."

"Cao Cao will not listen to peace proposals—he is too certain of his strength," said the envoy.

Kong Rong then wrote his letter and also gave orders to muster his men. But just at this moment a messenger came with the urgent news that a remnant troop of the Yellow Turbans had come to invade the prefecture. It was necessary to deal with them first so Kong Rong hastened to lead his army outside the city to oppose the rebels.

The rebel leader rode out to the front and said, "I know this district is

---

* Ancient Chinese philosopher, founder of Taoism.

rich and can well spare 10,000 *shi** of grain. Give me that and we will withdraw. Otherwise, we will batter down the city walls and destroy every single soul."

Kong Rong shouted back, "I am an official of the great Han, entrusted with the safety of their land. Do you think I will feed rebels?"

The rebel whipped his steed, whirled his sword, and rushed at the prefect. One of the officers rode out to fight with him, but after a very few bouts was slain. The soldiers fell into confusion and ran pell-mell into the city for protection. The rebels then laid siege to the city on all sides. Kong Rong was careworn and Mi Zhu, who now saw no hope for the success of his mission, was grieved beyond words.

The next day, Kong Rong ascended the gate tower to look but the sight of the enormous number of rebels around the city troubled him even greater. Suddenly, he saw a man armed with a spear riding in among the rebels and scattering them like chaff in the wind. Before long he had reached the city gate and called out, "Open the gate!" But the defenders dared not open it to a stranger and in the delay a crowd of rebels had followed him to the edge of the moat. He wheeled about and cut down half a score of them and the rest fell back. At this the prefect ordered the wardens to open the gate and let him in at once. As soon as he was inside, he dismounted, laid aside his spear, and climbed up the tower to bow humbly to Kong Rong.

He said that his name was Taishi Ci and he came from Donglai. His aged mother had sent him to help the prefect out of gratitude for his kindness to her. "I only returned home yesterday from the north and then I heard that your city was in danger from a rebel attack. My mother said you had been very kind to her and told me to come and help you. So I rode out all alone and here I am."

The prefect was overjoyed for he already knew the man by reputation as a valiant fighter, although the two had never met. When the son was away in the north the prefect had taken his mother, who dwelt about five *li* from the city, under his special care, and saw to it that she did not suffer from want. This had won over the old lady's heart and she had sent her son to show her gratitude.

Kong Rong showed his appreciation by treating the warrior with the greatest respect and gave him presents of clothing and armor, a horse and saddle.

Taishi Ci said, "Give me a thousand veteran soldiers and I will go out and drive them off."

---

* An old unit of weight measurement, one *shi* equaling 132 lbs (60 kilograms).

"You are a bold warrior, but they are numerous. You should not act too rashly," warned the prefect.

"My mother sent me because she was grateful to you. How will I be able to look her in the face if I cannot raise the siege? I prefer to conquer or perish."

"I have been told that Liu Bei is a true hero and if we could get his help there would be no doubt of success. But there is no one to send the message."

"I will go as soon as you have written the letter," said the warrior.

So the prefect wrote the letter and gave it to the bold warrior who, after a large meal, put on his armor, attached his bow and quiver to his girdle, and tied his haversack firmly to his back. With his spear in hand he rode out of the city gate to confront the huge number of enemies—all alone.

Along the moat gathered a large party of besiegers, who at once came to intercept the solitary rider. But, dashing in among them, he cut down several of them and finally fought his way through.

The rebel leader, hearing that a rider had left the city, guessed what his errand would be and followed him with several hundred horsemen. He spread his men out so that the warrior was entirely surrounded. Taishi Ci set aside his spear, took his bow and arrows, and shot one after another all around him. And as every twang of his bowstring sent an enemy rider to his death the pursuers dared not close in.

Thus he got away and rode in hot haste to Pingyuan to see Liu Bei. After greeting his host in proper manner he presented the letter from Kong Rong and explained his errand.

"Who are you?" asked Liu Bei.

"My name is Taishi Ci, a simple man from the east. I am not related to Prefect Kong by ties of kinship, nor even by ties of neighborhood, but I am bound to him by bonds of sentiment and I share his sorrows and misfortunes. The rebels have invested his city and destruction is imminent. He is distressed beyond measure, for there is no one to turn to for help. He knows that you are humane and righteous, able to aid people in difficulties. Therefore at his command I have braved all dangers and fought my way through his enemies to appeal to you for help."

As he listened, Liu Bei's face grew grave and he said, "So he knows of my existence?"

Then Liu Bei assembled 3,000 soldiers and set out to help raise the siege in Beihai. When the rebel leader saw their arrival he led out his army to fight them, thinking he could easily dispose of so small a force.

The three brothers and Taishi Ci were in the forefront of their troops. The rebel leader hastened forward to challenge. Taishi Ci was about to open the combat when Guan Yu rushed forth and engaged the enemy. As their two steeds met, the soldiers set up a great shout. But how could there be any doubt of the result? After a few bouts Guan Yu's great sword rose and fell, and with it fell, too, his opponent.

At this Zhang Fei and Taishi Ci rode out side by side. With their spears ready they dashed in among the rebels, while Liu Bei urged his men to advance. Like tigers among a flock of sheep, they slew the rebels wherever they went and none could withstand them. When the prefect saw how his brave rescuers had defeated the enemy he also sent out his men to join in the battle so that the rebels were trapped between two armies. Soon, the enemy force was completely broken and many men surrendered, while the remainder scattered in all directions.

The victors were welcomed into the city and a banquet was prepared in their honor. Mi Zhu was introduced to Liu Bei to whom he told the story of the murder of Cao Song by Zhang Kai and Cao Cao's vengeful attack on Xuzhou and his coming to beg for assistance.

Liu Bei said, "Prefect Tao is a kindly man of high character, and it is a pity that he should suffer this wrong through no fault of his own."

"You are a scion of the imperial family," said Kong Rong. "And this Cao Cao is hurting the people, a strong man abusing his strength. Why not go with me to rescue the sufferers?"

"Well, it is not that I dare to refuse but my force is weak and I must act cautiously," replied Liu Bei.

"Though my desire to help Prefect Tao arises from an old friendship, yet it is a righteous act as well. Could it be that your heart is not inclined toward the right?" said Kong Rong.

Liu Bei said, "All right. You go first and give me time to see Gongsun Zan from whom I may borrow more men and horses. I will come later."

"You surely will not break your promise?" said Kong Rong.

"What kind of man do you think I am?" said Liu Bei. "A saint once said, 'All men must die but he who is without faith cannot maintain himself.' Whether I get the men or not, I will certainly come."

So Kong Rong agreed to this arrangement. He told Mi Zhu to return immediately to report the news and he himself began to prepare for the expedition.

Taishi Ci, his mission completed, was ready to leave, too. He said to Prefect Kong: "My mother bade me come to your aid and luckily you are safe. My townsman Liu Yao, Governor of Yangzhou, has sent me a letter, asking me to go there and I must leave you now. I will see you again."

Kong Rong wanted to give him money and silk as rewards but he would not accept anything. When his mother saw him return she was very

pleased at his success. She said, "I'm very glad you can prove our gratitude to Prefect Kong." Soon he departed for Yangzhou.

While Kong Rong was marching toward Xuzhou, Liu Bei went away to
his friend Gongsun Zan and told him about his plan to help Tao Qian.

"Cao Cao is not your enemy. Why do you exert yourself for the sake of
another?" said Gongsun Zan.

"I have promised," answered Liu Bei, "and dare not go back on my
words."

"I will lend you 2,000 horse and foot soldiers."

"May I also ask you to let Zhao Yun come with us?"

Gongsun Zan agreed to this as well.

So the two forces marched toward the besieged city of Xuzhou, with
Liu Bei and his own men in the front and Zhao Yun with the borrowed
soldiers to the rear.

In due course, Mi Zhu returned to Xuzhou with the news that not only
would Kong Rong come but he had persuaded Liu Bei to offer help as
well. The other envoy, Chen Deng, came back and reported that Tian Kai
would also bring help. The good tidings set Tao Qian's heart at ease.

But both Kong Rong and Tian Kai, greatly in dread of Cao Cao's
strength, camped among the hills far away from the city, afraid to take
any immediate action. However, their arrival forced Cao Cao to divide
his army into several units, so postponing his attack on the city itself.
Soon Liu Bei also reached the place and went to see Kong Rong.

The prefect said, "The enemy is very powerful and Cao Cao handles his
army skillfully. We must be cautious. Let us tread carefully before we
strike a blow."

"What I fear is famine in the city," said Liu Bei. "They cannot hold out
very long. I will put Guan Yu and Zhao Yun with 4,000 soldiers under
your command while Zhang Fei and I try to break through Cao Cao's
camp and get into the city to consult the prefect."

Kong Rong was very pleased with this plan, so he and Tian Kai took up
positions on both sides of the hills, with Guan Yu and Zhao Yun on either
side to support them. Elsewhere, Liu Bei and Zhang Fei with a thousand
cavalry tried to get through Cao Cao's camp. However, when they got to
the flank of his camp there arose a great beating of drums, and their enemy, both horsemen and foot soldiers, rolled out like billows on the
ocean. Their leader was Yue Jin. He checked his horse and called out,
"Halt, you maniacs! Where do you come from?"

Without deigning to give a reply, Zhang Fei rode straight to attack
the speaker. After they had fought a few bouts Liu Bei waved his double
swords as a signal for his men to come on. Yue Jin was routed and fled

for his life. Zhang Fei led the pursuit and in this way they reached the city wall.

From the gate tower the prefect saw a red banner embroidered in white with the name of Liu Bei, so he at once ordered his men to open the gate. Liu Bei was then cordially welcomed into the official residence and a banquet was prepared in his honor. His men were also rewarded with feasts.

Tao Qian was delighted with Liu Bei, admiring his noble appearance and clear speech. He told Mi Zhu to present to Liu Bei the seal and insignia of the city.

"What does this mean?" asked Liu Bei, greatly startled.

Tao Qian said, "There is trouble everywhere in the country and the Emperor's rule is no longer maintained. You, sir, are a member of the imperial family and eminently suited to help restore the line of Han. I am but an old man without any ability and I want you to take over the city so that I can retire. Please do not refuse. I will report my action to the court."

Liu Bei rose from his seat and bowed to his host. "Scion of the Han House though I am, my merit is small and my virtue meager. I doubt if I am fitted for my present post, let alone the office of your city. I have come to your assistance out of a sense of righteousness. Do you suspect me of coming with greed in my heart to speak like that? May God bless me no more if I cherished such a thought!"

"It is a poor old man's real sentiment, sir," said Tao Qian.

Over and over Tao Qian repeated his offer, but how could Liu Bei accept it?

At last Mi Zhu said, "Now the enemy is right at the gate. We need to find a way to drive them off first. This matter can wait until the siege is raised."

Liu Bei said, "I will write to Cao Cao to seek peace first. If he refuses, then we will fight."

Orders were therefore given to the men in the camps to remain in their positions. Meanwhile, the letter was written and sent to Cao Cao.

When the arrival of the messenger with the letter was announced Cao Cao was holding a council with his officers. He opened it and found that it was from Liu Bei. The following is the letter in brief:

> *Since our last meeting fate has assigned us to different quarters of the world and I have not been able to pay my respects to you.*
> *It was owing to the vicious nature of Zhang Kai but not to any fault of Prefect Tao that your noble father was murdered some time ago. Now the remnants of the Yellow Turbans are disturbing the provinces and Dong Zhuo's partisans have the upper hand in the*

capital. I hope that you, Illustrious Sir, will place the critical condi-
tion of the country before your personal grievances and so divert
your forces from the attack on Xuzhou to the rescue of the state.
Such would be for the happiness of the city and the whole country.

Cao Cao let out a torrent of abuse after reading the letter. "Who does this Liu Bei think he is that he dares to write and exhort me. Besides, he even uses an ironic tone in the letter."

He issued orders to put the bearer of the letter to death and to press on with the attack. But his advisor Guo Jia remonstrated: "Liu Bei has come from afar to help Tao Qian and he is observing the rule of politeness before resorting to force. I think you should reply with fair words, sir, so that his heart may be lulled into a false feeling of safety. Then attack with vigor and the city will fall."

Cao Cao found this advice good so he entertained the messenger and asked him to wait for his reply. While this matter was being seen to, a horseman came riding up with bad news—Lu Bu had captured Yanzhou and was entering Puyang.

Now Lu Bu had fled to Yuan Shu's place after Li Jue and Guo Si, the two partisans of Dong Zhuo, succeeded in their attack on the capital. However, Yuan Shu despised him for his infidelity, and refused to accept him. Then he had tried Yuan Shao, who had made use of him in defeating Zhang Yan at Changshan. But his success filled him with pride and his arrogant demeanor so annoyed the other commanders that Yuan Shao was on the point of putting him to death. To escape this he had sought refuge with Zhang Yang, who accepted his services.

About this time a friend of his named Pang Shu, who had been protecting his family in the capital since his disappearance, restored them to him. When Li Jue learned about this he put Pang Shu to death and wrote to Zhang Yang, asking him to kill Lu Bu. So once again Lu Bu had to flee and this time he offered himself to Zhang Miao.

He arrived just as Chen Gong was being introduced to Zhang Miao. Chen Gong said to Miao, "The disruption of the empire has begun and warriors are seizing what they can. It is a shame that you, sir, with all the strength you have, do not strike for independence. Cao Cao is now on an expedition against the east leaving his own district defenseless. Lu Bu is the best fighter of the day. If you employ him to capture Yanzhou you could then proceed to establish your own rule."

Zhang Miao was very pleased with the scheme and resolved to implement it. Soon, Lu Bu was in possession of Yanzhou and Puyang. And the whole area was quickly conquered, except for the three counties that were desperately defended by the two new advisors of Cao Cao. Cao Ren had fought many battles but was defeated each time and the horseman had been sent by him to report the emergent situation at home.

Greatly disturbed, Cao Cao said, "If my own city is lost I have no home to return to. I must do my best to win it back."

"You can make use of this to do Liu Bei a favor and withdraw to recover Yanzhou," advised Guo Jia.

Cao Cao agreed. So he wrote to Liu Bei, gave the letter to the waiting messenger, and broke camp.

The news that the enemy had left was really gratifying to Tao Qian, who then invited his friends into the city and entertained all his rescuers with feasts as a token of his gratitude.

When the feasting was over, he asked Liu Bei to sit in the seat of the highest honor and addressed the assembly.

"I am old and feeble and my two sons lacked ability to hold so important an office as this. The noble Liu is a descendant of the imperial house. He is of lofty virtue and great talent, suitable to take over the rule of this district. I will be only too willing to retire so as to have some leisure to nurse my health."

Liu Bei replied, "I came at the request of Prefect Kong because it was the right thing to do. If I take the city, the world will denounce me as a wicked man."

Mi Zhu said, "You should not refuse. The House of the Hans is falling and their realm crumbling. Now is the time for doughty deeds and signal services. This is a fertile district, well-populated, and you are the man to rule over it."

"But I will never dare to accept."

"The prefect is a sick man," said another official of the city, "and cannot see to matters. You must not decline, sir."

Liu Bei said, "Yuan Shu belongs to a family of great ministers who held the highest offices of the state on four occasions in three generations. The whole country respects him. His prefecture is close by, too. Why not invite him to come?"

"Because he is a rotting bone in a dark tomb, not worth talking about," replied Kong Rong. "This opportunity is a gift from Heaven and you will never cease to regret its loss."

Liu Bei still obstinately refused. Tao Qian entreated him again with tears in his eyes. "I will die with my eyes open if you desert me."

Guan Yu also tried to persuade his brother. He said, "Brother, since Prefect Tao is so kind as to make you the offer, I think you should accept it for the time being."

"Why so much fuss?" cried Zhang Fei. "We haven't forced him to yield the place—it is he who wishes to give it to you."

"Do you all want me to do what is wrong?" objected Liu Bei.

Tao Qian continued to entreat Liu Bei, but again and again his offer was refused. Finally he said, "If you will never consent, I have another offer to make. Near here is a little town called Xiaopei, which is good enough to station an armed force. Perhaps you would care to encamp there so that you can keep watch over this city."

All those present urged Liu Bei to accept the new offer, so he gave in. With the feast of victory ended, the time came to say farewell. Liu Bei was very sad when Zhao Yun took his leave. Tears fell freely as he held his hands and said goodbye. Kong Rong and Tian Kai, too, returned to their own places.

Then Liu Bei and his two brothers took up their abode in Xiaopei. They repaired the city walls and put out proclamations to calm the inhabitants.

In the meantime, Cao Cao had marched back to his own district. His cousin Cao Ren met him and told him that Lu Bu was very strong and he had Chen Gong as his advisor. Yanzhou and Puyang were both lost and only three small towns in the entire district had held on desperately.

Cao Cao said, "Lu Bu is a fierce fighter but nothing more. He has no strategy and will not be a serious threat to us."

So he gave orders to make a strong camp and wait till they could think out some good plan. Lu Bu, knowing of Cao Cao's return, called two of his subordinate officers, Xue Lan and Li Feng, to him and assigned to them the task of holding Yanzhou. He said to them, "I have long waited for an opportunity to employ your skill. Now I give you 10,000 soldiers —you are to hold the city while I go forth to attack Cao Cao."

Both of them agreed. But Chen Gong, the strategist, came in hastily and asked, "You are leaving Yanzhou. Where are you going, General?"

"I am going to camp my men in Puyang to confront Cao Cao there," said Lu Bu.

"You are making a mistake," said Chen Gong. "These two will never be able to hold Yanzhou. Remember, about one hundred and eighty *li* to the south, on the road to Taishan, is a very advantageous position where you should place a great number of your best soldiers in ambush. Cao Cao will hasten back when he hears Yanzhou is lost and if you strike when half of his men have gone past this point you may capture him."

Lu Bu said, "I have my plans to camp in Puyang. How can you guess?"

So he left the two officers in command at Yanzhou while he himself went away.

Now when Cao Cao approached the dangerous part of the road near

Taishan, Guo Jia warned him of the possibility of an ambush. But his master only laughed. "Lu Bu is no strategist. Do you think he could have laid an ambush here?" So he told Cao Ren to besiege Yanzhou while he marched toward Puyang to fight Lu Bu.

When he heard of the enemy's approach, Chen Gong again advised: "The enemy will be fatigued after the long march here. We must attack quickly before they have time to recover."

Lu Bu replied, "Alone on my horse I can move around the country freely. Do you think I will be afraid of this Cao Cao? Let him set his camp. I will capture him after that."

By then Cao Cao had camped near Puyang. The following day he led out his officers and spread his men in the open country. Taking his position underneath the standard, he watched his opponents coming up and arranging themselves in battle formation. Lu Bu was in front and beside him were eight strong fighters. The two best ones were called Zhang Liao and Zang Ba. They had 50,000 men under their command.

The drums began their thunderous roll and Cao Cao, pointing to his antagonist, said, "You and I had never quarreled, why then did you invade my land?"

"The land of the Hans is the possession of all. What is your special claim?" retorted Lu Bu.

So saying, he ordered Zang Ba to ride forth and challenge. From Cao Cao's side came Yue Jin to accept the challenge. Lifting their spears they exchanged nearly two score bouts with no advantage to either. Then Xiahou Dun rode out to help his colleague; to match him, Zhang Liao went forth from Lu Bu's side. The four of them fought.

After some time Lu Bu lost patience and, raising high his halberd, urged his steed forward to join in the fighting. Seeing him approaching, both Xiahou Dun and Yue Jin fled, but Lu Bu pressed after them and Cao Cao's army suffered disastrous losses. Retreating far, they made a new camp. Meanwhile, Lu Bu recalled his men and returned to the city.

At Cao Cao's camp, a council was held to discuss ways to counter Lu Bu. Yue Jin said, "I went up the hill today and saw from the top an enemy camp to the west of Puyang. There were not many soldiers there, and after their victory today, they will be off their guard. Let us attack it and if we can seize the camp we will strike fear into the heart of Lu Bu. This is our best plan."

The plan was adopted and Cao Cao, accompanied by six of his bravest warriors and a large army, left for the camp by a secret road.

Lu Bu was feasting with his men when Chen Gong reminded him of the importance of the west camp and said that it might be attacked.

"They have lost a battle. I do not think they dare to come," replied Lu Bu.

"Cao Cao is a very capable commander," insisted Chen Gong. "You must keep a good lookout for him lest he attacks you by surprise."

Lu Bu agreed and sent three of his officers to defend the west camp.

However, by dusk Cao Cao had reached the camp and his army began an immediate attack on all sides. The defenders could not hold him off. They ran in all directions and the camp fell into Cao Cao's hands. Near the fourth watch, the three officers and their army arrived on the scene. Cao Cao sallied forth to meet them. Another battle then waged till dawn. About that time a rolling of drums was heard in the west and it was reported that Lu Bu himself was on his way to rescue the camp. Cao Cao abandoned the newly-captured place and fled.

Escape was not easy, for Cao Cao was chased from behind by the three officers, while in front of him was Lu Bu himself. Two of Cao Cao's officers fought Lu Bu, but were unable to ward him off. Cao Cao went toward the north. Soon, however, from behind some hills came more of Lu Bu's army; as they could not be beaten off, Cao Cao sought safety in the west. Here again his retreat was barred—four of Lu Bu's officers blocked his way ahead.

The fight became desperate. Cao Cao himself took the lead to try to break the enemy's line. Just then a clapper sounded and arrows like pelting rain flew toward him, completely blocking his way forward. Cao Cao, now at his wit's end, cried out in fear, "Who can save me?"

Then from among the riders dashed out Dian Wei with his double iron spears, crying: "Do not worry, my lord." He leapt from his steed, put aside his spears, and took out a dozen darts. Turning to his attendants, he said, "When the enemy is at ten paces, call out to me." Then he set off with mighty strides, plunging forward despite the flying arrows.

Lu Bu's horsemen followed and when they got near, his attendants shouted, "Ten paces!"

"Five, then call," shouted back Dian Wei and pushed on.

At five paces, his attendants called out again, "Five!"

Then Dian Wei spun round and flung his darts. With every fling a man fell from his saddle and in no time half a score were slain and the remainder all fled. Dian Wei quickly remounted his steed, set his twin spears, and rushed again into the fight with a ferocity that none of his opponents could withstand. Thus he was able to rescue Cao Cao. By and by, Cao Cao was joined by his other officers and together they looked for the way back to their camp.

But as evening fell the noise of pursuit again rose behind them and soon Lu Bu appeared. "Halt, you wretch!" he shouted, as he approached with his halberd ready to thrust.

All stopped and stared at each other: the men were weary, and their steeds spent. Fear gripped them. How they wished they could find some place of refuge!

> *You may come safely out of the plight,*
> *But can you resist a strong foe in pursuit?*

Whether Cao Cao could survive this calamity will be told in the next chapter.

CHAPTER TWELVE

Prefect Tao Thrice Offers Xuzhou to Liu Bei
Cao Cao Fights a Great Battle Against Lu Bu

The last chapter ended with Cao Cao in great danger. However, at that very moment help came. Xiahou Dun rushed forth with a body of soldiers from the south and immediately engaged Lu Bu in a fierce battle. They fought till dusk, when torrential rain forced both sides to withdraw and return to their own camps. When Cao Cao got back he rewarded Dian Wei handsomely and promoted him in rank.

Lu Bu called in his advisor, Chen Gong, for counsel after he reached his camp.

Chen Gong proposed a new scheme. He said, "Here in Puyang is a very wealthy man, by the name of Tian, who owns hundreds of servants. We can tell him to send a letter secretly to Cao Cao about your ferocity and the people's hatred of you. Feed him false information that you are going away, leaving the city to the care of Gao Shun only. Then end the letter by imploring Cao Cao to attack at once and promising your support. Thus our enemy will be deceived into entering the city and we will destroy them by setting fires at the four gates and laying an ambush outside. Even if he has an ability equal to encompassing the universe, Cao Cao will not be able to escape."

Lu Bu thought this trick might work so he arranged for the Tian family letter to be sent. Coming soon after his defeat, when Cao Cao felt uncertain as to what to do next, the letter was read with joy. It promised help and said that the secret signal should be a white flag with the word "Justice" written on it.

"Heaven is bestowing Puyang to me," said Cao Cao rapturously. So he rewarded the messenger very liberally and began to prepare for the expedition.

But his advisor Liu Ye warned him: "Lu Bu is no strategist, but Chen Gong is full of guile. You must be careful in case there is treachery in this letter. If you must go, divide your army into three sections, and enter with only one third of your men, leaving the others outside the city as a reserve."

Cao Cao agreed to take this precaution. When he arrived at Puyang he found the city gay with fluttering flags. Scanning carefully, he saw among them at the corner of the west gate the white flag with the inscription. His heart rejoiced.

At noon that day two officers came out of the gate as if to fight. Cao Cao ordered Dian Wei to oppose them. Neither, however, seemed to be able to withstand Dian Wei's attack and fell back into the city at once. During the confusion some soldiers were seen to escape and come outside to Cao Cao. They told him that they had been sent by the Tian family and handed him another secret letter which said: "At about the first watch tonight you will hear the beating of a gong on top of the gate tower. That will be the signal for you to start the attack. I will open the gate for you."

Cao Cao then told Xiahou Dun and Cao Hong to station their men outside the city as reserve forces while he led Li Dian, Dian Wei, and two other officers to go into the city. Li Dian entreated his master to stay outside the city and let them go in first as a precaution, but Cao Cao would not listen. "If I don't go, who will push ahead?" he said. So at the agreed time he led the way. The moon had not yet risen.

As they drew near the city they heard the sound of a bugle, then a loud shouting, and they saw torches illuminating the gates, which were suddenly thrown open and the drawbridge lowered down. Cao Cao, whipping up his steed, galloped in.

But when he reached the official residence of the city he noticed that the streets were completely deserted and he realized he had been tricked. Wheeling around he shouted to his followers to retreat. Unfortunately it was too late. At that very moment, an explosion of a signal bomb was heard close by and flaming fires at the four gates rose to the sky. Gongs and drums beat all around with a roar like rolling rivers and boiling seas. From the east and the west came two bodies of soldiers eager to attack.

Cao Cao dashed off toward the north only to find his way barred. He tried for the south gate, but here again he was stopped by two of Lu Bu's officers. His trusty henchman Dian Wei, with fierce eyes and gritted teeth, at last burst through and got out, with the enemy close behind him. But when he reached the drawbridge he glanced back and found that his master was not with him. Immediately he turned his horse and forced his way inside again. At the gate he met Li Dian.

"Where's our lord?" he asked.

"I can't find him, either," replied Li Dian.

"You go and get help from outside," shouted Dian Wei. "I'll go in to find him."

So Dian Wei slashed his way in once again, looking on every side for Cao Cao—but he was nowhere to be found. Dashing out of the city, Dian Wei ran up against Yue Jin, who also asked him the whereabouts of their lord.

"I've entered the city twice in search of him but can't find him," said Dian Wei.

"Let's go in together," said Yue Jin.

They rode up to the gate. But the noise of bombs from the gate tower frightened Yue Jin's horse, so it refused to enter. Therefore Dian Wei went in alone, braving the smoke and the flames, to search on every side.

When Cao Cao had been separated from his sturdy protector Dian Wei, he was unable to escape through the south gate, so again he made an attempt to reach the north gate. On the way, sharply outlined against the glow of the fires, he saw the figure of Lu Bu coming toward him, his halberd poised ready to kill. Cao Cao covered his face with his hand, whipped up his steed, and sped past. But Lu Bu came galloping up behind him and, tapping him on the helmet with his halberd, he cried, "Where is Cao Cao?"

Cao Cao pointed in the opposite direction at a dun-colored horse well ahead and said, "There, on that dun horse! That's he!"

Hearing this, Lu Bu left pursuing Cao Cao to gallop after the rider on the dun horse.

At once Cao Cao turned toward the east gate. Soon he fell in with Dian Wei, who took him under his protection and fought his way through, leaving a trail of death behind, till they reached the gate. Here the fire was raging ferociously and burning beams were falling on all sides. The ground was covered with sparks. Dian Wei warded off the burning pieces of wood with his lance and rode into the smoke, opening a way for his lord. Just as they were passing through the gate a flaming beam fell down from the gate tower, hitting Cao Cao's steed on the hind quarters and knocking it down. Cao Cao fended off the burning beam but his hand and arm were badly burned and his hair and beard singed.

Dian Wei turned back to rescue him. Luckily, Xiahou Yuan came along just then and the two helped him up. Setting him on Xiahou Yuan's horse, they got him out of the flaming city. But the fighting continued till daybreak.

At last Cao Cao returned to his camp. His officers crowded about his tent and inquired about his health. Cao Cao laughed when he thought of the night's experience.

"I blundered into that fool's trap, but I will have my revenge," he said.

"Let us think of a new plan soon," said Guo Jia.

"I will turn his trick to my own use. I will spread the false report that I was badly burned in the fire and that I died soon after I got back. Lu Bu will come to attack us as soon as the news gets abroad and I will have an ambush ready for him in the Maling Hills. I will get him this time."

"A fine scheme indeed!" applauded Guo Jia.

So the soldiers were set to mourning and the report went everywhere that Cao Cao was dead. Soon, Lu Bu was informed and he assembled his men at once to make a surprise attack, taking the road by the Maling Hills to his enemy's camp.

As he was passing the hills he suddenly heard the beating of drums as the ambush was sprung and enemy soldiers leapt out all around. Only by desperate fighting did he get out of the melee and with a sadly diminished force he returned to his camp at Puyang. There he strengthened the fortifications and could not be tempted forth to battle.

That year the land was infested with locusts which consumed every green blade. Famine soon followed and in that area grain rose to an exorbitant price. People even took to cannibalism. Cao Cao's army suffered from want and had to withdraw to Juancheng. Lu Bu, too, took his army to Shanyang to get provisions. So the fighting ceased temporarily.

Let us return to Xuzhou. The prefect, Tao Qian, then age sixty-three, suddenly fell seriously ill and summoned Mi Zhu to his chamber to make arrangements for the future.

Mi Zhu said, "Cao Cao abandoned his attack on our city because of Lu Bu's seizure of Yanzhou. Although they are both keeping the peace due to the famine, Cao Cao will surely renew the attack in the spring. When you tried to make Liu Bei accept the office of the city you were still in good health. Now you are ill and weak and you can use this as a reason for retirement. He will not refuse again."

The prefect was very pleased with this idea and invited Liu Bei over, saying that he wanted his counsel on military affairs. Liu Bei came to the city with his two brothers and a small escort. He was at once called in to the sick man's bedchamber. The greetings over, the prefect went straight to the real reason for his invitation.

"Sir, I have asked you to come for the sole reason that I am very ill and may die at any time. I look to you, sir, to consider the Han empire as more important than anything else, and so to take over the office of this district. Then I may close my eyes in peace."

"You have two sons, why not nominate them to the office?" asked Liu Bei.

"Both lack the requisite talents. I trust you will instruct them after I have gone, but do not let them meddle into the city affairs."

"But I am unequal to so great a responsibility."

"Let me recommend to you one who can assist you. This man is called Sun Qian and he can be entrusted with the administration of the city."

Turning to Mi Zhu, he said, "The noble Liu is the most prominent man of the day and you should serve him well."

Still Liu Bei declined again and again but just then the prefect, pointing to his heart to indicate his sincerity, passed away.

When the ceremonial mourning and wailing of the officials were over, the marks of office were brought to Liu Bei, but once more, he refused to accept. The following day, inhabitants of the city crowded before his residence. Bowing and crying, they entreated him to stay. "If you do not we cannot live in peace," they said with one voice. To these requests were added his two brothers' persuasion, till at length he consented to assume the administrative duties of the city. He first appointed Sun Qian and Mi Zhu as his official advisors and Chen Deng, his secretary. Then he called in his army from Xiaopei and issued a proclamation to placate the people. In the meantime, arrangements for the funeral were made. Liu Bei and all his army were dressed in mourning. After the sacrificial ceremony was over, the late prefect was buried by the side of the Yellow River. His testament was forwarded to the court.

News in Xuzhou reached the ears of Cao Cao, who was beside himself with rage. "I have not yet had my revenge but he has simply stepped in to command the district without so much as shooting an arrow. I will first put him to death and then dig up Tao Qian's corpse to avenge the death of my late father."

Orders were issued for the army to prepare for a new campaign against Xuzhou. But his advisor Xun Yu remonstrated: "In the past the founder of the Han Dynasty secured Guanzhong and later, Emperor Guangwu took Henei. They both consolidated their own positions for the command of the whole country. So when they advanced they could succeed, and when they retreated they could have a base to return to. In the end they accomplished their great designs, despite setbacks. And to you, sir, Yanzhou is your Guangzhong and Henei, which is a strategically important place and which you occupied first. If you leave many men here while you are on your expedition to attack Xuzhou, you will not be able to win the battle. But if you leave too few here, Lu Bu will seize the initiative to fall upon us and you will lose Yanzhou. If you fail to gain Xuzhou, where will you return to? Although Tao Qian has gone, Liu Bei now holds it, and since the people support him they will fight to death for him. To abandon this place for that is to give up the great for the small, to barter the root for the branch, and exchange safety for danger. I implore you to reconsider carefully."

Cao Cao replied, "It is not a good plan to keep soldiers idle here during a time of scarcity."

"If so, it would be more advantageous to attack the rebels in the east and feed our army on their supplies. Some remnants of the Yellow Turbans there have amassed a lot of grain and money by plundering wherever they could. Rebels like these are easily defeated. Destroy them, and you can feed your army with their grain. Moreover, this will please both the court and the common people."

This new scheme appealed strongly to Cao Cao and he quickly began his preparations to carry it out. Leaving Xiahou Dun and Cao Ren to guard Juancheng, he led the main body of his army to march toward the east.

When the rebels learned about Cao Cao's approaching they came out in a great force to oppose him. The two armies met at Goat Hill. Though numerous in number, the rebels were an undisciplined bunch, a mere pack of foxes and dogs without organization. Cao Cao ordered his strong archers and vigorous crossbowmen to check their advance. Then he ordered Dian Wei to challenge. From the rebel side came the assistant chief to give battle, but he was vanquished in the third bout. Cao Cao's army pushed forward and drove the rebels over the hill, where they encamped.

The following day the rebel leader himself led forth his army and deployed his men in battle array. A fighter, wearing a yellow turban on his head and a green robe over his body, advanced on foot to offer combat. Waving his iron mace, he shouted, "I am He Man the Devil, who dares to fight with me?"

Cao Hong uttered a great shout and jumped from his saddle to accept the challenge. Sword in hand he advanced on foot and the two engaged in a fierce struggle before the two armies. They exchanged some scores of passes but neither could gain any advantage over the other. Then Cao Hong feigned defeat and ran away. He Man went after him. Just as he got close, Cao Hong suddenly wheeled about and struck with all his might. Two slashes, and He Man lay dead.

At once Li Dian dashed forward into the midst of the enemy and laid hands on the rebel chief who, caught unprepared, became his captive. Cao Cao's men then charged ahead and scattered the rebels. The spoils of money and grain was immense.

The other rebel leader fled with a few hundred horsemen toward a hill. But while they were on their way, there suddenly appeared from behind the hill a company of men led by a very powerful-looking warrior. He was of medium height, thickset and stout, with a waist ten spans in girth. Whirling his long sword he barred their way. The rebel leader set his spear and rode toward him, but at the first encounter the warrior caught him under his arm and made him a prisoner. Terror-stricken, all the others dismounted from their horses and allowed themselves to be bound. The victor drove them all into an enclosure with high banks.

After a while Dian Wei, still pursuing the rebels, also reached a hill. The warrior came up to meet him.

"Are you also a rebel?" asked Dian Wei.

"I have some hundreds of them prisoners in an enclosure here," answered the warrior.

"Why not submit them to me?"

"I will if you can win this sword from my hand."

This angered Dian Wei so much that he raised his twin spears and attacked his opponent. The two engaged in combat, which lasted for four long hours, but neither could beat the other. Both rested for a while. The unknown warrior was the first to recover and renewed his challenge. They fought till dusk and then, as their horses were quite spent, the combat was once more suspended.

In the meantime, some of Dian Wei's men had run off to tell the story of this wondrous fight to Cao Cao, who greatly alarmed, hastened to the scene to watch, followed by his officers.

The next day the warrior rode out again to offer battle. Cao Cao was very much impressed by his powerful-looking physique. In his heart he rejoiced to see such a valiant hero and desired to gain his services for himself. So he told Dian Wei to feign defeat.

Dian Wei rode out in answer to the challenge. After some score of bouts he turned and fled toward his own side. The warrior followed him and came quite close but was driven away by a flight of arrows. Cao Cao hastily withdrew his men and then he secretly prepared a trap, sending some soldiers carrying hooks to lie in ambush.

So the following day Dian Wei was again sent out with a hundred or so horsemen. His adversary came out to meet him.

"You have been defeated by me. How dare you come again?" he laughed. So saying he rode forth to fight but after a faint show of fighting, Dian Wei turned to flee. His opponent, intent upon the pursuit, did not notice the trap, and soon both he and his horse fell into the pit. He was taken prisoner by the soldiers, who tied him up and took him to their chief.

As soon as he saw the prisoner, Cao Cao stepped down from his seat, sent away the soldiers, and with his own hands loosened the bonds. Then he brought out clothes for him to wear, bade him sit down, and asked him his name and place of birth.

"My name is Xu Chu from the district of Jiaoguo. When the rebellion broke out I gathered several hundred of my kinfolk to build a stronghold for protection. One day the robbers came, but I had told my men to prepare a lot of stones for me and I threw them, hitting someone every time I aimed. This drove off the robbers.

"Another time they came again and we were short of grain. So I made peace with them and agreed to exchange cattle for their grain. They delivered the grain and were driving away the cattle when the beasts took fright and ran back to their pens. I seized two of them by the tail, one with each hand, and hauled them backwards a hundred or so paces. The robbers were so scared that they dared not come back for the cattle. From then on they never troubled us again."

"I have long heard of your heroic exploits," said Cao Cao. "Will you join my army?"

"Yes, that is my strongest desire," replied Xu Chu.

So he called up his clan, some hundreds in all, and they formally submitted to Cao Cao. The strong man received the rank of a senior officer and received ample rewards. The two captured rebel leaders were executed and the area returned to peace.

Then Cao Cao returned to his own district and was met by Xiahou Dun and Cao Ren. These two told him that scouts had reported Yanzhou to be left defenseless, most of its garrison having given themselves up to plundering the surrounding country, and they suggested attacking it as soon as possible. "With these soldiers fresh from victory, the city will fall at a tap of the drum," they said.

Acting on their advice, Cao Cao led his army to march to Yanzhou without delay. The two officers in the city, Xue Lan and Li Feng, were quite unprepared for this sudden assault, but had to come out with their small force to fight. Xu Chu said to his new master that he would capture these two as a gift to him.

Cao Cao was very happy to hear it and ordered him out to challenge for battle. Li Feng, with his halberd, advanced to meet him. The combat was brief, as Li Feng fell in the second bout. Seeing this, his colleague retreated with his men but, to his dismay, he found the drawbridge was seized by the enemy. He dared not go back to the city, so he led his men toward another town. Then an arrow killed him and his soldiers scattered to the four winds. So Yanzhou was restored to Cao Cao.

Next an expedition was prepared to take Puyang. The army set out in perfect order with van leaders and commanders for the flanks and the rear. Cao Cao led the center; Dian Wei and Xu Chu were van leaders. When they approached Puyang, Lu Bu wanted to go out alone to fight his enemy but his advisor protested, begging him to wait the arrival of his officers.

"Who do I fear?" said Lu Bu.

So he threw caution to the wind and went to meet his foes. Holding his halberd he began to revile them. From Cao Cao's side, Xu Chu came out to fight with him and after a score of bouts neither combatant was any the worse.

"Lu Bu is not the type that a single man can overcome," said Cao Cao, and he sent Dian Wei to assist. Lu Bu withstood the combined attack but soon after four other officers joined in. The six opponents proved too many for him so he turned back toward the city.

However, the gate tower had been seized by the rich Tian family. When they saw him returning beaten, they immediately raised the drawbridge. Lu Bu shouted to them to open the gates, but the Tians said: "We have gone over to General Cao Cao." Lu Bu was so angry that he abused them roundly before he left for Dingtao. The faithful Chen Gong got away through the east gate, taking with him Lu Bu's family.

Thus Puyang came into Cao Cao's hands. The Tian family were forgiven their previous indiscretion of sending the false letters because of this new service.

Liu Ye said, "Lu Bu is a veritable tiger. To leave him alive would be a great danger. We must hunt him down while he has not yet recovered from defeat."

Cao Cao saw this was true. Therefore he decided to follow Lu Bu to Dingtao, leaving Liu Ye and others to guard Puyang.

Lu Bu, Zhang Miao, and Zhang Chao were assembled in the city but four of his major officers were out foraging for provisions. Soon Cao Cao's army arrived. However, it did not attack for several days and then retreated a long way to set up camp. It was harvest time and the soldiers were told to cut the wheat for food. Lu Bu's men reported this to him and he hurried over with his army, but when he saw that Cao Cao's camp lay near a thick wood he feared there might be an ambush inside and returned to the city. When Cao Cao heard that Lu Bu had come and gone, he guessed the reason.

"He was afraid of an ambush in the wood," he said. "We will put up a lot of banners there to deceive him. To the west of the camp is a long embankment, but there is no water in the stream below. We will lay an ambush there for Lu Bu when he comes to burn the wood. I'm sure he will come tomorrow."

So he hid all his soldiers behind the embankment, except fifty drummers and some villagers, who were told to raise a great deal of noise inside the camp, to make it seem that it was not empty.

Now Lu Bu had returned to tell his advisor what he had seen. "This Cao Cao is very crafty and full of wiles," said his advisor Chen Gong. "You mustn't underestimate him."

"I will use fire this time and burn out his ambush," said Lu Bu.

The following day he led a large force to Cao Cao's camp and there he saw banners flying everywhere in the wood. He ordered his men forward to set fire to all sides. But to his great surprise there was not a single soul. He wanted to make for the camp but just then he heard the beating of drums and doubt filled his mind. Suddenly, he saw a party of soldiers moving out from behind the camp and he galloped after them to give chase.

Then the signal bombs exploded and out from behind the embankment rushed six of Cao Cao's most valiant officers with their men. All of them dashed toward Lu Bu. He knew that he could not withstand them all so he fled into the open country. One of his officers was killed by an arrow and two-thirds of his men were lost. The defeated soldiers ran back to tell Chen Gong what had happened.

"We had better leave here," said Chen Gong. "An empty city cannot be defended."

So he and Gao Shun, taking Lu Bu's family with them, abandoned the city of Dingtao. When Cao Cao led his victorious army into the city he met with little resistance. Zhang Chao committed suicide and Zhang Miao fled to Yuan Shu's palace.

Thus the whole of Shandong fell under the power of Cao Cao. To consolidate his rule, he set out to calm the people and repair the city walls.

In the meantime, while retreating Lu Bu fell in with the four officers who had been out foraging. Soon Chen Gong also joined him so that he was by no means broken.

"I have but few men," he said, "but still enough to challenge Cao Cao." And so he took the road back toward the city to fight his enemy.

> *Thus does fortune alternate, victory, defeat,*
> *The happy conqueror today, tomorrow may retreat.*

The fate of Lu Bu will be told in the next chapter.

CHAPTER THIRTEEN

Li Jue and Guo Si Fight a Bloody Battle
Yang Feng and Dong Cheng Rescue the Emperor

The last chapter told of the defeat of Lu Bu, and his reunion with the other officers of his army by the riverside. When all his men had joined him he began to feel strong enough to fight it out with Cao Cao once again.

Chen Gong objected, "He is too strong to defeat right now. Wait until you find some place where you can entrench yourself first."

"Suppose I went to Yuan Shao?" said Lu Bu.

"Send someone to make inquiries first."

Lu Bu agreed. The news of the fighting between Cao Cao and Lu Bu had, however, reached Jizhou. One of Yuan Shao's advisers, Shen Pei, warned him, "If this savage Lu Bu gets possession of Yanzhou, he will certainly attempt to devour our district. For your own safety you should help to crush him."

Therefore Yuan Shao sent Yan Liang with 500,000 soldiers to help Cao Cao. Lu Bu's spy heard of this and at once returned to tell him. Greatly disturbed, Lu Bu called in the faithful Chen Gong for consultation.

"I hear Liu Bei has lately acquired Xuzhou. We can go to him," suggested Chen Gong.

Following this advice, Lu Bu started toward Xuzhou. When Liu Bei learnt of his coming, he wanted to go out and welcome him as a brave warrior. Mi Zhu was strongly against receiving him at all, saying that he was a cruel, bloodthirsty beast. "If you receive him, he will harm you," he added.

But Liu Bei replied, "How would misfortune have been avoided if he had not attacked Yanzhou? He cannot be our enemy now that he is seeking asylum."

"Brother, you're really too kind. Although it may be as you say, it's better to get prepared," said Zhang Fei.

The new prefect went out of the city to welcome Lu Bu and the two chiefs rode in side by side. They proceeded to the official residence and there, after the elaborate ceremonies of reception were over, they sat down to talk.

Lu Bu said, "After Wang Yun and I succeeded in slaying Dong Zhuo, there arose the rebellion of Li Jue and Guo Si. I drifted about from one place to another in the northeast and most of the nobles seemed unwilling to receive me. When Cao Cao wickedly invaded this district and you, sir, came to its rescue, I aided you by attacking Yanzhou and thus diverting a portion of his force. I did not expect then that I would be the victim of a vile plot and lose my officers and men. Now I have come to offer myself to you so that we may together accomplish great designs. What do you say to this, sir?"

Liu Bei replied, "When the late prefect died there was none to administer Xuzhou and so I assumed that task temporarily. Now that you are here, General, I should certainly yield this place to you."

So saying he handed to Lu Bu the insignia and the seal. Lu Bu was on the point of accepting them when he saw Guan Yu and Zhang Fei, who stood behind the prefect, glaring at him with angry eyes, so he put on a smile and said, "I am nothing but a fighting man, how could I rule a place like this?"

Liu Bei repeated his offer. Chen Gong said, "A strong guest does not intimidate his host. You need not fear, sir."

Then Liu Bei did not insist any longer. Banquets were held and lodgings prepared for the guest and his retinue. Lu Bu returned the feast the next day and Liu Bei went with his two brothers. Halfway through the banquet, Lu Bu invited his guest into the private quarters and the brothers followed him. Lu Bu told his wife and daughter to bow to their benefactor. As Liu Bei again showed excessive modesty, Lu Bu said, "My good younger brother, you needn't be so very modest."

Zhang Fei heard what he said and his eyes glared. "Our brother is one of the royal family. What sort of a man are you that dares call him 'younger brother?'" he cried. "Come out and I will fight you three hundred bouts."

Liu Bei hastily checked the impulsive Zhang Fei and Guan Yu persuaded him to go away. Then Liu Bei apologized to Lu Bu: "My unruly brother talks wildly after drinking. I hope you will not blame him."

Lu Bu said nothing. Soon after, the guests departed. But as he escorted Liu Bei to his carriage he saw Zhang Fei galloping up with his spear set for combat.

"Lu Bu, you and I will fight that duel of three hundred!" he shouted.

Liu Bei told Guan Yu to check him.

The next day Lu Bu came to take leave of his host. "Thank you for kindly receiving me but I fear your brothers and I cannot agree. I will seek some other asylum."

"General, if you go, my fault becomes grave. My rude brother has offended you and I will make him apologize to you later. Would you care for a temporary sojourn in the town of Xiaopei, where I was encamped for some time? That place is small and mean, but it is near and I will see to it that you are supplied with all you need."

Lu Bu thanked him and accepted the offer. He led his men there and took up residence. After he had gone, Liu Bei blamed Zhang Fei for his rudeness.

But this is not our concern for the moment. Let us return to Cao Cao. After he had subdued the whole of Shandong, he reported this to the throne and was rewarded with the title of General of Eminent Virtue and created a lord. At this time the rebellious Li Jue had made himself Chief Minister of War, and Guo Si styled himself Grand Commander. Their conduct was abominable but no one dared to criticize them. Two ministers, Yang Biao and Zhu Jun, said to the Emperor in private: "Cao Cao has a large army and many capable advisors and officers; it would be well for the country if he could lend his support to the imperial family and help to rid the government of these two evil men."

His Majesty wept, "I have long been insulted and bullied by these villains and should be very glad to have them removed."

"I have thought of a plan to estrange Li Jue and Guo Si and so make them destroy each other. Then Your Majesty can call Cao Cao in to cleanse the court," said Yang Biao.

"How will you manage it?" asked the Emperor.

"Guo Si's wife is very jealous and we can take advantage of her weakness to bring about a quarrel."

So the Emperor gave a secret edict for Yang Biao to act accordingly.

Yang Biao's wife was then instructed to make an excuse to visit Madam Guo at her house. In the course of their conversation, she said, "There is talk of a secret liaison between the General, your husband, and the wife of Minister Li. It is a great secret, but if Minister Li knew it he might try to harm your husband. I think you ought to stop them from seeing each other again."

Madam Guo was surprised. "I have wondered why he sometimes spends the night at their home," she said, "but I did not think there was anything shameful connected with it. I should never have known if you had not told me. I must put a stop to it."

By and by, when Madam Yang took her leave, her hostess thanked her warmly for the information she had given. Several days passed and Guo Si was again invited to dinner at Li Jue's home. His wife said, "This Li Jue is very deep and one cannot fathom his designs. As the saying goes, 'Two heroes cannot exist side by side'. If he tries to poison you, what would become of your poor wife?"

Guo Si paid no attention to her words but she finally prevailed on him to stay at home. In the evening, wine and food arrived from Li Jue's house and Guo Si's wife secretly put poison into the delicacies before she set them before her husband. He was going to taste them at once but she said, "It's unwise to consume things that come from outside. Let's try them out on a dog first."

They did and the dog died. This incident aroused Guo Si's suspicion of his friend Li Jue.

One day at court, Li Jue again persuaded Guo Si to have dinner at his place. After Guo Si arrived home in the evening, rather drunk because of too much wine, he happened to have a stomach upset. His wife said she suspected poison and hastily administered an emetic, which relieved the pain. Guo Si began to feel angry.

"We planned our grand scheme together. Now he wants to harm me. If I don't get in the first blow, I'll be his victim."

So Guo Si began to prepare his force for a sudden attack on Li Jue. Very soon this was told to Li Jue and he, in his turn, grew angry. "How dare Guo Si plot against me?"

Then he assembled his men and went to attack Guo Si. Several hundred thousand soldiers were involved in the conflict and the quarrel became so serious that they fought a pitched battle beneath the city walls. The common folk suffered greatly as they were plundered by both armies.

Then a nephew of Li Jue's suddenly surrounded the palace, put the Emperor and Empress in two carriages, and carried them off. The palace attendants were made to follow on foot. As they went out of the rear gate they met Guo Si's army, who began to shoot arrows at the cavalcade. They killed many attendants before Li Jue's army came up and forced them to retire.

Without asking for the Emperor's permission, the carriages were driven out of the palace and into Li Jue's camp, while Guo Si's men plundered the palace and carried off all the women who remained to their camp. Then the palace was set on fire.

As soon as Guo Si heard of the whereabouts of the Emperor he came over to attack Li Jue's camp. The Emperor was greatly alarmed.

Li Jue went out to give battle. His enemy could not prevail and retreated temporarily. Then Li Jue removed the imperial captives to Meiwu with his nephew as jailer. Supplies were reduced and hunger showed itself on the faces of the attendants. The Emperor sent someone to Li Jue to request five measures of rice and five sets of bullock bones for his attendants. The tyrant angrily replied, "The court gets food morning and evening; why ask for more?"

He deliberately sent them putrid meat and rotten grain that was too smelly to eat. The Emperor was greatly annoyed at the new insult.

Yang Qi, one of his attendants, entreated him to be patient. "He is very cruel. Under the present circumstances, Your Majesty has to put up with this and must not provoke him."

The Emperor lowered his head and was silent, but tears fell on his garments. Suddenly, someone came in with the tidings that a force of cavalry, their sabers glittering in the sun, was approaching to rescue them. Then they heard the gongs beat and the roll of the drums.

The Emperor told him to find out who it was. But it was Guo Si, and sadness fell again. Presently there arose a great shout, for Li Jue had gone out to fight with his opponent.

"I treated you well. Why did you try to kill me?" asked Li Jue.

"You are a rebel, why should I not slay you?" Guo Si retorted.

"You call me rebel when I am guarding the Emperor?"

"You have abducted him—do you call that guarding?"

"Why so many words? Let us settle the matter in a single combat without the aid of soldiers; the winner will take the Emperor and leave."

So saying the two fought in front of their armies, but neither could prevail over the other. Then they saw Yang Biao come riding up to them, crying, "Rest a while, Commanders! I have invited the officials to mediate a peace between you."

Therefore the two leaders retired to their camps. Soon Yang Biao, Zhu Jun, and three other officials came up and went to Guo Si's camp first, but to their horror, they were all thrown into confinement.

"We came with good intentions," they moaned, "and we are treated like this."

"Li Jue has run off with the Emperor, why can't I get his officials?" asked Guo Si.

"One has the Emperor and the other, his officials. What are you up to?" said the peacemaker, Yang Biao.

Guo Si lost patience and drew his sword, but one of his officers persuaded him not to slay the speaker. Then he released Yang Biao and Zhu Jun. The others, however, were kept in custody.

"Here we are, two officials of the throne, and we cannot help our lord. We have been born in vain," said Yang Biao.

Throwing their arms about each other, they wept and fell swooning to the ground. When Zhu Jun went home, he fell seriously ill and soon died.

Thereafter the two adversaries fought every day for nearly three months, each losing many men.

Now Li Jue was a firm believer in black magic. He often called witches to beat drums and summon spirits to his camp. His chief advisor, Jia Xu, used to remonstrate with him, but to no avail.

Yang Qi said to the Emperor: "I find that Jia Xu, although a close friend of Li Jue's, does not seem to have lost his loyalty to Your Majesty. I think Your Majesty should ask him for help."

Just then Jia Xu himself arrived. The Emperor sent away his attendants and said to him in tears, "Will you not pity the Hans and save my life?"

Jia Xu prostrated himself on the ground and said, "That is my strongest wish. But say no more, Your Majesty, let your servant try to work out a plan."

The Emperor dried his tears. Soon Li Jue came in with his sword girded on. The Emperor was so terrified that his face became the color of clay.

Li Jue said to the Emperor, "Guo Si has failed in his duty and imprisoned the court officials. He wished to slay Your Majesty and you would have been captured but for me."

The Emperor joined his hands together in salute and thanked him. He went away. Before long, Huangfu Li, an official from Xiliang, entered and the Emperor, knowing him as a man of persuasive tongue and also that he came from the same district as Li Jue, asked him to go to both factions to try to negotiate peace. He accepted the mission and first went to Guo Si, who said he was willing to release the officials if Li Jue would restore the Emperor to full liberty. He then went to the other side. To Li Jue he said, "Since I am a Xiliang man the Emperor has selected me to make peace between you and your adversary. Now Guo Si has consented to cease the quarrel—will you agree to peace?"

"I have overthrown Lu Bu, I have upheld the government for four years, and have many great services to my credit, as all the world knows. But Guo Si, a mere horse thief, has dared to seize the officials of state and to set himself up against me. I have sworn to slay him. Look around you. Don't you think my army large enough to break him?"

"Not necessarily," said Huangfu Li. "In ancient days Hou Yi,* proud of his skill in archery, gave no thought to great adversity and so perished. Lately, you have seen how powerful Dong Zhuo has been, but he

---

* Legendary king noted for his skill in archery.

was betrayed by Lu Bu who had received many benefits at his hands. In no time his head was hanging over the city gate. So mere force is not enough to guarantee safety. Now you are a high-ranking general, with all the symbols of rank and high office, and your descendants and all your clan occupy distinguished positions. You must confess that the state has rewarded you liberally. True, Guo Si has seized the officials of the state, but you have done the same to the Emperor. Who is worse than the other?"

Li Jue angrily drew his sword and shouted, "Did the Emperor send you to humiliate me? I will cut your head first."

One of his officers checked him. "Guo Si is still alive," he said. "To slay the imperial messenger would be giving him a good excuse to raise an army against you. And all the nobles would join him."

Jia Xu also tried hard to calm him down. The messenger of peace was urged to go away. But he would not be satisfied with failure. He remained there and cried loudly, "Li Jue will not obey the Emperor's command. He will kill his lord to set up himself."

One of the Emperor's attendants hastened to shut his mouth. "Do not utter such words. You will only bring harm upon yourself."

But Huangfu Li shrieked at him as well. "You are also an official of the state and yet you even back up the rebel. As the saying goes, 'When the Emperor is put to shame his ministers die'. If it were my lot to suffer death at the hands of Li Jue, so be it!"

And he continued with a torrent of abuse. When the Emperor heard of the incident, he at once called in Huangfu Li and sent him away to his home in Xiliang.

Now the majority of Li Jue's men were from Xiliang and he had also relied on the assistance of Qiang tribe soldiers. Huangfu Li had spread the story among them that Li Jue was a rebel and so were those who helped him, and that there would be a day of heavy reckoning. His words were readily believed and the morale of the soldiers sank. Li Jue sent one of his officers to arrest Huangfu Li; but the officer had a moral sense and, instead of carrying out his master's order, returned to say he could not be found.

Jia Xu tried to work on the feelings of the Qiang soldiers. He said to them in secret, "The Emperor knows you are loyal to him and have suffered from military campaigning. He has issued a secret command for you to go home and then he will reward you liberally in future."

The tribesmen had a grievance against Li Jue for not paying them, so they listened readily to the persuasions of Jia Xu and deserted. Then Jia Xu said to the Emperor, "Li Jue is greedy and unresourceful. Now he is enfeebled with the departure of the tribesmen. If you heap honors upon him, Your Majesty, he can be bought."

The Emperor agreed and raised him to the rank of Supreme Commander of the Army. This delighted him greatly and he credited his promotion to the power of the witches' prayers and incantations. He rewarded them most generously.

But his army was forgotten. Yang Feng was angry and he said to his colleague Song Guo: "We have taken all the risks and exposed ourselves to stones and arrows in his service, yet instead of giving us any reward he ascribes all the credit to those witches of his."

"Let us kill Li Jue and rescue the Emperor," said Song Guo.

"You start a fire inside as a signal and I will attack from without."

So the two agreed to act together in the second watch that very night. But they had been overheard and the eavesdropper told Li Jue. Song Guo was seized and put to death. That night Yang Feng waited outside for the signal and while waiting, out came Li Jue to look for him. Then a fight began, which lasted till the fourth watch. But Yang Feng got away and fled with his men to Xian in the west.

From then on, Li Jue's army was even more weakened and he felt more than ever the losses caused by his opponent's frequent attacks. Then came news that Zhang Ji, at the head of a large army, was coming down from the west to arrange peace between the two factions. He declared that he would attack the one who was not compliant. Li Jue, whose strength was much diminished, jumped at the opportunity and hastened to inform Zhang Ji of his willingness to accept a peace settlement. Guo Si, too, had to concede.

So the strife of the rival factions ended at last and Zhang Ji presented a memorial, asking the Emperor to go to Hongnong near Luoyang. The Emperor was delighted to have the opportunity to go back to the east, for he had long wished to revisit the old capital. Zhang Ji was rewarded with the title of General of Carriage and Cavalry and was highly honored. He saw to it that the Emperor and the court had good supplies of food and wine. Guo Si set free all his captive officials and Li Jue prepared transport for the Emperor and his followers to move to the east. Several hundred former palace guards were entrusted with escorting the cavalcade.

Their progress was without incident as far as Baling. It was fall and the cold west wind blew with great violence. Soon, above the howling of the blast, the trampling of a large body of horses could be heard. They stopped at a bridge and barred the way.

"Who is there?" cried a voice.

"The imperial chariot is passing. Who dares to stop it?" said Yang Qi, riding forward.

Two officers advanced, "General Guo has ordered us to guard the bridge and stop all spies. You say the Emperor is here—we must see him and then we will let you pass." So the beaded curtain was raised and the Emperor said, "I, the Emperor, am here. Why do you block my way, officers?" They all shouted, "Long live the Emperor! Long live the Emperor!" and fell away to allow the procession through.

But when they reported what they had done to Guo Si, he was very angry. "I meant to outwit Zhang Ji, seize the Emperor, and hold him in Meiwu. Why did you let him get away?" He put the two officers to death and set out to pursue the cavalcade himself.

As the cavalcade reached the town of Huayin a great shouting arose behind the travelers and a loud voice commanded the chariot to stop. The Emperor burst into tears.

"Out of the wolf's den, into the tiger's mouth! What is to be done?" cried the Emperor.

No one knew what to do, for they were all too frightened. But as the rebel army was closing upon them, they heard the beating of drums and from behind some hills came an armed force preceded by a great banner bearing the name of Yang Feng, the officer who had betrayed Li Jue.

Now after Yang Feng's defeat he had camped under the Zhongnan Mountains, but as soon as he knew of the Emperor's journey he came up to guard him. Seeing it was necessary to fight, he drew up his line of battle and one of Guo Si's fighters rode out and let forth a volley of abuse. Yang Feng turned to his men and shouted, "Where is Xu Huang?"

In response a valiant warrior galloped forth on his bay steed, carrying a heavy battle-ax. He made directly for his opponent and killed him with the first blow. At this Yang Feng led his men to press forward and routed Guo Si, who withdrew some twenty *li*. Yang Feng also called back his men and then he went to see the Emperor.

"You have rendered a great service by saving my life," said the Emperor graciously.

Yang Feng bowed and thanked him. The Emperor then asked to see the warrior who had slain the rebel. Presently Xu Huang was led to the chariot, where he bowed reverently to the Emperor.

Then the cavalcade proceeded, Yang Feng acting as escort as far as Huayin, where they halted for the night. A general there presented clothing and food to the Emperor, who spent the night in Yang Feng's camp.

The next day Guo Si, having mustered his men, reappeared in front of the camp and Xu Huang rode out to engage him in battle. But Guo Si's army was much greater in number and in no time the loyalist force was entirely surrounded, with the Emperor and Yang Feng in the center. At this critical moment, an army arrived from the southeast led by a galloping horseman and the rebels fell back. Then Xu Huang smote them and so scored a victory.

Their helper turned out to be Dong Cheng, a relative of the imperial house. The Emperor wept as he related what he had been through.

Dong Cheng said, "Do not worry, Your Majesty. General Yang and I pledge to kill both rebels and so purify the state."

The Emperor bade them travel east as soon as possible and so they set out immediately toward their destination.

Guo Si led his defeated army back and on the way he met Li Jue to whom he said, "The Emperor is going to Hongnong. If he reaches Shandong and gets settled there, he will surely send out a decree to the whole country, calling up the nobles to attack us—all our families will be in danger."

"Zhang Ji is holding Chang'an and is unlikely to venture out," said Li Jue. "Why don't we take this opportunity to launch a joint attack on Hongnong? We will kill the Emperor and divide the country between us."

Guo Si thought this a good scheme, so their armies merged and they united in plundering the countryside. Wherever they went they left destruction behind them. Yang Feng and Dong Cheng heard of their plot when they were yet a long way off, so they turned back to meet them and fought the rebels at Dongjian.

Seeing that the loyalist troops were few as compared with their own, the rebels planned to overwhelm them like a flood. So when the battle started they poured out in enormous numbers, covering the hills and filling the plains. Yang Feng and Dong Cheng fought desperately but only managed to protect the Emperor and the Empress from harm. The officials, attendants, archives and records, and all the paraphernalia of the court, were left unguarded. The rebels ravaged Hongnong, but the two got the Emperor safely away to travel to the north of Shanxi.

When the rebels showed signs of pursuit the two loyalists sent people to mediate peace terms with them while also despatching a secret edict to Hedong asking for help from three former "White Wave Rebels." Li Yue, one of the three, was actually a brigand, but their need was desperate.

These three being promised pardon for their faults or crimes and a grant of official rank, naturally responded to the call. Thus the loyalists were strengthened and they planned to recapture Hongnong. Meanwhile, the rebels laid waste to whatever place they reached, slaying the aged and the weak and forcing the strong to join their ranks. When going into battle they forced these people-soldiers to the front and called them the "dare-to-die" soldiers.

The rebel force was very strong. When Li Yue, the late brigand, approached, Guo Si bade his men scatter clothes and booty along the road. The former robbers could not resist the temptation so a scramble began. The rebels fell upon the disordered ranks and defeated them completely. At this, Yang Feng and Dong Cheng escorted the Emperor toward the north.

But the rebels pursued. Li Yue said, "The danger is grave. Pray mount a horse and go in advance, Your Majesty."

The Emperor replied, "But I cannot abandon my officials."

All the officials wept and struggled on as best they could. One of the three "White Wave Generals" was killed in battle. The enemy came over very near and the Emperor had to leave his carriage and went on foot to the bank of the Yellow River, where they found a boat to carry him to the other side. The weather was very cold and the Emperor and Empress cuddled up close to each other, shivering. They reached the river but the banks were too high and they could not get down into the boat. However, some rolls of white silk were found and they rolled up the two imperial personages in the silk and thus they lowered the Emperor down into the boat. The brother of the Empress carried her on his back and got into the boat. Then Li Yue took up his position in the prow, leaning on his sword.

The boat was too small to carry everybody and those unable to get onboard clung to the cable, but Li Yue cut them down and they fell into the water. After the royal family had been ferried over the river the boat came back for the others. There was a desperate scramble to get on board and Li Yue chopped off the fingers of those who persisted in clinging to the boat.

The lamentation rose to the heavens. When they finally got to the other bank, only a core of the Emperor's retinue remained. A bullock cart was found in which the Emperor traveled to Dayang. They had no food and at night sought shelter in a poor, tile-roofed house. The owner gave them some boiled millet but it was too coarse to swallow.

The Emperor rested for some time in Yang Feng's camp and then was requested to stop at a small town called Anyi, now the temporary capital. But the town did not contain a single building of any substance and the Emperor and his followers had to live in thatched huts devoid even of doors. They surrounded these with a fence of thorns as a protection, and within the Emperor held a counsel with his ministers. Soldiers camped around the fence.

Li Yue and his fellow ruffians showed their true colors. They wielded power as they wished and officials who offended them were beaten or abused, even in the presence of the Emperor. They purposely provided unstrained wine and coarse food for the Emperor's consumption. The poor man struggled to swallow what they sent. Li You and his friend Han Xian recommended to the throne more than two hundred convicts, common soldiers, sorcerers, leeches, and such people to be give official rank. As seals could not be engraved pieces of metal were hammered into some sort of a shape.

A famine occurred that same year and people were reduced to eating grass from the roadside. Corpses of starved people could be seen everywhere. Then two prefects from the neighboring districts sent the Emperor some food and clothing and he began to enjoy a little repose.

Dong Cheng and Yang Feng wanted to send workmen to restore the palaces in Luoyang, with the intention of moving the throne there. Li Yue, however, was opposed to this but the two of them argued that Luoyang was really the capital when compared to the paltry town of Anyi, and removal would be only reasonable. In the end, Li Yue gave in.

"You may get the Emperor to Luoyang but I will remain here," he said.

But hardly had the Emperor started on his journey than Li Yue secretly sent his men to arrange with Li Jue and Guo Si to capture him again. However, this plot leaked out and the Emperor and his escort pressed on to Qi Pass as rapidly as possible. Li Yue heard this and, without waiting for his accomplices to join him, he set out to act alone.

At about the fourth watch during the night, just as the cavalcade was passing the Jishan Mountains, a voice was heard shouting, "Stop those carriages! Li Jue and Guo Si are here!"

This frightened the Emperor greatly and his terror increased when he saw the whole mountainside suddenly lit up by fire.

The rebel party of two,
Erstwhile split in twain,
Is now joined by a third
For a most wicked aim.

How the Emperor was to escape this peril will be told in the following chapter.

CHAPTER FOURTEEN

Cao Cao Moves the Throne to Xudu
Lu Bu Raids Xuzhou at Night

The last chapter closed with the arrival of Li Yue, who shouted out falsely that Li Jue and Guo Si had come to recapture the Emperor. But Yang Feng recognized his voice and ordered Xu Huang to go out and fight him. Xu Huang killed the traitor in the first bout and then dispersed his followers, so the imperial cavalcade got safely through Qi Pass. Prefect Zhang Yang came to welcome the Emperor at Zhidao and supplied him plentifully with food and other necessaries. For his timely help the Emperor conferred a very high rank upon him, who then took his leave and camped near Luoyang.

The Emperor presently entered Luoyang, where he found total destruction. The palaces and halls had been burned out and the streets were overgrown with grass and brambles. What remained of the old palaces and courts were broken roofs and toppling walls. A small palace was hastily built and the officials presented their congratulations, standing in the open air among thorn bushes and brambles. The reign title was changed from Xing Ping to Jian An.

That was a year of grievous famine. The Luoyang people, reduced in number to a few hundred households, had nothing to eat and they prowled about outside the city, stripping the bark off trees and grubbing up the roots of plants to stave off hunger. All officials, except those of the highest ranks, went out into the country to gather firewood for fuel. Many died between ruined walls of dilapidated houses. At no time during the last days of Han did misery press harder than at this period.

Yang Biao went to see the Emperor and said, "Your Majesty's decree to call in Cao Cao was issued to me some time ago but has never been acted upon. Now he is very strong in Shandong and it would be well to link him with the government so that he might support the ruling house."

The Emperor replied, "There is no need to tell me about this again. Send for him when you will."

So the decree was prepared and an envoy bore it into Shandong.

In the meantime, Cao Cao had heard that the Emperor was back in Luoyang. He called together his advisors to consult them on the matter.

Xun Yu said, "Of old, King Wen* of Jin supported Emperor Xiang of the Zhou Dynasty and all the feudal lords backed him. The founder of the Hans also won popular favor by arranging the funeral ceremony for Emperor Yi, who never really occupied the throne. Now the present Emperor has been an exile on the dusty roads. To take the lead in offering an army to restore him to honor is to have an unrivaled opportunity to win universal respect. But you must act quickly or someone else will get in there before you."

Cao Cao was very pleased with his words and at once prepared his army to move. Just at this moment the imperial envoy was announced with the very command he wanted and he set out without delay.

At Luoyang everything remained to be done. The city walls had fallen and there were no means of rebuilding them. But worse was yet to come. Soon reports arrived that Li Jue and Guo Si were on their way to invade the city.

The frightened Emperor asked Yang Feng, "What can be done? There is still no answer from Shandong and our enemies are near."

Yang Feng and Han Xian said, "We will fight to the death to protect Your Majesty."

Dong Cheng objected, "The fortifications are weak and our military resources are small. If we fight, we can hardly hope for victory. And what if we are defeated? I think we had better move into Shandong."

The Emperor agreed to this and the journey began without further preparations. There being few horses, the officials had to follow on foot. However, no sooner had they left the capital than they saw a thick cloud of dust out of which came all the clash and clamor of an advancing army. The Emperor and his consort were dumb with fear. Then a single horseman emerged, who turned out to be the envoy returning from Shandong. He rode up to the chariot, bowed and said: "General Cao has received the order and is coming with all the military forces of Shandong, but on hearing that Li Jue and Guo Si had again approached the capital he has sent Xiahou Dun in advance. With him are ten capable warriors and 50,000 proven soldiers. They will guard Your Majesty."

All fear was swept away. Soon after, Xiahou Dun and his staff arrived

---

* 697 B.C.–628 B.C., ruler of the Kingdom of Jin in the period of Spring and Autumn. He helped Emperor Xiang of the Zhou Dynasty return to the throne and later became head of the feudal lords.

and they were presented to the Emperor who cordially addressed them.

Then another large army was found to be approaching from the east. At the Emperor's command Xiahou Dun went to ascertain their identity. He soon returned to say that they were Cao Cao's infantry.

In a short while Cao Hong and his officers came to pay their respects to the Emperor.

Cao Hong said: "When my cousin heard of the approach of the rebels he feared that the first batch of officers and men he had sent might be too weak, so he sent me to march quickly and reinforce them."

"He is indeed my trusty general," said the Emperor.

So orders were given for them to escort the Emperor in advancing forward. By and by scouts came to report that the rebels were coming up very quickly. The Emperor bade Xiahou Dun divide his force into two parts to oppose them. So the army threw out two wings with cavalry in front and foot behind. They attacked with great ferocity and the rebels were utterly overwhelmed. The Emperor was then asked to return to Luoyang and the army encamped outside the city.

Soon Cao Cao came with his great army and after setting up camp he went into the city to seek an audience with the Emperor. He knelt at the foot of the steps but was allowed to stand before the Emperor and be thanked.

Cao Cao replied, "Having been the recipient of great bounty from the state I have always longed to repay it with my services. The two rebels have committed countless crimes and their days are numbered. I have an army of 200,000 soldiers who are fully equal to destroying the rebels and securing the safety of Your Majesty. I hope Your Majesty will put the interests of the state first and take good care of your health."

High honors were then conferred on Cao Cao, who then resumed his battle with the rebels.

Knowing that Cao Cao had traveled far, Li Jue and Guo Si planned to attack his army while it was fatigued from its long march, but their advisor Jia Xu was opposed to this.

"No, this will not do. Cao Cao has valiant officers and brave soldiers. The only way is to surrender so as to seek pardon for the wrongs you have committed," said Jia Xu.

Li Jue was very angry at his suggestion and accused him of disheartening the army. He drew his sword to slay him but the other officers interceded and saved Jia Xu. That night, Jia Xu stole out of the camp all by himself and went home to his native village.

Soon the rebels decided to offer battle. In reply, Cao Cao sent out three warriors with a small company of horsemen to dash into the rebel army three times before forming the battle array. Then two nephews of Li Jue rode out. At once from Cao Cao's side dashed out Xu Chu, and in a moment one of them was cut down. The other was so startled that he fell out of his saddle. He, too, was slain. The victor rode back to his own side with the two heads. When he offered them to his master, Cao Cao patted him on the back and said, "You are really my most valiant warrior!"

Next there was a general advance, Xiahou Dun and Cao Ren leading the two wings and Cao Cao commanding the center. They advanced to the roll of the drum. The rebels fell back before them and fled. Sword in hand, Cao Cao himself led his army in pursuit. Many were killed and many more surrendered. Li Jue and Guo Si flew toward the west in panic, like dogs from a falling house. Having no place of refuge they took to the hills and became robbers.

The army returned and camped again outside the city. Yang Feng and Han Xian said to one another, "This Cao Cao has done a great service and he will be the man in power. There will be no place for us." So they told the Emperor that they wished to pursue the rebels and under this excuse withdrew to camp at Daliang.

At Cao Cao's camp an envoy of the Emperor came to summon him to the palace. Cao Cao noticed that the man looked remarkably well and could not understand why, since everyone else looked hungry and famine-stricken. So he asked, "You look very well, sir—how come?"

"Only this—I have been a vegetarian for thirty years."

Cao Cao nodded. "What office do you hold?" he asked the envoy.

"Well, I used to serve under Yuan Shao but I came here when the Emperor returned. Now I am one of the secretaries. I am a native of Dinglao and my name is Dong Zhao."

Cao Cao rose from his seat and said, "I have long heard of your name. How happy I am to meet you!"

Then wine was brought into the tent and Xun Yu was called in and introduced. While they were talking a messenger came in to report that a small force was moving eastward. Cao Cao was about to order the man to find out whose men these were when the visitor said, "They are Yang Feng and Han Yi, running off to Daliang because you have come."

"Do they distrust me?" said Cao Cao.

"They are no strategists, unworthy of your attention."

"What about this departure of Li Jue and Guo Si?"

"Tigers without claws, birds without wings, will not be able to escape from your grip very long. They are not worth thinking about."

Cao Cao saw that he and his guest had much in common, so he began to consult him on state affairs.

Dong Zhao said, "You, sir, have swept away the rebellion with your noble army and have become the mainstay of the throne, an achievement comparable to the five lords in the Zhou Dynasty. But the officials will look at it in very different ways and not all favorably to you. I think you would not be wise to remain here and I advise a change of capital to Xudu in Henan. However, it must be remembered that the Emperor, after the long exile, had only recently returned to the capital and the attention of all the people is concentrated on Luoyang, hoping for a period of rest and tranquillity. Another move will displease many. But the performance of extraordinary service may mean the procurement of extraordinary achievement. It is for you to decide."

"That is exactly what I have been thinking!" cried Cao Cao, smiling and seizing his guest's hand. "But are there not dangers? What about Yang Feng at Daliang and the court officials here?"

"That is easily managed. Write to Yang Feng and set his mind at rest. Say plainly to the officials that there is no food in the capital here and so you are going to another place where there is no problem of scarcity. When the high-ranking officials hear this they will approve."

Cao Cao was so pleased with his advice that when his guest took leave he held his hand once more and said gratefully, "I am indebted to you for whatever success I may accomplish."

Dong Zhao thanked him and left. Cao Cao secretly discussed the change of capital with his advisors.

Now a certain official named Wang Li, who was a student of astrology, said to a friend: "I have been studying the night sky. Since last spring there have been signs in the movements of the stars indicating that a new ruler will emerge. The aura of the Hans will soon be exhausted and prosperity will rise in the districts of Jin and Wei."[*]

He also presented to the Emperor a secret memorial which said: "The Mandate of Heaven has its course and the five elements[†] are out of proportion. 'Earth' is attacking 'Fire' and the successor to the empire of Han is in Wei."

When Cao Cao heard of his sayings and the memorial, he sent someone to warn the astrologer. "Your loyalty is well known, but the ways of Heaven are past finding out. The less said, the better."

Then he asked Xun Yu to expound the meaning of the astrologer's words. The advisor said, "The element of fortune for the Hans is 'fire;'

---

[*]   In Central China.

[†]   Referring to wood, earth, gold, fire, and water, through which ancient Chinese philosophers tried to explain the origin and inter-connectedness of things in the world.

yours is 'earth'. Xudu is under the influence of 'earth' and so your fortune depends on getting there. 'Fire' can produce 'earth', as 'earth' can multiply 'wood'. These agree with what Dong Zhao and the astrologer have forecast and you have only to bide your time."

Xun Yu's explanation helped Cao Cao make up his mind. The next day at court he said, "The capital is deserted and cannot be restored, nor can it be supplied easily with food. Xudu is a prosperous city, standing close to a fruitful district. It is everything that a capital should be. I venture to request that the court move there."

The Emperor dared not oppose and the officials were too in awe of Cao Cao to have any independent opinion, so a day was chosen for the journey. Cao Cao commanded the escort and the officials all followed. When they had traveled some distance they saw before them a high mound and from behind this arose the beating of drums. Then Yang Feng and Han Xian came out and barred the way. In the forefront stood Xu Huang, who shouted, "Cao Cao, where are you taking the Emperor?"

Cao Cao rode forth to take a good look at the speaker and was quite struck by Xu Huang's powerful physique. He ordered Xu Chu to go and fight him. The combat was ax against broadsword and the two men fought more than half a hundred bouts without advantage to either side. Then the gongs sounded and Cao Cao drew off his men.

In his camp a council was called. Cao Cao said, "Yang Feng and Han Xian are nothing but Xu Huang is a fine officer and I was unwilling to use force against him. I want to win him over to our side."

At this moment, an officer called Man Chong said, "Do not let that trouble you, sir. He is an old acquaintance of mine. I will disguise myself as a soldier this evening and steal over to the enemy's camp to talk to him. I promise I will persuade him to submit to you willingly."

That night Man Chong, in disguise, got over to the other side and made his way to the tent of Xu Huang, who sat there by the light of a candle. He was still wearing his coat of mail. Suddenly, Man Chong appeared in front of him and saluted to him. "You have been well since we parted, old friend?" he asked.

Xu Huang stood up in surprise, gazed into the face of the speaker a long time, and then said: "Are you Man Chong of Shanyang? How come you are here?"

"I am an officer in General Cao's army. I saw you in front of the army today and I wanted to have a word with you. So I risked my life to come here."

Xu Huang invited him to sit down. Then Man Chong said, "There are few warriors as bold as you on the earth. Why then do you commit yourself to such people as Yang Feng and Han Xian? My master is the most prominent man in the world, a man who respects the wise and appreciates the valiant, as everyone knows. Your valor today won his entire admiration and so he took care that the attack was not too fierce for you. Now he has sent me to invite you to join him. Why don't you leave darkness for light and help him in his magnificent cause?"

Xu Huang sat for a long time, pondering over the offer. Then he said with a sigh, "I know my masters are doomed to failure, but I have all along followed their fortunes and do not like to leave them."

"But you know the fine bird selects its tree and the wise servant chooses his master. He who meets a worthy master and lets him go is a fool."

"I am willing to do what you say," said Xu Huang, rising to thank him.

"Why not put these two to death as a gift for an audience with General Cao?" suggested Man Chong.

"It is very wrong for a subordinate to slay his master. I will never do that."

"You are really a true man."

Then Xu Huang, taking only a score or so horsemen with him, left that very night to desert to Cao Cao. Soon the news was reported to Yang Feng, who, at the head of a strong company of horsemen, set out to capture the deserter. He called out to him to come back.

But when Yang Feng was getting near he was ambushed. Suddenly the whole mountainside was lit up with torches and out sprang Cao Cao's men, he himself being in command. "I have been waiting here a long time. Do not try to run away," he cried.

Yang Feng was terrified and attempted to draw off but was quickly surrounded. Han Xian came to his rescue and a confused battle began. Yang Feng succeeded in breaking through but Cao Cao kept up the attack on the disordered army. A great number of their men gave in and the two leaders found they had too few men left to continue the battle, so they escaped to seek shelter at Yuan Shu's place.

When Cao Cao returned to camp the newly surrendered man was presented and well received. Again, the cavalcade set out for the new capital. In due time they reached it. Soon after that great construction work began. They built palaces and halls as well as an ancestral temple, an altar, and public offices. The city walls were repaired, storehouses were built, and all put in order.

Then came the rewards. Here Cao Cao exercised full power. Every reward or punishment, if any, was based upon his sole decision. Thirteen were raised to the rank of nobility. He himself was made the Grand Commander and Lord of Wuping. His important advisors filled high offices and his warriors became generals and high-ranking officers. All good service received full recognition.

Cao Cao became the leader of the court. All memorials went first to him and were then submitted to the Emperor.

When state matters were in order a great banquet was given in his private quarters to all his advisors and officers, and affairs outside the capital were the subject of discussion. Cao Cao said, "Liu Bei has his army at Xuzhou and he carries on the administration of the prefecture. Lu Bu fled to him when defeated and Liu Bei gave him Xiaopei to live in. If these two agreed to join forces and attack us, my position would be most serious. What good plan do you have to destroy them?"

Xu Chu rose and said: "Give me 50,000 men and I will present their heads to you."

Xun Yu said, "You are brave, but you are no strategist. The new capital has just been established and we cannot start another war. However, there is a certain tactic known as "the Rival Tigers." Liu Bei has no decree authorizing him to govern Xuzhou. You, sir, can procure one for him and so confer upon him the right to administer the district. When you send the decree you can enclose a secret note telling him to get rid of Lu Bu. If he does, he will have lost a vigorous warrior from his side and he could be dealt with as the occasion arises. If he fails then Lu Bu will slay him. Either way, they will wrangle and destroy each other. This is the Rival Tigers tactic."

Cao Cao agreed that this was a good plan, so he petitioned for a formal appointment, creating Liu Bei a general and a lord, fully authorized to govern Xuzhou. He then sent the decree to Liu Bei together with a secret note.

By that time Liu Bei had heard of the change of capital and he was about to offer his congratulations when an imperial messenger was announced. He at once went outside the city gate to welcome him. The decree was reverently received and a banquet was prepared for the messenger.

The messenger said, "This decree was obtained for you entirely through the effort of General Cao."

Liu Bei expressed his gratitude to Cao Cao. Then the messenger offered his secret letter. After he had read this Liu Bei said, "This matter has to be further considered."

The banquet over and the messenger conducted to his lodging, Liu Bei at once called in his men to discuss the letter.

"Lu Bu is a bad man," said Zhang Fei. "What does it matter if we kill him?"

"But he came to me for protection in difficulty. How can I put him to death? That would be bad, too."

"It's not easy to be a good man," replied Zhang Fei.

Liu Bei would not consent. The following day when Lu Bu came to offer congratulations, he was received as usual.

"I have come specially to felicitate you on your receipt of the imperial bounty," said Lu Bu.

Liu Bei thanked him in due politeness. Just then he saw Zhang Fei rush into the hall, drawing his sword to slay Lu Bu. He hastily interfered and stopped him.

Lu Bu was surprised and asked, "Why do you want to kill me?"

"Cao Cao says you are treacherous and tells my brother to kill you," shouted Zhang Fei.

Liu Bei shouted again and again to him to go away. After he left, Liu Bei led Lu Bu into the inner hall, where he told him the whole story and even showed him the secret letter. Lu Bu wept as he finished reading.

"This is Cao Cao's scheme to sow discord between us," he said.

"Don't be anxious," said Liu Bei. "I pledge never to commit such an infamous crime."

Lu Bu repeatedly expressed his gratitude and Liu Bei treated him with wine. They remained talking and drinking till late.

After Lu Bu left, his two brothers asked, "Why didn't you kill him?"

Liu Bei said, "This is Cao Cao's plot. He fears that Lu Bu and I may attack him so he's trying to separate us and make us 'swallow' each other, while he steps in and takes the advantage. Do you think I should fall into his trap?"

Guan Yu nodded assent, but Zhang Fei added, "I still want to get him out of the way lest he should trouble us later."

"This is not what a noble man should do," said his eldest brother.

Soon, the messenger returned to the capital with a letter of reply from Liu Bei. The letter only said that it would take some time to carry out the plan. But the messenger told Cao Cao how Liu Bei would not kill Lu Bu.

"The plan has failed—what next?" asked Cao Cao.

Xun Yu replied, "I have another tactic, called 'the Tiger and the Wolf,' in which the tiger is made to gobble up the wolf."

"Let us hear it," demanded his master.

"Send someone to Yuan Shu to spread the rumor that Liu Bei expresses his wish to subdue the southern districts in a secret petition to the Emperor. Yuan Shu will be very angry and attack him. Then you will order Liu Bei to dispose of Yuan Shu and so set them destroying each other. Lu Bu will certainly think that is his chance and turn traitor. This is the Tiger and the Wolf tactic."

Cao Cao found this a good scheme and did as he was advised. When Liu Bei received the false edict from Cao Cao that ordered him to capture Yuan Shu, he related it to Mi Zhu, who pronounced it a trick.

"It may be," said Liu Bei, "but the royal command is not to be disobeyed."

So the army was prepared and the day of the departure fixed. Sun Qian reminded him that a trusty person should be left behind to guard the city and Liu Bei asked which of his brothers would undertake this task.

"I'll guard the city," volunteered Guan Yu.

"I'm constantly in need of your advice. How can you stay behind?"

"Let me guard the city," said Zhang Fei.

"You'll fail," said Liu Bei. "After one of your drinking bouts you'll lose your temper and flog the soldiers. Besides, you're rash and will not listen to anyone's advice. I'll be worried all the time."

"From now on I won't drink any wine. I won't beat the soldiers and I'll always listen to advice," promised Zhang Fei.

"I fear the mouth doesn't correspond to the heart," said Mi Zhu.

Zhang Fei became angry. "I've followed my brother these many years and never broken faith. Why should you be so contemptuous of me?" he bellowed.

Liu Bei said, "Though you say so, I don't feel quite assured." Then he ordered Chen Deng to help his youngest brother to guard the city and keep him sober so that he would not do anything foolish.

Chen Deng agreed to undertake this duty and the final orders for departure were given. The army, composed of 300,000 horse and infantry, left Xuzhou and marched toward Nanyang.

When Yuan Shu heard that a memorial had been presented by Liu Bei proposing to take possession of his district he broke out into a violent abuse of his enemy. "That weaver of mats! Maker of straw sandals! He has been audacious enough to get hold of a large district and elbow his way into the ranks of the lords. I was just going to attack him and now he dares to scheme against me! How I detest him!"

He at once gave orders to prepare an army of 100,000 men under Ji Ling to attack Xuzhou. The two armies met at Xuyi, where Liu Bei had encamped on a plain with hills behind and a stream on his flank as protection, for his army was small.

Ji Ling, his opponent, was a native of Shandong. He used a very heavy three-edged sword. After he had made camp he rode out and began abusing his enemy. "Liu Bei, you rustic bumpkin, how dare you invade this land?"

"I have a decree from the court ordering me to destroy your master, who behaves improperly. If you oppose me you will be assuredly punished," replied Liu Bei.

Ji Ling angrily rode out, brandishing his weapon. But Guan Yu cried, "You wretch, do not attempt to show off your prowess!" and rode forth to meet him. The two fought and after thirty exchanges neither could prevail over the other. Then Ji Ling called for a rest. So Guan Yu rode back to his own army and waited for him.

When the moment to renew the combat came, Ji Ling sent out one of his officers to take his place. But Guan Yu said, "Tell Ji Ling to come: I must fight it out with him."

"You are a nameless person and unworthy to fight with our general," replied the officer.

This reply angered Guan Yu, who made just one attack on his opponent and laid him dead on the ground. At this success Liu Bei urged on the army and Ji Ling's men were defeated. They retired to the mouth of the Huaiyin River and declined all open challenges. However, he would send his men to make sudden and stealthy attacks on Liu Bei's camp to try to do what mischief they could, yet all these attempts were to no avail.

But the armies will be left facing each other while we relate what happened in Xuzhou.

After Liu Bei had gone on his expedition Zhang Fei placed his advisor Chen Deng in charge of the routine business of the city, keeping military affairs under his own supervision. After thinking over his promise to his brother for some time he gave a banquet to all his colleagues. When every guest had taken his seat he made a speech.

"Before my brother left he told me to keep clear of the wine cup for fear of accidents. Now, gentlemen, you may drink deep today but from tomorrow wine is forbidden, for we must keep the city safe. So drink your fill." And with this he himself rose to fill the wine cups for his guests.

When he came to an officer called Cao Bao, the latter declined it, saying that he never drank as he was forbidden by heaven.

"What! a fighting man not drinking wine!" cried the host. "I want you to take just one cup."

Cao Bao was afraid to offend so he drank.

After the wine had gone round once the host began to drink huge goblets, and so swallowed an enormous quantity of liquor. He became quite intoxicated. Yet he would drink more and insisted on a cup with every guest. Again it was Cao Bao's turn, who again declined.

"Really, I cannot drink any more," said Cao Bao.

"You drank just now—why refuse this time?"

Zhang Fei pressed him, but still Cao Bao resisted. Then Zhang Fei in his drunken madness lost control of his temper and said, "If you disobey the order of your general you will be flogged a hundred times." And he called in his guards.

Here Chen Deng interfered, reminding him of the strict injunction of his brother.

"You civilians attend to your civil business and leave us alone," said Zhang Fei.

The only way out for Cao Bao was to beg for remission and he said, "Please pardon me for my son-in-law's sake."

"Who is your son-in-law?"

"Lu Bu."

"I did not mean to have you beaten, but if you think of frightening me with the threat of Lu Bu, I will. I will beat you as if I were beating him."

The other guests interposed to beg him off, but their drunk host was obdurate and the unhappy officer received fifty blows. Then at the earnest pleadings of the others the remainder of the punishment was canceled.

The banquet came to an end and the beaten man left, burning with resentment. That night he sent a letter to Xiaopei relating the insult he had received from Zhang Fei. In the letter he also told Lu Bu of Liu Bei's absence and proposed that a sudden raid be made that very night before Zhang Fei recovered from his drunken fit. Lu Bu at once summoned Chen Gong for counsel.

"Xiaopei is only a place to occupy temporarily," said Chen Gong. "If you have a chance to seize Xuzhou, do so. Otherwise you will live to regret it."

Lu Bu got ready at once and was soon on the way with five hundred cavalry, while Chen Gong was to follow with the main body. Gao Shun, too, was to follow him.

Xiaopei being only about forty *li* away (one gets there almost as soon as one is mounted), so Lu Bu was under the wall at the fourth watch. It was a clear moonlit night. No one on the gate tower was aware of the impending danger. Lu Bu came up close to the wall and called out, "Prefect Liu's secret messenger is here!"

Some of the guards on the wall were Cao Boa's men and they called to him. He came and when he saw who it was he ordered the gates to be opened. Lu Bu gave the secret signal and the soldiers entered with loud shouting.

Zhang Fei was in his room sleeping off the effects of wine. His servants hastened to arouse him and told him that Lu Bu had got the gates open and was in the city. Zhang Fei hastily got into his armor and laid hold of his mighty spear but he had hardly mounted his horse at the gate when his foe came up. He rushed at him but being still half intoxicated made but a poor fight. Lu Bu, knowing his prowess, did not press him hard and Zhang Fei made his way with eighteen of his native men to the east gate and there galloped out, leaving his brother's family to their fate.

Cao Bao, seeing Zhang Fei had but a very small force and was still half drunk as well, pursued. Zhang Fei saw who it was and became mad with rage. He galloped toward him and, after a few passes, Cao Bao had to flee, but Zhang Fei chased him to the edge of the moat and pierced him in the heart from behind. His frightened steed carried him into the moat and both were drowned.

Once outside the city, Zhang Fei collected his men and they rode off toward the south.

Lu Bu having seized the city by surprise set himself to restore order. He put a guard over the residence of Liu Bei, so that no one should disturb his family.

Zhang Fei with his few followers went to Liu Bei's camp and told him about Cao Bao's betrayal and Lu Bu's sudden raid on the city. All were greatly distressed.

"Possession is not worth rejoicing over, nor is loss worth grieving about," said Liu Bei with a sigh.

"Where are our sisters-in-law?" asked Guan Yu.

"They're trapped in the city."

Liu Bei fell silent.

Guan Yu stamped his foot and reproached: "Remember what you said when you promised to guard the city and what orders our brother gave you? Now the city is lost and our sisters-in-law trapped. What's to be done now?"

Zhang Fei was overwhelmed by remorse. He drew his sword to kill himself.

> He raised the cup in pledge,
> None might say nay;
> Remorseful, he drew the sword,
> Himself to slay.

Zhang Fei's fate will be told in the next chapter.

CHAPTER FIFTEEN

Taishi Ci Fights a Fierce Battle with Sun Ce
Sun Ce Competes with the White Tiger

A t the close of the last chapter Zhang Fei was about to end his life by his own hand. But his brother Liu Bei rushed forward and caught him with his arms, snatched away the sword, and threw it on the ground.

"Brothers are like hands and feet; wives are like clothing," said Liu Bei. "One may mend his torn dress, but who can reattach a lost limb? We three, by the Oath of the Peach Garden, swore to seek the same day of death. The city's lost, it's true, and my family trapped, but I couldn't bear that you should die in the prime of your life. Besides, the city is not really mine. I'm sure Lu Bu won't harm my family so we can still seek to rescue them. You've made a mistake, worthy brother, but is it one deserving of death?"

And he wept. His brothers were much affected and their tears fell in gratitude.

As soon as the news of Lu Bu's successful seizure of Xuzhou reached Yuan Shu, he sent promises of valuable presents to Lu Bu to induce him to join in a further attack on Liu Bei. The presents were said to be 50,000 measures of grain, 500 horses, 10,000 taels of gold and silver, and 1,000 rolls of fine silk. Lu Bu was tempted by the bait and ordered Gao Shun to lead 500,000 men to attack Liu Bei from the rear. But Liu Bei got wind of the threatened attack, so under cover of the rain he turned eastward to take Guangling before the attacking force came up.

However, Gao Shun demanded the promised reward from Ji Ling, who put him off by saying that he had to wait for Yuan Shu's decision and asked him to return first.

With this answer Gao Shun went back to Lu Bu, who could not decide what to do. Then Yuan Shu sent him a letter that said that although Gao Shun had gone to attack Liu Bei, yet Liu Bei had not been destroyed and no reward could be given till he was actually captured. Lu Bu railed at what he called a breach of faith, and was inclined to attack Yuan Shu himself. However, his advisor opposed this course.

"No, you should not," he said. "Yuan Shu is in possession of Shouchun with a large army and a good supply. You must not treat him lightly. Rather ask Liu Bei to take up his quarters at Xiaopei as one of your wings and, when the time comes, let him lead the attack. Then both the Yuans will fall before you and you will be very powerful."

Finding this advice good, he sent a letter to Liu Bei asking him to return. Meanwhile, Liu Bei's attack on Guangling was unsuccessful and most of his men were lost during a raid on his camp by Yuan Shu. On his way back he met the messenger sent by Lu Bu, who presented the letter. Liu Bei was quite content with the offer but his brothers were not inclined to trust Lu Bu.

"Since he treats me kindly, I shouldn't suspect him," said Liu Bei.

So he went back to Xuzhou. Lu Bu, fearing that Liu Bei might doubt his sincerity, restored his family to him first; when the ladies, Gan and Mi, saw their lord, they told him that they had been kindly treated and guarded by soldiers against any harm, and provisions had never been wanting.

"I knew he wouldn't harm my family," said Liu Bei to his brothers.

However, Zhang Fei still hated Lu Bu and would not accompany his brother into the city when he went to express his thanks. Instead, he went to escort the two ladies to Xiaopei.

At the interview Lu Bu said, "I didn't wish to take the city but your brother behaved very badly, drinking and flogging the soldiers, and I came to guard it lest some evil should befall."

"But I had long wished to yield it to you," said Liu Bei.

Then Lu Bu pretended to wish to give the city back to Liu Bei who, however, would not hear of it and returned to Xiaopei. His two brothers would not take the situation kindly and were very discontented.

Liu Bei said, "One must accept one's lot and wait for a chance. It's the will of Heaven and I can't struggle against fate."

Lu Bu sent presents of grain, silk, and other things to Liu Bei and so peace reigned in the area again.

Let us now return to Yuan Shu. As the story runs, he was giving a great banquet for his officers and men when reports came of a victory gained by Sun Ce (son of the late Sun Jian) over the prefect of Lujiang. Yuan Shu summoned the victor, who came and bowed to him at the foot of the audience hall. Yuan Shu, sitting on high, asked for details of the battle and then told him to take a seat at the banquet.

It must be told here that after the unhappy death of his father Sun Ce had returned to the south, where he had devoted himself to peaceful ends, inviting to his side able men and learned scholars. Afterwards when a quarrel broke out between his mother's brother, prefect of Danyang, and Tao Qian, the late prefect of Xuzhou, he moved his family to Qua, while he himself went to serve under Yuan Shu, who admired him greatly.

"If I had a son like him," said Yuan Shu, "I should die without regret." He employed Sun Ce as an officer and sent him on various expeditions, all of which were successful.

After the banquet, Sun Ce returned to his camp very bitter over the arrogant and patronizing airs of his master. Instead of retiring to his tent he went for a stroll under the moonlight.

"Here I am, a mere nobody and yet my father was such a hero!" he cried out—and wept in spite of himself.

Then someone suddenly appeared and said, laughing loudly, "What's this, Bo-fu?* While your noble father was alive, he made free use of me. If you have any difficulty to solve, why don't you refer it to me instead of weeping here alone?"

Looking at the speaker Sun Ce saw it was Zhu Zhi, who had been in his father's service. Sun Ce then dried his eyes and the two sat down to talk.

"I wept from regret at being unable to continue my father's work," he said.

"Why stay here bound to the service of a master? Why not borrow an army from Yuan Shu with the excuse of an expedition to rescue your uncle in the east? Then you can accomplish great designs."

While these two were talking another man suddenly came up and said, "I know what you two are planning, noble sirs. I have a hundred bold fellows who can help you in what you wish to achieve."

The speaker was one of Yuan Shu's advisors named Lu Fan. Sun Ce asked him to sit down and join their discussion.

"The only fear is that Yuan Shu may refuse to lend you the soldiers you need," said the newcomer.

"I still have the Imperial Seal that my father left me—that should be a good pledge."

"Yuan Shu earnestly desires possession of that," said Zhu Zhi. "He'll certainly lend you men for that purpose."

The three talked over their plans, gradually settling the details, and the next day Sun Ce obtained an interview with his patron. Assuming the appearance of deep grief he said, "I have been unable to avenge my father. Now the Prefect of Yangzhou is opposing my uncle and my mother and

---

* Sun Ce's familiar name.

family are in danger. I would like to borrow a few thousand fighting men from you, sir, to rescue them. In case you might lack confidence in me I am willing to deposit the Imperial Seal, left to me by my late father, as a guarantee."

"Let me see it if you have it," said Yuan Shu, overjoyed. When the seal was given to him, he said: "I do not really want the seal but you may as well leave it with me for the time being. I will lend you 3,000 men and 500 horses. Return as soon as peace can be made. As your rank is hardly sufficient for such powers, I will petition to obtain for you higher rank with the title of general, and you can soon start."

Sun Ce thanked his patron most humbly and soon put the army in motion, taking with him his two new friends as well as his father's former officers. On the way he saw a body of troops in front of him, and at their head was a dashing leader of handsome and refined appearance. As soon as this man saw Sun Ce he dismounted and bowed to him. It was Zhou Yu, native of Shucheng.

In the past when Sun Jian was fighting the tyrant Dong Zhuo, the family had moved to Shucheng, in modern Anhui, and as Zhou Yu and Sun Ce were of the same age, they became exceedingly good friends and later sworn brothers. Sun Ce, being older by two months, became the elder brother. Zhou Yu was on his way to visit his uncle when the happy meeting took place.

Naturally Sun Ce confided his projects and inmost ideas to his friend, who at once promised fidelity and service. They decided to work out the grand design together.

"Now that you've come to my side the design is as good as accomplished," said Sun Ce in great joy. Then he introduced Zhou Yu to his two new friends.

Zhou Yu said, "Do you know of the two Zhangs of this region? They'll be most useful men in working out your schemes."

"Who are they?" asked Sun Ce.

"Their names are Zhang Zhao and Zhang Hong. Both are men of transcendent genius who choose to live in seclusion here for the sake of tranquillity in these troubled times. Why don't you invite them to help you, brother?"

Sun Ce lost no time in sending letters and gifts, but they both declined. Then he visited them in person and was greatly impressed by their speech. At last, by dint of large gifts and much persuasion, he got them to promise to join him. They were given substantial offices.

The plan of attack upon Qua was the next matter for discussion. The prefect, Liu Yao, was a scion of the imperial family. He had long ruled in

Yangzhou but Yuan Shu had driven him across the river to Qua. Hearing of the planned attack on him he summoned his officers for counsel. One of his officers, called Zhang Ying, volunteered to defeat the enemy.

"I will take an army and entrench at Niuzhu. No army can get past that, whatever its strength," he boasted.

He was interrupted by another who shouted, "And I will lead the van!"

All eyes turned to this man: it was Taishi Ci who, after raising the siege of Beihai, had come to visit Liu Yao and stayed on.

Hearing him offer to undertake the hazardous post of van leader Liu Yao said: "But you are still young and not yet equal to such a charge. Better stay by my side and wait for my orders."

Taishi Ci withdrew sulkily. Soon Zhang Ying led his army to Niuzhu and stored a huge quantity of grain for future consumption. When Sun Ce approached, Zhang Ying went to meet him and the two armies faced each other on the sand banks of Niuzhu. Zhang Ying roundly abused his opponent and Huang Gai rode out to attack, but before the combat had proceeded far, there arose an alarm of fire in Zhang Ying's camp. He hastily turned back and then Sun Ce advanced in full force, compelling the enemy to abandon their position and flee to the hills.

Now the fire was started by two men named Jiang Qin and Zhou Tai, both from the Jiujiang district, who in these troubled times had got together a band of men and lived by plundering the country along the Yangtze River. They knew Sun Ce by reputation as a man who treated able men very liberally and wished to join him. So they came with their band, three hundred strong, and helped him in this way to recommend themselves to him.

Sun Ce welcomed them and gave them ranks. After taking possession of the large stores of grain and arms abandoned by the runaways, and enlisting a large number of those who surrendered into his own ranks, he moved to attack Shenting.

After his defeat Zhang Ying returned to his master and related his misfortune. Liu Yao was so angry that he would have put him to death if not for the pleadings of his two advisors, who suggested sending him to command the garrison in Lingling. Liu Yao himself set out to meet the invaders at Shenting. He camped south of the hills. Sun Ce camped on the opposite side of the hills.

Sun Ce inquired of the local men if there was a temple to honor Emperor Guang-wu of the East Han Dynasty in the vicinity, and was told that there was one on the summit of the hills.

"I dreamed last night that he summoned me so I will go and pray there," said Sun Ce.

He was advised not to go as the enemy was on the other side and he might fall into an ambush.

"The Emperor's spirit will help me. What do I have to fear?"

So he put on his armor, took his spear and mounted, taking with him twelve of his officers as an escort. They rode up the hills to the temple where they burned incense and bowed reverently. Then Sun Ce knelt down and made a vow: "If I, Sun Ce, succeed in my design to restore the grand cause of my late father, then I will rebuild this temple and order sacrifices for the four seasons."

When they had remounted he said, "I'm going to ride over the ridge and make a survey of the enemy's position."

Again his followers begged him not to, but he was obstinate and they rode away together, noting the villages below. Scouts quickly reported the presence of horsemen on the ridge to Liu Yao but he only said, "It is certainly Sun Ce's trick to induce us to fight. Do not go out."

Taishi Ci, the bold warrior, jumped up and cried out, "What better chance to capture him than this!"

So, without orders he armed himself and rode out of the camp. "If there be any valiant men among you, follow me!" he called out to his fellow men.

No one moved save a minor officer who said, "He is really a valiant warrior. I will go with him." So he also went. The others only laughed at the pair.

Now having seen all he wished to see, Sun Ce thought it time to return and wheeled round his horse. But when he was coming down the summit someone shouted from above, "Stay, Sun Ce!"

He turned and saw two horsemen coming at full speed down the next hill. He halted and drew up his escort right and left, he himself with his spear ready.

"Which of you is Sun Ce?" shouted Taishi Ci.

"Who are you?" was the reply.

"I am Taishi Ci of Donglai, coming to take him prisoner."

"Then I am he," said Sun Ce, laughing. "Come, both of you together. I am not afraid of you. If I were, I should not be Sun Bo-fu!"

"You and all your crowd come on and I will not flinch," cried Taishi Ci, putting his horse at a gallop and setting his spear.

Sun Ce braced himself and the combat began. Fifty bouts were fought and still neither combatant had the advantage. Sun Ce's followers whispered their admiration and amazement. Seeing that the spearmanship of his opponent showed no weak point, Taishi Ci decided to resort to guile. Feigning defeat, he induced Sun Ce to pursue him. However, he did not retreat by the road he had come but took a path leading to the back of the hill. Sun Ce followed, shouting: "He who retreats is no hero!"

Taishi Ci thought to himself: "He has twelve helpers but I have only one. If I capture him here, the others will get him back. I must lead him further so that they will not find him and then try." So fleeing and fighting by turns he led Sun Ce, an eager pursuer, down to the plain.

Here, Taishi Ci suddenly wheeled about and attacked. Again they exchanged half a hundred bouts without result. Sun Ce made a fierce thrust, which his opponent evaded by gripping the spear tightly. Then Taishi Ci did the same but his spear was also firmly gripped by his opponent. Neither was wounded but each exerted himself to pull the other out of the saddle and they both ended up falling to the ground.

Their steeds galloped off out of sight, while the two men, each dropping his spear, began a hand-to-hand struggle. Soon their fighting robes were in tatters. Sun Ce snatched the short lance that his opponent carried at his back while Taishi Ci tore off the other's helmet. Sun Ce tried to stab him with the short lance but Taishi Ci fended off the blow with the helmet as a shield.

Then a great shouting arose. Liu Yao had sent more than a thousand soldiers to support Taishi Ci. Sun Ce was now in great danger and he became much alarmed. At this moment, however, his twelve followers also arrived on the scene. It was only then that each of the two combatants let go of the other. Taishi Ci quickly found another steed, took his spear, and mounted. Sun Ce, whose charger had been caught by Cheng Pu, also mounted and a confused battle began between the dozen men on the one side and a whole thousand on the other. They fought on and on till they drifted to the foot of the hills when Zhou Yu came to the rescue. Liu Yao, too, had come up with the main body of his army. But by that time dusk was falling and a heavy storm swept up, which put an end to the fight. Both sides drew off and returned to camp.

The next day Sun Ce led his army to the front of Liu Yao's camp and his challenge was accepted. The two armies were drawn up. Sun Ce held up the short lance he had seized from Taishi Ci and waved it before the line of battle while his soldiers were ordered to shout: "If Taishi Ci had not fled he would have been stabbed to death."

On the other side, Taishi Ci held up Sun Ce's helmet and the soldiers shouted back: "Sun Ce's head is here already."

Both sides thus yelled defiance at each other, one side boasting and the other side bragging. Then Taishi Ci rode out to challenge Sun Ce to a duel. His rival would have accepted, but Cheng Pu said, "You need not trouble yourself, sir. I will fight him." And he rode forth.

"You are no antagonist to me," said Taishi Ci. "Tell your master to come."

This infuriated Cheng Pu, who rode at his opponent, and they fought many bouts. Suddenly the duel was stopped by the sound of the gong on Liu Yao's side.

"Why did you draw off?" asked Taishi Ci. "I was just going to capture the wretch."

"I have just heard that Qua has been taken by Zhou Yu. A certain man called Chen Wu was in league with him and secretly led him into the city. Now that my base is lost I cannot remain here for long. I must hasten to Moling to get help from there."

Liu Yao's army retreated but was not pursued. Taishi Ci, too, went with his master. At Sun Ce's camp, the advisor Zhang Zhao said, "Zhou Yu's seizure of Qua is the cause of this move. They are in no mood to fight. A night raid on their camp will finish them."

Divided into five divisions for the surprise attack, that night the army hastened toward the enemy camp. The attack was a great success and their opponents scattered in all directions. Taishi Ci alone could not withstand a whole army so he escaped with a few followers to Jingxian.

Now Sun Ce acquired a new adherent in the person of Chen Wu, who was rather an odd-looking man of medium height with sallow complexion and red eyes. But Sun Ce held him in high esteem, gave him an officer's rank, and put him in the van for the attack on Xue Li at Moling. As van leader he and half a score horsemen made a dash into the enemy's formation, killing many as they went. So Xue Li would not fight but remained within the walls of his city. As Sun Ce was attacking the city a messenger came with the news that Liu Yao and his ally, Ze Rong, had gone to take Niuzhu. Sun Ce was very angry and at once moved back to fight Liu Yao. His two opponents were ready for battle.

"I am here," Sun Ce shouted. "You had better surrender."

An officer came out from behind Liu Yao to accept the challenge but in the third bout he was captured. Sun Ce carried him under his arm and turned to ride back to his own army. Seeing his colleague thus captured, another of Liu Yao's men rode out to his rescue and got quite close. But just as he was going to thrust, Sun Ce's soldiers shouted to warn him of an enemy behind his back. At this Sun Ce turned and cried out in such a thunderous voice that his opponent fell out of his saddle from mere fright. He cracked his skull and died. When Sun Ce returned to his own lines, he threw his prisoner to the ground. And he was also dead, crushed to death between the arm and the body of his captor. So in a few moments Sun Ce had disposed of two enemies, one crushed to death and the other frightened to death. From then on he was known as the Formidable Little Lord.

After Liu Yao's defeat the greater portion of his force surrendered and the number of those put to death exceeded 10,000. Liu Yao and Ze Rong sought refugee with Liu Biao.

Another attack on Moling was the next move. As soon as Sun Ce arrived there, he called out across the moat to Xue Li and ordered him to surrender. But from the gate tower someone shot a furtive arrow which wounded Sun Ce in the left thigh and he fell from his steed. Hastily his officers picked up their wounded chief and returned to the camp, where the arrow was pulled out and the wound dressed.

By Sun Ce's command the story was spread abroad that the injury had been fatal and all the soldiers gave out cries of lamentation. The camp was broken up. The defenders of the city led by their chief Xue Li and two other officers launched a night chase, but fell into a carefully prepared ambush and presently Sun Ce himself appeared on horseback, shouting, "Sun Ce is here!"

His sudden appearance created such a panic that the soldiers dropped their weapons and knelt on the ground. Sun Ce gave orders not to kill them but their leaders fell, one from a spear thrust as he turned to run away, another from an arrow; the chief commander Xue Li was slain in the confusion of the battle. Thus Sun Ce gained possession of Moling. Having calmed the people he set out again to Jinxian where Taishi Ci was in command.

By then Taishi Ci had assembled 2,000 strong young men in addition to his own troops for the purpose of avenging his former master, Liu Yao. Sun Ce, on the other hand, consulted Zhou Yu on how to capture Taishi Ci alive. Zhou Yu's plan was to attack the city on three sides, leaving the east gate free for flight. At some distance from the city an ambush was to be prepared on three separate roads, where their target, his men fatigued and horses spent, would fall an easy prey.

The new recruits under Taishi Ci were mostly local hillmen unaccustomed to discipline. Besides, the walls of the city were pitiably low. That night Sun Ce ordered Chen Wu, striped of his long robe and armed with a dagger, to climb up the wall and set fire to the city. Seeing the flames spreading, Taishi Ci made for the east gate. As soon as he got outside, Sun Ce followed in pursuit. The chase was maintained for quite some time, when the pursuers stopped. Taishi Ci rode for as long as he could, finally halting to rest in a spot surrounded by reeds. Suddenly, a tremendous shouting was heard. Taishi Ci was about to move when tripping ropes arose on both sides, throwing him and his horse down on the ground. He was taken prisoner and carried off to Sun Ce's camp. As soon as Sun Ce heard the news he rode out to meet him. Ordering the soldiers to disperse, he loosened the cords that bound Taishi Ci with his own hands. He took off his own embroidered robe and put it over the captive's shoulders. Then he invited him into his camp.

"I know you are a real hero," said Sun Ce. "Liu Yao was a fool not to employ you as his chief officer, so he was beaten."

Taishi Ci, overcome by this generosity, agreed to surrender.

Sun Ce seized his hand and said, laughing: "If you had taken me at that fight we had near the temple, would you have killed me?"

"Who knows?" said Taishi Ci, smiling.

Sun Ce laughed again and they entered his tent, where his former rival was placed in the seat of honor at a banquet.

Taishi Ci said, "I am thinking of going back to muster as many of the soldiers of my late master as I can. They will turn against him after his recent defeat and they will be a great help for you. But can you trust me so far as to let me go?"

"This is exactly what I most desire. I will make an agreement with you that I expect you back by noon tomorrow."

Taishi Ci agreed and went off. All the other officers said he would never return.

"He is trustworthy and will not break his word," said Sun Ce.

None of the officers believed he would come back. The next day they planted a bamboo stick outside their camp and just as its shadow marked noon Taishi Ci returned, bringing with him about a thousand men. Sun Ce was very pleased and all his officers had to admit that he had rightly judged this man.

Sun Ce now had an army of several hundred thousand soldiers and the east was his. He improved the conditions of the people and maintained order so that adherents and supporters increased daily. He was known to the local people as Sun Long, or Sun, the Junior. On hearing of his army's approach people would flee in terror, but when they saw that his men were ordered not to loot or make any attempt on their houses, they rejoiced and presented the soldiers with oxen and wine, for which they were duly rewarded. Happiness filled the countryside. The former soldiers of Liu Yao were kindly treated. Those who wished to join his army were allowed to stay, while those who preferred not to be soldiers were sent home with presents. Thus Sun Ce won the respect and praise of the people in the region and became very powerful.

He settled his mother and the rest of his family in Qua and appointed his brother, Sun Quan, to guard the city of Xuan together with Zhou Tai.

And he himself headed for another expedition to the south to conquer Wujun and its neighboring districts. At that time Wujun was ruled by Yan Bai-hu, or the White Tiger, who styled himself Virtuous Prince of Eastern Wu. Hearing of Sun Ce's approach, he sent his brother Yan Yu to oppose him. The two armies met at the Maple Bridge.

Yan Yu, sword in hand, took his stand on the bridge. This was reported to Sun Ce, who prepared to accept the challenge. One of his advisors tried to dissuade him: "The commander's fate is bound up with that of his army and should not risk himself for a mere ruffian. I hope you will remember your own status, sir."

"Your words are as good as precious stones, sir, but I fear my men will not exert themselves if I myself do not share their danger," replied Sun Ce.

Then he ordered Han Dong to take up the challenge. But before he reached the bridge two other officers, Jiang Qin and Chen Wu, had already got under the bridge by boat, from where they shot out a flight of arrows and drove off the enemy soldiers on the bank. Then the two men rushed up and fiercely attacked Yan Yu, who fled in fright. Han Dong pursued Yan Yu up to the city gate, where he escaped.

Sun Ce advanced by both land and water and laid siege on Suzhou. For three days no one came out to offer battle. Then at the head of his army he came to the city gate and summoned his enemy to surrender. From the gate tower an officer of inferior rank stood out with one hand resting on a beam, while with the other he used to point as he abused those below. Quickly Taishi Ci reached for his bow and arrow.

"See me hit that fellow's left hand," he said to his companions.

Even before the sound of his voice died away, the bowstring twanged, the arrow flew and pierced the officer's left hand to lodge in the beam, thus firmly pinning the hand to the beam. Both sides, those on the wall and those below it, marveled at such marksmanship.

The wounded man was taken away. When the White Tiger heard of this he was greatly upset. "How can we hope to withstand an army with such men as this in it?" he said.

And his thoughts turned toward a peace. He sent his brother Yan Yu out to see Sun Ce, who received him politely, invited him into his tent, and set wine before him.

"And what does your brother propose?" asked Sun Ce.

"He is willing to share this district with you," was the reply.

"The rat! how dare he put himself on a level with me?' cried Sun Ce.

He commanded that the messenger be put to death. Yan Yu started up and drew his sword, but out flew Sun Ce's blade and the victim fell to the ground. His head was hacked off and sent into the city to his brother.

This had its effect. The White Tiger saw resistance was hopeless, so he abandoned the city and fled. Sun Ce pressed on with the invasion. Soon, Huang Gai captured Jiaxing and Taishi Ci took Wucheng. The district was quickly subdued. The White Tiger rushed off toward Hangzhou in the south, plundering wherever he went, till the local people organized themselves under the leadership of one Ling Cao and drove him fleeing toward Guiji.

The Lings, father and son, then went to meet Sun Ce, who employed them in his service as a reward for their part in dealing with the White Tiger. The army began to cross the river.

The White Tiger gathered his men and took up a position at the western ferry but he was there attacked by Cheng Pu and escaped to Guiji that night. The prefect of the place, Wang Lang, was sympathetic with the White Tiger and wanted to support him. But when he proposed this, one of his men stood forth and objected, "No! No! Sun Ce as a leader is humane and just, while the White Tiger is a savage ruffian. Better capture him and give him over to Sun Ce as a peace offering."

The prefect turned angrily toward the speaker, who was an official named Yu Fan, and ordered him to be silent. He withdrew, sighing deeply. And the prefect went to the aid of the White Tiger, with whom he joined forces at Shanyin.

Soon Sun Ce's army came to the spot. When both sides were in battle array Sun Ce rode out and addressed Wang Lang: "I have come with an army of justice and benevolence and my aim is to restore peace to Zhejiang. Why do you assist the ruffian?"

Wang Lang replied, "Your greed is insatiable. You have taken possession of the Wu districts and now you want to annex my area. Today I am going to avenge the Yans!"

This response greatly angered Sun Ce. He was about to rush forth and give battle when Taishi Ci flew out and engaged Wang Lang. Before they had exchanged many passes Wang Long's officer, Zhou Xin, came out to help him. At once Huang Gai rode out to meet him. On both sides sounded thunderous drums and a ferocious fight ensued between the two pairs.

Suddenly, confusion started in the rear of Wang Lang's army caused by a surprise onslaught of a small troop led by Zhou Yu and Cheng Pu. Wang Lang was startled and immediately turned to engage his new enemy. But attacked from both the front and the rear, he was in a hopeless position. So together with the White Tiger and Zhou Xin, he fought desperately, only just managing to reach the shelter of the city. The drawbridge was then raised, the gates closed, and preparations made to repel a siege.

Sun Ce followed right up to the city wall and divided his men so as to attack all four gates. Seeing how fiercely his enemy raided the city, Wang Lang proposed sallying forth and fighting it out with Sun Ce, but the White Tiger argued that it was hopeless to struggle against so strong a force. He advised the prefect to strengthen his defense and remain behind the shelter of the ramparts until hunger forced the besiegers to retreat. Wang Lang agreed and the siege went on.

For several days a vigorous attack was maintained but with little success. Sun Ce sought counsel with his officers. His uncle Sun Jing said, "Since they are holding the city with such resolution it will be difficult to dislodge them. But the bulk of their supplies are stored at Chadu, which is not far from here. Our best plan is to seize that place, thus attacking where the enemy is unprepared."

Sun Ce said with joy: "Your plan is wonderful, uncle. The enemy will surely be crushed." So he issued orders to kindle fires at the four gates and leave the banners standing all around, to create an appearance of soldiers in position, while the army was to break camp and go south.

Zhou Yu said, "When you go away, sir, the besieged will undoubtedly come out and follow you. We can prepare a surprise attack for them."

Sun Ce replied, "I have thought about that. The city will be captured tonight."

Then the army set out.

Wang Lang heard that the besiegers had gone and he went up to the tower to investigate. He saw beneath the city wall fires blazing, smoke rising, and banners fluttering in the wind as usual. He did not know what to make of it all and suspicion filled his heart.

Zhou Xin said, "Sun Ce has gone and this is only a trick to deceive us. Let us go out and smite him."

The White Tiger said, "Maybe he is attacking Chadu. Let us pursue."

"That place is our base of supply," said Wang Lang, "and must be defended. You two lead the way and I will follow with the reserve force."

So the White Tiger and Zhou Xin went forth with 5,000 men and came to a dense forest, some twenty *li* from the city, at about the first watch. Suddenly drums rolled and lighted torches sprang up on all sides. Frightened, the White Tiger turned to retreat. At once an enemy officer appeared in front who, by the glare of the torches, he recognized as Sun Ce. Zhou Xin came to his aid and made a rush at Sun Ce, but fell under his spear. The men surrendered. However, the White Tiger managed to cut his way out.

Wang Lang soon heard of the loss and, not daring to return to the city, fled in haste to the coast.

Sun Ce then turned back to capture the city and appease the people. The following day a man came bringing the head of the White Tiger as an offering to him. This man was a native of this district named Dong Xi. He was of medium height with a square face and wide mouth. Sun Ce was very pleased and employed him as an officer in his army. After this the whole district came under Sun Ce's rule. Having placed his uncle in command and Zhu Zhi as the prefect, he returned to the east.

While Sun Ce was absent a band of brigands suddenly made an attack on the city of Xuan, left in the care of his brother Sun Quan and an officer called Zhou Tai. The onslaught was made on all sides at once, and late in the night the enemy got the upper hand. Zhou Tai helped Sun Quan onto a horse and tried to escape, but scores of robbers came up with swords to assault them. Zhou Tai, without horse or mail, met them on foot and slew more than ten of them. Then a brigand rode directly at him with his spear ready to strike, but Zhou Tai laid hold of his opponent's weapon and pulled him down from his horse. Then he mounted the robber's horse and, thrusting this way and that with the spear, he fought his way out and rescued his young master Sun Quan. He himself, however, received more than a dozen wounds.

These wounds being caused by metal would not heal but swelled enormously, and the brave soldier's life hung in the balance. When Sun Ce returned and learned about this, he was deeply grieved. Then Dong Xi said, "I once fought with some pirates and suffered many spear wounds. Fortunately a kind official named Yu Fan recommended to me a very good doctor who cured me in two weeks."

"Is he also called Yu Zhong-xiang?" asked Sun Ce.

"Yes, he is."

"I know he is truly an upright man. I will invite him to my service."

So Sun Ce sent Dong Xi and Zhang Zhao to go and find this man and he came with them. He was treated graciously and appointed an official. Then the question of finding a doctor for the dying man was brought up.

"The doctor's name is Hua Tuo, native of Peiguo. He has perfectly marvelous skill in the art of medicine. I will ask him to come," said Yu Fan.

Shortly after came the famous doctor, a man of youthful complexion yet snowy hair. He looked more like a saint who had transcended this life. He was treated very courteously and taken to see the sick man.

"The case is not difficult," said the doctor and he prepared special dressings that would heal the wounds in a month. Sun Ce was greatly pleased and rewarded the doctor very handsomely.

Next Sun Ce went into the mountains to destroy the brigands, thus bringing peace to the whole region. To protect his rule, he assigned officers to guard all the strategically important positions, and this done, commended to the court what he had achieved to acquire official recognition. Then he sent gifts to Cao Cao to reach an understanding with him while at the same time he wrote to Yuan Shu, demanding the return of the Imperial Seal.

Yuan Shu, however, secretly ambitious, did not want to return it. He wrote back and made some excuses to justify himself. In his own place he hastily summoned his trusted subordinates to a council.

"Sun Ce borrowed an army from me to start his expedition to the east and now he has acquired the whole area. Instead of feeling grateful to me he demands back the Imperial Seal. He is really impudent. What steps can I take to destroy him?"

One of his subordinates said, "Sun Ce has the natural barrier of the Yangtze River and a powerful army and abundant supplies. You cannot do anything against him now that he is so strongly placed. Better remove Liu Bei first in revenge for having attacked you without cause, and then deal with Sun Ce. I have a scheme to capture Liu Bei in a very short time."

> *Instead of going to the east to destroy a tiger,*
> *He leads his army to Xuzhou to attack a dragon.*

What his scheme was will be told in the next chapter.

CHAPTER SIXTEEN

Lu Bu Performs a Feat in Archery
Cao Cao Loses a Battle at Yushui River

"What is your plan to attack Liu Bei?" asked Yuan Shu.

The advisor replied, "Though Liu Bei, now camped in Xiaopei, can easily be taken, Lu Bu is strongly positioned in the vicinity. And I think he would help Liu Bei because of the grudge he bears against you for not giving him the money and grain you promised. Now you can send Lu Bu a present to win him over to your side so that he will keep quiet while you deal with Liu Bei. You can deal with him after this is done. Then Xuzhou will be yours."

Yuan Shu took his advice and sent a large quantity of millet with a letter to Lu Bu. The gift pleased Lu Bu immensely and he treated the messenger with great cordiality. Feeling sure of no trouble from him, Yuan Shu dispatched a big army led by Ji Ling and some other officers to invade Xiaopei.

When Liu Bei heard about this he called in his officers and advisors for a council. Zhang Fei was for an open war with the enemy but Sun Qian said that they lacked both men and supplies to fight and suggested asking Lu Bu for help.

"Do you think that fellow will do anything?" asked Zhang Fei cynically.

Liu Bei favored Sun Qian's advice and at once wrote a letter to Lu Bu. It read as follows:

> *Thanks to you, General, I have been able to take shelter in Xiaopei. Your kindness is as great as the heavens. Yuan Shu, out of his desire for revenge, is sending an army to assault this place and its destruction is imminent unless you intervene. I earnestly hope you will dispatch a force to relieve us from this crisis. I will be most grateful.*

After reading this Lu Bu discussed the matter with Chen Gong to whom he said, "Earlier, Yuan Shu sent me grain and a letter with the intention of restraining me from assisting Liu Bei. Now Liu Bei has also written to me asking for help. It seems to me that Liu Bei can do me no harm now that he is stationed in Xiaopei, but if Yuan Shu overcomes Liu Bei then he can combine with the forces of the north against me and I will never be able to sleep secure. It will be a better course if I assist Liu Bei." So he assembled his army and set out for Xiaopei.

Now Yuan Shu's army had arrived at its destination and soon the country to the southeast of the town fluttered with banners of war by day and blazed with watch fires by night, while the rolling of drums resounded to the skies.

The few men at Liu Bei's disposal were led out of the town and arrayed for battle to make a brave show, but it was good news to him to hear that Lu Bu had arrived with his army and camped only one *li* away. When Ji Ling, commander of Yuan Shu's force, heard of this he at once wrote to Lu Bu to reproach him for his treachery. Lu Bu smiled as he read.

"I know how to make both of them bear no grudge against me," he said.

So he issued invitations to both leaders to ask them to a banquet at his camp. Liu Bei was ready to accept the invitation and go to the banquet but his two brothers tried to dissuade him.

"You shouldn't go, brother," they said. "Lu Bu must have some evil intentions in his heart."

"I've treated him very well. I don't think he'll harm me," replied Liu Bei.

Then he mounted and rode away and his two brothers followed. Soon they were inside Lu Bu's camp.

The host said, "I have come specially to rescue you from the danger. I hope you will not forget this when you are powerful."

Liu Bei thanked him and was invited to take a seat. The two brothers took up their usual places behind him as guards.

Presently Ji Ling was announced. Liu Bei was greatly startled and rose to avoid him.

Lu Bu said, "I have asked both of you here for a counsel together. Have no fear."

Liu Bei, being quite ignorant of his true intention, was very uneasy. In a moment his fellow guest entered. Seeing Liu Bei seated in the tent, he was extremely surprised and at once turned to leave. The attendants tried to stop him but in vain. Lu Bu went forth and pulled him back easily, as if he were as light as a child.

"Do you want to slay me?" Ji Ling asked.

"Not at all," replied Lu Bu.

"Then you are going to slay the Long Ears (Liu Bei)?"

"No, not that."

"Then what do you mean?"

"Liu Bei and I are as close as brothers. Now he is besieged by you, General, and so I have come to his rescue."

"If so, you want to slay me," said Ji Ling.

"That does not make sense. All my life I have disliked fighting but loved making peace. And now I want to settle the quarrel between you two."

"May I ask how you are going to do it?"

"I have a way to let it be determined by Heaven."

Then he drew Ji Ling inside the tent to meet Liu Bei. The two men faced each other, full of suspicion in their hearts, but their host made them take their seats on both sides of himself.

The banquet began. After several rounds of wine, Lu Bu spoke: "I hope you two gentlemen will listen to me and put an end to your quarrel."

Liu Bei made no reply but Ji Ling said, "I have come with an army of 100,000 men at the express order of my master to take Liu Bei. How can I cease the fighting?"

"What!" exclaimed Zhang Fei in wrath, drawing his sword. "Few as we are, we regard you no more than mere dirt. What are you compared with a million Yellow Turbans? You dare to hurt our brother?"

Guan Yu hastened to silence him. "Let's see what General Lu has to say first," he said. "Afterwards, there will be time for us to go back to our camps and fight."

"I beg you both to come to an understanding. I cannot let you fight," said Lu Bu.

Now on one side, Ji Ling was discontented and angry; on the other, Zhang Fei was dying for a fight. Lu Bu lost his temper. He turned to his attendants and ordered, "Bring me my halberd!" Both guests turned pale as they saw him with his powerful weapon in hand.

Lu Bu continued, "I have been trying to persuade you to make peace, for that is the command of Heaven. It will be put to the test."

He then commanded his men to take the halberd outside and set it up far away beyond the gate. Then he said to the two guests, "That gate is 150 paces from here. If I can hit the tiny center branch of the halberd-head with an arrow, you must both withdraw your armies. If I miss, you can go and prepare for immediate battle. I will compel you to honor the result by force."

Ji Ling thought to himself, "That small mark at that far distance! How could he not miss it?" So he assented, feeling sure that he would have plenty of fighting after his host had missed the mark. Liu Bei was, of course, willing.

Lu Bu told them to sit down again and drink one more cup of wine. When they finished the wine, the host called for his bow and arrows. Liu Bei silently prayed that he would hit the mark.

Lu Bu folded back his sleeves, fitted an arrow to the string, and pulled the bow to its utmost stretch. A slight exclamation escaped him as the bow curved like the harvest moon sailing through the sky and the arrow sped like a comet falling to the earth. Clop! and it struck the slender tongue of the halberd head full and square. From all sides rose a roar of acclamation to greet this wonderful display of archery.

> *Oh, Lu Bu was a wonderful archer,*
> *And the arrow he shot sped straight;*
> *By hitting the mark he saved his friend*
> *That day at his camp's gate.*
> *Hou Yi, the archer of ancient days,*
> *Brought down each mocking sun;*
> *And the apes that gibbered to frighten You Ji*
> *Were shot by him, one by one.*
> *But we sing of Lu Bu that drew the bow,*
> *And his feathered shaft that flew;*
> *For a myriad men could doff their mail*
> *When he hit the mark so true.*

Lu Bu laughed with delight at the success of his shot. Dropping his bow to the ground he seized his guests by the hands and said, "The will of Heaven indeed! And now you must cease fighting!"

He ordered his soldiers to pour out large goblets of wine and each drank. Liu Bei secretly rejoiced at this great piece of luck; his fellow guest sat silent for some time. Then Ji Ling said to Lu Bu, "I dare not disobey your command, General, but when I go back, what will my master say and will he believe me?"

"I will write a letter to him to explain everything," said Lu Bu.

After a few more rounds of wine Ji Ling took the letter and departed.

"You would be in danger but for me," Lu Bu again reminded Liu Bei of the debt he owed him. Liu Bei thanked him humbly and then left with his two brothers. The next day, all the soldiers dispersed.

When Ji Ling got back he told his master about the feat of archery and the peace-making that followed. Then he presented Lu Bu's letter. Yuan Shu was beside himself with rage.

"That is how he repays me for all the grain I sent him!" he cried. "How dare he protect Liu Bei with this bit of play-acting! I will lead a large army myself to destroy Liu Bei and take Lu Bu as well."

"You should not act too much in a hurry, my lord," said Ji Ling. "Lu Bu is so powerful that no one can compete with him. Besides, he has the wide territory of Xuzhou. He and Liu Bei together make a formidable combination, not easy to break. I was told that he has a daughter by his wife, Lady Yan, who is of marriageable age and as you have a son, you could arrange a matrimonial alliance with him. If his daughter were married to your son he would certainly slay your enemy for you. This is the tactic of 'Blood is thicker than water.' A mere acquaintance cannot separate relations."

This scheme appealed to Yuan Shu, who soon sent Han Yin with gifts to go and act as the matchmaker. When Han Yin saw Lu Bu he spoke of the immense respect his master had for him and his desire to ensure a permanent alliance between the two families through marriage.

Lu Bu went in to consult his wife. Now Lu Bu had two wives and one concubine. He first married a lady of the Yan family and she was the legal wife. Then he took Sable Cicada as a concubine and while living in Xiaopei he had married Cao Bao's daughter, who became the second wife. Lady Cao had died young leaving no child. Neither had Cicada born him any children. So he had but one child, this daughter, whom he loved dearly.

When he broached the subject to his, wife she said, "I hear Yuan Shu has dominated this part of the country these many years. He has a large army and his area is very prosperous. One day a Yuan family member will become emperor and our daughter may hope to be an empress. But how many sons does he have?"

"Only this one."

"Then we should accept the offer. Even if our daughter doesn't become an empress, our city will be safe from now on."

Lu Bu decided to give consent to the marriage proposal and so treated the messenger with great hospitality. Han Yin went back to report the good news. The wedding gifts were then prepared and sent again by Han Yin to the bride's family. The were received with joy and the messenger was cordially entertained and well accommodated.

The next day Chen Gong went to see the messenger in his lodging, and after the usual greetings, the two men sat down to talk. After the servants had been sent out of earshot Chen Gong said, "Who originated this scheme to unite Yuan Shu with Lu Bu by marriage so that Liu Bei's head may fall?"

Han Yin was terrified. "I beg you not to let it get abroad," he entreated.

"I will certainly keep it a secret. But if there is any delay some other person will surely see through the trick, and that spells failure."

"What can be done then? Please help me."

"I will see Lu Bu and get him to send the girl immediately. How about that?" said Chen Gong.

"If so, my master will be much indebted to you for your kindness," replied Han Yin.

Chen Gong took his leave and sought an interview with Lu Bu.

"I hear your daughter is to be married to Yuan Shu's son. A very good match indeed, but when is the wedding?" he asked.

"That has yet to be considered," answered Lu Bu.

"Since olden days there have been fixed rules as to the period between sending presents and consummation of a marriage: emperors, one year; nobles, six months; high officials, three months; and common people, one month."

Lu Bu replied, "I think the imperial rule will apply since Heaven has already put into Yuan Shu's hands the Imperial Seal and he will surely ascend the throne one day."

"No, it won't."

"The nobles' rule, then?"

"No, nor that."

"The high officials' rule?"

"Not even that."

Lu Bu laughed. "Then you mean me to go by the rule for common people?"

"Not that either," replied Chen Gong.

"Then what do you mean?"

Chen Gong explained: "In the midst of the present troubles, when there is great rivalry between the lords, don't you see that the others will be exceedingly jealous of your marriage alliance with such a family as the Yuans? If you set the wedding date a long time away, it is not unlikely that when the day arrives the wedding party will fall into an ambush on the road, and the bride carried off. Then what is to be done? My opinion is that you would have done better to refuse. But since you have consented, then you should send your daughter to Shouchun at once, before the lords hear of it. You can arrange to let her stay in a separate house till you have selected the wedding day. The odds against any failure are lower."

"What you say is quite right," said Lu Bu with pleasure.

He went in to tell his wife about this. So the trousseau was prepared that very night and a beautiful wedding carriage drawn by fine horses was readied for use. The escort consisted of Han Yin and two military officers and the procession was seen out of the city amid the sound of drums and pipes.

Now at this time Chen Deng's father had retired from office and was resting at home. Hearing this burst of music he inquired about the occasion and his servants told him.

"They're playing the trick of 'Blood is thicker than water,'" the old man said. "Liu Bei's in danger."

Therefore in spite of his infirmities he went to see Lu Bu.

"What brings you here, sir?" asked Lu Bu.

"I hear you are dying and I have come to mourn," replied the old man.

Lu Bu was greatly surprised. "Why do you say that?" he asked.

"Some time ago Yuan Shu sent you presents so that you would not interfere when he came down to slay Liu Bei, but later by that miraculous shot you succeeded in effecting the withdrawal of his army. Now he suddenly proposes a marriage alliance with you. His intention is to take your daughter as a hostage. The next move will be an attack on Xiaopei and if that place is lost, Xuzhou will also be in peril. Furthermore, whatever he may ask in future—grain or men or anything else—if you yield, you will exhaust yourself and make yourself hated all around. If you refuse, you will be neglecting the duties of a relative and that will be an excuse for an open attack on you. Besides, this Yuan Shu intends to call himself Emperor, which is rebellion, and you will be part of the rebel family. Surely this will not be tolerated by the whole country!"

Lu Bu was much disturbed to hear this. "I have been misled by Chen Gong!" he cried.

So he hurriedly ordered Zhang Liao to bring back the wedding party. When they had returned he threw Han Yin into prison and sent someone else to tell Yuan Shu that the girl's trousseau was not ready and that he would send her there when it was. The old man also suggested handing over Han Yin to the court in the new capital, but Lu Bu hesitated as to which course to take.

At this time his men came to report to him that Liu Bei was recruiting soldiers and buying horses in Xiaopei for no apparent reason.

"He is simply doing his duty as a general. There is nothing to be alarmed about," said Lu Bu.

Just then two of his officers came in and said, "On your order we went into Shandong to purchase horses. We had bought three hundred but when we came to the border area of Xiaopei on our way back, some robbers snatched half of them. Later we heard that the robbers were actually Zhang Fei and his men in disguise."

Lu Bu was very angry at this and immediately set out on an expedition against Xiaopei. When Liu Bei heard about it he was startled and hastened to lead out his army to confront it—the two armies faced each other in battle array. Liu Bei rode to the front and asked: "Why do you bring your army here, brother?"

Lu Bu said angrily, "I saved you from grave danger last time when I shot that arrow. Why then did you steal my horses?"

"I did buy some horses because we needed them. But I would never dare to take yours."

"You let Zhang Fei snatch one hundred and fifty horses from me. Can you deny it?"

At this Zhang Fei rode out, his spear set, and cried, "Yes, I took your horses, what are you going to do about it?"

Lu Bu responded angrily, "You goggle-eyed thief! You are always trying to provoke me."

Zhang Fei retorted, "I took your horses and you get angry, yet you did not say anything when you stole my brother's city."

Lu Bu rode forward to give battle and Zhang Fei advanced to engage him. A violent fight began and the two warriors exchanged more than a hundred bouts, but still neither could prevail over the other. Then Liu Bei, fearing that his brother might get hurt, hurriedly beat the gongs as a signal to withdraw from the battle. His army then returned into the city. Lu Bu, however, did not retreat but besieged the city on all sides.

Liu Bei called his brother to him and blamed him as the cause of all this misfortune.

"Where are the horses?" he asked.

"I put them in the temples," replied Zhang Fei.

Liu Bei then sent a messenger to Lu Bu's camp to offer to return the stolen horses and to propose peace. Lu Bu was disposed to agree but Chen Gong objected. "You will fall into his hands if you don't remove him now."

Under his influence Lu Bu rejected the request for peace and pressed harder with his attack on the city.

Liu Bei sought advice from Mi Zhu and Sun Qian.

Sun Qian said, "The one person that Cao Cao detests is Lu Bu. Let us then abandon the city and seek refuge from him and borrow his army to destroy Lu Bu. This is the best policy."

"If we try to get away, who will take the lead and break through the encirclement?" asked Liu Bei.

"I will fight to death," said Zhang Fei.

So Zhang Fei led the way. Guan Yu was placed in the rear and in the center was Liu Bei himself with the non-fighting portion. At about third watch during the night they started out through the north gate under the bright moonlight. They met some opposition but the two officers that tried to stop them were driven off by Zhang Fei and they broke through the besieging force without difficulty. Zhang Liao came to pursue them but was held off by Guan Yu. It seemed that Lu Bu was not bothered at their flight, for he took no trouble to prevent it. He entered the city to calm the residents and, after appointing Gao Shun to guard the place, he returned to Xuzhou.

Liu Bei approached the new capital and encamped outside the city. He sent Sun Qian to see Cao Cao and relate the events that brought him there. Cao Cao was very friendly and said that he regarded Liu Bei as his own brother. He invited Liu Bei to enter the capital.

Leaving his two brothers at the camp, Liu Bei, accompanied by Sun Qian and Mi Zhu, went to see Cao Cao, who received him with great respect. The story of Lu Bu's perfidy was again related.

"He is a faithless fellow," said Cao Cao. "You and I will attack him together."

Liu Bei thanked him. A banquet was then prepared and it was late evening before the visitor left for his own camp.

Xun Yu went in to see his master and said, "Liu Bei is quite a figure. You should destroy him otherwise he will be your undoing in future."

Cao Cao made no reply and his advisor retired. Presently, Guo Jia came and Cao Cao asked him: "I have been advised to kill Liu Bei. What do you think of this advice?"

"Very bad advice indeed," said Guo Jia. "You, sir, are raising an armed force to uphold justice and to relieve the people from oppression. Only by truth and rectitude can you secure the support of the noble-minded. Your only fear is lest they should stay away. Now Liu Bei is famous as a hero. He has come to you for help and protection—to put him to death will not only harm a good man but alienate all the wise men and put fear into the hearts of all the able advisors. Where, then, will you find those whose help you need? To remove the danger represented by one man and thus injure yourself in the eyes of all is a sure means of destruction. The pros and cons of these matters need to be carefully weighed."

"Exactly what I think," said Cao Cao, greatly pleased with these remarks.

The next day he petitioned the Emperor to give Liu Bei the governorship of Yuzhou in Henan.

However, another of his advisors also tried to warn him of Liu Bei's potential threat. He said, "Liu Bei is sure to rise to the top. He will never remain in the subordinate position. You had better remove him."

Cao Cao replied, "Now is the time to make use of distinguished men. I will not forfeit the regard of the world for the sake of removing one individual. Guo Jia and I both see this issue in the same light."

Therefore he rejected all persuasions against Liu Bei but provided him with 3,000 soldiers and a large quantity of grain. It was decided that Liu Bei was to take office in Yuzhou and then march to Xiaopei to call together his former men for an attack on Lu Bu.

When Liu Bei reached Yuzhou he sent someone to inform Cao Cao, who began to prepare an army to subdue Lu Bu. But just at that time urgent news came that Zhang Ji, who had been attacking Nanyang, had died from a wound by a stray arrow. His nephew Zhang Xiu had succeeded to the command of his army and with Jia Xu as his advisor he had formed a league with Liu Biao and camped at Wancheng, intending to attack the capital and carry off the Emperor.

Cao Cao was placed in a dilemma. He would like to destroy this combination but he feared lest Lu Bu would take the advantage of his absence to raid the capital. So he sought advice from Xun Yu.

"This is easy," said Xun Yu. "Lu Bu is a simpleton, easily taken in by any little advantage that presents itself. All you need to do is to obtain promotion for him, giving him some additional title, and tell him to make peace with Liu Bei. Then he will not want to start an expedition against the capital."

"Good," said Cao Cao and he acted as he was advised. An officer was sent to Xuzhou with the official announcement of a title for Lu Bu and a letter urging peace, while he went on with preparations to relieve the other danger. When ready he led a huge army to march forward in three divisions with Xiahou Dun as the van leader. Soon they arrived at Yushui River, where they encamped.

In Zhang Xiu's camp, Jia Xu had succeeded in pointing out to his master the hopelessness of resistance.

"You would do better if you surrendered since his army is too strong for you to oppose," he said.

Seeing the truth of this, Zhang Xiu sent Jia Xu to his opponent's camp to offer submission. Cao Cao talked with the messenger and was greatly impressed by his ready and fluent speech. So he tried to win him over to his service.

Jia Xu replied, "I was formerly with Li Jue and was blamed by all. Now I am with Zhang Xiu, who followed all of my advice—I cannot bear to abandon him."

He left and the next day he introduced his master to Cao Cao, who treated him very well. Then Cao Cao entered the city with a small force while the greater part of his army remained in camp outside, where the line of tents extended some ten *li*. Inside the city banquets were given every day to entertain Cao Cao.

One day Cao Cao returned to his quarters in a more than usual merry mood and he asked his attendants if there were any singing girls in the city. The son of his elder brother heard the question and said to him in private, "Last night I saw by a fleeting glance a perfectly beautiful woman who lives next door to us. They told me she is the wife of Zhang Xiu's uncle."

Cao Cao told his nephew to go and bring her to him. He did so supported by an armed escort, and very soon the lady stood before Cao Cao.

She was a beauty indeed and Cao Cao asked her who she was.

"I am Zhang Ji's wife, born of the Zhou family," she replied.

"Do you know who I am?"

"I have known Your Lordship by reputation for a long time. I am happy to be permitted to bow before you," she said humbly.

"It was for Your Ladyship's sake that I allowed Zhang Xiu to submit; otherwise, his whole clan would be exterminated."

"Indeed I owe my very life to you. I am most grateful."

"It is a blessing from heaven for me to set eyes upon you. Stay here for the night and then come with me to the capital, where we can enjoy a life of luxury together. What do you say to that?"

She thanked him. That night she stayed in his bedchamber.

"Zhang Xiu will surely suspect if you continue to live in the city and besides, gossip wll begin to spread," she said.

"I will go with you to my camp outside the city tomorrow," said Cao Cao.

So the following day Cao Cao left the city to stay in his tent, where Dian Wei was appointed as a special guard to bar the entrance to anyone not permitted. Therefore Cao Cao was divorced from affairs outside and he passed days in idle dalliance with the lady, quite content to let time flow by.

Soon Zhang Xiu's people told him about this and he was very angry at the shame brought upon the family. He confided his trouble to Jia Xu who said, "Keep quiet about this. There should be no leaks. Wait until he comes again to attend to business." And then he told his master his plan to punish Cao Cao in great secret.

Not long after this Zhang Xiu had an interview with Cao Cao. He told him that, as many of his men were deserting, it would be well to put them in the center. Cao Cao agreed and so Zhang Xiu was able to move his soldiers and place them in four camps, ready to start an attack at any time.

But Dian Wei, the special guard of Cao Cao's tent, was a man to be feared, being both brave and powerful. It was hard to get near to him. So Zhang Xiu discussed the matter with an officer called Hu Ju-er, a man of enormous strength and great stamina. He could carry a burden of 600 pounds (272 kg) and travel 700 *li* in a day.

The officer said, "The fearsome thing about Dian Wei are his double iron spears. Invite him to a wine party and make sure that he is quite drunk before you send him back. I will mingle among his escort and so get into his tent to steal his weapons. Then we need not be afraid of him."

Zhang Xiu was very pleased with this. So the necessary arms were prepared and orders given to his men in the four camps. When the date to strike the blow came, Dian Wei was invited and plied with copious wine so that he was quite intoxicated when he left. And, as arranged, Hu Ju-er mingled with his escort and made away with the weapon.

That night when Cao Cao was drinking with the lady, he heard the voices of men and the neighing of horses outside. He sent someone to find out what was the matter, and the man returned to say that it was Zhang Xiu's soldiers doing the night patrol. Cao Cao was assured.

At about the second watch he was again disturbed by some noise in the camp and was told that one of the fodder carts was on fire.

"Some soldiers must have dropped a spark. There is nothing to be alarmed about," said Cao Cao.

But very soon the fire spread on all sides and he was startled. He called Dian Wei, but his trusted warrior was asleep after too much wine.

However, the beating of gongs and rolling of drums stirred Dian Wei in his dreams and he jumped up. Yet he could not find his spears. By this time the enemy had reached the outer gate. He hastily snatched a short sword and rushed out. At the gate he saw a big crowd of horsemen with spears bursting in. He dashed at them, slashing all around, and a score of them fell to his sword. But no sooner had the horsemen left than the foot soldiers came up. The spears stood around him like reeds on the river bank. Being totally without mail he was soon covered with wounds but he still fought desperately till his sword was blunted and no longer of any use. Throwing it aside, he seized a couple of soldiers and with their bodies as weapons felled half a score of his opponents. The others dared not approach, but they shot arrows at him. These fell as thick as rain, yet he still blocked the front entrance to Cao Cao's tent against any assailants.

In the end the mutineers broke in by the rear entrance and one of them wounded him in the back with a spear thrust. Uttering loud cries, he fell. The blood gushed from his wounds like torrents and Dian Wei died. Even after he was dead, for some time no one dared to come in through the front gate.

In the meantime, Cao Cao, relying on Dian Wei to hold the enemy at bay, had fled in haste through the rear gate. Only his nephew accompanied him on foot. Then Cao Cao was wounded by an arrow in the right arm and his steed, too, was struck by three arrows. Fortunately it was a fine breed of horse and in spite of its wounds it bore its master swiftly to the banks of Yushui River.

Here some of the pursuers approached and his nephew was hacked to pieces. Cao Cao rode, splashing, into the river and reached the other side, but there an arrow struck his steed in the eye and it fell. By then his eldest son had caught up with him and he immediately dismounted and yielded his horse to his father, who galloped on. His son was killed but he himself got away. Soon after he met several of his officers who had rallied a small portion of their men.

The Qingzhou soldiers under Xiahou Dun seized the occasion to plunder the people. When Yue Jin learned about this he ordered his men to fall upon them and slew many of them. Thus he protected and appeased the people. The plunderers, meeting Cao Cao on the road, knelt down howling loudly, and told him that Yue Jin had mutinied and attacked them. Cao Cao was greatly surprised and when he was joined by his veteran officers he gave orders to capture Yue Jin.

When Yue Jin saw his master approaching with a big retinue he at once set his men to get into positions and make a camp. They did not understand what this meant and asked, "The Qingzhou soldiers have accused you of turning traitor; why don't you explain now that our lord has arrived? Why first make a camp?"

Yue Jin replied, "Our enemies are close behind us. It is necessary to prepare for defense or we will not be able to withstand them. Explanation is a small matter but defense is very important."

Almost immediately after the camp was finished, Zhang Xiu fell upon them in two divisions. Yue Jin himself rode out to face them. Zhang Xiu hastened to withdraw. The other officers, seeing Yue Jin advance thus boldly, also attacked and Zhang Xiu was overcome. They pursued him for as long as a hundred *li* until his force was nearly annihilated. With the miserable remnant he finally fled to Liu Biao.

Cao Cao called in his officers and men. It was only then that Yue Jin went to tell his master of the misconduct of the Qingzhou soldiers and why he had attacked them.

"Why didn't you tell me before you set up camp?"

Yue Jin gave him the same reason as he had given to his men.

Cao Cao said, "At a time of great stress you still strived to maintain order and strengthen your defense, giving all your attention to duty but no thought to slander, and thus turning defeat into victory. Even distinguished generals in ancient times could not excel you!"

He rewarded Yue Jin with a pair of gold pieces and a noble title but reprimanded Xiahou Dun for neglecting his duty to discipline his men. Sacrifices in honor of the dead warrior Dian Wei were instituted. Cao Cao himself led the wailing to mourn over his death. Turning to his officers he said, "I have lost my eldest son and my dear nephew but I do not grieve so deeply for them as for Dian Wei. And I cry for him alone." All were greatly moved.

Orders were then issued for the army to return to the capital—but nothing will be said here about the journey back.

Let us now turn to Lu Bu and what happened in Xuzhou. Now Cao Cao's messenger, bearing the imperial decree, reached the city and was met by Lu Bu, who conducted him into his residence where the decree was read. It conferred on him a new title, General-Conqueror of the East, accompanied by a special seal for the mandate. A private letter from Cao Cao was also handed over and the messenger detailed the high esteem in which Lu Bu was held by the prime minister. Lu Bu was very flattered.

At that moment a messenger from Yuan Shu was announced. When the man was called in, he said that Yuan Shu's plan to declare himself emperor and select his heir apparent were well under way and that he wanted the princess—meaning Lu Bu's daughter—to be sent to his place as soon as possible.

"Has the rebel gone so far as that?" cried Lu Bu in a rage.

He put the messenger to death. Then he drafted a letter of thanks and sent it to the capital through Chen Deng; he also sent the unfortunate matchmaker, Han Yin, wearing a large wooden collar around his neck. He also replied to Cao Cao's private letter asking to be confirmed in his governorship of Xuzhou.

On receiving the message, Cao Cao was pleased to hear of the rupture of the marriage arrangement and at once executed Han Yin.

However, Chen Deng secretly advised Cao Cao to destroy Lu Bu as soon as possible, saying that he was as vicious as a wolf, brave but stupid, and faithless.

"I know Lu Bu quite well," said Cao Cao. "He is wickedly ambitious, and it will be hard to keep him in his place for long. You and your father are the only people that can tell me about his schemes and you must help me to get rid of him."

"I will certainly be at your service if you are going to take action against him," pledged Chen Deng.

As a reward Cao Cao obtained a handsome monthly grant of grain for the father and a prefecture for the son. When he took his leave, Cao Cao held him by the hand and said, "I will depend on you for affairs in the east." Chen Deng offered his obeisance. Then he returned to Lu Bu, who asked him how things went. Chen Deng told him of the rewards he and his father had received.

Lu Bu burst into anger. "You did not ask Xuzhou for me yet you got something for yourselves. Your father advised me to help Cao Cao by breaking off the marriage alliance with Yuan Shu, and now I get nothing at all of what I asked for while you and your father get both wealth and position. I have been betrayed by you two!"

He drew his sword and threatened to kill him.

Chen Deng laughed and said, "Oh, General, how can you be so ignorant?"

"Me? Ignorant?"

"When I saw Cao Cao, I said that maintaining you was like feeding a tiger. The tiger must be kept fully fed or he would eat men. But he laughed and replied, 'No, not like that. I treat him like a falcon. Do not feed it until the foxes and hares have been removed. Hungry, the bird is of use; fully-fed and it flies away.' I asked him who were the beasts of prey. He named Yuan Shu, Sun Ce, Yuan Shao, Liu Biao and others."

Lu Bu threw aside his sword and laughed. "Yes, he truly understands me."

But just as they were talking, news came of the advance of Yuan Shu on Xuzhou and Lu Bu was quite taken aback.

> *When an alliance was broken, war started,*
> *After a failed marriage an army marched.*

What might happen to Lu Bu will be told in the next chapter.

CHAPTER SEVENTEEN

Yuan Shu Expeditions Eastward
with Seven Divisions
Cao Cao Unites Three Forces to Attack Yuan Shu

As Governor of Huainan, a spacious and prosperous region, Yuan Shu was very powerful. Later the possession of the Imperial Seal added to his self-esteem. And he began to seriously think of assuming the title of Emperor. So he assembled all his subordinates and addressed them as follows:

"Of old the founder of the Han Dynasty was only an official of a very low rank and yet he became ruler of an empire. Now, after four hundred years of rule, the Hans have exhausted their fortune. They no longer have authority; and the country is the scene of turbulent unrest. My family has held the highest offices of the state for four generations and is universally respected. Therefore I intend to assume the imperial dignity in response to the will of Heaven and the desire of the people. What do you all think of this?"

Yan Xiang rose at once to oppose. "No, you should not do this. In the past, the ancestor of the House of Zhou was of distinguished virtue and had many merits. Later when King Wen ruled the House of Zhou he had already acquired two-thirds of the empire, yet he still served the Emperor of the Shang Dynasty as his lord. Your family is honorable but it is not so glorious as that of the House of Zhou in its prime. The Hans may be weak but they are not so abominably cruel as Emperor Zhou of the Shang Dynasty. Indeed, what you propose should never be done."

Yuan Shu heard his words with great anger. "We Yuans came from Chen, who was a descendant of the ancient Emperor Shun. So I am of royal descent and my element of fortune is 'earth,' which agrees with the heavenly revelation that 'fire,' the element for the Hans, is to be replaced by 'earth.' Secondly, there is an oracle which says, 'He who succeeds the Hans must be on the high roads.' My name, Gong-lu, means 'the high road.' It fits exactly. Thirdly, I possess the Hereditary Seal of the State. If I do not become lord of all I will be acting against Heaven's rule. My mind is made up. Whoever dares to object will be put to death."

So he declared himself the new Emperor and his subordinates were given official titles of ministers. He rode in a carriage decorated with a dragon and a phoenix and offered sacrifices to Heaven and Earth after the manner of an Emperor in the north and south suburbs. A girl of the Feng family was made the Empress and his son, the Heir Apparent. Then he sent his men to Xuzhou to press for an early wedding of Lu Bu's daughter with his son, so that the palace entourage might be complete.

But when he heard of the fate of his marriage ambassador he was very angry and began at once to plot revenge. Zhang Xun was made the general commander leading an enormous army of more than 200,000 men in seven divisions, each with its own leader and instructed to make a specific town his objective. The Governor of Yanzhou was ordered to superintend the supply of provisions, but he declined the office and so was put to death. General Ji Ling was in command of the reserve forces to help wherever he was required. Yuan Shu himself led 30,000 soldiers to reinforce the seven divisions and he appointed three veteran officers to supervise and see that the various armies did not lag behind.

Lu Bu found out from his scouts that Xuzhou, Xiaopei, and five other towns were the immediate targets under attack. The armies were marching fifty *li* a day, and plundering the countryside as they advanced.

He summoned his advisers to a council, to which came Chen Gong as well as Chen Deng and his father. When all had assembled Chen Gong said, "This misfortune is provoked by Chen Deng and his father, who fawned upon the court in order to obtain ranks and appointments for themselves. Now they shift the blame on to you, General. Just put these two to death and send their heads to Yuan Shu and the armies will withdraw."

Lu Bu assented and had the two arrested. But the son, Chen Deng, only laughed. "What is this anxiety about?" he said. "These seven armies are no more to me than so many heaps of rotting straw. They are not worth thinking about."

"If you can show us how to overcome them I will spare your life," said Lu Bu.

"General, if you will listen to my words the city will be perfectly safe," said Chen Deng.

"Let us hear what you have to say."

"Yuan Shu's men are numerous but they are only a motley crowd, not an army under a leader. There is no mutual trust. I can keep them at bay with a firm defense or overcome them by surprise strategies. What is more, I have another plan by which not only the city can be protected but Yuan Shu will be captured."

"Go ahead and tell us," said Lu Bu.

"Yang Feng and Han Xian, two of the seven leaders of our enemies, are old servants of the Han Dynasty who fled from fear of Cao Cao and, being homeless, sought temporary refuge with Yuan Shu. Naturally he despises them and they, in their turn, are dissatisfied to be in his service. A letter from you will secure their help as our allies from the inside, and with Liu Bei to help us on the outside we can certainly capture Yuan Shu."

"You must deliver the letters yourself," said Lu Bu.

Chen Deng agreed. Then Lu Bu prepared a memorial to report the situation to the court, wrote the letters to the two leaders and to Liu Bei, and finally sent Chen Deng, with a small escort, to wait for Han Xian on the road. When Han Xian's army had halted and pitched camp, Chen Deng went to see him.

"What are you here for?" asked Han Xian. "You are Lu Bu's man."

"I am an official of the great Hans. Why do you call me Lu Bu's man? But you, General, used to be an imperial officer, now serve under a traitor. You cancel out the grand services you rendered in protecting the Emperor and I do not think it a worthy exchange. Besides, Yuan Shu is by nature a suspicious person and he will surely harm you later. If you do not take this opportunity to work against him it will be too late to regret."

Han Xian sighed. "I would give my allegiance to Han if there should be any opportunity."

Then Chen Deng gave him the letter from Lu Bu. After reading it he said, "I see. Please go back and tell your master that General Yang and I will turn our weapons around and smite Yuan Shu. Look out for a signal flare and ask your master to come to our aid."

As soon as Chen Deng had got back and reported his success, Lu Bu divided his men into five divisions of 10,000 soldiers each. He himself went to oppose Yuan Shu's main body under the chief commander, Zhang Xun, and sent the others to four points to meet their enemies. The rest were left to guard the city.

Lu Bu camped thirty *li* from the city. Soon his enemy came up. Knowing that he was no match for Lu Bu, the enemy commander retreated twenty *li* to await reinforcements.

That night, in the second watch, Han Xian and Yang Feng arrived and at once the flare was lighted as arranged. Lu Bu's men were admitted into the camp, causing great confusion. Taking advantage of this Lu Bu launched a fierce attack and Zhang Xun fled in defeat. Lu Bu pursued till daylight, when he fell in with one of Yuan Shu's other armed forces led by

Ji Ling. The two armies faced each other, but just as they were beginning to engage in battle Yang Feng and Han Xian also came up to join the attack and Ji Ling was forced to fly.

Lu Bu went in pursuit but soon from the rear of some hills appeared another force, marching toward him with all the pomposity of a royal expedition. It was preceded by flags bearing the dragon and the phoenix, representations of the sun and moon, and all kinds of imperial emblems. And beneath a yellow silken umbrella sat Yuan Shu on horseback, clad in golden mail with a sword handle showing at each wrist.

Riding in front of his army Yuan Shu railed at his opponent, calling him a traitor and a slave. Lu Bu said nothing but rode forward to give battle and one of Yuan Shu's officers advanced to take the challenge. They met, but at the third bout, the man was wounded in the hand, at which he fled leaving his spear on the ground. Lu Bu waved on the advance and his men prevailed. The other side fled, leaving much spoil, including clothing, mail, and horses.

Yuan Shu's defeated men had not gone far, however, when another strong troop, led by Guan Yu, appeared before them and barred their way of escape.

"You rebel! Get down and be slain!" cried Guan Yu.

Yuan Shu fled in great trepidation and his army melted in all directions. Guan Yu led his men to fall upon them with great slaughter. Yuan Shu and the remnant of his army retreated back to his own district.

Victory being now secure, Lu Bu, in company with Guan Yu, Yang Feng, and Han Xian, returned to Xuzhou, where he entertained his guests with banquets and rewarded all, including the soldiers. These over, Guan Yu took his leave, while Han Xian and Yang Feng were both recommended by Lu Bu to be magistrates of two cities in Shandong.

Lu Bu consulted his advisors about whether he should keep these two in Xuzhou but Chen Gui was opposed to it. "Let them hold those places in Shandong, which will all be yours within a year." Lu Bu agreed and so they were sent to station their armies there and, in the meantime, to await court confirmations of their posts.

"Why not retain them here?" asked Chen Deng secretly of his father. "They can be used for our plan against Lu Bu."

"But if they helped him, on the other hand, he would be made even stronger," said his father.

Chen Deng could only but admire his father's foresight.

Yuan Shu returned home burning to avenge his defeat, so he sent a messenger to Sun Ce to borrow soldiers from him. Sun Ce was very angry at the request. He said, "He does not return me the Imperial Seal but assumes the title of Emperor on the strength of it and betrays the Hans. He is an out-and-out rebel! I am just going to lead my army to punish him. How dare he expect me to help him?"

So he refused. His letter refusing help added to Yuan Shu's anger. "What impudence!" he cried. "That callow youth! I will smite him before I deal with Lu Bu." It was only after earnest dissuasion from one of his advisors that he gave up this course.

Having sent the letter of refusal to Yuan Shu, Sun Ce thought it wise to take measures for his own safety. So he stationed an army at the mouth of the river. Soon after, an envoy from Cao came with a decree bearing his appointment as Prefect of Guiji and ordering him to raise an army against Yuan Shu.

Sun Ce was inclined to carry out these orders and he called a council to discuss the matter at hand. But Zhang Zhao opposed this course. He said, "Although recently defeated, Yuan Shu still has many men and ample supplies. He is not to be treated lightly. You had better write to Cao to persuade him to lead an expedition to the south and we will support him. If our two armies join forces Yuan Shu will certainly be defeated. If, by the remotest chance, we lose, we have Cao to come to our rescue." This plan was adopted and a messenger was sent to lay it before Cao Cao.

Back in the capital Cao Cao's first thought was to dedicate sacrifices to his lost warrior Dian Wei. He conferred rank upon his son and took him into his own house to be cared for.

Presently Sun Ce's messenger arrived with the letter from his master and next came a report that Yuan Shu, being short of food, had raided Chenliu. Cao Cao thought the moment opportune, so he issued orders for the expedition south, leaving Cao Ren to hold the city. The force consisted of 170,000 horse and foot soldiers, with wagons of food to the number of over a thousand. Messages were sent to summon Sun Ce, Liu Bei, and Lu Bu to launch a joint attack.

When the army reached Yuzhou, Liu Bei was already there to welcome Cao Cao and was called into his tent. After the usual salutations Liu Bei produced two heads.

"Whose are these?" asked Cao Cao in surprise.

"The heads of Han Xian and Yang Feng."

"How did this happen?'

"They were sent by Lu Bu to station in two cities in Shandong but they allowed their soldiers to plunder the people and bitter complaints arose. So I invited them to a banquet during which my brothers slew them when I gave the signal by dropping a cup. All their men gave in at once. I must apologize for my fault."

"You have removed an evil, which is a grand service: why talk of a fault?"

And he praised Liu Bei for what he had done.

When the joint army reached the borders of Xuzhou, Lu Bu came to meet them. Cao Cao spoke graciously to him and conferred upon him the title of General of the Left Division, promising to confirm his governership of Xuzhou as soon as he returned to the capital. Lu Bu was very pleased.

Then the three armies were made into one force, Cao Cao being in the center and the other two on the wings. Xiahou Dun and Yue Jin were van leaders.

On Yuan Shu's side a major officer named Qiao Sui was appointed van leader with 50,000 men. The armies met in the confines of Shouchun. The two van leaders rode out and opened battle. Qiao Sui fell in the third bout and his men fled into the city. Then came news that Sun Ce's fleet was near and would attack on the west while the three land corps of Cao Cao, Liu Bei, and Lu Bu attacked on the three other sides—the city was in a perilous state.

At this juncture Yuan Shu summoned his advisors for immediate consultation. Yang Da-jiang said, "Shouchun has suffered from flood or drought for several years and the people are on the verge of famine. Now the war adds to their distress and anger, and resistance would be uncertain. I think it would be better not to fight, but to hold on till the besiegers are conquered by lack of supplies. Your Majesty can move over to the other side of the river with your palace guards so as to be ready for the harvest season and to avoid open confrontation with the enemy."

Yuan Shu took his advice. Leaving four officers with a large army to guard the city, he ordered a general move to the other side of the Huai River. Not only the army went over but all the accumulated wealth of the Yuan family, gold and silver, jewels and precious stones, were shipped across the water.

Cao Cao's army of 100,000 men needed daily a vast quantity of food, and as the country around had been famine-stricken for several years nothing could be got there. So he tried to hasten the military operations and capture the city. On the other hand, the defenders knew the value of delay and simply held on. After a month's vigorous siege the fall of the city seemed as far off as it was at first and supplies were very short. Letters were sent to Sun Ce who sent 100,000 measures of grain, but it was still not enough to feed the empty stomachs of the men. When the usual distribution became impossible, Wang Hou, head of the granaries, went to see Cao Cao, asking what was to be done.

"Serve out with a smaller measure," said Cao Cao. "That will save us for a time."

"But if the soldiers complain, what then?"

"I know what to do."

As ordered, Wang Hou issued grain in short measures. Cao Cao secretly sent people to find out how the men reacted to this. When he found that complaints were general and that they blamed him for fooling them, he sent a secret summons to Wang Hou. When he came Cao Cao said, "I want to borrow something from you to pacify the soldiers. You must not refuse."

"What do you want, sir?"

"I want to borrow your head and expose it before the soldiers."

"But I have done nothing wrong?" exclaimed the terrified man.

"I know that, but if I do not put you to death there will be a mutiny. After you are gone your wife and children will be in my care. So you need not grieve on their account."

Wang Hou was about to protest further but just then at a signal from Cao Cao, the executioners hustled him out and he was beheaded. His head was exposed on a tall pole and a notice said that in accordance with military law Wang Hou had been put to death for embezzlement and the deliberate use of a short measure in issuing grain.

This appeased the discontent. Next followed a general order threatening death to the various commanders if the city was not taken within three days. Cao Cao in person went up to the very walls to superintend the work of filling up the moat. The defenders kept up constant showers of stones and arrows. Two inferior officers, who left their positions in fear, were slain by Cao Cao himself. Then he dismounted and joined in piling earth into the moat, thus inspiring his officers and men to exert themselves so that work progressed steadily and no one dared to be a laggard. The army became invincible and the defenders of the city could not withstand their onslaught. In a very short time the walls were scaled, the gates battered in, and the besiegers were in possession. The officers of the garrison were captured alive and were executed in the market place. All the paraphernalia of the illegitimate imperial state was burned and the whole city wrecked.

When the question of crossing the river in pursuit of Yuan Shu came up Xun Yu opposed it and said: "The country has suffered from poor crops for years and we will be unable to get grain. An advance will weary the army, harm the people, and possibly end in disaster. I advise a return to the capital to wait till the spring wheat has been harvested and we have plenty of supplies."

Cao Cao hesitated, but before he had made up his mind there came an urgent message for help from the capital which said that Zhang Xiu, with the support of Liu Biao, was ravaging the country all around and that there was rebellion in a number of places. Cao Hong, who had been entrusted with the defense of the region, could not cope with it and had been worsted already in several battles.

Cao Cao at once wrote to Sun Ce asking him to deploy decoy troops across the river so as to prevent any move on the part of Liu Biao, while he returned immediately to the capital to deal with Zhang Xiu. Before departure he directed Liu Bei to camp at Xiaopei again and made him a sworn brother of Lu Bu's so that they might live in peace and aid each other.

When Lu Bu had left for Xuzhou Cao Cao said to Liu Bei, "I am leaving you at Xiaopei for a special purpose, which is to plan 'a pit for the tiger.' Take advice only from Chen Deng and his father and there can be no mishap. I will come to your assistance when needed."

So Cao Cao marched back to the capital, where he heard that the two rebels Li Jue and Guo Si had been slain by two men called Duan Wei and Wu Xi, who presented their heads before him. Besides, Duan Wei had also brought Li Jue's whole clan to the capital. Cao Cao ordered all of them to be put to death at various gates and their heads exposed. This harsh punishment, however, met with approval from the people, who clapped in joy.

In the Emperor's palace a large number of officials were assembled at a peace banquet. Both Duan Wei and Wu Xi were rewarded with titles and sent to guard the old capital Chang'an. They thanked the Emperor in gratitude and marched away.

Then Cao Cao sent in a memorial stating that Zhang Xiu was in rebellion and proposing an expedition to destroy him. The Emperor himself went in his chariot to see Cao Cao off when he started on the journey in summer, the fourth month of the third year of the period Jian An. Xun Yu, Cao Cao's chief advisor, was left in military command of the capital.

The army marched away. Before long they passed through a wheat district and noticed that the crop was ready for harvesting. However, the peasants had fled from fear as the army approached and the wheat remained uncut. Cao Cao made it known to all the villagers and officials in the region that he was sent on the expedition by command of the Emperor to capture a rebel and save the people, and although he could not avoid moving his army in the harvest season he would put to death whoever trampled down the wheat. He assured the people that the military law was very severe and the people should have no fear of damage. The people were so pleased that they lined the road and bowed in gratitude. When the soldiers passed wheat fields they dismounted and pushed aside the stalks so that none was trampled down.

One day, when Cao Cao was riding through the fields, a turtledove suddenly flew up, startling his horse so that it swerved into the standing wheat field and a large patch was trampled down. Cao Cao at once called the officer in charge of military discipline and asked him to announce the sentence for his crime of trampling down the wheat.

"How can I deal with your crime?" asked the officer.

"I made the rule and I have broken it. How else can I convince others?"

He laid hold of the sword by his side as if to take his own life. All hastened to prevent him. Then Guo Jia said, "In the ancient book of Spring and Autumn, it says, 'No law is to be applied to the lord of all.' You are the supreme leader of a mighty army and must not harm yourself."

Cao Cao pondered for a long time. At last he said, "Since there exists such a practice I may escape the death penalty."

Then with his sword he cut off his hair and threw it down on the ground. "I cut off my hair in place of my head," he said.

Then he sent a man to exhibit the hair to the whole army with the words, "The prime minister, having trodden down some wheat, ought to have been beheaded by the terms of the order; but here is his hair cut off as an attack on the head."

This deed was a stimulus to discipline all through the army so that not a man dared to be disobedient. A poet wrote:

> *A myriad soldiers march along and all are brave and bold,*
> *And their myriad inclinations by one leader are controlled.*
> *That crafty leader shore his locks when forfeit was his head,*
> *Oh full of schemes wert thou, Cao Cao, as every one has said.*

On hearing of the approach of Cao Cao and his army, Zhang Xiu wrote to Liu Biao for help. Then he led his men out of the city under the command of two officers named Lei Xu and Zhang Xian. When the deployment was complete Zhang Xiu took his position in front and pointing at Cao Cao he railed: "You shameless hypocrite! You are no different from a beast!"

This put Cao Cao in a rage and he sent out Xu Chu to give battle. Zhang Xian came to meet him but fell in the third bout. His soldiers fled and were pursued to the very walls of Nanyang, only managing to get inside just before the pursuit closed in. The city was then closely besieged. Seeing that the moat was very wide and deep and an approach to the wall would be difficult, they began to fill up the ditch with earth. Then with sand bags, brushwood, and bundles of grass they built a great mound near the wall so that they could look over into the city.

Cao Cao rode around the city carefully, inspecting the defense in the city. Three days later he issued an order to make a mound of earth and brushwood at the northwest angle, as he would mount the walls at that point. However, little did he know that he was observed from within the city by Jia Xu, who went to his chief and said, "I know what Cao Cao intends to do and I can defeat him by turning his trick on himself."

Even amongst the strongest there is one who excels;
Someone sees through your trick, as crafty as you he is.

What countermove Jia Xu had in mind will be told in the next chapter.

CHAPTER EIGHTEEN

Jia Xu Engineers a Great Victory
Xiahou Dun Loses An Eye

At the close of the last chapter it was told that Jia Xu had guessed Cao Cao's intention and had also devised a counter-move. He said to his master, "I saw Cao Cao very carefully reconnoitering the city and he certainly noticed that the southeast corner of the wall had been lately restored with mud bricks, which look quite new and that the abatis is badly out of repair. He will try to force an entrance there. But to fool us he is making a feint attack at the northwest point. He is piling up straw and making ostentatious preparations there in order to cajole us into withdrawing from the real point of attack and to defend the northwest. His men will scale the walls in the dark and try to enter at the southeast."

"Suppose your hunch is correct, what must we do?" asked Zhang Xiu.

"This is easy. You issue an order for our best and bravest soldiers to have a hearty meal, take only the lightest equipment, and conceal themselves in the houses near the southeast corner. Then disguise the townspeople as soldiers and send them to pretend to defend the northwest. Tonight we will let the enemy climb up the walls and enter the city and, once they are inside, give the signal and the concealed soldiers will rush out upon them. We may even capture Cao Cao himself."

The stratagem appealed very much to Zhang Xiu and he decided to adopt it. Soon scouts reported to Cao Cao that the defenders of the city had moved to the northwest, where noisy preparations for defense were going on. The opposite corner was left undefended.

"They have fallen into my trap," said Cao Cao gleefully.

He told his men to secretly prepare shovels and hooks and all the gear needed for scaling the walls, and at the same time kept up the attack on the northwest corner all day.

But at the second watch they dispatched the veterans to the opposite corner, where they climbed the wall, broke up the abatis and got into the city, apparently without disturbing any of the guards. There was no sign of life anywhere as they entered. But just as they were leaving the wall, suddenly a bomb exploded and they found themselves in an ambush. They turned to retreat, but Zhang Xiu immediately fell on the rear. Cao Cao's men were totally defeated and fled out of the gate into the country. Zhang Xiu kept up the pursuit till daybreak, when he withdrew into the city again.

Cao Cao then rallied his army and mustered his men. He had lost 50,000 men and much baggage, while two of his captains, Lu Qian and Yue Jin, were wounded.

Cao Cao being thus worsted, Zhang Xiu wrote to Liu Biao to urge him to cut off his retreat so that he might be utterly destroyed.

Liu Biao was beginning to prepare an army for this purpose when a scout came to say that Sun Ce had encamped at the mouth of the river. His advisor Kuai Liang proposed that the expedition depart immediately, arguing that Sun Ce's move was part of Cao Cao's strategy to pose an appearance of threat so as to discourage them from pursuing him.

"Cao Cao would certainly come to our harm if he were allowed to escape this time," concluded Kuai Liang.

Therefore Liu Biao moved out with his army to camp at Anzhong to block Cao Cao's way of retreat, leaving Huang Zu behind to hold firmly the point of vantage. Zhang Xiu, having been informed of his ally's movement, went with Jia Xu to smite Cao Cao once more.

In the meantime Cao Cao's army, marching at a slow pace, had arrived at the Yu River. Suddenly he uttered a great cry, and when his officers asked him the reason, he replied, "I remember that it was here, only a year ago, that I lost my great warrior Dian Wei. I cannot hold back my tears."

Therefore he gave orders to halt while he administered a solemn memorial service to lament over his lost hero. At the ceremony he himself burned incense and wailed and bowed. The army was much affected by his devotion. After that he offered sacrifices to his deceased nephew and his eldest son, as well as all his lost soldiers—and even his steed, which had been killed by an arrow.

The next day a messenger sent by Xun Yu came from the capital with the news that Liu Biao had gone to Zhang Xiu's assistance and was camped at Anzhong, thereby cutting his road of retreat. In his letter to his advisor Cao Cao stated: "I have been marching only a short distance each day and of course knew of the pursuit. But my plans are laid and, as I get near Anzhong, my enemy will be broken. You need not have any fears."

Then he hastened his march till he came close to where Liu Biao had taken up position. Zhang Xiu still followed. During the night, Cao Cao ordered his men to open a secret way through a pass, where he laid an ambush.

With the first light of dawn the two armies of Liu Biao and Zhang Xiu met. As Cao Cao's force looked small, they thought he had escaped so they boldly advanced into the pass to smite him. All at once the ambushed soldiers rushed out and both the attackers' forces were badly mauled. The fighting ended, Cao Cao's men left the pass and encamped.

Meanwhile, the two defeated leaders collected together their beaten men and held a conference.

"How come we fell for his wicked ruse?" said Liu Biao in disbelief.

"We will try to get him again," replied his colleague.

And so they joined forces at Anzhong.

But at that time Xun Yu discovered through his spies that Yuan Shao was preparing an attack on the capital, so he at once wrote to Cao Cao who, much disturbed by this news, set out homeward at once. When Zhang Xiu heard this through his scouts he wanted to follow the retreating army. Jia Xu strongly opposed the idea and said it would surely lead to a defeat. However, Liu Biao was also of the opinion that it was wrong to lose such a chance and so finally pursuit was decided upon.

They had not marched very far before they came upon Cao Cao's rear force, who fought with great vigor and bravery, so that the pursuers were beaten off and returned home discomfited.

Zhang Xiu said to Jia Xu, "This defeat comes from my not following your advice."

"Now set your army in order and pursue," said Jia Xu.

"But we have just suffered defeat!" cried both leaders. "Do you now want us to pursue again?"

"Yes, and the result will be a great victory if you go immediately. I will guarantee that with my head."

Zhang Xiu was persuaded but his colleague was unconvinced and would not accompany him. So only one army started in pursuit.

However, this was enough. Cao Cao's rear force was thoroughly routed and abandoned their wagons and their baggage in their hasty flight. Zhang Xiu pursued, but suddenly a troop came out from behind some hills and checked him. Fearful to push further, he hastened back to Anzhong.

Feeling quite confused, Liu Biao asked the adviser to explain his apparent inconsistency. "When our veteran and brave soldiers were going to pursue those who retreated you said our men would lose the day; and when our defeated men pursued the victors you predicted victory. You were right in both cases, but I hope you would enlighten me as to how?"

"It is easy to explain. You, generals, although skilled leaders, are not a match for Cao Cao. Though he had lost a battle he would certainly place able warriors in the rear to guard against pursuit. Our men are good, but not a match for them. That was how I knew we would be defeated. Now Cao Cao's hurried retreat can only be interpreted by trouble in the capital and after he had beaten off our men, I knew he would retreat at his utmost speed and not take his usual precautions. I ventured to take advantage of his laxity."

Liu Biao and Zhang Xiu could not but admire his wisdom.

On the advice of Jia Xu, Liu Biao returned to Jingzhou, while Zhang Xiu took up his position at the neighboring Xiangcheng, so that each strengthened the other as the lips protect the teeth.

When Cao Cao, during his retreat, heard that his army was being pursued he hastily turned back to support the rear. By then, however, the pursuing army had already drawn off. The defeated men said: "Had it not been for the troop that came out of the hills we would all have been captured."

"What troop?" asked Cao Cao in surprise.

The leader of the troop, taking his spear and dismounting, came forward to bow to Cao Cao and introduced himself as Li Tong, an officer of some rank.

Cao Cao asked him where his troop was stationed.

Li Tong replied, "I am holding the nearby city of Runan. When I heard of the battle, sir, I came specially to lend you any help I could."

To show his gratitude Cao Cao conferred upon him an honorable title and commanded him to guard the region west of Runan as a defense against Zhang Xiu and Liu Biao. Then Li Tong thanked him and took his leave.

On his return to the capital, Cao Cao offered a memorial on the good services rendered by Sun Ce, who was duly created Lord of Wu as well as General-Captor of Rebels. The envoy bearing the decree to the south bore also an order urging Sun Ce to subdue any attack from Liu Biao.

Cao Cao went to his house, where he received the ceremonial calls of his subordinates. These finished, Xun Yu asked, "You, sir, marched very leisurely to Anzhong; how come that you felt certain of victory?"

Cao Cao replied, "He who finds his retreat cut off will fight desperately. I went slowly to entice them into following so that I could smite them. Basing my movement on these considerations I felt secure."

Xun Yu bowed to him in admiration.

Just then Guo Jia entered. "Why are you so late?" asked his master.

The late comer drew a letter from his sleeve and said: "Yuan Shao has sent you this in which he says he desires to attack Gongsun Zan and wishes to borrow provisions and men from you."

"I heard he was going to attack the capital—I suppose my return has made him change his mind," said Cao Cao.

Then he opened the letter and read it. It was couched in very arrogant language.

"He is so exceedingly rude that I wish to attack him," said Cao Cao to Guo Jia. "Only I think I am not quite strong enough. What should be done?"

Guo Jia replied, "My lord, you know well who lost, and why, in the conflict between Liu Bang and Xiang Yu; the former won only by superior strategies. Xiang Yu was the stronger, but in the end he was overcome. Your rival has ten weak points, whereas you have ten strong ones. Although his army is large, it is not irresistible.

"Yuan Shao is too caught up in ceremony and show while you, on the other hand, are more practical. He is often antagonistic and tends to force things, whereas you are more conciliatory and try to guide things to their proper courses, giving you the advantage of popular support. His extravagance hinders his administrative ability while your better efficiency is a great contribution to the government, granting you the edge of a well-structured and stable administration. On the outside he is very kind and giving but on the inside he is grudging and suspicious. You are just the opposite, appearing very exacting but actually very understanding of your followers' strengths and weaknesses. This grants you the benefit of tolerance. He lacks commitment where you are unfaltering in your decisions, promptly acting on your plans with full faith that they will succeed. This shows an advantage in strategy and decisiveness. He believes a man is only as good as his reputation, which contrasts with you, who looks beyond this to see what kind of person they really are. This demonstrates that you are a better judge of moral character. He only pays attention to those followers close to him, while your vision is all-encompassing. This shows your superior supervision. He is easily misled by poor advice, whereas you maintain sound judgment even if beset by evil council. This is a sign of your independence of thought. He does not always know what is right and wrong but you have an unwavering sense of justice. This shows how you excel in discipline. He has a massive army, but the men are poorly trained and not ready for war. Your army, though much smaller, is far superior and well provisioned, giving you the edge in planning and logistics, allowing you to execute effectively. With your ten superiorities you will have no difficulty in subduing Yuan Shao."

"How can I be worth as much as you say?" said Cao Cao, smiling.

"What he says agrees exactly with what I think," said Xun Yu. "Yuan Shao's army is not formidable in spite of its size."

"The really dangerous enemy is Lu Bu," said Guo Jia. "Since Yuan Shao is going north to destroy Gongsun Zan, we ought to strike at Lu Bu and so clear away the threat from that side, which is a better policy. Otherwise if we attack Yuan Shao, Lu Bu will seize the opportunity to make an attempt on the capital. That would be disastrous."

Cao Cao agreed with his advisors and began to discuss with them plans for an attack on Lu Bu. Xun Yu was of the opinion that they should first secure the fidelity and aid of Liu Bei before taking any action. So a letter was dispatched to Liu Bei while they waited for his assurance of aid. Then, in order to pacify Yuan Shao, his emissary was treated with great kindness and a decree obtained from the Emperor to confer extra honors on him, creating him governor of the four prefectures in the north. A private letter was also sent to him approving his attack on Gongsun Zan and promising assistance. Yuan Shao was very pleased with Cao Cao's reply and his army set out.

Let us now shift our attention to Lu Bu in Xuzhou. Chen Deng and his father, secret allies of Cao Cao, were playing their game. At every feast and gathering they would utter the most extravagant compliments of Lu Bu. Chen Gong was greatly displeased and took an opportunity to talk about this to his master. "These two flatter you to your face, but it is hard to tell what they harbor in their hearts. You ought to be more careful on your guard."

"Hold your tongue!" was the angry reply. "You are simply slandering them without the slightest cause. Do you want to harm good men?"

"He turns a deaf ear to loyal words and we will suffer," sighed Chen Gong as he went away, sad at heart.

He thought seriously of abandoning Lu Bu, but that would be too painful a wrench. Besides, he feared people would mock him.

So the days passed sorrowfully for him. One day, with a few horsemen, he rode out to the country near Xiaopei to hunt. On the high road he saw a messenger galloping along in hot haste and began to wonder what it might mean. He gave up the hunt, rode across the country and intercepted the rider.

"Where are you from? Who sent you?" asked Chen Gong.

The messenger was too terrified to reply, for he knew to which party his captors belonged. Chen Gong ordered his men to search him and found a letter, the secret reply to Cao Cao's letter from Liu Bei. The messenger and the letter were both taken straight to Lu Bu. He questioned the man, who said he had been sent by the prime minister to Liu Bei with a letter and was now taking back the reply. He was ignorant of the content of the letter. Lu Bu tore it open and read it.

The letter said, "I have received your command concerning the destruction of Lu Bu and never for a moment dare I venture to disregard it. But my force is weak and I must act with extreme discretion. If you move your main body, then I will hasten forward as the van and in the meantime my men will be getting ready and weapons prepared. I await your command."

Lu Bu was furious. "That wretch Cao Cao!" he cried. "How dare he act thus!"

The unhappy messenger was put to death and counter-moves planned. Chen Gong and Zang Ba, together with the outlaws in the Taishan Mountains, were ordered to take Yanzhou in Shandong. Gao Shun and Zhang Liao were to attack Liu Bei in Xiaopei. Two other officers were to go and conquer the west regions. Lu Bu himself took command of the center force ready to offer help wherever needed.

The departure of the army under Gao Shun and Zhang Liao against Xiaopei was reported to Liu Bei, who at once assembled his men for a council. Sun Qian suggested sending an urgent message to inform Cao Cao of their danger and his advice was accepted. In response to the chief's call, Jian Yong, a fellow townsman of Liu Bei's, offered to take the message. So a letter was written and the man set out at once on his journey.

At the same time preparations were made for defense. The four gates of the city were to be defended by the three brothers and Sun Qian, while the center force was left in the care of Mi Zhu and his brother. These two were Liu Bei's brothers-in-law, he having taken their sister as a second wife. Hence they were suitable men to guard the family.

In due course Gao Shun came up to the south gate. Liu Bei ascended the tower and asked, "I have nothing against your master. Why do you come here with an army?"

"You have plotted with Cao Cao to injure my master. Now your treachery is exposed and you had better surrender."

So saying, he gave the signal to attack. But Liu Bei only kept the gate closed tight.

The next day Zhang Liao led an attack on the west gate, which was protected by Guan Yu, who addressed him from the wall. "You appear no ordinary figure. Why waste yourself on a rascal?" he asked.

Zhang Liao hung his head and made no reply.

Knowing that he was a man of loyalty and high principles, Guan Yu said no more, as he was unwilling to wound him. Nor did he go out to attack.

Zhang Liao then drew off and proceeded to the east gate, and Zhang Fei went out to give battle. This was immediately reported to Guan Yu, who came over quickly. He saw Zhang Fei going out, but Zhang Liao was already withdrawing. Zhang Fei wished to pursue, but his brother held him back.

"He's afraid and so has gone away—we'd better pursue," said Zhang Fei.

"No," said his brother. "As a warrior he's not inferior to either of us, but I've tried to move him with straight words and they've sunk deep. He's repentant now and that's why he won't fight with us."

Zhang Fei understood. He ordered the soldiers to firmly guard the gate and did not go out to give battle.

When Liu Bei's messenger reached the capital, he went to see Cao Cao and told him what had happened. Cao Cao called in his advisors and said to them, "I wish to attack Lu Bu. I do not fear Yuan Shao, but Liu Biao and Zhang Xiu may attack me in the rear."

Xun Yu said, "These two have been too recently defeated to do something so rash. But Lu Bu is a remarkable fighting man, and if he joins forces with Yuan Shu and they set themselves to conquer the Huai and Si regions, it will be difficult to overcome him."

Then Guo Jia said, "Let us seize the present moment when his allies have not yet made up their minds. Smite before they are fully prepared."

Cao Cao assented. Fifty thousand men led by the Xiahou brothers and two other officers were sent in advance, while Cao Cao followed with the main force. Jian Yong also went with them.

Soon scouts informed Gao Shun of Cao Cao's movements. He at once relayed it to Lu Bu, who dispatched three officers and two hundred cavalry to assist him and ordered him to post his army thirty *li* from the city to meet Cao Cao's army. He himself followed with the major body.

When Liu Bei saw the enemy retreating from the city, he knew Cao Cao's army was close at hand. So, leaving only the Mi brothers and Sun Qian to guard the city and his home, he and his two brothers marched all their men out of the city and made a camp so that they might be ready to assist Cao Cao.

Now the division of Cao Cao's army under Xiahou Dun, having marched out in advance, arrived first and came upon Gao Shun. He at once rode out with spear set and offered a challenge. Gao Shun accepted and the two leaders fought half a hundred bouts. Then Gao Shun began to weaken and turned to ride back to his own army. His adversary pressed him hard and he fled to the rear of his army. Xiahou Dun still gave chase and followed him right into the enemy's country. At this moment, Cao

Xing, another of Lu Bu's officers, secretly took his bow, fitted an arrow and, when Xiahou Dun had come quite near, shot at him. The arrow hit him full in the left eye. He cried out in pain, and reaching up, pulled out the arrow, and with it the eye.

"Essence of my father, blood of my mother, I cannot throw this away," he cried, and he put the eye into his mouth and swallowed it.

Then, resuming a firm grip of his spear, he charged after this new enemy. There was no escape for Cao Xing. He was overtaken and fell with a spear wound full in the face. Soldiers on both sides were stricken dumb with amazement.

Having thus slain the man who had wounded him, Xiahou Dun rode back toward his own side. Guo Sheng went in pursuit and, waving on his men, attacked so vigorously that he won the day. Xiahou Yuan came to the rescue of his elder brother, and both fled. The defeated army retreated to Jibei and encamped there.

Having scored this victory, Gao Shun returned to attack Liu Bei. And as Lu Bu opportunely also arrived with Zhang Liao, these three joined forces to attack the three brothers.

> *Dauntless was Dun, that warrior bold,*
> *His courage had been proved of old;*
> *But smitten sore one hapless day,*
> *He might not in the battle stay.*

The fate of Liu Bei will be told in the next chapter.

CHAPTER NINETEEN

Cao Cao Assembles His Forces at Xiapi
Lu Bu Perishes at the White Gate Tower

At the close of the last chapter, the three brothers were being attacked by Lu Bu and his two valiant officers. Gao Shun and Zhang Liao went to smite Guan Yu, while Lu Bu attacked Zhang Fei's camp. Both brothers went out to give battle, while Liu Bei's force waited in reserve. Lu Bu divided his army and attacked from the rear and both Guan Yu and Zhang Fei were forced to flee. Liu Bei, with a few score horsemen, rushed back to Xiaopei. As he approached the gate with Lu Bu pressing hard on him, he shouted to the soldiers on the wall tower to lower the drawbridge. Lu Bu was so close behind that the archers were afraid to shoot lest they should wound their lord, and so Lu Bu got inside the gate. The guards were unable to hold him back so they scattered in all directions. Lu Bu led his force into the city.

Liu Bei saw the situation was too desperate for him to go to his residence. He had to abandon his family. He hastened through the city and escaped by the west gate. Alone on horseback, he fled for his very life.

When Lu Bu reached Liu Bei's house he was met by Mi Zhu, who said: "I hear that a great man does not harm another man's wife. Your rival for the empire is Cao Cao, and my master, always mindful of the good turn you did him when you shot the wonderful arrow from your camp, would not be ungrateful. He was forced to seek help from Cao Cao and I hope you will pity him."

Lu Bu replied, "Your master and I are old friends—how could I bear to harm his family?"

Therefore he sent Liu Bei's family to Xuzhou, with Mi Zhu to take care of them. Then he led his army into Yanzhou in Shandong, leaving Gao Shun and Zhang Liao to guard Xiaopei.

During the turmoil, Sun Qian had also managed to flee the city. Liu Bei's two younger brothers, each with a handful of men, had got away to the hills. As Liu Bei was retreating from the scene of his defeat, he heard someone coming up behind him. When he got closer the person proved to be Sun Qian.

"Alas! I don't know the fate of my brothers, whether they are alive or dead, and my family are lost to me! What can I do?" said Liu Bei.

Sun Qian replied, "I see nothing better than getting away to Cao Cao. We can plan our future moves later."

Liu Bei had no better plan to propose and the two men directed their way to the capital, choosing bypaths rather than highways. When their small supplies ran out they would enter a village to beg. Whenever his name was mentioned people vied with each other to offer all that was needed.

One day they sought shelter at a cottage. A young hunter named Liu An came out and bowed low to him. Hearing who the visitor was the hunter wished to lay before him a dish of game, but though he sought for a long time nothing could be found for the table. So he came home, killed his wife, and prepared a portion for his guest. While eating, Liu Bei asked him what meat it was. The hunter told him it was wolf. Liu Bei believed him and ate his fill. The next day at daylight, just as he was leaving, he went to the stables in the rear to get his horse, and passing through the kitchen, he suddenly saw the dead body of a woman lying on the ground. The flesh of one arm had been cut away. Quite startled, he asked what this meant, and then he knew what he had eaten the night before. He was deeply affected at this proof of his host's regard for him, and tears rained down as he mounted his steed at the gate.

"I wish I could go with you," said Liu An, "but as my mother still lives I cannot go so far from home."

Liu Bei thanked him and went away with his companions. On the road, they saw not far off a thick cloud of dust. When the troop came nearer they found they were men of Cao Cao's army, and with them they made their way to the central camp to see Cao Cao, who wept at the sad story of Liu Bei's distress, the loss of the city, his brothers, and his family. When Liu Bei told him of the hunter who had sacrificed his wife to feed them, Cao Cao sent the hunter a hundred ounces of gold as a reward.

They continued to march to Jibei, where they were welcomed to camp by Xiahou Yuan. When Cao Cao heard that his brother was still ill from the wound he had received in the eye he went to the sick man's bedside to see him, and had him removed to the capital for careful treatment.

Presently the scouts, sent out to find tidings of Lu Bu, returned to say that he had allied himself with the outlaws in the Taishan Mountains and they were launching a joint attack on Yanzhou. On hearing this, Cao Cao dispatched Cao Ren with 3,000 soldiers to take Xiaopei, while he, together with Liu Bei, moved against Lu Bu. As they came near Xiao Pass on their journey to Shandong they were stopped by the four Taishan brigands with a large force. However, they were easily beaten back and were pursued right up to the pass.

The scouts told Lu Bu, who was then back in Xuzhou and was planning to start an expedition to lift the siege at Xiao Pass, the hidden spy of Cao Cao's. He unwittingly left the protection of his city to Chen Deng's father, another of Cao Cao's men, and set out with the son.

As Chen Deng was starting out his father said to him, "Remember the words of Cao Cao, that the business of the east is in our hands. Now is the moment, as Lu Bu is about to fall."

"Don't worry, father, I'll take care of the things on the outside. But if he returns beaten you must arrange with Mi Zhu to keep him out of the city. I'll find a means of escape," said Chen Deng.

"His family is here and so are many of his trusted men. How can I avoid them?'

"I also have a scheme to settle them."

Then he went to see Lu Bu, to whom he said: "Xuzhou is surrounded and this city will be fiercely attacked. We ought to prepare for probable retreat and I think it will be wise to store grain and money in Xiapi. We could retreat there if the day went adversely. Why not see about this in good time?"

"Your words are indeed wise. I will also send my family there," said Lu Bu.

The family then left under escort and with them was sent much grain and silver. And the soldiers marched to the relief of the pass. About half way there, Chen Deng said: "Let me go to the pass first to find out how things are so that you, my lord, may advance with confidence."

Thus Chen Deng parted company with his chief and went alone to the pass, where he was received by Chen Gong. He said, "The general is greatly annoyed by your inaction. He's going to investigate it."

"The enemy is great in force and we can't be too careful," said Chen Gong. "We're holding the pass and you should persuade our master to take steps to guard Xiaopei."

Chen Deng pretended to agree. That evening he went up to the pass from where he could see Cao Cao's army below. That night he wrote three letters, tied them to arrows, and shot them into Cao Cao's camp.

The next day he left the pass and hastened back to Lu Bu. "Those bandits all want to give up the pass to the enemy, but I have left Chen Gong to hold it. You had better make an attack tonight and help him."

"Had it not been for you the pass would have been lost," said Lu Bu.

Then he sent Chen Deng back to tell Chen Gong to light a fire that night as a signal for simultaneous action. So Chen Deng returned to the pass to see Chen Gong—but to him he told a different story. He said, "Cao Cao's men have found a secret way through the pass and I fear Xuzhou is in grave danger. You ought to go back at once."

At this news the pass was abandoned. Chen Gong began to turn back toward Xuzhou. After he was gone, Chen Deng lit a fire on top of the pass.

Lu Bu advanced under the cover of darkness to reclaim the pass. Presently he bumped into Chen Gong's men, and as neither recognized the other in the dark, a fierce battle ensued among themselves. Nor was the trick discovered till daylight came.

While these things were going on, Cao Cao noted the signal fire and advanced as fast as possible. The outlaws from the mountains, who alone remained to hold the pass, were easily driven out and they scattered in all directions.

When daylight came and Chen Deng's trick was exposed, Lu Bu and Chen Gong set off together for Xuzhou. But when they arrived and summoned the guards to open the gate, there came instead a thick shower of arrows. At the same time Mi Zhu appeared on the defense tower and shouted, "You stole my master's city and it must be returned to him now. You must not enter here again."

"Where is Chen Gui?" cried Lu Bu in wrath.

"I have slain him," was the reply.

"Where is that son of his?" said Lu Bu, turning to Chen Gong.

"Do you still hold to your delusion, general, that you ask where this specious rogue is?"

Lu Bu bade his men search throughout the ranks, but he was not to be found. Then they decided to go to Xiaopei. But before they had got halfway, there suddenly appeared the troops under the command of Gao Shun and Zhang Liao.

"Why are you here?" asked Lu Bu.

They replied, "Chen Deng came to tell us that you had been surrounded and wanted help, so we came at once."

"Another trick of that false rogue!" said Chen Gong.

"I will not let him live!" roared Lu Bu indignantly.

They went with all speed to Xiaopei, only to find as they drew near the ensigns of the enemy displayed all along the walls, for the city had been taken by Cao Ren on Cao Cao's orders.

While Lu Bu stood at the foot of the rampart reviling the traitor, Chen Deng himself appeared on the wall tower. Pointing to Lu Bu, he cried:

"Did you think that I, an official of the Han Dynasty, would serve a rebel like you?"

Lu Bu in his wrath was about to make a desperate attack but suddenly a great noise was heard and an army came up behind him. It was led by none other than his old foe Zhang Fei.

Gao Shun went to engage him, but he had no chance of success. Lu Bu then joined in the fight. But at this juncture another powerful army appeared, and the leader this time was Cao Cao himself, and his men rushed to the attack. Aware that he had no hope of victory, Lu Bu went away toward the east, with Cao Cao in pursuit. His army marched till they were quite worn out yet still another force appeared before them under the command of Guan Yu. Holding his sword ready to strike he called out: "Do not try to flee, Lu Bu, Guan Yu is waiting for you."

Lu Bu hastened to combat him. Soon Zhang Fei closed in from behind. By desperate efforts Lu Bu and his men cut their way through the press and got free. After this they started for Xiapi as fast as they could. Lu Bu was joined by his officer, Hou Cheng, who helped keep the pursuers at bay.

So the two brothers, Guan Yu and Zhang Fei, were together again after their separation. Both shed tears of joy as they told each other what had happened.

"I was on the Haizhou road when I heard of the battle here," said Guan Yu. "I lost no time in coming."

"And I had been camped in the Mangdang Hills for some time. It's such great luck for us to be together again."

After this exchange of information they marched off together to find their eldest brother. It was a very moving meeting. The two younger brothers wept as they made their salutations to Liu Bei, whose heart was mixed with sadness and joy. He then presented them to Cao Cao. Together, they all went into the captured city of Xuzhou.

Mi Zhu presently came with the welcome news of the safety of the family. And the two Chens, betrayers of Lu Bu, came to pay their respects to Cao Cao. A grand banquet was prepared for the officers at which Cao Cao presided as host and Chen Gui and Liu Bei occupied the seats of honor. At the close of the banquet, Cao Cao praised most highly the merits of the two Chens and rewarded them with a very high salary, besides giving the son the title of general.

Cao Cao was very pleased with his success and at once began to plan a scheme to capture Xiapi, the sole place now left to Lu Bu, where he had taken refuge.

Cheng Yu said, "If we pressed him too hard Lu Bu might put up a desperate fight and throw himself into the arms of our arch enemy Yuan Shu. These two as allies will be difficult to overcome. Rather, we should send a capable man to guard the route to Huainan, so as to protect you against Lu Bu on the one hand and ward off Yuan Shu on the other. Moreover, some of Lu Bu's men are still at large in Shandong. We need to take precautions against them as well."

Cao Cao replied that he would clear up the whole of Shandong and asked Liu Bei to take care of the south.

"I will certainly obey your command," said Liu Bei.

So the following day Liu Bei went south with his two brothers and Sun Qian, leaving Mi Zhu and Jian Yong at Xuzhou. Meanwhile, Cao Cao led his army to besiege Xiapi.

Lu Bu felt very secure in his refuge. With his good store of grain and the protection of the river, he thought his defense was unbeatable and he could sit back and relax. So he allowed Cao Cao's army to approach without interference.

Chen Gong said, "You ought to attack Cao Cao's army before they have time to establish camps and strengthen defenses. Their soldiers will be tired and your fresh troops will certainly defeat them."

But Lu Bu only replied, "We have suffered too many defeats lately to take any risk. Wait till they actually attack and you will see them drowning in the water."

So he neglected his loyal advisor's words and waited till the enemy had settled into their camp. This done, the attackers came to the very gate of the city. From the foot of the wall Cao Cao demanded to speak to Lu Bu. At his call, Lu Bu ascended the wall tower.

Cao Cao said, "I hear that your family and that of Yuan Shu are likely to be united by marriage, so I have come with an army against you. Yuan Shu is guilty of treason while you have to your credit the destruction of Dong Zhuo. For what reason have you sacrificed all your merits to throw in your lot with a rebel? It will be too late for regrets when this city has fallen. But if you surrender and help me to support the ruling house you will win yourself the rank of a lord."

Lu Bu replied, "If you will retire we may be able to discuss the matter."

But Chen Gong, standing beside his master, began to rail at Cao Cao, calling him a rebel, and shot an arrow that struck his plumed helmet.

"I swear I will slay you!" cried Cao Cao, outraged, pointing his finger at Chen Gong.

Then the attack on the walls began.

"They have come from afar and cannot maintain this for long," said Chen Gong. "General, you go out with your horse and foot soldiers and take up a position outside, leaving me to maintain the defense with the remainder of our men. If he engages you, I will come out and strike at his rear ranks; if he attacks the city, you can come to our aid. In a few days their supplies will be exhausted and we can beat them off easily. In this way we can aid each other and our enemy will become trapped between two horns."

"You are right," said Lu Bu.

So he went back to his residence to pack up. As it was in the depth of winter he told his attendants to pack plenty of cotton padded clothing. His wife overheard and asked him where he was going. He told her of Chen Gong's plan.

She said, "My lord, you're leaving your city, abandoning your wife, and going out all by yourself with a paltry force. Should any untoward event happen, will I ever see you again?"

Lu Bu hesitated, and for three days made no move. Then Chen Gong came to see him again and said, "The enemy are all around the city now and unless you go out soon you will be quite hemmed in."

"I think it would be better to maintain a resolute defense," said Lu Bu.

"Our enemy is short of food and has sent men to the capital for supplies. These will soon arrive and you should go out with some veterans and intercept the convoy. That loss will be a heavy blow to the enemy."

Lu Bu agreed and went to tell his wife about the new plan. She wept and said, "If you go, do you think those others equal to the defense of the city? If anything should go wrong you would be very sorry. You abandoned me at Chang'an and it was only through the kindness of Pang Shu that I was hidden from our enemies and rejoined you later. Who would have thought you would leave me again? But General, you have bright prospects before you, please don't think of your poor wife." She wept bitterly.

Lu Bu was torn by indecision and he went to tell Cicada about it. She said, "You're my lord, you mustn't be careless and ride out alone."

"Don't worry. With my mighty halberd and the Red Hare, the fastest steed in the world, who dares to come near me?" Lu Bu comforted her.

He went out to tell Chen Gong, "That story about supplies for Cao Cao is all false, one of his many ruses. I mustn't venture out."

Chen Gong sighed—he felt all was lost.

"We'll all die without a burying place," he said to himself.

From then on Lu Bu remained in his own quarters with his women folk, drinking freely to drown his sorrows. One day two of his advisors went in to see him and proposed seeking help from Yuan Shu, who had become very strong again in Huainan.

"You have previously talked about a matrimonial alliance with him, General. Why not write to him to suggest renewing the bond of marriage again? If he could send an army here, it would be easy to destroy Cao Cao," they said.

Lu Bu accepted the advice and the two advisors were sent as messengers to Yuan Shu.

They said, "We must have a strong escort with us to force a way through."

So Lu Bu sent Zhang Liao and He Meng with a thousand soldiers to conduct his messengers beyond the pass. They started that night at the second watch, with Zhang Liao leading and He Meng bringing up the rear. They got out of the city, crept past Liu Bei's camp, and got beyond the danger zone. Then half the escort went on and Zhang Liao led the remainder back toward the city. At the pass he found Guan Yu waiting. However, at that moment Gao Shun came to his assistance and they escaped to the city.

The two messengers presently reached Shouchun, paid their respects to Yuan Shu, and presented the letter.

"What is this?" said Yuan Shu. "Formerly he slew my messenger and repudiated the marriage; now he wants to ask for it again."

"It is all due to the vile plans of that monster Cao Cao. I pray you, noble sir, to consider it carefully," replied one of the messengers.

"But if your master were not hemmed in by his enemy and in imminent danger he would never have thought of renewing this proposal of marriage."

The messengers said, "As the saying goes, when the lips are gone the teeth are cold. If you do not help him now, it will not be to your benefit either."

Yuan Shu said, "Lu Bu is unreliable; tell him that I will send soldiers after the girl has arrived here."

This was final and the two messengers could not but take their leave. When the party reached Liu Bei's camp they decided to try to get through after dark, the two messengers going first while He Meng and the soldiers bringing up the rear. They tried that every night and the two messengers crept across without being discovered. But the escort found their advance cut off by Zhang Fei. He Meng tried to fight but was captured in the very first bout—his five hundred men fled and many were killed.

The prisoner was taken to Liu Bei, who sent him on to the main camp, where he related the proposal of marriage and the scheme to save the city. Cao Cao was angry and ordered the execution of the prisoner at the main gate.

Then he sent orders to each camp to exercise the greatest diligence, with threats of rigorous punishment for any officers that permitted any communication between the besieged and the outer world.

All were quite intimidated. Liu Bei returned to camp and cautioned his brothers. "We are guarding the very route to Huainan and you must be extremely careful not to allow any breach of this command."

Zhang Fei was angry. "We've just captured one enemy officer," he said, "and there's no word of praise or reward for us but new orders and threats. What do you make of that?'

"You're wrong to complain," said Liu Bei. "He has a huge army to command and must rule by strict discipline. Otherwise how can he control such a force? Don't disobey him, brothers."

They promised obedience and withdrew.

In the meantime the messengers had got back to Lu Bu and told him what Yuan Shu had said, and that the army would come only after the girl was sent.

"How can she be sent?" asked Lu Bu.

"That is the difficulty. He Meng's capture means that Cao Cao knows the whole plan of getting help from the south. I do not see how anyone but you could hope to get through the siege lines."

"Suppose we try today?" said Lu Bu.

"This is an ill-omened day—you must not go today. Tomorrow is a very lucky day, especially in the night, for any military action."

Then Lu Bu ordered Zhang Liao and Gao Shun to get ready 3,000 soldiers for the venture and to prepare a light carriage. He would lead for the first two hundred *li*. Then they would escort the bride-elect the remainder of the way to her new home.

The next night, toward the second watch, Lu Bu wrapped up his daughter in soft cotton, bound her about with a mailed coat, and carried her on his back. Then with his mighty halberd in hand, he mounted his steed and rode at the head of the cavalcade out of the city gate. The two officers followed.

In this way they approached Liu Bei's camp. The drums at once beat the alarm and the two younger brothers barred the way.

"Stop!" they shouted.

Lu Bu had no desire to fight—all he wished to was to get through, so he made for a side road. Liu Bei also came in pursuit and the two parties engaged. Brave as he was, Lu Bu was hampered by a girl on his back, whom he was desperately anxious to shield from hurt. Soon, two of Cao Cao's most powerful officers rushed forth to attack him and he had no alternative but to give up his project and return into the city. The besiegers returned to camp well pleased that no one had got beyond their lines. After this Lu Bu became even more depressed and found consolation only in the wine cup.

The siege had gone on for two months and still the city held. At this time reports came to say that Zhang Yang, Prefect of Henei, had been inclined to come to the help of Lu Bu. But one of his subordinates had assassinated him and was bringing his head as an offering to Cao Cao when he also was slain by one of the prefect's friends. The man had then fled. Hearing this report, Cao Cao ordered an officer to chase and slay the escaped man. Then he called a general council, at which all his advisors were present.

Cao Cao said, "Though it is rather fortunate for us that Zhang Yang, who meant to hurt us, is no more, yet we are still threatened in the north by Yuan Shao and to the east by Liu Biao and Zhang Xiu. We are stuck here with no success against the city. I think we should leave Lu Bu to his fate for the time being and return home. What do you say to this?'

Xun Yu at once objected. "You must not act like this," he said. "Lu Bu has lost many battles and his fighting spirit is broken. The spirit of the leader expresses that of his men, and when the leader fails his men have no desire to fight. Chen Gong is clever but it is too late for him to do anything. Now that Lu Bu has not regained his vigor and Chen Gong has not come up with a better scheme, it only needs a speedy attack and we will win."

Guo Jia said, "I have a plan to overcome the city at once—a plan better than having 200,000 men."

"I suppose you mean to drown the city," said Xun Yu.

"That's it," said Guo Jia, smiling.

Cao Cao embraced the suggestion with joy and set his men to cut the banks of the Yi and Si rivers. He moved his men to the high ground, from where they watched the city of Xiapi become submerged in water. Only the east gate tower remained clear of water.

The besieged soldiers hastened to inform their leader. But Lu Bu was not alarmed. "Why should I fear?" he said. "My good horse can go as well through water as over land." And he again returned to the wine cup for consolation, drinking deeply with his wife and concubine.

The continual drinking bouts told at last and Lu Bu began to look haggard. Seeing himself in a mirror one day he was startled at the change. "I am injuring myself with too much wine; no more drink from this day onward."

He then issued an order to forbid the drinking of wine under penalty of death.

Now one of his officers, Hou Cheng, had fifteen horses stolen by his stablemen, who intended to give them to Liu Bei. The thieves were eventually slain and the horses retrieved. His colleagues came to congratulate him on this. To celebrate the occasion he brewed some wine, intending to have a good drink with his guests. However, he was afraid that his chief might accuse him of disorder, so he sent several bottles of wine to his place and said, "By virtue of your renown I have recovered my horses. My colleagues have come to share my joy and I have prepared a little wine for this occasion. But I dare not drink it without your permission. So I have come to present you some to show my respect to you."

Lu Bu responded angrily and said, "I have just forbidden drinking, yet you dare to brew wine and give a wine party. Are you plotting against me?" Then he ordered the officer to be instantly executed. However, a number of his colleagues came in to plead for him and after a time Lu Bu softened.

"You ought to lose your head for this deliberate disobedience, but for the sake of your colleagues the punishment will be reduced to a hundred strokes."

They tried to beg him off this, but only succeeded in reducing the number of blows to fifty.

When the sentence had been carried out and the offender was permitted to return home, his colleagues came sadly to console him.

"Hadn't it been for you I would've been put to death," said Hou Cheng.

Song Xian said, "All he cares for is his women, there's no pity for any one else. We're no more than the weeds by the roadside."

Wei Xu said, "The city's besieged and the water's drowning us out. We can't take much more of this, for we may die any day."

"He's cruel and faithless. Let's leave him," proposed Song Xian.

"That's not a good policy. Rather, let's seize him and hand him over to Cao Cao," said Wei Xu.

"I was punished because I got my horses back again, yet he counts on his own steed for success. If you two will open the gate and seize Lu Bu, I'll steal his Red Hare and present it to Cao Cao."

They settled on how to carry out the plot. That very night, Hou Cheng sneaked into the stable and made away with the Red Hare. He hastened to the east gate, which was opened by Wei Xu, who then made a pretense of pursuing him.

Hou Cheng reached Cao Cao's camp, presented the horse, and told him what had been arranged. His two colleagues would show a white flag as a signal and open the gates to his army. Hearing this, Cao Cao had scores of notifications written out, which were attached to arrows and shot over the walls. This is one of them: "General Cao Cao has received a command from the Emperor to destroy Lu Bu. Those who interfere with the operations of his grand army, whatever their rank, will be put to death, together with his whole family on the day that the city is captured. Should any one capture Lu Bu or bring his head he will be well rewarded. Let all take note of this."

The next day at daylight a tremendous hubbub was heard outside the city and Lu Bu, halberd in hand, hastened out to see what it meant. As he went from gate to gate inspecting the defenses, he blamed Wei Xian for letting Hou Cheng escape and get away with his fine horse. He threatened to punish him. But just then the besiegers began a fierce attack as the white flag had appeared and Lu Bu was forced to turn all his energy to defense. The assault lasted till noon, when the attacking force drew off for a time.

Lu Bu took a short rest in the tower and fell asleep in his chair. Song Xian sent away his attendants, and when they had gone he stole his master's weapon, the powerful halberd. Then he and Wei Xu fell upon Lu Bu together, and before he was fully awake had bound him with cords, trussing him up so that he could not move. Lu Bu shouted for his men, but they were driven off by the two traitors and could not come close. Then a white flag was shown and the besiegers again approached the city. The traitors shouted out that Lu Bu was a prisoner. But Xiahou Yuan could hardly believe it till they threw down the famous halberd.

The gates were flung open and the enemy entered the city. Gao Shun and Zhang Liao, who were at the west gate, were surrounded by water and could not get out. They were captured. Chen Gong made a dash to the south gate but was also taken. Presently, Cao Cao entered the city and at once gave orders to turn the streams back into their usual courses. Then he put out proclamations to soothe the people.

He and Liu Bei seated themselves side by side in the White Gate tower, with Guan Yu and Zhang Fei in attendance. The captives were brought before them. Lu Bu looked pitiable. Although a very tall man he was tied up in a veritable bundle.

"The bonds are too tight," he cried. "Pray loosen them."

"A tiger must be bound tight," replied Cao Cao.

Seeing the three traitors standing by, Lu Bu asked: "I treated you all well enough—how could you turn against me?"

Song Xian said, "You listened to the words of your women, but rejected the advice of your men. Was that what you mean by 'well enough'?"

Lu Bu was silent. Then Gao Shun was brought forward.

"What have you to say?" asked Cao Cao.

Gao Shun sulkily held his tongue and was ordered out to be executed. Next Chen Gong was led in.

"I hope you have been well since we last saw each other, sir?" asked Cao Cao.

"Your ways were crooked and so I left you," said Chen Gong.

"You say my ways were crooked—why then do you serve Lu Bu?"

"Though he is no strategist, he is not deceitful and wicked as you are."

"You say you are wise and resourceful. What about your situation now?'

Turning toward Lu Bu, Chen Gong said, "This man would not follow my advice. Had he done so we would not now be your captives."

"What do you say to that?" asked Cao Cao.

"There is death for me today and that is the end," shouted Chen Gong.

"Very well for you—but what of your mother and your wife?"

"It is said that he who rules with due regard to filial piety does not harm a man's family; and he who governs by benevolence does not cut off the sacrifices at a man's tomb. My mother and my wife are in your hands. Since I have been taken prisoner I beg you to slay me at once. I am ready to die."

Cao Cao's heart still leaned toward mercy, but Chen Gong turned and walked away, repulsing the attendants who would stop him. Cao Cao rose from his seat to escort him with tears in his eyes. But Chen Gong never even looked back. Turning to his men Cao Cao said, "Let his mother and family be taken to the capital at once and be well looked after. Whoever dares to show negligence will die."

Chen Gong heard him but uttered no words. He stretched out his neck to receive the blow. Tears sprang to the eyes of all present. His remains were honorably buried in the capital.

A poem lamenting his fate said:

> *Neither in life nor in death did he yield.*
> *How dauntless was he, a hero indeed!*
> *But his lord heeded not his words,*
> *In vain he possessed great talents.*
> *His loyalty deserves our respect*
> *And his loss to his family our pity.*
> *Who could be as brave as he was*
> *That day he died at the White Gate?*

While Cao Cao sadly escorted Chen Gong on his way to death, Lu Bu appealed to Liu Bei: "Noble sir, you sit there an honored guest while I lie bound at your feet. Will you not utter a word to alleviate my state?'

Liu Bei nodded. As Cao Cao returned to his place his prisoner called out: "Your only worry, sir, is myself and I am now willing to obey you. You command and I will help you. Together the world will be at our feet."

"What do you think?" said Cao Cao, turning to Liu Bei.

"You are willing to forget the episodes of Ding Yuan and Dong Zhuo?'

"Truly you are not the most faithless," said Lu Bu, looking at Liu Bei.

"Strangle him," said Cao Cao.

As he was led away the prisoner turned once more to Liu Bei: "You long -eared rogue! You forget now how my arrow hit the mark and saved you!"

Just then someone shouted, "Lu Bu, you coward! Death is but death. What is there to be so scared of?"

Everyone turned to look—the guards were hustling in Zhang Liao.

Lu Bu was strangled to death and then beheaded.

A poet wrote the following upon the death of Lu Bu:

> *The flood spreads wide, the city drowns,*
> *The day its lord is made captive,*
> *Leaving aside his steed of a thousand* li *a day*
> *And his powerful halberd that scares everyone away.*
> *The tiger erstwhile so fierce and so proud,*
> *Now whines meekly for mercy to be shown.*
> *Little did he doubt of the traitor's words*
> *Of a falcon flown at will and hungry kept.*
> *Unable to resist the tearful plea of his wife*
> *Poor fool! He ignored Chen Gong's wise advice.*
> *In vain he now rails against the long-eared Liu Bei*
> *For his lack of gratitude and faith.*

And another poem said this of Liu Bei:

> *Bound tightly is the hungry tiger, eater of men,*
> *Since the blood of his victims is fresh and not yet dry.*
> *Liu Bei spoke no word in favor of Lu Bu,*
> *To whom even a father's life was not sacred.*
> *How could he save him to be a menace to Cao Cao?*

It was recorded earlier that the executioners were hustling Zhang Liao forward. Pointing to him as he stood there, Cao Cao said, "His face is familiar."

"You were not likely to forget me; we met before in the city of Puyang," said Zhang Liao.

"So you remember it too?"

"Yes, more is the pity."

"Pity for what?'

"That the fire that day was not fierce enough to burn you to death, you rebel."

Cao Cao began to get angry. "How dare you insult me?" he cried and lifted his sword to kill the bold speaker.

The undaunted Zhang Liao never changed color, but stretched out his neck for the blow. Then a man behind Cao Cao caught his arm and in front of him another dropped to his knees. They pleaded, "Oh, sir, please stay your hand."

> *Lu Bu whining was not spared,*
> *Railing Zhang Liao far better fared.*

Who pleaded with Cao Cao for Zhang Liao's life will be told in the next chapter.

CHAPTER TWENTY

Cao Cao Goes Hunting at Xutian
Dong Cheng Receives a Secret Decree in the Palace

The last chapter said that Cao Cao was checked in his angry attack upon Zhang Liao. It was Liu Bei who held his arm and Guan Yu who knelt before him.

"A man as loyal-hearted as he is should be saved," said Liu Bei.

Guan Yu said, "I have always known him as loyal and righteous. I will vouch for him with my own life."

Cao Cao threw aside his sword. "I also know him to be a man of loyalty and goodness—I was just testing him," he said.

He loosed the prisoner's bonds with his own hands, took off his own robe, and placed it around his shoulders. Then he led him to a seat of honor. This kindly treatment touched Zhang Liao's heart and he yielded. So he was given a rank and a title and was sent on a mission to win over Zang Ba who, hearing what had happened, came forthwith and offered his submission. He was graciously received and in his turn, he brought in several of his former colleagues, with the exception of Cang Xi, who remained obstinate. All these former enemies who came over were kindly treated and given posts of responsibility. Lu Bu's family were sent to the capital.

After the soldiers had been rewarded with feasts the camp was broken up and the army moved back. Passing through Xuzhou the local people lined the roads and burned incense in honor of the victors. They also petitioned that Liu Bei should be their governor.

Cao Cao replied: "Liu Bei has rendered great services. You must wait till he has received an audience with the Emperor and obtained his reward. After that he will be sent here."

Then he left a major officer of his to be in command of Xuzhou for the moment. When the army arrived at the capital, rewards were granted to all those who had been in the expedition. Liu Bei was retained in the capital, lodging in an annex to his residence. The next day at court, Cao

Cao celebrated the services of Liu Bei and presented him to Emperor Xian. Dressed in court robes, Liu Bei bowed at the lower end of the audience arena. The Emperor called him into the hall and asked him about his ancestry.

Liu Bei replied, "Your humble servant is the son of Liu Hong, grandson of Liu Xiong, who was a direct descendant of Prince Jin of Zhongshan, who was a son of His Majesty Emperor Jing."

The Emperor told his secretary to bring forth the *Book of Genealogy*. Consequently Liu Bei's royal origin was proved, as the book had listed in a detailed family tree that he was, indeed, a descendant of Prince Jin of Zhongshan, who was the seventh son of the fourth Emperor Jing in West Han Dynasty.

The Emperor compared this with the registers of the imperial house and found by them that Liu Bei was his uncle by descent. The Emperor was greatly pleased and requested Liu Bei to go into one of the side chambers, where he might perform the ceremonial obeisance prescribed for a nephew to his uncle. In his heart he rejoiced to have this heroic warrior-uncle as a powerful supporter against Cao Cao, who really held all the power in his own hands, leaving him a mere puppet. He conferred upon his uncle the rank of general and the title of Lord of Yicheng.

When the banquet was concluded Liu Bei thanked the Emperor and went out of the palace. And from this time onwards he was generally known as Liu, the Imperial Uncle.

When Cao Cao returned to his place, Xun Yu and his fellow advisors went to see him. Xun Yu said, "It is no advantage to you, sir, that the Emperor recognizes Liu Bei as an uncle."

"He is now formally recognized as the Emperor's uncle, which only makes it easier for me to order him about in the name of the throne. He will not dare to disobey. Besides, I will keep him here under the pretense of having him near his sovereign and he will be entirely in my hands. I have nothing to fear. The man I fear is the powerful Yang Biao, who is a relative of the two Yuans. If he should conspire with them, much harm might be done. He will have to be removed at once."

Hence Cao Cao secretly ordered one of his men to accuse Yang Biao of intriguing with Yuan Shu and on this false charge the innocent man was arrested and imprisoned. He seemed to be destined to die.

But at that time Kong Yong, Prefect of Beihai, happened to be in the capital and he remonstrated with Cao Cao. "Minister Yang comes from a family famed for virtue for at least four generations. It is not right to charge him on account of the Yuans."

"It is the Emperor's idea," replied Cao Cao, trying to shift responsibility.

"In the old days, Duke Zhou,* the regent, made the young Emperor Cheng put Duke Shao to death. Could Duke Zhou have pretended ignorance?'

Cao Cao could not answer and had to relinquish, but he took away Yang Biao's office and banished him to his family estate in the country.

Indignant at Cao Cao's tyranny, a certain official sent up a petition impeaching him for having removed a high-ranking minister of the state from office without the Emperor's approval. Cao Cao's angry reply to this was the arrest of the brave man and his execution, an act that terrified all the other officials and reduced them to silence.

At Cao Cao's place, Cheng Yu advised him to take an even bolder step. He said, "Sir, your prestige is growing daily—why not seize the opportunity to take the throne?"

"There are still too many supporters of the court," said Cao Cao. "I must be careful. I am going to propose a royal hunt to try to find out the best line to follow."

The hunting expedition decided upon, his men got together swift horses, famous breeds of falcons, and pedigree hounds, and prepared bows and arrows in readiness. Moreover, a strong force of guards was mustered and positioned outside the city.

Then Cao Cao went in to propose the hunting expedition to the Emperor, who objected by saying that he feared it was an improper thing to do.

Cao Cao replied, "In ancient times rulers took four expeditions yearly, one at each of the four seasons in order to exhibit their military strength. Now that the whole country is in turmoil it would be wise to launch a hunting expedition to champion military training."

The Emperor dared not argue with him so the full paraphernalia for an imperial hunt joined the expedition. He rode a saddled horse, carried an inlaid bow, and his quiver was filled with gold-tipped arrows. His chariot followed behind. The three brothers were in the imperial train, each with a bow and quiver. Each wore a breastplate inside his robe and held his special weapon, while their escort followed them. Cao Cao rode a duncolored horse called Flying Lightning at the head of a huge procession.

The hunt took place in Xutian and the army deployed as guards around the hunting arena, which extended over some two hundred square *li*. Cao Cao rode almost side by side with the Emperor, following

---

* An important minister in West Zhou Dynasty. After the death of his brother, Emperor Wu, he became regent, helping the young emperor suppress rebellions by various lords.

only at the close distance of a horse' head. Behind them were all of Cao Cao's trusted officers. The imperial officials, civil and military, lagged far behind, for who dared to press forward into the midst of Cao Cao's partizans?

That day, when the Emperor reached the hunting ground, he saw his newly-found uncle respectfully bowing to him by the roadside.

"I would like to see you display your hunting skill, Uncle," said the Emperor.

Liu Bei mounted his steed at once. Just then a hare emerged from the grass. Liu Bei shot and hit it with the first arrow. The Emperor applauded at this fine display of archery. Then he rode away over a slope. Suddenly, a deer broke out of the thicket. He shot three arrows at it but all missed.

"You try," said the Emperor turning to Cao Cao.

"Lend me Your Majesty's bow and arrows," he replied, and taking the inlaid bow and the golden-barbed arrows, he pulled the bow and hit the deer in the shoulder at the first shot. It fell still in the grass.

Now the crowd of officers, seeing the golden-barbed arrow sticking in the wound, concluded at once that the shot was the Emperor's, so they rushed up, shouting "Long live the Emperor!" Cao Cao rode out, pushing past the Emperor, and acknowledged the congratulations.

All turned pale. What did this mean? Liu Bei's brother Guan Yu was especially angry. His bushy eyebrows stood up fiercely and his red phoenix eyes glared as he, sword in hand, urged his horse forward to cut down the audacious minister for his impertinence. However, his eldest brother hastily waved him back and shot at him a meaningful glance so that he stopped and made no further move.

Liu Bei bowed toward Cao Cao and said, "A truly wonderful shot, sir. Few can hope to match your mastery!"

"I owe this to the enormous good fortune of the Emperor," said Cao Cao with a smile. Then he turned his steed to congratulate the Emperor. Nevertheless, he did not return the bow but hung it over his own shoulder instead. The hunt finished with banqueting. When the entertainment was over they all returned to their own lodgings in the capital.

Guan Yu was still thinking of Cao Cao's breach of decorum. He asked Liu Bei, "Brother, why did you prevent me from killing that rebel and so ridding the world of a scoundrel? He had insulted the Emperor."

"When you throw stones at a rat, beware of the vase," quoted Liu Bei. "Cao Cao was only a horse's head away from our Lord and in the midst of a crowd of his own men. In that momentary burst of anger, if you struck and failed, and harm had come to the Emperor, what an awful crime would have been laid on us!"

"If we don't get rid of him today, more evil will come of it," said Guan Yu.

"But be discreet, my brother. Such matters can't be lightly discussed."

The Emperor sadly returned to his palace. With tears in his eyes he related what had occurred in the hunting expedition to his consort, Empress Fu. He said, "From the day of my accession one vicious minister has succeeded another. I was first the victim of Dong Zhuo's tyranny, which was then followed by the rebellion of Li Jue and Guo Si. You and I have suffered miseries such as no others have endured. Then came this Cao Cao. I thought he would maintain the imperial dignity, but he has seized all the power of the state and does as he wishes. He works continually for his own glorification and rides roughshods over all others. I never see him but I am on tenterhooks. In the hunting field today he even pushed ahead of me to acknowledge the cheers of the crowd. He was so extremely impertinent that I feel sure he has sinister designs against me. And then, alas, it will be the end of both you and me!"

The Empress said in despair, "In a whole court full of nobles who have eaten the bread of Han, is there not one who will save his country?"

Hardly had she finished her words there stepped in a man who said, "Do not grieve, Your Majesties! I can recommend someone to destroy the evil Cao Cao."

The Emperor turned to look at the speaker and found that it was none other than the father of the Empress, Fu Wan.

"Have you also heard of Cao Cao's wanton and perverse behavior today?" asked the Emperor, drying his eyes.

"Who could have failed to notice his impudence after he shot that deer? But the whole court is full of his clan or his close followers. With the exception of the relatives of the Imperial House there is not one loyal enough to step forward and deal with the rebel. I am old and have no authority to do anything, but there is your grand uncle, General Dong Cheng, who could do it."

"I know he has had much experience in dealing with state troubles. I will call him in to discuss this."

Fu Wan replied, "Every one of your attendants is a partizan of Cao Cao's and this must be kept a strict secret or the consequence will be most serious."

"Then what can be done?" inquired the Emperor.

"The only plan I can think of is to send gifts of a robe and a jade girdle to Dong Cheng, and in the lining of the girdle hide a secret edict authorizing him to take certain steps. When he gets home and has read the edict he can formulate plans day and night, and neither the spirits above nor the demons below will know anything about it."

The Emperor approved and the old man went away. The Emperor then with his own hand drew up a decree in blood drawn by biting his finger. He gave the document to his consort and she sewed it into the purple lining of the girdle. When the sewing was done he put on the robe and tied the girdle. Next, he summoned Dong Cheng to the palace.

Dong Cheng came and after the usual ceremony was over the Emperor said, "I was talking with the Empress last night of those terrible days of rebellion and we thought of your good service then, therefore I have called you in to reward you."

The general knelt down and bowed in gratitude. The Emperor led him out of the Reception Hall to the Ancestral Temple and later to the Gallery of Worthy Ministers, where the Emperor burned incense and bowed. After this he took Dong Cheng to look at the portraits. The first one they saw was the centerpiece, the picture of Emperor Gao-zu, founder of the Han Dynasty.

"From where did our great ancestor start his grand cause and how did he establish his great empire?" asked the Emperor.

"Your Majesty is teasing me," said Dong Cheng, rather startled at the question. "Who could have been unaware of the heroic achievements of our Sacred Ancestor? He began life as a minor official in Sishang. There gripping his sword he slew the White Serpent and rose in uprising against the rule of Qin. Speedily he conquered the whole empire—in three years he had destroyed Qin, and in five years Chu. Thus he established a dynasty that will endure forever."

"Such heroic forefathers! Such weakling descendants! How sad it is!" said the Emperor.

Pointing to the portraits right and left he continued, "Are not these two Zhang Liang and Xiao He?"

"Yes, they are. Your great ancestor relied much on their efforts."

The Emperor glanced about him: his attendants were rather far away. Then he whispered to Dong Cheng, "You, like these two, will stand at my side."

"My poor services are of no worth—how can I compare with those two?" said Dong Cheng.

"I remember how you saved me last time at the western capital. I have never forgotten but I have nothing to reward you with." Then, pointing to his own robe, the Emperor continued: "You must wear this robe of mine, bound with my own girdle, and it will be as though you are always near your Emperor."

Dong Cheng bowed gratefully. Taking off his robe and girdle, the Emperor presented them to his faithful general and whispered, "Examine it closely when you get home, and do not fail my expectations."

Dong Cheng understood. He put on the robe and the girdle, took his leave, and left the chamber.

However, news had traveled very fast and presently Cao Cao was informed of the meeting. He at once went to the palace and arrived just as Dong Cheng was leaving the gate. They met face to face and Dong Cheng could in no way avoid him. He stood at the side of the road and made his obeisance.

"Where have you been, sir?" asked Cao Cao.

"His Majesty summoned me into the palace and has given me this robe and girdle."

"Why did he give you these?"

"He had not forgotten that I saved his life in the days of the Li and Guo rebellion."

"Take it off and let me see it."

Knowing that a secret decree was hidden away somewhere in the garments, Dong Cheng was afraid Cao Cao would find out, so he hesitated. But the tyrant called his guards to force Dong Cheng to take off the girdle and give it to him at once. Then he looked it over very carefully.

"It certainly is a very handsome girdle," he said. "Now take off the robe and let me look at that."

Dong Cheng's heart was melting with fear but he dared not disobey. So he handed over the robe.

Cao took it and held it up against the sun, minutely examining every part of it. When he had done this he put it on, secured it with the girdle and, turning to his followers, said: "How is it for length?"

"Beautiful!" they said in chorus.

Turning to Dong Cheng he said, "Will you give these to me?"

"My Emperor's presents to me I dare not give to another. Let me give you another robe and girdle instead."

"Is there not some intrigue connected with these presents?"

"How would I dare to do such a thing?" said Dong Cheng, trembling. "If you are so set upon these then I must give them up."

"How could I take away what your Emperor has given you? I was only joking," said Cao Cao.

He returned both the robe and girdle and their owner made his way home. That night, alone in his library, he took out the robe and looked over every inch of it most carefully but found nothing.

"He gave me these and told me to look at them carefully. That means there is something to be looked for but I can find no trace of it. How can it be?" he thought to himself.

Then he lifted the girdle and examined that. The jade plates were carved into the semblance of small dragons interlaced among flowers. The back was of purple silk. All was sewn together most carefully and neatly and he could find nothing out of the ordinary. Feeling greatly puzzled, he laid the belt on the table but presently picked it up and scrutinized it again. He spent long hours over it until he was so sleepy that he leaned over on the small table, his head resting on his hands. He was almost asleep when sparks from the light fell down upon the girdle and burned a hole in the lining. He hastily shook it off, but the mischief was done; a small hole had been burned in the silken lining, and through this there appeared something white with blood marks. He hastily ripped it open and drew out the decree, written by the hand of the Emperor himself in characters of blood. It read:

> *Of human relationships, that between father and son stands first; of the various social ties, that between the Emperor and his officials stands the highest. Today the wicked Cao Cao is a real tyrant, treating even me with indignity. Supported by his faction and his army he has corrupted the principles of government. He confers rewards and inflicts punishments at will, thus reducing me to a nonentity. I grieve over this day and night for fear that the empire would be ruined.*
>
> *You are a high-ranking general of the state and my own relative. You must recall how difficult it was for our great founder to establish the regime and assemble together the loyal and right-minded to destroy this evil faction and restore the prerogatives of the throne. Such a deed will be an extreme joy to the spirits of my ancestors. This decree, written in blood drawn from my own fingers, is confided to you. Be most discreet and do not fail in executing my design. Given in the spring of the third month of the fourth year of Jian An (A.D. 199).*

So ran the decree and Dong Cheng read it with streaming eyes. There was no sleep for him that night. Early in the morning he returned to his library and re-read it. No plan suggested itself. He laid the decree down on the table and sought in the depths of his mind for some scheme to destroy Cao Cao, but could not decide upon any. And as he was very tired he dozed off on the table.

It so happened that an official named Wang Zi-fu, with whom he was on terms of great intimacy, came to visit him and, as usual, walked into the house unannounced and went straight to the library. His host did not wake up and the visitor noticed, hardly hidden by his sleeve, the Emperor's writing. Wondering what this might be he drew it out, read it, and put it in his own sleeve. Then he called out, "How carefree you are! I'm surprised you can still get to sleep."

The host started up and at once found the decree missing. He was aghast, terrified out of his wits.

"So you want to make away with Cao Cao? I'll go and tell him," said his visitor.

"Then, good brother, that is the end of the Hans," said his host in tears.

"I was joking," said his friend. "My forefathers also served the Hans and lived on their bounty. Am I devoid of loyalty? I'll help you as far as I can."

"It's a great fortune for the country that you think like this," said Dong Cheng.

"But we need a more private place than this to talk over such plans and pledge ourselves to sacrifice all in the cause of Han."

Dong Cheng began to feel very satisfied. He produced a roll of white silk and wrote his own name at the top and signed it, and his friend followed suit. Then the visitor said, "General Wu is my best friend, he can be trusted to join us."

The host replied, "Of all the officials of the court, Zhong Ji and Wu Shu are my best friends. Certainly they'll assist us."

As they were discussing a servant came to announce the arrival of none other than these two men.

"This is providential," said Dong Cheng and he told his friend to hide behind a screen.

The two guests were led into the library and after an exchange of civilities and a cup of tea, Zhong Ji mentioned the shooting of the stag at the hunting expedition.

"Were you not angry at that?" he asked the host.

Dong Cheng answered, "Yes, I am, but what can we do?"

Wu Shu interjected, "I want to slay this fellow, I swear I do! Only I can't get anyone to back me up."

"I'd have no regret even though I should perish for my country," said Zhong Ji.

At this moment Wang Zi fu appeared from behind the screen and said in jest, "You two want to kill Cao Cao! I have to let him know about this. And Dong Cheng is my witness."

"A loyal minister does not mind death. If we are killed we will be Han ghosts, which is better than one who curries favor from a traitor of the state."

The host laughed. "We were just saying we wanted to see you two on this matter. He's only joking."

Then he drew forth the decree and showed it to the two newcomers, who also wept as they read it. They were asked to add their names.

Wang Zi-fu said, "Please stay for a few moments. I'm going to get my best friend to come here."

He left the room and very soon returned with his friend, who also wrote his name in the presence of all the others.

After this the host invited them to the inner hall to drink to the success of their plan.

While they were drinking, a new visitor, Ma Teng, Prefect of Xiliang, was announced.

"Say I am indisposed," said the host, "and cannot receive visitors."

The doorkeeper took the message to Ma Teng who said angrily, "Last night at the palace gate I saw him come out in robe and girdle. How can he pretend illness today? I have not come from mere idleness. Why does he refuse to see me?"

The doorkeeper went in again and told his master what the visitor had said and that he was very angry. Dong Cheng asked his guests to wait for him and went to receive the new visitor. After the greetings Ma Teng said, "I am going to return home soon. I have already had an audience with the Emperor and wished to bid you farewell. Why did you want to put me off?"

"My poor body was suddenly taken ill—that is why I failed to welcome you when you came," said the host.

"You do not look ill, though—your face wears the very bloom of health," said the guest bluntly.

His host could find nothing to say. The visitor shook out his long sleeves and rose to depart. He sighed deeply as he walked down the steps, saying to himself, "Not one of them is any good, there is no one to save the country."

This speech sank deeply into Dong Cheng's heart. He stopped his guest and said, "Who is no good to save the country? Who do you mean?"

"My breast is still bursting with rage over that incident at the hunting expedition the other day. But you, a near relative of the Emperor, can pass your time in wine and idle dalliance without any thought of doing away with the rebel. Can you be counted as one who will save the country?"

Though his words sounded true Dong Cheng's doubts were not set at rest. Pretending great surprise he replied, "The prime minister is an official of the highest rank and has the full confidence of the Emperor. Why, then, do you utter such things against him?"

"So you find that ruffian a good man, eh?" said Ma Teng indignantly.

"Please lower your voice: there are eyes and ears very near us."

"Those who covet life and fear death are not the ones to discuss any great undertakings."

So saying he rose to leave. By this time his host's doubts were cleared—he was sure that Ma Teng was loyal and patriotic. So he said, "Do not be angry any more. I will show you something."

Then he invited him into the library and showed him the decree. As Ma Teng read it his hair stood on end—he ground his teeth and bit his lips till the blood came.

"When you take action, remember the whole force of my army is ready to help," he offered.

Dong Cheng introduced him to the other three and then the pledge was produced and Ma Teng was asked to sign his name. He did so, at the same time smearing his lips with blood as he said the oath. "I swear I would rather die than betray this pledge."

Pointing to the five he said, "If there are ten of us we can accomplish our design."

"True and loyal men are but few," said Dong Cheng. "One of the wrong sort will spoil all."

Ma Teng told them to bring in the name list of all the officials. He read on till he came to the name Liu of the Imperial clan. Clapping his hands he cried, "Why not consult him?"

"Who?" cried the others altogether.

Ma Teng very slowly and deliberately spoke his name.

> *To a relative of the state comes the Emperor's decree,*
> *And a scion of the ruling house can prove his loyalty.*

The name of Ma Teng's hero will be told in the next chapter.

CHAPTER TWENTY-ONE

Cao Cao Brews the Wine and Talks about Heroes
Guan Yu Slays Che Zhou to Regain Xuzhou

At the end of the last chapter Ma Teng was about to disclose the name of a person who could be trusted with effecting the Emperor's decree.

"Who is it?" was the question they asked him.

Ma Teng answered, "Liu Bei, Governor of Yuzhou. He's here and we can ask him to help."

"Though he is an uncle of the Emperor, he is at present a partizan of our enemy. I don't think he'll support us," said Dong Cheng.

"But I noticed something during the expedition," said Ma Teng. "When Cao Cao advanced to acknowledge the cheers of the crowds Liu Bei's sworn brother Guan Yu was behind him. I saw him reaching for his sword to cut down Cao Cao. However, Liu Bei checked him with a warning look and he did not. He would willingly destroy Cao Cao, only he thought the tyrant had too many claws and teeth around him. You can ask him. I'm sure he'll consent."

Here Wu Shu interrupted. "Don't be too hasty," he cautioned. "Let's consider the matter more carefully."

They dispersed. The following night Dong Cheng went to Liu Bei's lodging, taking with him the decree. As soon as he was announced Liu Bei came to greet him and led him into a private room where they could talk freely. The two younger brothers, as always, stood at his sides.

"It must be something unusually important that has brought you here tonight, sir," said Liu Bei to his guest.

"If I had ridden forth by daylight, Cao Cao might suspect, so I came by night."

Then wine was served and while they were drinking Dong Cheng said, "Why did you hold back your brother the other day at the hunting expedition when he was going to slay Cao Cao?"

Liu Bei, greatly startled, asked: "How did you know?"

"Nobody noticed but I saw."

Liu Bei could not deny any more. "My brother could not help getting very angry at Cao Cao's presumptuous behavior," he explained.

The visitor covered his face and wept. "Alas, if all the officials were like him, there would be no worries for lack of tranquillity," he sighed.

Now Liu Bei suspected that he might be sent by Cao Cao to test him so he cautiously replied, "Why worry about lack of tranquillity while Prime Minister Cao is running the government?"

Dong Cheng changed color and rose from his seat. "You, sir, are an uncle of His Majesty and so I showed you my innermost feelings. Why do you try to deceive me?"

"Because I feared you might be deceiving me, and I wanted to find out," replied Liu Bei.

At this Dong Cheng showed him the decree. Liu Bei was deeply affected with sorrow and indignation. Then the guest produced the pledge, on which were only six names.

"Since you are acting on the decree of the Emperor, I must do all I can to help," said Liu Bei. At Dong Cheng's request he put down his name and signature underneath the others and handed it back.

"Now we need to get but three more, which will make ten, and we will be ready to act."

"But you must move with the greatest caution and not let this get abroad," warned Liu Bei.

The two talked till an early hour in the morning, when the visitor left.

In the meantime, Liu Bei, in order to guard against possible attacks from Cao Cao, began to devote himself to gardening, planting vegetables, and watering them with his own hands. His brothers were puzzled.

"Why do you neglect great matters of the country but tend to such lowly things?" they asked.

"This isn't something you'll understand, brothers," he replied. And they said no more.

One day when the two brothers were absent and Liu Bei was busy in his garden, two officers came with an escort from Cao Cao's palace and said: "The prime minister commands that you go and see him at once."

"For what important affair?" he asked nervously.

"We know nothing. We were ordered to come and invite you."

All he could do was to obey. When he went in to see Cao Cao, the latter laughed and said, "That is a great business you have in hand at home."

At this remark Liu Bei's face turned the color of clay. But Cao Cao took him by the hand and led him straight to his back garden. "The business of learning to grow vegetables is not easy."

Liu Bei breathed again. "Hardly a business, just to while away the time," he said.

Cao Cao said, "I happened to notice the green plums on the trees today and my thoughts turned back to a year ago when we were thrashing Zhang Xiu. We were marching through a parched district and everyone was suffering from thirst. I suddenly thought of a scheme. Lifting my whip I pretended to be pointing at something in the distance and said, 'There is a plum orchard ahead.' The soldiers heard it and it made their mouths water and they were no longer thirsty. Now I owe a debt to the plums and we will pay it today. Besides, I have brewed some wine which has been heated very hot so I have invited you, sir, to come and share the fruit and the wine with me."

Liu Bei was quite composed by this time and went with his host to a small summer house, where the wine cups were already laid out and in the dishes were green plums. They sat facing each other and drank to their hearts' content.

As they drank, the weather gradually changed. Dark clouds scudded across the sky and a storm was in the making. Some servants pointed out a mass of clouds that looked like a dragon hung in the sky. Both of them went over to the window and leaned against the railing to look at it.

"Do you understand the evolution of dragons?" asked Cao Cao of the guest.

"Not in detail."

"A dragon can assume any size, can rise in glory or hide from sight. Assuming gigantic sizes, it can generate clouds and evolve mists; reduced in form, it virtually disappears from our vision. Rising, it can soar to the heavens; sinking, it hides among the deep waves of the ocean. This is the season of late spring and the dragon chooses this moment for its metamorphosis, like a man realizing his ambitions and dominating the world. As an animal the dragon can compare with the hero of the human world. Now you, Xuan-de, with your experience, must know the heroes of the present day. Tell me who they are."

"How can my dull eyes recognize heroes?"

"Don't be so modest."

"Thanks to your kindly protection I have a post at court, but as to heroes, I really do not know who they are," said Liu Bei.

"You may not know them by their faces but you have at least heard of their names," insisted Cao Cao.

"Yuan Shu, with his rich resources—is he one?"

His host laughed. "A rotting bone in the graveyard. I will put him out of the way sooner or later."

"Well, Yuan Shao, then. The highest offices of state have been held in his family for four generations and his friends are many. He is firmly posted in Jizhou and he has many able men under his command. Surely he is one."

"A bully and a coward. He is fond of grandiose schemes but is indecisive; he attempts great things but grudges the necessary toil. He loses sight of everything else for just a little advantage. He is not a hero."

"There is Liu Biao. He is renowned as one of the Wise Eight and his fame has spread on all sides. He must be a hero."

"He is merely a man of vain reputation, not a hero."

"Sun Ce is young and valiant, a leader in the east. Is he a hero?"

"He is relying on his father's reputation—he is no hero."

"What about Liu Zhang?" asked Liu Bei again.

"Though he belongs to the reigning family, he is nothing more than a guard dog. How could he be counted as a hero?" sneered Cao Cao.

"How about Zhang Xiu, Zhang Lu, Han Sui?"

Cao Cao clapped his hands and laughed very loudly. "These mediocre people are not worth mentioning."

"Apart from these I really know none."

"Now heroes are men who cherish lofty aspirations in their hearts and know how to accomplish them. They have all-embracing schemes and the whole world is at their mercy."

"Who can be such a hero?" asked Liu Bei.

Pointing first at his guest and then at himself, Cao Cao said, "The only heroes in the world are you and me."

Liu Bei was so frightened at the remark that his chopsticks rattled to the floor. Just at that moment a tremendous peal of thunder announced the onrush of the rain. Liu Bei calmly stooped down to recover the fallen article. "How powerful was that thunder! It was quite a shock!" he said.

"What? Are you afraid of thunder?" said Cao Cao, laughing.

Liu Bei replied, "The wise man in the ancient days paled at a sudden peal of thunder or a fierce gust of wind. How can one not fear?"

Thus he was able to conceal the real cause that so startled him.

> *Constrained to lodge in a tiger's lair.*
> *He played a waiting part.*
> *But when Cao disclosed the real heroes*
> *Then terror gripped his heart.*
> *But he cleverly used the thunder peal*
> *As excuse for turning pale.*
> *Oh, quick to seize occasions thus!*
> *He surely must prevail.*

The shower had just stopped when all of a sudden there appeared two men rushing into the garden with swords in their hands. Pushing past the attendants, they forced their way to the pavilion where Cao Cao and Liu Bei were drinking. These two newcomers turned out to be Guan Yu and Zhang Fei.

The two of them had been outside the city practicing archery. On their return they heard that their brother had been led away by two of Cao Cao's officers. They hastened to his house and were told that their brother was in the back garden with his host. Fearing something might have gone amiss they rushed in. Now when they saw their brother quietly talking with Cao Cao and sipping wine, they took up their usual places behind him, their hands on their swords.

"Why did you come?" asked Cao Cao.

"We heard that you, sir, had invited our brother to a wine party and we came to amuse you with a little sword play," said Guan Yu.

"This is not a Hongmen Banquet,"* replied Cao Cao. "What use do we have for two swordsmen?"

Liu Bei smiled. The host ordered wine to be served to them to allay their fear and, soon after, the three took their leave and returned home.

"We were nearly frightened to death," said Guan Yu.

Liu Bei told his brothers about what happened at Cao Cao's place. They asked him why he should say that he was afraid of thunder.

He explained: "Remember I've been learning gardening these days. That is to convince Cao Cao that I have no ambition at all. But I little expected that he'd name me as one of the two heroes. I was so startled that my chopsticks dropped to the ground. I thought he had some suspicions. Happily, the thunder at the moment supplied the excuse I wanted."

"How very clever you are!" they said in admiration.

On the following day Cao Cao again invited Liu Bei over, and while the two were drinking, an officer, who had been dispatched to find out what Yuan Shao was doing, came to present his report.

He said, "Yuan Shao has completely overpowered Gongsun Zan."

"Do you know the details?" asked Liu Bei at once.

"They were at war and Gongsun Zan had the worse of it, so he acted on the defensive. He built a wall around his city and on that erected a high tower, where he stored a huge quantity of grain. He took up his quarters there but his troops still passed in and out of the city without ceasing,

---

* Referring to the banquet given by Xiang Yu to his rival Liu Bang (later founder of the Han Dynasty), in which sword play was performed in an attempt to stab the guest. Hongmeng is situated near modern Sian.

some to give battle and others returning to rest. When one of them was surrounded by the enemy, the others asked Gongsun Zan to rescue him. He said, 'If I rescue one, then later on everyone else will want to be helped and will not exert himself.' So he did not go. This disgusted his men and many went over to the enemy so that his army diminished.

"He tried to seek help from the capital but the messenger was captured by Yuan Shao's men. Then he sent a letter to Zhang Xiu to arrange with him for a joint attack against Yuan Shao, but the letter was again intercepted. His enemies disguised themselves as Zhang Xiu's men and lit a fire outside the city, the signal given in the letter, to flush him out. Thus Gongsun Zan fell into an ambush. He lost heavily and retreated back into the city, where he was besieged. Later, Yuan Shao's men dug a subterranean passage to his tower and set fire to it. Gongsun Zan could not escape. So he slew his wife and committed suicide. The flames destroyed his whole family.

"Yuan Shao has added the remnants of the vanquished army to his own and so become yet stronger. However, his brother Yuan Shu in Huainan, is so arrogant and cruel that his army and the people have turned against him. Therefore he sent a messenger to his brother to say that he would yield to him the title of Emperor, which he had assumed. Yuan Shao, however, also demanded the Imperial Seal, and Yuan Shu promised to bring it to him in person. Now he has abandoned Huainan and is about to set out for Hebei. If the two brothers join forces it will not be easy to overwhelm them. We must take immediate action to prevent this from happening."

Liu Bei heard the story with sorrow in his heart, for he remembered Gongsun Zan's kindness to him in the past. Moreover, he was anxious to know the fate of Zhao Yun.

He thought to himself, "What better chance am I likely to get to set myself free?"

So he rose and said to Cao Cao, "If Yuan Shu goes over to join his brother he will surely pass through Xuzhou. Give me an army and I will intercept him on the way. That will finish Yuan Shu."

"Present a petition to the Emperor tomorrow and then you can start on the expedition," said Cao Cao, smiling.

So the next day Liu Bei went to obtain permission from the Emperor and Cao Cao gave him command of 50,000 soldiers, horse and foot, and sent Zhu Lin and Lu Zhao to accompany him.

Liu Bei went to bid farewell to the Emperor, who wept as he saw him leave. As soon as he reached his lodging he set about preparing for immediate departure, returning his official seal and assembling his weapons. The army started the march at once.

Dong Cheng hurried out of town to see him off.

"You need not worry about my leaving—this journey will assuredly help with the scheme," said Liu Bei.

"Keep your mind fixed on that," said Dong Cheng, "and never forget what His Majesty requires of us."

They parted. Liu Bei's brothers asked him why he was in such a hurry to get away.

He replied, "I've been a bird in a cage, a fish in a net. This is like the fish regaining the open sea and the bird soaring into the blue sky. Now I'm no longer in confinement." And he gave orders for the army to move faster.

Now Guo Jia and Cheng Yu had been away inspecting stores and supplies when Liu Bei left. As soon as they heard of his expedition they went to see their master, asking him why he had let Liu Bei go in command of an army.

"He is going to cut off Yuan Shu's advance to Hebei," said Cao Cao.

Cheng Yu said, "Formerly, when he was governor of Yuzhou, we entreated you to put him to death, but you would not hear of it. Now you have even given him an army. You have allowed the dragon to reach the sea, the tiger to return to the mountains. What control will you have in future?"

Guo Jia also remonstrated: "Even if you would not put him to death you need not let him go. As the proverb says, 'Release control of the enemy for one day and an age-long harm ensues.' Please consider this matter more carefully."

Cao Cao recognized that these were prudent counsels, so he sent Xu Chu and five hundred men with imperative orders to bring Liu Bei back.

Liu Bei was marching as rapidly as possible when he noticed a cloud of dust to the rear and remarked to his brothers, "These must be Cao Cao's men coming to pursue us."

He halted and made a stockade and ordered his brothers to be in readiness, one on each side. Presently the messenger arrived and found himself in the midst of an army, ready for battle. He dismounted and entered the camp to speak to Liu Bei.

"Sir, on what business have you come?" asked Liu Bei.

"The prime minister has sent me to request that you return as he has further matters to discuss with you."

"When a general has once taken the field, even the royal command can be of no effect. I bade farewell to the Emperor and received the prime minister's command, so there can be nothing further to talk about. Please return at once with that reply to your master."

The messenger was undecided what action to take. He knew of the friendship that existed between his master and Liu Bei and besides, he had no orders to fight. He could only return with this reply and ask for further instructions. So he left. When he related what had occurred to his master, Cao Cao still hesitated to take any action. His advisers pointed out to him that this refusal to return indicated betrayal.

"Still, two of my men are with him," said Cao Cao. "He will not dare to betray me, I think. Besides, I sent him myself and I cannot go back on my own orders."

So Liu Bei was not pursued.

A poem was written in praise of Liu Bei:

> *He fed the horses, disciplined his men,*
> *And marched forth in a hurry,*
> *Intent to accomplish his King's behest*
> *Deeply engrained in his memory.*
> *At last he had escaped from confinement,*
> *Like a tiger breaking loose from its cage.*
> *He had shaken the shackles from his feet,*
> *As a dragon soaring to heaven's gate.*

When Ma Teng heard that Liu Bei had departed, he felt that it would be difficult to carry out the Emperor's decree in a short time. Meanwhile, pressing business at the frontier urged him to go back and he, too, left the capital for his own district in the west.

On Liu Bei's arrival at Xuzhou the governor, Che Zhou, went to meet him. After the official banquet was over, his former subordinates, Sun Qian and Mi Zhu, came to pay their respects to him. Then he proceeded to his residence to see his family.

Scouts were sent out to discover what Yuan Shu was doing. They came back with the news that his arrogance had driven away two of his officers to the mountains. His forces thus reduced, he wrote to his brother, saying that he would yield his imperial title to him. Yuan Shao at once sent for him. So he packed up the palace fittings, got the remnants of his army in order, and marched toward Xuzhou.

When he neared Xuzhou, Liu Bei led out his officers and men to oppose him. They were met first by Ji Ling. Zhang Fei rode out and attacked without a word. In the tenth bout Ji Ling was slain and the defeated soldiers fled in all directions.

Then Yuan Shu came up with his army. Liu Bei placed his brothers and Cao Cao's two officers on his two sides and began to abuse him. "You wicked rebel, I have the Emperor's decree to destroy you. Yield at once and you may avoid punishment."

"Base weaver of mats and mean maker of straw sandals, how dare you make light of me?" replied Yuan Shu and he gave the signal to attack.

The four officers on Liu Bei's right and left fought back with their soldiers. They smote the enemy till corpses littered the plain and blood flowed in streams. Many soldiers deserted. After the defeat, Yuan Shu was further attacked by his former subordinates, who robbed him of all his supplies, completing his destruction. Yuan Shu tried to retreat to his home but the bandits barred the road.

He had to seek refuge in Jiangting, with only a thousand or so men left of all his army. And these were but the old and the weakly ones, able neither to fight nor flee. It was then the height of summer and their food was nearly exhausted. The whole provision consisted of thirty measures of wheat. This was made over to the soldiers and the members of his household went hungry. Many died of starvation. Yuan Shu could not swallow the coarse food that the soldiers lived on. One day he ordered his cook bring him some honey water to quench his thirst.

"There is no water with honey, save that tainted with blood," replied the cook.

This was the last straw. Yuan Shu sat up on his couch and rolled out onto the floor with a loud cry. Blood gushed from his mouth and thus he died. It was the sixth month of the fourth year of the reign of Jian An.

> *The last days of Han approached and weapons clashed in every quarter,*
> *The misguided Yuan Shu, lost all sense of honor,*
> *Forgetful of his forefathers, who had filled the State's highest offices.*
> *Madly aspired to make himself Emperor,*
> *Resting his outrageous claim on the possession of The Seal,*
> *And arrogantly boasting that thus he fulfilled the design of Heaven.*
> *Alas! Sick unto death he vainly begged for a little honey water;*
> *He died, alone on his empty bed.*

Yuan Shu being dead, his nephew escorted his coffin and his family toward Lujiang. There, the magistrate, Xu Miao, slew all the survivors. Among the possessions he found the Imperial Seal, which he at once took to the capital and presented to Cao Cao, for which service he was made a prefect.

When Liu Bei heard that Yuan Shu was dead, he prepared a report to the throne and sent it to Cao Cao. He also sent the two officers appointed by Cao Cao back to the capital, but kept the army to defend Xuzhou.

Then he personally went through the countryside to call back the people to resume their lives.

Cao Cao was angry when his two officers returned without the army and wanted to put them to death. Xun Yu reasoned with him.

"The power was in Liu Bei's hands and they had no alternative," he said. So they were pardoned.

"You should instruct Che Zhou to try to destroy him," said Xun Yu.

Accordingly he sent secret orders to Che Zhou, who took Chen Deng, who had earlier betrayed Lu Bu, into his confidence. Chen Deng proposed placing an ambush near the city gate to attack Liu Bei on his return from the country. "I will attack his escort with arrows from the city walls," he added. Che Zhou agreed to try this.

Chen Deng then went to tell the scheme to his father who, however, bade him go and warn Liu Bei of the danger. He at once rode away to do so. Before long he met the two younger brothers, to whom he related the story.

Now the two brothers had returned earlier and Liu Bei was still some distance behind. As soon as Zhang Fei heard of the plot, he wanted to attack the ambushing force, but Guan Yu said he had a better plan.

He said, "He's laid an ambush there. It'll be to our disadvantage if we go and attack. I think we can do this—in the night, we'll pretend to be Cao Cao's men and lure him out to meet us. We'll slay him then."

Zhang Fei approved of the plan. Now the soldiers, who used to serve under Cao Cao, had his army banners and wore the same armor. At about the third watch, they came to the city wall and hailed the guards to open the gate, saying that they were Zhang Liao's troops sent from the capital. This was reported to Che Zhou, who sent hastily for Chen Deng to discuss the matter.

"If I don't receive them they will suspect my loyalty," he said. "Yet if I do I may be victim of a trick."

So he went up on the wall and said it was too dark to distinguish friends from foes and they must wait till daylight. The men shouted back that Liu Bei had to be kept in ignorance and they begged him to let them in. Still he hesitated. But the shouting only grew louder.

Presently, Che Zhou put on his armor, placed himself at the head of a thousand men, and went out. He galloped over the drawbridge and shouted, "Where is Zhang Liao?"

Then lights blazed around and he recognized Guan Yu, with his sword drawn.

"Wretch!" cried Guan Yu. "How dare you plot to slay my brother?"

Che Zhou was too frightened to make a good defense, and after a few bouts, he turned to re-enter the gate. But as he reached the drawbridge flights of arrows met him, for Chen Deng had betrayed him. So he turned aside and galloped along under the wall. But Guan Yu came quickly in pursuit. His sword was raised aloft and as it came down the poor man was slain and his head cut off.

Guan Yu shouted up to those on the wall, "I have slain the rebel Che Zhou. You others need not fear if you only surrender."

The soldiers threw down their spears and gave in. As soon as order was restored Guan Yu took the head to show Liu Bei and told him the story of the plot.

"But what will Cao Cao think of this?" said Liu Bei. "And he may come."

"If he does come, Zhang Fei and I will meet him," said Guan Yu.

But Liu Bei was grieved beyond measure. Nevertheless, there was no alternative for him and he entered the city. The elders of the people knelt in the road to welcome him. Then he hurried to his residence and looked for his youngest brother, only to find that Zhang Fei had already exterminated the entire family of Che Zhou.

Liu Bei said, in distress, "We've slain one of Cao Cao's trusted officers. How will he stand that?"

"I have a plan to withstand Cao Cao," said Chen Deng.

> *Just from grave danger extricated,*
> *An impending war must be averted.*

What plan Chen Deng had in mind will be told in the next chapter.

CHAPTER TWENTY-TWO

Yuan Shao and Cao Cao Both Take the Field
Guan Yu and Zhang Fei Capture
Two Enemy Officers

hen Deng said, "Cao Cao's only fear is Yuan Shao. He is strongly positioned in the four northern districts, with a million fighting men and many able officers and advisors. Why not write to him for help?"

Liu Bei replied, "But we have never had any dealings with each other and he is unlikely to assist the person who has just destroyed his brother."

"There is someone here whose family has been on intimate terms with the Yuans for a hundred years. Yuan Shao would surely come if he would write."

"And who is this?"

"A man you know well and respect greatly. Can you have forgotten him?"

"You surely mean Zheng Xuan," said Liu Bei suddenly.

"That is he," said Chen Deng, smiling.

Now Zheng Xuan was a scholar of great talent, who had once studied under Ma Rong. This man was rather peculiar as a teacher. Whenever he lectured he would assemble his students in front of a curtain, behind which sang and danced singing girls, while young maids stood in attendance all around. Zheng Xuan attended these lectures for three years and never once let his eyes wander to the curtain or to the girls around.

Naturally the master admired his pupil. After he had finished his studies and gone home his teacher said, "Only one man has penetrated the inner meanings of my instructions, and that one is Zheng Xuan."

In the Zheng household the waiting maids were familiar with Mao's edition of the Odes.* Once one of the maids behaved against Yuan's wishes, so as punishment she was made to kneel in front of the steps.

---

* Works of poetry allegedly composed by two Maos in the beginning of the West Han Dynasty (206 B.C.– A.D. 24)

Another girl made fun of her, quoting from an ode:

> *What are you doing there in mire?*

The kneeling girl answered back, quoting from another ode:

> *'Twas but a simple word I said,*
> *Yet brought it wrath upon my head.*

Such was his highly refined household. In the reign of Emperor Huan he was a minister, but when the ten eunuchs began to control the government he gave up office and retired into the country to Xuzhou. Liu Bei had known him before, had consulted him on many occasions, and greatly respected him.

Liu Bei was glad that he had remembered this man and with no time to lose, he and Chen Deng went to ask Zheng Xuan to write the letter, which he generously consented to do. Afterwards, Sun Qian was entrusted with delivering the letter. He set out at once.

Yuan Shao read the letter and thought to himself, "Liu Bei destroyed my brother and I ought not to help him, but out of consideration for the writer of this letter I have to go." Therefore he assembled his officers and advisors to discuss an attack on Cao Cao.

Tian Feng, one of his advisors, said, "Do not raise an army. The people are worn out and the granaries are empty with these constant wars. Let us rather report our recent victory against Gongsun Zan to the throne. If that does not reach the Emperor, then present a petition to accuse Cao Cao of hindering our communication with the Emperor. Then raise an army to occupy Liyang. At the same time, assemble a fleet in Henei and prepare a large quantity of weapons. When all this is done, send out your best officers and men to occupy key points on the borders—within three years you will accomplish your great design."

Another advisor named Shen Pei objected, "I do not agree. With the military genius of our lord and the powerful strength of the north, to dispose of Cao Cao is as simple as turning one's hand. It is not necessary to wait."

Another advisor, Ju Shou, supported Tian Feng and said, "Victory does not always belong to the powerful. Cao Cao is a good commander and his soldiers are brave and well drilled. He will not sit down quietly waiting to be surrounded as Gongsun Zan did. I think it unwise if you abandon the good plan to inform the throne of our recent success, but send out an army against Cao Cao without any valid excuse."

However, his view was refuted by the advisor Guo Tu who said: "This is wrong. No expedition against Cao Cao can lack an excuse. I think you, sir, should take this chance to achieve your own great design. I suggest you accede to Minister Zheng's request and ally yourself with Liu Bei for the destruction of Cao Cao. This would win the approval of Heaven and the support of the people. A double blessing indeed!"

Thus the four advisors differed and wrangled and Yuan Shao could not decide which to follow. Then there came two other advisors, Xu You and Xun Shen, and, seeing them, their master said: "These two are very experienced. Let us see what they think of this."

The two made their obeisances and Yuan Shao said, "Minister Zheng has written to me, asking me to support Liu Bei in an attack on Cao Cao. Now am I to send an army or not to send an army?"

They cried with one voice, "You should send an army for you will be stronger in number and in strength against Cao Cao. Besides, you will be acting under the just cause of destroying a traitor and helping the House of Han."

"Exactly what I think," said Yuan Shao. So the discussion focused on the expedition.

Sun Qian was sent back with Yuan Shao's consent and instructions for Liu Bei to get ready to cooperate.

General provisions were immediately made for the expedition. The army was to be composed of 300,000 men, half infantry and half cavalry. The two most valiant officers, Yan Liang and Wen Chou, were named generals and Tian Feng and several others were to be advisors. They were to march toward Liyang.

When these were complete Guo Tu said, "In order to justify the righteousness of your attack on Cao Cao, it would be well to issue a manifesto with a summary of his various crimes."

Yuan Shao approved of this and Chen Lin, well known as a scholar, who had served in court in the late Emperor's reign, was entrusted with the composition of such a document. And in no time the manifesto was completed. It reads as follows:

"A perspicacious ruler prepares against political upheavals; a loyal minister asserts authority in times of trouble. Therefore, a man of extraordinary talents precedes an extraordinary situation, and of such a man the achievements will be extraordinary. For indeed, the ordinary man is quite unequal to an extraordinary situation.

"In former days, after gaining ascendancy over a weakling emperor of the powerful Qin Dynasty, Zhao Gao* wielded the whole authority of

---

* A powerful eunuch in the Qin Dynasty, who controlled the state after the death of the first emperor of Qin.

the throne, overruling the government. All punishment and reward came through him and his contemporaries were pressed into silence. Slowly but surely evolved the tragedy of Wangyi Palace, when the emperor was forced to commit suicide and the imperial tablets perished in the flames. This disgrace has since been held as a bitter lesson for later generations.

"In the latter days of Empress Lu* of the Hans the world saw Lu Chan and Lu Lu, brothers of the Empress and fellows in wickedness, monopolizing the rule of the government. Within the capital they commanded two armies and without, they ruled the feudal states of Liang and Chao. They arbitrarily controlled all state affairs and decided every matter in the imperial palaces. This dominance of the base over the noble saddened the hearts of the people throughout the land. Therefore two lords, Zhou Bo and Liu Zhang, raised an army to vent their wrath. They destroyed the rebellious ministers and restored the crown prince to his royal state. Thus they enabled the imperial rule to flourish and the glory of the Emperor to be manifested. This is an instance of how ministers asserted authority.

"This Cao Cao, now a high-ranking minister, is in truth the grandson of a certain eunuch named Cao Teng who, together with two other eunuchs, stirred up trouble in the country. They were wicked and greedy beyond measure. They were immoral and preyed upon the populace. Cao Cao's father, Cao Song, who begged to be adopted by the eunuch, presented gold and jewels at the gates of the influential and contrived, through bribery, to sneak his way into office, where he could subvert authority. Thus Cao Cao is the depraved descendent of a monstrous excrescence, devoid of all virtue in himself, ferocious and cunning, delighting in disorder and reveling in public calamity.

"Now I, Yuan Shao, a man of war, first displayed my might in the destruction of the evil eunuchs. Later, when the ruffian Dong Zhuo invaded the official circle and abused the government, I grasped my sword and issued the call to restore order in the country. I assembled warriors, selected the best, and took them into my service. In this mission I came into contact with this Cao Cao and conferred with him to further my scheme. Knowing that he was but of mediocre talent I gave him command of a subordinate force and looked to him to render such petty service as he was able. Much have I suffered from his stupidities and his shortcomings, yet I tried to overlook his rash attacks and hasty retreats,

---

*   Wife of Liu Bang, founder of the Han Dynasty, who tried to establish her own rule after her
     husband's death.

his losses and shameful defeats, his repeated destruction of whole armies. Again and again I sent him more troops and filled the gaps in his depleted ranks. I even recommended him to be appointed Governor of Yanzhou. I added to his honors and increased his authority, hoping that eventually he would justify his position with a real victory.

"But Cao Cao availed himself of the opportunity to overstep all bounds, to give free rein to violence and evil. He robbed the common people, persecuted the good, and injured the virtuous. Bian Rang, Prefect of Jiujiang, was a man of remarkable talents and enjoyed nationwide reputation. Honest in speech and correct in demeanor, he never curried Cao Cao's favor with flattery. So he was put to death and his head exposed, his family utterly destroyed. From that day to this, scholars have deeply mourned over his loss and popular resentment has steadily grown. One man raised his arm in anger and the whole country followed him so that Cao Cao was smitten at Xuzhou and his district was snatched by Lu Bu. He fled eastward without shelter or refuge.

"My policy is for a powerful central empire and obedient feudal lords, just like a tree with a strong trunk and weak branches. Also, I do not involve myself in partisanship. Therefore, I again raised my banners, donned my armor, and moved forward to uphold justice. My drums rolled in an assault on Lu Bu, who immediately fled. I saved Cao Cao from destruction and restored him to a position of authority. In doing so I must confess that I was probably being unkind to the people of Yanzhou but doing a great service to Cao Cao.

"Later it happened that the imperial cavalcade moved west and a horde of rebels rose and attacked our lord. The course of government was hindered. At that moment my territory was threatened by forces from the north which I had to deal with. Therefore, I sent one of my officers to Cao Cao, asking him to see to the repair of the temples and the protection of the youthful sovereign, upon which Cao Cao gave the rein to his inclinations. He arbitrarily ordered the removal of the court. He brought shame upon the ruling house and subverted the laws. He assumed control of the three highest offices and dominated the administration. Offices and rewards were conferred according to his will, while punishment was at his word. He glorified whole families of those he loved; he exterminated whole clans of those he hated. Open critics were executed; secret opponents were assassinated. Officials sealed their lips and only exchanged glances when they met in the streets. Secretaries merely recorded court meetings and ministers only filled offices.

"The late Yang Biao, a man who had served the three highest offices of state, was—because of some petty grudge—though guiltless, charged with a crime. He was beaten and subjected to every form of cruelty. This wanton act was a flagrant disregard of the constitutional laws.

"Another victim was Councilor Zhao Yan. He was faithful in remonstrance, honest in speech, endowed with the highest principles of rectitude. He was listened to at court. His words carried enough weight with the Emperor to cause him to modify his intention and confer rewards for outspokenness. Desirous of deceiving the Emperor and stifling all criticism, Cao Cao presumed to arrest and put to death this censor, in defiance of all legal procedure.

"Another evil deed was the destruction of the tomb of Prince Liang, the brother of the late Emperor. His tomb was an impressive sight surrounded by pines and cypresses, mulberries and lindera trees. Cao Cao led soldiers to the cemetery and stood by while it was desecrated, the coffin destroyed and the remains exposed. They stole the gold and jewels of the dead. This deed brought tears to the eyes of the Emperor and rent the hearts of all men. Cao Cao also created special military posts for grave diggers and gold seekers whose tracks were marked by desecrated tombs and exhumed bodies. Indeed, while assuming the position of the highest office of state, he indulged in the inclinations of a bandit, polluting the state, oppressing the people, a bane to gods and men.

"He added to this by setting up minute and vexatious prohibitions so that there were nets and snares spread in every pathway, traps and pitfalls laid in every road. A hand raised was caught in a net, a foot advanced was taken in an entanglement. Therefore the men of Yanzhou and Yuzhou districts became poverty-stricken and the inhabitants of the metropolis groaned and murmured in anger.

> *Read down the names through all the years*
> *Of ministers that all men curse*
> *For greed and cruelty and lust;*
> *Than Cao you will not find a worse.*

"For the past months I have been investigating the cases of evil deeds in the provinces, so I have been unable to reform him. I have given him repeated opportunities hoping that he would repent. But he has the heart of a wolf, the nature of a wild beast. He nourishes evil in his bosom and desires to pull down the pillars of the state, to weaken the House of Han, to destroy the loyal and true and to stand out conspicuously as the chief of criminals.

"Formerly, when I attacked Gongsun Zan in the north, that obstinate bandit and perverse bravo resisted my might for a year. Before he could be destroyed this Cao Cao wrote to him that, under the pretense of assisting the imperial armies, he would covertly lead them to destruction. The plot was discovered through his messengers and Gongsun Zan also perished. This blunted Cao Cao's ardor and his plans failed.

"Now he is camped at Ao Granary with the river to strengthen his position. Like the mantis in the fable, who threatened the chariot with its forelegs, he thinks himself invincible. But with the dignity and prestige of Han to support me I will confront the whole world. I have spearmen by the million, horsemen by thousands of squadrons, and most fierce and vigorous warriors. I have enlisted expert archers and strong bowmen. Geographically I am also stationed at strategically important positions. Bingzhou leads to the Taihang Mountains and Qingzhou, to the Ji and Luo Rivers. My army can course down the Yellow River to attack him in the front, as well as take the route through Wan and Ye districts via Jingzhou to smite his rear. Powerful as thunder and swift as the tiger, my army is irresistible. For my army to deal with Cao Cao is like kindling roaring flames to burn down rootless grass or overturning the ocean to extinguish smoldering embers. Is there any hope that he can escape destruction?

"Of the soldiers of Cao Cao, those who can fight are from the north or from other camps and they all desire to return home. They weep whenever they glance toward the north. The others are either common folks from Yanzhou or Yuzhou, or remnants of the armies of Lu Bu and Zhang Yang. These have been forced to render their service, and they take it only as a temporary expedient. All have been wounded and regard their captors as enemies. If I but give out the call at the mountain tops, and wave the white flag to show them they may surrender, they will melt away like dew before the sun and no blood needs to be shed. The victory will be mine.

"Now the Hans are failing and the bonds of the empire are weak. The sacred dynasty has no supporter and the ministers are impotent to cope with the difficulties. Within the capital the responsible ministers are crestfallen and helpless. Such loyal and high principled men as are left are browbeaten by this tyrant. How can they manifest their virtue?

"Cao Cao has surrounded the palace with seven hundred veteran soldiers, the ostensible object being to guard the Emperor, but the covert design being to hold him prisoner. I fear this is but the first step in his scheme to usurp the throne and so I hasten to take action. Now is the time for loyal ministers to sacrifice their lives, the opportunity for officers to perform meritorious deeds. Can I fail to urge you?

"Furthermore, he has forged commands in the name of the state to call for military assistance. I fear lest some generals in distant districts may obey his behest and send troops to help him. If they did they would bring everlasting shame onto themselves. No wise man should do so.

"In no time the forces of my four prefectures* will be moving out simultaneously. When this call reaches Jingzhou they will unite with the army of General Zhang Xiu. All districts ought to organize volunteers and station them along their borders, to demonstrate their force and prove their loyal support of the court. This will be an extraordinary service to render to the state.

"Whoever brings the head of Cao Cao will be created a nobleman, with feudal rights over 5,000 households and a money reward of fifty millions. I welcome those who serve under Cao Cao to come over to my side. No questions will be asked of their past faults. I publish abroad this notice so that all may realize that the country is in real danger."

Yuan Shao read this denunciation of Cao Cao with great joy. He at once ordered copies to be posted everywhere, in towns and cities, at ferries and passes. Copies found their way to the capital and one made it to Cao Cao's residence. That day he happened to be in bed with a bad headache. Servants took the paper to the sick man's room. He read it and was so frightened that his hair stood on end and cold shivers went down his spine. He broke out into a cold perspiration and his headache vanished. He bounded out of bed and asked Cao Hong, "Who wrote this?"

"They say it is Chen Lin's writing," he replied.

Cao Cao laughed. "Literary genius must be backed up by military strategy. Chen Lin may be a very elegant writer, but what if Yuan Shao's fighting capacity falls short?"

He called his advisers together to consider the next move. When Kong Rong, Prefect of Beihai, heard of this he went to see him. "You should not fight with Yuan Shao," he said. "He is too strong. The only way out is to make peace."

Xun Yu said, "He is impotent. Why is it necessary to seek peace?"

Kong Rong replied, "His land is wide and his men strong. He has many fine strategists, loyal officials, and valiant fighters. How can you say that he is impotent?"

Xun Yu laughed and said, "His army is a rabble. Each of his four most important advisors has his shortcomings: Tian Feng is bold but rude to his master; Xu You is greedy and unwise; Shen Pei is domineering but stupid; and Feng Ji is resolute but useless. These four, being of such incompatible temperaments, will create confusion rather than enforcing

---

* Yuan Shao's territory included the four prefectures of Jizhou, Youzhou, Qingzhou, and Bingzhou in north China.

efficiency. The two generals, Yan Liang and Wen Chou, know nothing but foolhardy courage and can be disposed of in one battle, while the rest are poor, rough stuff. What is their use, even if they number a million?"

Kong Rong could not answer and Cao Cao laughed. "They are just as Xun Yu has described," he said.

Then Cao Cao issued orders. Two officers, Liu Dai and Wang Zhong, were to lead an army of 50,000 men to attack Liu Bei in Xuzhou, displaying banners bearing his name.

This Liu Dai had been governor of Yanzhou but had surrendered to Cao Cao after the fall of the city. Cao Cao had given him a rank in his army and so he was asked to accompany Wang Zhong on the expedition.

Cao Cao himself took command of a large army of 200,000 men for a simultaneous attack on Yuan Shao at Liyang.

When Cheng Yu pointed out to him that Liu Dai and Wang Zhong were unequal to their task, Cao Cao said that he was aware of this. "They are not meant to fight Liu Bei," he said. "It is merely a feint." Then he said to the two officers: "Do not make any rash attacks until I have overcome Yuan Shao. Liu Bei will be the next to be destroyed."

Liu Dai and Wang Zhong's army went forth at the same time as Cao Cao marched out his grand army to Liyang, where Yuan Shao's forces were positioned some eighty *li* away. Both sides dug trenches and made fortified camps, but made no move. This went on for two months.

There was dissension in Yuan Shao's camp. Xu You was in conflict with his colleague, Sheng Bei, and Ju Shou resented the rejection of his plan. So they were at war with each other and would not consider how to deal with their real enemy. Yuan Shao also could not make up his mind. Tired of the inaction, Cao Cao then ordered several of his officers to occupy key points of defense while he himself marched back to Xudu.

Now the army sent against Liu Bei encamped a hundred *li* from Xuzhou. In the center were banners bearing the name of Cao Cao, but no attacks followed. Their spies were very busy finding out about the war in the north. On the other side, Liu Bei, since he was uncertain of the strength of the force against him, dared not move either. He, too, was trying to get news of the war between Yuan Shao and Cao Cao.

Suddenly, orders came for the Cao army to launch an attack against Liu Bei and then discord rose between the two officers.

Liu Dai said, "The prime minister has ordered an attack on the city—you advance."

Wang Zhong replied, "But the prime minister named you first."

"I'm the commander in chief—it's not my place to go first."

"Then let's go together," said Wang Zhong.

"We'll draw lots and let it be decided by fate," said Liu Tai.

They drew lots and it fell to Wang Zhong, who was compelled to advance toward Xuzhou with half the force.

When Liu Bei heard of the threatened attack he called Chen Deng for consultation.

Liu Bei said, "There is dissension in Yuan Shao's camp at Liyang, so they do not advance. We do not know where Cao Cao is. They say his personal banner is not displayed in the Liyang camp. Why, then, is it shown here?'

Chen Deng replied, "His tricks take a hundred forms. He certainly regards the north as more important and has gone there to supervise, but he deliberately shows his flag here instead of there, and I feel sure it is only meant to mislead us. He cannot be here."

Then Liu Bei asked his two brothers, "Which one of you will go and find out the truth?"

Zhang Fei volunteered at once.

"You're unsuited for this," said Liu Bei. "You're too impetuous."

"If Cao Cao's here then I'll haul him out!" said Zhang Fei.

"Let me go first and find out," said Guan Yu.

"If you go I'll have no fear," said Liu Bei.

So Guan Yu set out with 3,000 soldiers. It was then early winter and snow was falling from a somber sky. Braving the snow, they deployed near Wang Zhong's camp. Guan Yu rode out and summoned Wang Zhong to a parley.

"The prime minister is here—why don't you surrender?" said Wang Zhong.

"Ask him to come to the front. I have something to say to him," replied Guan Yu.

"Is the prime minister likely to come out to see someone like you?"

Guan Yu angrily dashed forward and Wang Zhong set his spear to meet him. Guan Yu rode till he came close to his antagonist, then suddenly wheeled away. Wang Zhong went after him, following up a slope. Just as they passed over the crest, Guan Yu turned back and, with a mighty shout he flourished his weighty sword. Wang Zhong could not withstand it and fled. But Guan Yu, shifting the huge sword to his left hand, laid hold of his victim with his right hand by the straps of the man's breastplate, lifted him out of the saddle, and rode away to his own lines with the captive laid across the pommel of his saddle. Wang Zhong's men scattered.

The captive was brought to Xuzhou, where he was summoned into the presence of Liu Bei.

"Who are you? What office do you hold? How dare you falsely display the ensigns of the prime minister?" asked Liu Bei.

"I was simply obeying orders," said Wang Zhong. "The prime minister told me to give the impression that he was present. Really he is not there."

Liu Bei treated him kindly, giving him food and clothing, but put him in prison till his colleague could be captured.

Guan Yu said, "I know you have peaceful intentions in mind so I have captured the man instead of slaying him."

Liu Bei said to Zhang Fei, "I was afraid that with your hasty and impulsive temper you would have slain this man, so I could not send you. There is no advantage in killing persons of this sort. While alive, they are often useful for amicable settlements."

At this Zhang Fei said, "You've got this Wang Zhong; now I'll go and capture the other man."

"Be careful," said his elder brother. "Liu Dai was once governor of Yanzhou and he was one of the lords who fought at Tigertrap Pass to destroy Dong Zhuo. He's not to be treated lightly."

"I don't think he's worth mentioning. I'll bring him in alive, just as my brother did with this other."

"But if you kill him, it'll upset my great design," said Liu Bei.

"If I do, I'll forfeit my own life," said Zhang Fei.

So he was also given 3,000 men for the task.

The capture of his colleague made Liu Dai careful. He strengthened his defenses and stayed behind them. He took no notice of the daily challenges and continual insults that followed Zhang Fei's arrival.

After some days Zhang Fei thought of a plan. He ordered his men to prepare a raid on the enemy's camp that night, but he himself spent the day drinking. Pretending to be very intoxicated he intentionally found fault with a soldier, who was severely flogged and then bound by his hands and feet in the camp. Zhang Fei said, "Wait till I am ready to sally forth tonight—you will be offered as a sacrifice to the flag." At the same time he gave secret orders to the guards to let the man escape.

The man crept out of camp and went over to the enemy, to whom he betrayed Zhang Fei's plan of a night attack. As the man bore signs of savage punishment, Liu Dai did not suspect his tale. He made careful arrangements, setting his men in ambush outside his camp so that it was empty.

That night, however, Zhang Fei divided his men into three parties, and only thirty men were ordered to make a show of attacking the camp and lighting a fire. Two larger bodies of men were to go round to the rear of the camp and attack simultaneously, once they saw the fire started.

The plan was carried out as he had designed. At midnight Zhang Fei, with his veterans, went to cut off Liu Dai's road of retreat. The thirty men commanded to start a fire made their way into the camp and were successful. When the flames arose, Liu Dai's men who had been lying in ambush rushed out to attack, only to find themselves assailed on both sides. This confused them and as they knew nothing of the number of their attackers they were panic-stricken and scattered.

Liu Dai, with a company of his men, got clear of the fight and fled, but he ran straight into Zhang Fei. Escape was impossible and after only one bout he was captured by Zhang Fei and his men surrendered.

Zhang Fei immediately sent news of this success to his brothers.

Liu Bei was very pleased. He said to Guan Yu, "Yi-de's always been rather impetuous, but this time he's acted wisely."

They rode out of the city to welcome their brother.

"You said I was too rough; how about now?" said Zhang Fei to his brothers.

"If I hadn't put you on your mettle you'd not have developed this stratagem," said Liu Bei.

Zhang Fei laughed. Then the captive Liu Dai was brought forth. Liu Bei at once dismounted and loosened the cords. "My young brother was rather hasty. Please pardon him."

He was welcomed into the city, where his colleague was also released and both were cared for.

Liu Bei said to them, "I was forced to put Che Zhou to death when he tried to kill me, but the prime minister mistook it as defection and sent you two generals to punish me. I have received much kindness from him and certainly would not dream of betraying him. I will appreciate it if you can explain this to the prime minister when you get back."

"We are deeply grateful that you spare our lives and we will tell the prime minister that we can guarantee your loyalty on the lives of our two households."

The next day, the two leaders and their army were allowed to depart unharmed. But before they had gone ten *li* they heard the beating of drums and there appeared Zhang Fei, barring the road.

"My brother is not in his right mind. How could he set free you two captives?"

This made the two men tremble with fear, but as the fierce-eyed warrior with uplifted sword charged toward them they heard another man galloping up and shouting, "Don't behave so disgracefully!"

The newcomer was Guan Yu, whose appearance relieved the two men of all fear.

"Our brother has released them. Why do you disobey his order and try to stop them?" he cried.

"If they're let go today they'll surely come back," said Zhang Fei.

"Wait till they do, then you may kill them," replied Guan Yu.

The two leaders with one voice cried, "Even if the prime minister slays our whole clan we will never come again. Please pardon us."

Zhang Fei said, "If Cao Cao himself comes I'll destroy him completely. Not even a single fragment of armor will remain. But for this time I leave you your heads."

Clapping their hands to their heads the two men scuttled off, while the two brothers returned to the city.

"Cao Cao will certainly come," they said.

Sun Qian advised, "This is not a city that can hold out for long. We should send part of our forces to the two neighboring towns of Xiaopei and Xiapi. The three places can assist each other against Cao Cao."

Liu Bei agreed and told Guan Yu to guard Xiapi, to which he also sent his two wives, the ladies Gan and Mi. The former was a native of Xiaopei, while the latter was Mi Zhu's sister. Sun Qian and three others were left to defend Xuzhou and Liu Bei went to station in Xiaopei with Zhang Fei.

The two released officers returned to the capital and explained to Cao Cao that Liu Bei had not rebelled. But he became exceedingly angry with them. "You shameful cowards, what use do you have?"

He roared to the guards to take them away for instant execution.

> *How can a dog or a pig expect to conquer in a tiger's strife?*
> *Minnows and shrimps that with dragons contend already have done with life.*

The fate of the two officers will be told in the next chapter.

CHAPTER TWENTY-THREE

Mi Heng Strips and Rails at Cao Cao
Ji Ping Is Tortured for Poisoning Cao Cao

At the close of the last chapter the two unsuccessful officers, Liu Dai and Wang Zhong, were in danger of death. However, Kong Rong remonstrated with Cao Cao, saying, "You knew these two men were no match for Liu Bei. If you put them to death because they failed, you will lose the support of your men."

Therefore the death sentence was not carried out but they were deprived of rank and status. Cao Cao would have led an army himself to attack Liu Bei, but the weather was too inclement. So it was decided to wait until the spring. In the interval there would be time to arrange peace with Zhang Xiu and Liu Biao.

So an envoy was sent to Zhang Xiu and in due time he reached his destination. He first had an interview with Jia Xu, to whom he extolled Cao Cao's virtues. Jia Xu seemed to be impressed, and kept him as a guest at his home.

The next day the advisor went in to see Zhang Xiu and told him that Cao Cao had sent a messenger to negotiate peace. While the discussion was in progress another messenger from Yuan Shao was announced and he was called in. The man presented Yuan Shao's letter, which also proposed terms of peace. Jia Xu asked him how his master's war with Cao Cao was progressing.

"The war is suspended for the moment on account of the cold weather," replied the messenger. "As you, General, and Liu Biao are both well respected officers of the state, I have been sent to request your help."

Jia Xu laughed. "You can return to your master and say that he could not even tolerate rivalry from his own brother. How could he put up with that of all the officers of the state?"

So saying he tore the letter into fragments before the messenger's face and angrily sent him away.

Zhang Xiu said, "But his master, Yuan Shao, is stronger than Cao Cao.

You have torn up his letter and driven away his man. What if he comes to attack us?"

"Better to join hands with Cao Cao," said Jia Xu.

"Between us there is still an unavenged enmity. He will not really accept me."

Jia Xu said, "There are three advantages in joining hands with Cao Cao. First, he has an order from the Emperor to restore peace in the country. Secondly, as Yuan Shao is very strong, the little help we can offer will not be appreciated, while we will loom large and be well treated by Cao Cao. Thirdly, Cao Cao has ambitious designs and he will ignore all private feuds in order to impress the whole country of his magnanimity. I hope, General, you will see these things clearly and hesitate no longer."

Zhang Xiu was persuaded and received Cao Cao's messenger, who again eulogized the virtues of his master. "If my master had any thought of the old quarrel he would hardly have sent me to make peace, would he?" he added.

Zhang Xiu, now convinced, proceeded with Jia Xu to the capital, where formal submission was made. At the interview he bowed low at the entrance, but Cao Cao, hastening forward, took him by the hand and helped him to his feet. "Please forget that little fault of mine," said Cao Cao.

Zhang Xiu and Jia Xu were both rewarded with high ranks.

Cao Cao then asked Zhang Xiu to write to his friend Liu Biao to seek his support.

Jia Xu said, "Liu Biao favors scholarly men. If some famous scholar can be delegated with the job he would submit immediately."

Then Xun You suggested that Kong Rong was the right person to take up the task. Cao Cao agreed and sent him to speak with Kong Rong about this.

Xun You went to see Kong Rong and said, "The prime minister wants a scholar of reputation to act as a messenger to Liu Biao. Can you undertake this task?"

Kong Rong replied, "I have a friend called Mi Heng whose talents are ten times greater than mine. He ought to be constantly at the side of the Emperor and not merely be sent as a state messenger. I will recommend him to the Emperor."

So he wrote the following memorial:

"I hear great waters flow across the land and the Emperor seeks out men of talent from all directions. In olden times, when Emperor Wu of West Han desired to enlarge his borders, crowds of scholars responded to his call.

"Being intelligent and holy, Your Majesty ascended the throne. You have fallen upon evil days, but have been diligent, modest, and untiring in your efforts. Now from on high have descended gods and on all sides appear men of genius.

"I, your humble servant, know of a certain scholar, Mi Heng by name, of Pingyuan, a young man of twenty-four. His moral character is excellent, his talents eminent. As a youth he took a high place in study and penetrated into the very secret of learning. What he saw he could repeat, what he heard once he never forgot. His character conforms with high principles and his thoughts are divine. His mental calculations and mnemonic feats can be compared with the best in history. Loyal and honest, he cherishes the noblest of aspirations. He regards the good with deferential respect, he detests the evil with uncompromising hatred. Even the most renowned officials in ancient days could not surpass him in unflinching candor and severe rectitude.

"Hundreds of hawks are not worth one osprey. If Mi Heng be given a court appointment, notable results must follow. Ready in debate, quick of speech, his overwhelming intelligence wells up in profusion—in solving problems and unraveling difficulties he has no peer.

"In former days Jia Yi* asked to be sent to a vassal state to tame its king and Zhong Jun† offered to bring the ruler of a southern kingdom with a long rope. The brave conducts of these youths have been much admired. Examples of extraordinary talents also occur in our time. And Mi Heng is no less capable. Should he be got, then all possibilities may be realized; the dragon may leap into the celestial paths and fly along the Milky Way; fame will extend to the poles of the universe and hang in the firmament with rainbow glory. He will add to the glory of all the officials in court and enhance the majesty of the palace. The music from Heaven must possess fantastic beauty and the palace of the Emperor should contain rare treasures.

"Men like Mi Heng are rare. As with the singing of the most beautiful songs of old, the best performers are sought, and the fastest horses are looked for by the most skillful judges of horses, so I, ever humble, dare not conceal this man. Your Majesty is careful in the selection of servants and should try him. Let him be summoned as he is, simply clad in his plain robe, and should he not appear worthy then may I be punished for the fault of deception."

---

* A poet and political theorist during the West Han Dynasty.

† An official in the West Han Dynasty, who volunteered to negotiate peace between Han and South Yue.

The Emperor read the memorial and passed it on to Cao Cao, who duly summoned Mi Heng. The young man came, but after his formal salutations were over he was left standing and not invited to sit down. Looking up to heaven he sighed deeply and said, "Wide as the universe is, it cannot produce a single man."

"Under my orders are scores of men who are all recognized heroes. What do you mean by saying there is not a single man?" said Cao Cao.

"I should be glad to hear who they are," said Mi Heng.

"Xun Yu, Xun You, Guo Jia, and Cheng Yu are all men of profound wisdom and prophetic vision, superior to Xiao He and Cheng Ping, who served the founder of West Han; Zhang Liao, Xu Chu, Li Dian, and Yue Jin are bravest warriors, better than the two generals, Cen Peng and Ma Wu, who fought for the first emperor of East Han. Lu Qian and Man Chong are my secretaries; Yue Jin and Xu Huang are my van leaders; Xiahou Dun is one of the country's marvels, and Cao Ren the most successful officer of the age. Now how can you say there are no men?"

"Sir, you are quite mistaken," said Mi Heng with a smile. "I know all these men you have just named. None of them is equal to what I mean by 'man.' Xun Yu is qualified only to pose at a funeral or ask after a sick man; Xun You, to be a tomb warden; Cheng Yu, to shut doors and bolt windows; Guo Jia, to recite poems; Zhang Liao, to beat drums and clang gongs; Xu Chu, to lead cattle to pasture; Yue Jin, to be a clerk at a criminal court, and Li Dian, to deliver dispatches and notices; Lu Qian, to make armor; Man Chong, to drink wine and eat brewers' grains; Yue Jin, to carry planks and build walls; and Xu Huang, to kill pigs and slay dogs. Xiahou Dun should be styled 'Whole Body' General and Cao Ren should be called 'Money-grubbing Prefect.' As for the remainder, they are mere clothes horses, rice sacks, wine butts, and flesh bags."

"And what special gifts do you have?' said Cao Cao angrily.

"I know everything in the sky above and the earth beneath. I am conversant with the Three Religions and the Nine Systems of Philosophy. I could make my Emperor the rival of the wise, ancient rulers Yao and Shun and compare in virtue with Confucius and his best disciple, Yan Yuan. Can I be discussed on equal terms with common people?"

At that moment only Zhang Liao was present at Cao Cao's side and he raised his sword to slay the impudent speaker but Cao Cao said, "I need a drummer to play on festive occasions. I can use him for the job."

Instead of indignantly refusing this role, Mi Heng accepted the position and went out.

"He was very insolent," said Zhang Liao, "Why not put him to death?"

"He enjoys some sort of a reputation and is known to people far and near. If I put him to death, they will say I am intolerant. As he boasts of ability, I have made him a drummer to humble him."

A few days later, Cao Cao instituted a banquet to which a great many guests were invited. He gave orders for the new drummer to play. The old drummer told Mi Heng that he should wear new clothes to beat the drum. But Mi Heng took his place with the other musicians clad in old and worn garments. The piece chosen was an old tune and from the very first taps on the drum the effect was exquisite, profound as the notes from metal and stone. The performance stirred so deeply the emotions of the guests that they even shed tears.

The attendants said sternly, "Why didn't you put on your new robe?"

Mi Heng stripped off his frayed and torn robe and stood there facing them, naked as he was born. The assembled guests covered their faces. Then the drummer drew up his under garments.

"Why do you behave so rudely at this sacred place?" reproached Cao Cao.

"To flout one's king and insult one's superiors is real rudeness," cried Mi Heng. "I bare the form bestowed to me by my parents to reveal my clean body."

"So you are clean! And who is foul?"

"You do not distinguish between the wise and the foolish, which is to have foul vision; you do not read the Odes or the Histories, which is to have foul speech; you are deaf to honest words, which is to have foul ears; you are not conversant with past and present events, which is to be foul without; you cannot tolerate the nobles, which is to be foul within; you harbor thoughts of rebellion, which is to have a foul heart. I am the most famous scholar in the world and you make me a drummer boy—that is like Yang Huo belittling Confucius or Zang Chang vilifying Mencius. You aspire to be the greatest of nobles, yet you insult men of wisdom like this!"

Now Kong Rong, who had recommended Mi Heng to the Emperor, was among the guests and he feared for the life of his friend. So he tried to calm the storm.

"Mi Heng is as guilty as a common prisoner," he said slowly. "He is not worth your notice, sir."

Pointing to Mi Heng, Cao Cao said, "I will send you to Jingzhou as my messenger and if Liu Biao surrenders to me I will give you a post at court."

But Mi Heng would not go. So Cao Cao ordered two of his men to go with him. They were to prepare three horses, set Mi Heng in the middle one and drag him along the road between them.

On the day they departed Cao Cao told his subordinates of various ranks to assemble at the east gate to see the messenger start. Xun Yu said,

"When Mi Heng comes we will not rise to salute him."

So when Mi Heng came, dismounted, and entered the waiting room, they all sat stiff and silent. Mi Heng wailed loudly.

"Why are you doing that?" asked Xun Yu.

"Should not one wail when one walks among corpses in coffins?" said Mi Heng.

"We may be corpses," they cried together, "but you are a headless wild ghost."

"I am an official of Han and I will not be a partisan of Cao Cao's," he said. "How can I have no head?"

They were so angry that they wanted to kill him, but Xun Yu checked them. "He is but a paltry thing, not worth soiling your blades with."

"I may be paltry yet I still have the soul of a man and you are mere worms," said Mi Heng.

They all went away very angry.

Mi Heng began his journey and presently reached Jingzhou, where he saw Liu Biao. But under the pretense of extolling his virtue, he held him in derision. Liu Biao was annoyed and sent him away to see Huang Zu.

"Why didn't you put the fellow to death for his impudence?" asked his men.

Liu Biao explained, "Mi Heng ridiculed Cao Cao several times, but Cao Cao did not kill him for fear of losing popular favor. So he sent him to me in an attempt to use my hand to slay him so that I will suffer the loss of my good name. Now I have sent him on to Huang Zu to let Cao Cao see that I have seen through his scheme." His clever caution met with general approval.

At that time a messenger from Yuan Shao also arrived with proposals for an alliance and it was necessary to decide which side to support. All the advisors were called together to consider the question.

Han Song said, "Now that the two powerful men Yuan Shao and Cao Cao are at war with each other, it is your chance, General, to destroy them and accomplish your own great plans. But if you have no schemes for the present, then I think you should choose to support the one that is more likely to win the war. Now Cao Cao is an able general and has many capable men in his service. It seems to me that he may destroy Yuan Shao and then move his armies across the river. I fear, General, that you would be unable to withstand him. So I think it would be wise to support Cao Cao. He will treat you with respect."

Liu Biao said, "You go to the capital first and see how things stand. That will help me to decide."

Han Song replied, "The positions of master and servant are clearly defined. Now I am your man and I am prepared to go all lengths for you and obey you to the last. If you are ready to serve the Emperor and follow Cao Cao, then you can send me as your envoy. But if you are still undecided, then I must warn you: Suppose the Emperor gives me an office when I get there then I will become his servant and will not be ready to face death for you."

"You go and find out what you can. I have some plans."

So Han Song took his leave and went to the capital to see Cao Cao, who gave him rank and made him Prefect of Lingling. The advisor Xun Yu was unhappy about this and said to his master, "This man has come to spy out how things are. He has done nothing to deserve reward and yet you give him an office like this. And there is no news from Mi Heng. You have sent him away but you do not ask his whereabouts. Why?"

"Mi Heng shamed me too deeply before all the world so I have borrowed Liu Biao's hand to remove him. It is not necessary to ask about him," said Cao Cao.

Then Han Song was sent back to Jingzhou to persuade his former master to surrender. When he saw Liu Biao he was full of praise for the virtues of the court and was keen on persuading him to send his son to serve under the Emperor. Liu Biao became very angry, charged him with treachery, and threatened him with death.

"You failed me, General, but I did not betray you!" cried Han Song.

Kuai Liang reminded Liu Biao that Han Song had foretold this possibility before he left and Liu Biao, who was just and reasonable, pardoned him.

The news arrived that Mi Heng had been put to death by Huang Zu. It so happened that the two of them were drinking together for some time. Both being the worse for liquor, they had begun to discuss the worth of people.

"You were in the capital," said Huang Zu. "Who was there of worth?"

"The big boy was Kong Rong and the little one Yang Xiu. There was no one else of note."

"What about me?" asked Huang Zu.

"You are like a god in a temple; you sit still and receive sacrifices but do not answer the prayers of your worshippers."

"Do you regard me as an image of clay?" cried Huang Zu in a rage.

So he put the impudent speaker to death. Even at the very point of death Mi Heng never ceased his railing and abuse.

Liu Biao sighed deeply when he heard of his fate. He had the victim honorably interred by the side of Parrot Isle. And a later poet wrote the following to mourn over Mi Heng:

Huang Zu could brook no rival; at his word
Mi Heng met death beneath the cruel sword.
His grave on Parrot Isle may yet be seen,
The river flowing past it, coldly green.

Cao Cao heard of the young man's death with pleasure. "The putrid bookworm has just cut himself up with his own sharp tongue," he said.

As there was no sign of Liu Biao coming to join him, Cao Cao began to think of coercion by force. The advisor, Xun Yu, dissuaded him from this course of action.

He said, "Yuan Shao is not subjugated and Liu Bei is not destroyed. To attack Liu Biao would be to neglect the vital in favor of the immaterial. Destroy the two chief enemies first and the east is yours at one blow."

Cao Cao took the advice.

After the departure of Liu Bei, Dong Cheng discussed day and night with his comrades, trying to evolve plans for the destruction of Cao Cao, but they could see no chance to attack. On the New Year's Day court gathering, he found Cao Cao even more odiously arrogant and overweening. He was so disgusted with the tyrant that he fell ill. Hearing of his illness, the Emperor sent the court physician to see him.

The court physician was a famous doctor from Luoyang, named Ji Ping. At the Emperor's order he came to Dong Cheng's house and devoted himself wholly to the treatment of his patient. Living in his place and seeing him at all times he soon found that some secret grief was sorely troubling him. However, he dared not ask questions.

On the evening of the lantern festival, the physician asked for leave but Dong Cheng kept him back and the two men had some wine together. They sat drinking for some time and by and by Dong Cheng dropped off to sleep dressed as he was.

Presently his good friend Wang Zi-fu and the three others were announced. As they were coming in Wang Zi-fu cried, "Our business is settled!"

"Really? Tell me all about it," said Dong Cheng excitedly.

"Liu Biao has joined Yuan Shao and an army of 500,000 men is on its way here by ten different routes. Moreover, Ma Teng and Han Sui are coming from the north with a force of 720,000 men. Cao Cao has moved every soldier outside the capital to meet the combined armies and the city is virtually unguarded. As it's the lantern festival tonight there will be a great banquet in Cao Cao's house in celebration. If we gather the servants of our five families, we can muster more than a thousand men, and while he's at the banquet we can surround his place and finish him off.

We mustn't miss this chance!"

Dong Cheng was more than delighted. They decided to assemble inside the inner gate of his house at the second watch. Dong Cheng called his servants and armed them, put on his own armor, and mounted his horse. Then the small army marched straight into Cao Cao's house, Dong Cheng leading with his sword drawn. He found his intended victim at a table in his private quarters. Dong Cheng cried, "Stay, you arch rebel!" and dashed at Cao Cao, who fell at the first blow.

…Just then Dong Cheng woke up and found it was all a dream. But he was still cursing his enemy.

"Do you really wish to destroy Cao Cao?" said Ji Ping, going forward to his half awakened patient.

This brought him to his senses. Dong Cheng, terror stricken, could not reply.

"Do not be frightened, sir," said the doctor, "Although I am only a physician I never forget my Emperor. For many days I have seen you sighing with grief but I have never ventured to ask the reason. Now you have shown it in your dream and I know your real feelings. If I can be of any use I will help. Nothing daunts me."

Dong Cheng covered his face and wept. "I fear you may not be true to me," he cried.

Ji Ping at once bit off a finger as a pledge of his faith. Then Dong Cheng showed the doctor the Emperor's decree. "I am afraid our schemes will come to nothing," he said. "Liu Bei and Ma Teng are gone and there is nothing we can do. That was the real reason I fell ill."

"It is not worth troubling you gentlemen with, for Cao Cao's life lies in my hands," said Ji Ping.

"How can that be?"

"Because he often has severe headaches. When this happens, he sends for me. Next time he calls me I only have to give him one dose of poison and he will certainly die. There is no need of any weapons."

"If only you could do it! You would be the savior of the Han Dynasty!"

Then Ji Ping went away leaving his late patient a happy man. Dong Cheng strolled into the garden and there he saw one of his slaves whispering with a waiting maid in a dark corner. This annoyed him and he called his attendants to seize them. He would have put them to death but for the intervention of his wife. At her request he spared their lives but both were beaten, and the lad was thrown into a dungeon. Feeling bitter at his treatment the slave escaped in the night, climbed over the wall and went straight to Cao Cao, where he betrayed his master's secret.

Cao Cao at once had him taken into a private chamber and questioned, at which the servant gave the names of the conspirators and told as much as he knew. He said his master had a piece of white silk, with writing on it, but he did not know what it was. He also told Cao Cao that he had lately seen the doctor biting off one of his fingers as a pledge of fidelity.

The runaway slave was kept in a secret part of Cao Cao's house while his late master, only knowing that he had escaped, took no special means to find him.

Soon after this, Cao Cao feigned a headache and sent for Ji Ping as usual.

"The rebel is done for," thought Ji Ping, and he made a secret package of poison, which he took with him to the prime minister. Cao Cao was in bed when he got there and ordered him to prepare the medicine for him.

"One draught will cure this disease," said Ji Ping. He asked the attendants to bring him a pipkin and he prepared the potion in front of them. When it had simmered for some time and was half dried up the poison was added, and soon after the physician presented the draught. Cao Cao, knowing it was poisoned, made excuses and would not swallow it.

"You should take it hot," said the doctor. "Then there will be a gentle perspiration and you will feel better."

"You are a scholar," said Cao Cao, sitting up, "and know what is the correct thing to do. When the Emperor is ill and has to take medicine, his officials first taste; when the father is ill, his son first tastes the medicine. You are my confidant and should drink first. Then I will swallow the remainder."

"Medicine is to treat disease; what is the need of tasting it first by someone else?" replied Ji Ping. But he guessed now the secret had been discovered so he dashed forward, seized Cao Cao by the ear, and tried to pour the potion down his throat. Cao Cao pushed it away and it spilt onto the bricks, which at once were spoiled. Before Cao Cao could speak his servants had already seized the poor doctor.

Cao Cao said, "I was not ill. I only wanted to test you. So you really thought to poison me."

He sent for a score of sturdy jailers who carried off the prisoner to the back courtyard to be interrogated. Cao Cao took his seat in a pavilion and the hapless physician, tightly bound, was thrown to the ground before him. The prisoner betrayed no trace of fear.

Cao Cao said "You are merely a physician—I know you would not dare to poison me. Someone must have incited you to commit this crime. If you tell me I will pardon you."

"You are a rebel—you flout the Emperor and injure your superiors. The whole country wishes to kill you. Do you think I am the only one?"

Cao Cao again and again pressed the prisoner to confess what he knew, but he only replied that no one had sent him; it was his own desire.

"As I have failed I will die," he added.

Cao Cao angrily ordered the jailers to give him a severe beating and they flogged him for several hours. His skin hung in tatters, the flesh was battered, and the blood from his wounds ran down the steps. Then fearing he might die and his information be lost, Cao Cao told them to cease and remove him. They took him off to a quiet place where he might recover a little.

The next day Cao Cao gave a banquet to which he invited the court officials, including his five enemies. Dong Cheng made an excuse of being unwell and did not show up. The others dared not stay away as they feared they would be suspected.

Tables were laid in the inner hall and after several courses the host said, "There is not much to amuse us today but I have a man to show you that will sober you."

"Bring him in," he said, turning to the jailers, and the bold doctor appeared, securely fastened in a wooden collar. He was placed where all could see him.

"You officials will not know that this man is connected with a gang of evil doers who desire to overturn the government and even injure me. However, Heaven has defeated their plans, but I desire that you should hear his confession."

Then Cao Cao ordered the jailers to beat the prisoner. They did so till he lay unconscious. They revived him by spraying water over his face. As soon as came to, he glared at his oppressor and ground his teeth.

"Cao Cao, you hateful rebel! What are you waiting for? Why not kill me?" cried Ji Ping.

Cao Cao replied, "The conspirators were only six at first—you made the seventh."

Here the prisoner broke in with more abuse, while Wang Zi-fu and his three friends exchanged glances, looking as though they were sitting on a rug full of needles. Cao Cao continued his torture of the prisoner, beating him into unconsciousness and reviving him with cold water, but the victim refused to ask for mercy. Finally Cao Cao realized the futility of this approach and so he told the jailers to remove him.

At the close of the banquet, when the guests were dispersing, the four of them were invited to remain behind to supper. They were so terrified that their souls seemed no longer to inhabit their bodies, but there was no way out for them. Presently Cao Cao said, "I should not have retained you but there is something I want to ask you about. I do not know what you four have been arranging with Dong Cheng."

"Nothing at all," answered Wang Zi-fu.

"And what is written on the white silk?" asked Cao Cao.

They all said they knew nothing about it.

Then Cao Cao ordered the runaway slave to be brought in. Wang Zi-fu asked, "Well, what have you seen and where?"

The slave replied, "You six hid yourselves in a room and secretly wrote your names down on a white scroll. You cannot deny that."

Wang Zi-fu replied, "This wretched creature was punished for misbehavior with one of Dong Cheng's maids and now because of that he slanders his master. You must not listen to him."

"Ji Ping tried to poison me. Who told him to do that if it was not Dong Cheng?"

They all said they knew nothing about who it was.

"If you confess tonight," said Cao Cao, "you might be pardoned. But if the plot is exposed, you will not be able to escape punishment."

They vigorously denied that any plot existed. However, Cao Cao called up his henchmen and the four men were put into confinement.

The next day Cao Cao went with a large following to Dong Cheng's place to ask after his health. Dong Cheng came out to receive his visitor, who at once asked, "Why did you not come last night?"

"I am not quite well yet and have to be very careful about going out," replied Dong Cheng.

"Presumably you were suffering from a sadness for the nation, eh?" said Cao Cao.

Dong Cheng started.

Cao Cao continued, "Have you heard of the Ji Ping affair?"

"No—what is it?"

Cao Cao smiled coldly. "How can it be that you do not know?"

Cao Cao turned to his attendants and told them to bring in the prisoner, to cure his host's illness.

Dong Cheng was scared out of his wits and did not know what to do. Soon, the jailers led in the physician to the steps of the hall. At once the bound man began to rail at Cao Cao as a rebel and a traitor.

"This man," said Cao Cao, pointing to Ji Ping, "has implicated Wang Zi-fu and three others, all of whom are now under arrest. There is one more whom I have not caught yet."

"Who sent you to poison me?" interrogated Cao Cao, turning toward the physician. "Quick, tell me."

"Heaven sent me to slay a traitor."

Cao Cao angrily ordered the jailers to beat him again, but there was no unharmed part of his body that could be beaten. Dong Cheng sat looking at him and felt as if his heart were transfixed with a dagger.

"You were born with ten fingers—how is it you now have only nine?"

Ji Ping replied, "I bit off one as a pledge when I swore to slay a traitor."

Cao Cao told his men to bring a knife and they lopped off his nine other fingers.

"Now they are all off—that will teach you to make pledges."

"Still I have a mouth that can swallow a traitor and a tongue that can curse him," said Ji Ping.

Cao told them to cut out his tongue.

But before they could do this, Ji Ping said, "No. I cannot endure any more punishment, I will have to speak out. Loosen my bonds."

"Loosen them," said Cao Cao to his guards. "There is nothing to fear."

As soon as he was free Ji Ping stood up, and turning his face toward the direction of the Emperor's Palace he bowed and said, "It is Heaven's will that your servant has been unable to remove the evil." And the brave and loyal doctor killed himself by hitting his head on the steps.

His body was quartered and exposed.

This happened in the first month of the fifth year of the reign of Jian An. A certain historian wrote a poem to lament the doctor's death:

> There lived in the sad days of Han
> A brave doctor of the name Ji Ping
> Who risked his very life
> His Emperor to save.
> Alas! he failed, but lasting fame
> Is his. He feared not death
> And cursed the traitorous Minister.
> To the last of his breath.

Seeing his victim had passed beyond the realms of punishment, Cao Cao had the slave led in.

"Do you know this man?"

"Yes," cried Dong Cheng. "So the runaway slave is here—he ought to be put to death."

"He reported your plot to me and is my witness," said Cao Cao. "Who dares to kill him?"

"Why do you, sir, heed the unsupported tale of a runaway slave?"

"I have Wang Zi-fu and the others in prison," said Cao Cao. "How can you refute the evidence?"

He then ordered his men to arrest Dong Cheng and to search his bedroom. Soon, they found the decree and the pledge signed by the officials loyal to the Emperor.

Cao Cao read it and laughed. "Those lowly rats! I will not let them get away with this!"

He gave orders to arrest the whole household, without exception. Then he returned to his house with the incriminating documents and called all his advisors together to discuss the dethronement of the Emperor and the setting up of a successor.

> *Several lines written in blood accomplished nothing;*
> *One inscribed pledge brought mountains of sorrow.*

The fate of the Emperor will be told in the next chapter.

CHAPTER TWENTY-FOUR

Cao Cao Kills Lady Dong, the Emperor's Concubine Liu Bei Seeks Refuge with Yuan Shao after His Defeat by Cao Cao

The last chapter closed with the discovery of the decree and the assembly of Cao Cao's advisors to consider the deposition of Emperor Xian. Cheng Yu spoke strongly against this: "Sir, the reason why you impress the world and rule the government is because you act in the name of the House of Han. In these times of turmoil and rivalry among the nobles, such a step as the deposition of the ruler will certainly bring about war against you and should be minimized."

After reflection Cao Cao abandoned the design. But Dong Cheng and his four friends, with every member of their households totaling seven hundred or more, were taken and put to death at the four gates of the city. Both officials and the people all wept at such brutal slaughter.

A poet composed the following to praise the loyal Dong Cheng:

> *A secret decree in a girdle sewn,*
> *In red blood written, the Emperor's own,*
> *To the staunch and faithful Dong addressed,*
> *Who had saved him once when enemies pressed,*
> *And who, sore grieved at his sovereign's fate,*
> *Expressed in dreams his ceaseless hate.*
> *Speak not that he had failed*
> *For his glory remained.*

Another poet wrote of the sad fate of Wang Zi-fu and his friends:

> *Undaunted they signed the silken roll,*
> *And pledged themselves to save their King from shame.*
> *Alas! black death of them took heavy toll,*
> *To write their names upon the roll of fame.*

But the slaughter of the five officials and their entire households did not appease the wrath of the cruel minister. As the Emperor's concubine was the sister of Dong Cheng, Cao Cao, sword in hand, went into the palace to slay her. The Emperor loved her tenderly, the more so as she was then in the fifth month of pregnancy. That day the Emperor and the Empress were sitting in their room, secretly wondering why nothing seemed to have been done about the decree. The sudden appearance of the angry minister, armed as he was, frightened them greatly.

"Does Your Majesty know that Dong Cheng conspired against me?" asked Cao Cao.

"Dong Zhuo died long ago," replied the Emperor.

"Not Dong Zhuo—Dong Cheng," roared Cao Cao.

The Emperor trembled with terror but he gasped out, "Really, I did not know."

"So the cut finger and the decree written in blood are all forgotten, eh?"

The Emperor could not answer. Cao Cao commanded his guards to go and take Lady Dong.

"This girl is five-months pregnant. Please have pity for her!" pleaded the Emperor.

"If Heaven had not interposed I would be a dead man. How could I leave this woman to work evil on me by and by?"

The Empress also begged: "Imprison her in one of the palaces till her confinement. Do not harm her now."

"Do you wish me to spare her offspring so that he will grow up to avenge his mother?" retorted Cao Cao.

"I pray that my body may be spared mutilation and not put to shame," said Lady Dong.

Cao Cao bade his men bring her the white silk cord. The Emperor wept bitterly.

"Please do not hate me in the nether world," said the Emperor to her. And his tears fell like rain.

The Empress also wept bitterly.

Cao Cao said furiously, "Stop this affectation." So saying he told the guards to take her away and strangle her in the courtyard.

> *In vain had the fair girl found favor in the sight of her lord,*
> *She died, and the fruit of her womb perished.*
> *Heartbroken her lord sat, powerless to save,*
> *Hiding his face while tears gushed forth.*

When leaving the palace, Cao Cao gave strict orders to the guards to bar entrance to any imperial relatives by marriage. He told them sternly, "If anyone enters without my permission, put him to death; and the guards will share the same punishment for failing to perform their duty."

To make sure that nothing would go amiss he appointed 3,000 of his own trusted men as imperial guards, with Cao Hong in command.

Then Cao Cao said to his councilor, Cheng Yu: "The conspirators in the capital have been removed but there are yet two others, Ma Teng and Liu Bei. These must not be left at large."

Cheng Yu replied, "Ma Teng is strong in the west and could not be easily captured. Send him a letter of kind words so that he will not suspect. Then entice him to come to the capital and he will be at your mercy. Liu Bei is now in Xuzhou, strongly positioned, and not to be lightly treated either. Furthermore, Yuan Shao is at Guandu and his one desire is to attack you. Any attempt on the east will send Liu Bei to him for help. If he comes here while you are away, what then?"

"You are wrong," replied Cao Cao. "Liu Bei is an outstanding figure. If we wait till he is fully fledged and winged, he will be more difficult to deal with. Yuan Shao may be strong but he is not to be feared. He is too undecided to act."

As they were discussing another advisor, Guo Jia, came in and Cao Cao referred the matter to him.

"I want to attack Liu Bei but I fear Yuan Shao might take advantage. What do you think of it?"

"Yuan Shao is slow and hesitant by nature and his advisors are jealous of each other. He is not to be feared. Liu Bei is getting together a new army and has not yet won their hearts. You could secure the east in one battle."

Being in harmony with Cao Cao's own opinion, this advice pleased him and he prepared an army of 200,000 men to move in five divisions against Xuzhou.

Scouts took the news of these preparations to Xuzhou. Sun Qian at once informed Guan Yu and Liu Bei in the two neighboring towns. Liu Bei discussed the matter with him and decided that help must be sought from Yuan Shao. So Sun Qian went north, taking with him a letter from Liu Bei. When he arrived there, he went to see the advisor Tian Feng first, and asked to be introduced to Yuan Shao. Tian Feng took him to his master, to whom Sun Qian presented the letter.

But Yuan Shao was of melancholy countenance and his dress was all awry.

Tian Feng asked, "You do not look well today, sir. What is the matter?"

"I am going to die," replied Yuan Shao.

"How can you say so?"

"I have five sons, but only the youngest is clever enough to understand my ideas. Now he is suffering from a disease which places his life in jeopardy. Do you think I have any heart to talk about other matters?"

"But," said Tian Feng, "the present combination of circumstances is unparalleled. Cao Cao is going to attack the east and the capital will be empty. You can enter it with your army of justice and so perform a good service to the Emperor and save the people from sorrow. You have only to make up your mind to act."

"I know the chance is excellent but I am distressed and fear failure."

"What are you distressed about?" said Tian Feng.

"Among my sons only this special one is remarkable and if anything happens to him I will die."

Thus he was determined not to dispatch any army. He said to Sun Qian: "Go home and tell Liu Bei the reason why I cannot do anything and say that if anything should happen he can come over to me and I will find some means to help him."

Tian Feng struck the ground with his staff. "What a pity!" he cried. "To miss such a unique opportunity just because of the illness of a child. All is lost now!"

He went out, sighing deeply. Seeing that no aid could be obtained Sun Qian returned in great haste. When he related what had happened, Liu Bei was extremely alarmed and did not know what to do.

"Don't be troubled, brother," said Zhang Fei. "Cao Cao's army is coming from a long distance and will be exhausted. We can make a sudden attack before they have time to camp."

"That agrees with the rules of war," said Liu Bei. "I've always thought you were just a bold warrior, but that move against Liu Dai shows that you're becoming a strategist, too."

So he divided his forces between the two of them to carry out his plan that night.

Now while Cao Cao was in the midst of his march toward Xiaopei a strong gust of wind sprang up and broke the staff of one of the banners. Cao Cao called a halt to the march and asked his advisors what this portended.

Xun Yu asked, "From what direction did the wind blow and what was the color of the flag?"

"The wind was from the southeast and the flag was blue and red."

"There is only one interpretation—there will be a raid on the camp tonight."

Cao Cao nodded. At that moment, Mao Jie entered and reported a similar incident. Cao Cao asked him what it might mean.

"To my mind, it means a night raid," he replied.

Pity this descendant of Hans,
Who placed his faith on a night raid.
But the broken staff of a banner warned his enemy.
Why should Heaven favor the wicked?

"This is evidently providence," said Cao Cao and he began to make preparations. He divided his army into nine sections, placing eight of them in ambush all around and leaving only one to put up a show of making a camp.

There was but little moonlight as Liu Bei and Zhang Fei marched their respective armies toward Cao Cao's camp. They had left only Sun Qian to guard Xiaopei. Zhang Fei, since he was the originator of the stratagem, led the way with his light cavalry. As they drew near they found the camp almost empty. Then suddenly lights flashed out all about them and Zhang Fei saw he had fallen into a trap. The ambushing troops came simultaneously from all the eight directions.

Zhang Fei, dashing this way and rushing that, tried desperately to fight his enemies in front and behind to clear a way. But his soldiers, being originally Cao Cao's men, gave in and went over to their old master when the situation became critical.

Zhang Fei met Xu Huang and the two engaged in a fierce battle, but soon he was also attacked by another enemy from behind. At last Zhang Fei cut his way out, followed by only a score of his men. He wanted to return to Xiaopei but the road of retreat was cut off. He thought of making for Xuzhou, but felt certain that way would also be barred. No other way seemed open and so he made for the Mangdang Hills.

In the meantime, Liu Bei was still unaware of what had happened to his youngest brother. As he drew near Cao Cao's camp he heard a great noise. Then he was attacked in the rear and very soon had lost half of his force. Next came Xiahou Dun to assault him. Liu Bei fled but was again pursued by Xiahou Yuan. Glancing about, he found he had less than fifty men supporting him. He hastened in the direction of Xiaopei.

But before long he saw that place in flames. He had to change his plan and went toward Xiapi. However, he found the whole countryside swarmed with his enemy and it was impossible for him to get through. He thought to himself, "Yuan Shao has told Sun Qian that I can find refuge with him if things go awry. I'd better go to him till I can form some other plan of my own." So he decided to take the Qingzhou road but it was also blocked. He finally managed to escape into the open country and made his way north. He was not pursued but his few remaining followers were all captured.

He hastened alone toward Qingzhou, traveling more than three hundred *li* a day. When he reached the city he called the guards to open the gate for him. The guards asked who he was and went in to tell their master Yuan Tan, the eldest son of Yuan Shao. The young man was greatly surprised, but he opened the gates and went to meet Liu Bei, whom he treated with due respect.

Liu Bei told him about his defeat by Cao Cao and expressed his wish for asylum. He was invited to stay at the guesthouse temporarily, while the young man wrote to inform his father. Then he provided an escort to accompany Liu Bei on his journey further north.

At the border of Pingyuan he was met by Yuan Shao himself with a big retinue. Liu Bei offered a humble obeisance, which Yuan Shao hastened to return and said, "I have been very distressed that, on account of my son's illness, I failed to come to your aid. It is great joy to see you now—the one desire of my life is satisfied."

Liu Bei replied, "I am but a wretched man of ill fortune. I have long desired to serve under you, but fate has hitherto denied me that privilege. Now, attacked by Cao Cao, my family lost, I remembered that you, General, are generous enough to receive men from all sides. Therefore I have put aside my feeling of shame to come to you. I trust that I may be found worthy and one day I will prove my gratitude."

Yuan Shao was very pleased and treated him exceedingly well. So from then on Liu Bei settled down in Jizhou with Yuan Shao.

After the capture of Xiaopei, Cao Cao pressed on toward Xuzhou. After a short struggle and the flight of the majority of the defenders, the city was surrendered by Cheng Deng. Cao Cao led his army into the city, restored order, and pacified the people. His next target was Xiapi, where Guan Yu was holding out and guarding Liu Bei's family.

Xun Yu said, "Guan Yu is there, protecting his brother's family, and he will defend the city to the last. If you do not take it quickly Yuan Shao will get it."

"I have always admired Guan Yu, both for his fighting skills and his noble character. I want him to enter my service. Better send someone to persuade him to come over to my side."

"He will not do that," said Guo Jia, "His sense of loyalty is too firm. I fear anyone who goes to speak with him will be harmed."

Then a man stepped out and said, "I know him slightly and I will go."

The speaker was Zhang Liao. Cheng Yu said to him, "Though you are an old acquaintance of his I don't think he is the kind of person to be persuaded. But I have a scheme that will leave him with no alternative and then he will have to enter the service of our minister."

They set the fatal trap beside the lordly tiger's tail,
They hide the hook with fragrant bait to catch the mighty whale.

How was Guan Yu going to be entrapped? This will be told in the next chapter.

CHAPTER TWENTY-FIVE

Guan Yu Proposes Three Conditions on Top of a Hill

Cao Cao Breaks the Siege at Baima

At the close of the last chapter Cheng Yu was about to disclose his plan to induce Guan Yu to betray his brothers. He said, "As Guan Yu is an unusually brave warrior, he can only be reached by superior strategy. Let us send some of the soldiers who have recently surrendered into Xiapi, where they can say they have escaped. They will thus be our men in the city. Then arrange an attack and a feigned defeat to entice Guan Yu to move away from the city. In the meantime, send veteran troops to cut his escape route. Only then can Zhang Liao go and talk to him."

Cao Cao accepted the scheme and a few score of the men who had lately been Liu Bei's men in Xuzhou were sent to Xiapi. Guan Yu believed the story they told him and let them stay in his place.

After this part of the game had been played, Xiahou Dun led 5,000 men to offer battle. At first Guan Yu would not accept the challenge; however, provoked by men sent to hurl insults at him from the foot of the wall, his temper got the better of him and he moved out with 3,000 soldiers. They exchanged some ten bouts and then Xiahou Dun turned to run away. Guan Yu pursued. His opponent stopped and engaged him for a few bouts and fled again. Thus alternately fighting and retreating, he succeeded in enticing Guan Yu to move away from the city for twenty *li*. Then Guan Yu, suddenly remembering the risk to the city, turned his men homeward.

Soon, the sound of a signal bomb was heard and out moved two bodies of men to bar his way. They were commanded by Cao Cao's fiercest fighters, Xu Huang and Xu Chu. Guan Yu fought his way through and hastened forward but from both sides a hundred or so archers let forth arrows that flew like locusts on the wing. Advancing was impossible and he was forced to turn back, but was again attacked by the joint forces of his two enemies. He fought furiously to drive them off and got onto the road to his own city, but soon Xiahou Dun came up again and attacked as fiercely as before. Evening came and still Guan Yu was hemmed in, so he finally went up a low hill, upon which he encamped for a rest.

He was surrounded on all sides by enemies. Looking toward his city, he saw it lit up in raging fire. But he did not know that it was the soldiers sent by his enemy that had opened the gate to Cao Cao, who had gone in with his mighty force. They had started the fire in order to upset Guan Yu, and indeed the sight alarmed him very much.

In the night he made several efforts to escape from the hill, but every attempt was checked by flights of arrows. At daybreak he prepared for one more effort, but before moving he saw a horseman riding up at full speed and he recognized him as his old acquaintance Zhang Liao. When within speaking distance, Guan Yu asked, "Have you come to fight me?"

"No," replied Zhang Liao. "I have come to see you because of our old friendship."

He threw aside his sword, dismounted and came forward to greet him. And the two sat down on top of the hill.

"You must have come to talk me round then," said Guan Yu.

"Nor that either," said Zhang Liao. "Sometime ago you saved me—how can I not save you?"

"Do you mean you have come to help me?"

"Not exactly that," replied Zhang Liao.

"Then what are you doing here if you have not come to help me?"

"Well, at present nothing is known of the fate of your elder brother, nor whether your younger brother is alive or dead. Last night your city fell into the hands of Cao Cao, but neither soldiers nor people were harmed and guards were assigned to look after the family of Liu Bei lest they should be alarmed. I come to tell you how well they have been treated."

"This is certainly trying to talk me round," said Guan Yu indignantly. "Though escape is impossible I am not perturbed. I look upon death as a journey home. Go away quickly and I will go down at once to fight you."

"The world will laugh at you when they hear of this," said Zhang Liao, laughing loudly.

"I will die for loyalty and righteousness. Who will laugh at me?" said Guan Yu.

"You will be guilty of three faults if you die now."

"Tell me what they are," said Guan Yu.

"First of all, you and your elder brother pledged to live and die together in the Peach Garden. Now your brother has only suffered a defeat and you want to fight to death. If your brother rises again by and by and wants your help, where is he to find you? That would be a betrayal of the Peach Garden oath. Secondly, your brother left his family in your care and, if you should die, the two ladies would be left without a protector. That would be a betrayal of trust. Thirdly, although your military skill stands unmatched and your learning profound, yet you do not aid your brother in his noble attempt to maintain the Han Dynasty. On the contrary, you are after a vain reputation and are ready to go through fire and water to die a valiant fool. What is the sense in that? That would be a betrayal of righteousness. These are the three faults and I feel it my duty to point them out to you."

Guan Yu thought for some time. Then he said, "You say I have three faults. What do you desire me to do?"

"You are surrounded on all sides. You will not be able to escape death if you do not yield. There is no advantage in a meaningless death. Therefore your best course is to yield to Cao Cao till you hear news of Liu Bei and can rejoin him. Thus you will ensure the safety of the two ladies and also keep inviolate the Peach Garden oath. In addition you will preserve a useful life. I hope you will reflect carefully on these three advantages."

"You have spoken of three advantages—now I have three conditions. If the prime minister concedes then I will discard my armor. If he refuses, then I prefer to be guilty of the three faults and die."

"Why shouldn't the prime minister concede? He is most liberal and broad minded. Please let me hear your conditions."

"The first is that as my elder brother and I have sworn to support the Hans I now submit to the Emperor and not to his minister, Cao Cao. The second condition is that provisions equal to my brother's status be made for the two ladies and that no one must be allowed to approach their gates. The third is that I should be allowed to rejoin my brother as soon as I hear where he is, be it thousands of *li* away. I require all these to be satisfied—failing a single one, I will not submit. So, I think you had better hasten back and report them to Cao Cao."

Zhang Liao lost no time in riding back to Cao Cao. When he spoke of Guan Yu's intention to submit to the Hans but not to Cao Cao, the latter smiled and said, "I am the Prime Minister of Han, so I am Han. I grant this."

Zhang Liao then spoke of suitable provisions for the two ladies and their security from disturbance, to which Cao Cao replied, "I will give them twice the regular amount for Liu Bei. As for securing them from being disturbed, that is simple. The ordinary domestic law is enough. Why should I not agree to it?"

Zhang Liao continued: "The last condition is that whenever he gets news of the whereabouts of Liu Bei, he must go to him."

At this Cao Cao shook his head. "Then what is the use of my keeping him? I cannot consent to this."

Zhang Liao replied, "You must have heard the story of the ancient scholar Yu Rang who once said that his attitude toward his king was decided by whether the king treated him as an ordinary person or as a man of genius. Liu Bei has won Guan Yu's heart by treating him kindly and liberally—you can surely win him over by being kinder and more liberal."

"You are quite right. I will grant the three conditions," said Cao Cao.

Then Zhang Liao went back to the hilltop to break the news to Guan Yu.

"I have another request: I want the army to withdraw temporarily so that I may enter the city to tell the two ladies what has been arranged. After that I will submit."

Zhang Liao rode back once more with this new request and Cao Cao ordered his army to retreat thirty *li*.

"Do not do this," said Xun Yu. "I fear this might be a trick."

"He will certainly keep his promise," said Cao Cao. "He is a man of high principles."

The army retreated and Guan Yu and his forces re-entered the city, where he saw that the people were going about their normal lives. He came to his brother's residence and went in to see the two ladies, who hastened to meet him. He bowed to them below the steps and apologized: "It is my fault to cause you so much alarm."

"Where is our lord?" they asked.

"I do not know where he has gone."

"What do you intend to do, brother?"

"Yesterday I went out of the city to fight. I was trapped on a hilltop, surrounded on all sides by the enemy. Zhang Liao came to urge me to yield. I proposed three conditions, all of which were agreed, and the enemy drew off to allow me to return to the city. As I have not got your permission, sisters, I dare not take any action."

They asked what the conditions were and Guan Yu told them. Then Lady Gan said, "When Cao Cao's army came in we thought we would certainly die. But it turned out that we were hardly disturbed, not a soldier has dared enter our doors. You have accepted the conditions, brother, and there is no need to ask for our consent. Our only fear is that he will not let you go to look for your brother later."

"Do not be anxious. I will see to that."

"You must decide everything and need not ask us womenfolk."

Guan Yu withdrew and then with a small escort went to see Cao Cao, who came to the outermost gate to welcome him. Guan Yu dismounted and made obeisance. Cao Cao hastened to return his salute with the greatest cordiality.

"The leader of a defeated army is grateful for your graciousness that has preserved his life," said Guan Yu.

"I have long admired you for your loyalty and high principles. This happy meeting gratifies a desire I have held my whole life," replied Cao Cao.

"Sir, you have granted the three requests which my friend petitioned on my behalf. I sincerely hope you will keep your promise," said Guan Yu.

"I have given my word. How can I break faith?" replied Cao Cao.

"Whenever I hear where my brother is I must certainly go to him, even though I need to find him through fire and water. There may be no time for me to take leave. I trust you will understand."

"Should Liu Bei prove to be alive you would certainly be allowed to go to him. But I fear that in the confusion of battle he may have lost his life. Set your mind at rest and let me make inquiries."

Guan Yu thanked him. Then a banquet was prepared in his honor. The next day the army started on its homeward march.

For the journey to the capital a carriage was prepared for the two ladies and Guan Yu was its guard. On the road they rested at a certain post station and Cao Cao, anxious to compromise Guan Yu's reputation by tricking him into forgetfulness of his duty, assigned him to the same apartment as his sisters-in-law. Guan Yu stood the whole night outside their door with a lighted candle in his hand without betraying any trace of fatigue. Cao Cao's respect for him could not but increase.

Back in the capital Cao Cao assigned a dignified residence to Guan Yu, which he immediately divided into two enclosures: the inner one for the two ladies and the outer one for himself. He placed ten reliable guards at the women's quarters.

Guan Yu was presented to Emperor Xian, who conferred upon him the rank of general. Soon after, Cao Cao gave a great banquet, inviting all his advisors and fighting men. Guan Yu was treated as a distinguished guest and was asked to sit in the seat of honor. Besides, he was also given presents of silks and gold and silver vessels, all of which he sent into the ladies' quarters for their use and keeping. In fact, from the day of his arrival in the capital, Guan Yu was treated with marked respect and distinction, banquets and feasts following each other in quick succession.

Cao Cao also gave him the ten most lovely girls to wait on him. These girls were also sent to be maids of his two sisters-in-law.

Every third day Guan Yu would go to the door of the ladies' quarters to inquire after their well-being, and then they would ask him if there was any news of their husband. This brief interview would always close with the ladies saying, "Brother, you may retire as you wish." Only then did Guan Yu dare to leave.

When Cao Cao heard of this strict observance of the proprieties he thought all the more of the man for it.

One day Cao Cao noticed that the robe Guan Yu was wearing was old and frayed. Guessing his measurements Cao Cao had a new one made of fine brocade and presented it to him. He took it but wore it under the old robe.

"Why so very thrifty?" laughed Cao Cao.

"It is not thrifty," was Guan Yu's reply. "The old robe was a gift from my brother and to wear it is like seeing him. I cannot allow the new gift to eclipse his old one."

"How very loyal!" said Cao Cao sighing. But in spite of his praises he was rather displeased in his heart.

One day when Guan Yu was at home a servant came in to say that the two ladies had thrown themselves to the ground, weeping for no obvious reasons, and asked him to go in and see. Guan Yu set his dress in order, went over, and knelt by the door. "Why is this grief, sisters?" he asked.

Lady Gan replied, "Last night I dreamed that your brother had fallen into a pit. I woke up and told Lady Mi and we thought he must be dead. So we weep."

"Dreams are not to be credited," he replied. "You dreamed of him because you were thinking of him. Pray do not grieve."

Just then Cao Cao sent his men to invite Guan Yu to another banquet so he took leave of the ladies and went. Seeing Guan Yu looked sad and tearful his host asked him the reason.

"My sisters-in-law have been weeping for my brother and I cannot help feeling sad, too."

Cao Cao smiled and tried to cheer up his guest with kind words. After being urged to drink some quantity of wine Guan Yu became quite intoxicated and sat stroking his beard, "What a useless thing I am! I could do no service for my country and I have betrayed my elder brother."

"Do you keep count of the hair in your beard?" asked his host, trying to divert his thoughts.

"Yes, some hundreds, perhaps. During fall, a few drop out and in winter I use a black silk bag to keep the hair from being broken," replied Guan Yu.

Cao Cao at once had a bag made for him to protect his beard. Soon after, when they were at court, the Emperor asked about the bag he saw hanging from Guan Yu's breast.

"My beard is rather long, Your Majesty," said Guan Yu. "So the prime minister has given me a bag to protect it."

The Emperor told him to take off the bag and show him his beard in all its fullness—it fell in rippling waves below his breast.

"Really a most beautiful beard!" said the Emperor.

From then on he was often known as "The Warrior with the Beautiful Beard."

Another time, after a banquet, Cao Cao walked with Guan Yu to the gate of his house to see him off. He noticed that his charger was very thin.

"Why is he so thin?" asked Cao Cao.

"My worthless body is rather heavy and really too much for him. He is always out of condition."

Cao Cao at once told his men to lead out one of his horses and before long it appeared, red like glowing charcoal, a handsome creature in every way.

"Do you recognize it?" asked Cao Cao.

"Why, is it Lu Bu's Red Hare?" cried Guan Yu.

"Surely it is," said Cao Cao, and he gave the horse, fully caparisoned, to his guest. Guan Yu bowed many times and thanked him again and again till Cao Cao began to feel displeased and said, "I have given you gold and silk and lovely girls but have never won a bow of gratitude from you before. This horse seems to please you better than all the rest. Why do you think so poorly of the damsels and so much of the steed?"

"I know this horse can go a thousand *li* a day and I am very lucky to have it. Now as soon as I find out where my brother is I can get to him in a single day," replied Guan Yu.

Cao Cao was astonished to hear the answer and he began to regret giving him the horse, but Guan Yu took his leave and went away.

> *His fame spread far and wide in the days of the Three Kingdoms.*
> *Dividing his dwelling proved the purity of his heart.*
> *The crafty minister desired to win him to his side,*
> *But felt that failure was foredoomed, however much he tried.*

Cao Cao said to Zhang Liao, "I have treated him well enough but he still desires to leave me. Do you know why?"

"I will try to find out," said Zhang Liao.

So he went to see his friend the next day. When they had greeted each other politely, Zhang Liao said: "I recommended you to the prime minister and I hope he has treated you well."

"I'm deeply grateful for his kindness," said Guan Yu. "But though my body is here, I'm always thinking of my brother."

"I am afraid you are wrong. If one does not discriminate in his relations with people he is not the most admirable type of man. Even Liu Bei could not have treated you so well as the prime minister does. Why then do you always maintain this desire to get away?"

"I know only too well that he has been most kind but I have also received great kindness from my brother. We have sworn to die together and I cannot betray him. I cannot remain here, but before I go I will render him some service to show my gratitude."

"What if Liu Bei has left the world—where will you go?" asked Zhang Liao.

"Then I will follow him to the nether world."

There could no longer be any doubt as to Guan Yu's intentions and Zhang Liao told Cao Cao exactly how matters stood.

Cao Cao sighed. "To serve one's chief with unswerving fidelity is a proof of the highest principle of all," he said.

Xun Yu advised, "He said he would leave only after he had performed some service. If he gets no chance of doing such a thing, he will not be able to go."

Cao Cao agreed.

In the meantime, Liu Bei had been with Yuan Shao. He was sorrowful day and night and, when asked by his host, he said, "I have no news of the whereabouts of my two brothers, nor of what has happened to my wives since they fell into the hands of Cao Cao. I cannot help feeling sad as I have failed toward my country and my family."

"I have long wished to attack Cao Cao," said Yuan Shao. "Now spring is here and just the time for an expedition." So he discussed plans for the destruction of Cao Cao with his advisors.

Tian Feng at once opposed this. "Last time when Cao Cao attacked Xuzhou and the capital was undefended you let the chance slip by. Now that Xuzhou has been captured and his army's fighting spirit is very strong with this victory it will be madness to attempt to defeat it. Better to wait for another chance."

"Let me think about it," said Yuan Shao.

He told Liu Bei about Tian Feng's words and asked him for advice.

Liu Bei replied, "Cao Cao is a rebel. I think you are failing in your duty if you do not attack him."

"You are right," said Yuan Shao.

And he made up his mind to start the expedition. However, the advisor Tian Feng again intervened.

Yuan Shao said angrily, "You fellows value scheming but despise fighting. You will make me neglect my duty."

Tian Feng bowed to the ground and said to him: "If you do not listen to my words you will fail in the battle."

Yuan Shao became so angry that he wanted to put him to death. Liu Bei pleaded for the poor advisor and in the end Yuan Shao spared his life and put him into prison.

Seeing the fate of his colleague another advisor, Ju Shou, called together his whole clan and distributed among them all his possessions. "I'm going with the army," he said to them. "If we win then nothing can exceed our glory, but if we fail, my life is at risk."

His relatives wept as they bade him farewell.

Yuan Shao appointed one of his best officers, Yan Liang, to be commander of the vanguard force to go and attack the city of Baima. Ju Shou said to his master, "Yan Liang is very brave but he is too narrow-minded to hold such a post without someone else to assist him."

"He is my best officer. You people are not in a position to measure him," said Yuan Shao.

The army marched to Liyang and the prefect sent an urgent message to the capital. Cao Cao hastily prepared for a counter-attack. As soon as Guan Yu heard the news he went to see Cao Cao and asked to be sent with the first body of the army.

"I dare not trouble you, General. If need arises, I will call upon you to help."

So Guan Yu retired. Soon, the army marched out in three divisions. On the road more messages were received from the prefect asking for urgent help. The first division led by Cao Cao himself arrived at Baima and took up a position on some hillsides. In the wide plain in front of them Yan Liang had arranged his army in battle array—it was twice as strong as Cao Cao's.

Cao Cao was much alarmed to see his enemy so strongly deployed and, turning back, he said to Song Xian: "I hear you used to be one of Lu Bu's best officers. You go and fight this Yan Liang."

Song Xian took the order and mounted to the front with his spear set. Yan Liang was on horseback under the big banner with his sword lying crossways. Seeing an opponent approaching he uttered a loud shout and galloped toward him. The two met, but after only three bouts, Song Xian was slain by a mighty slash from the other's sword.

"What a powerful warrior!" cried Cao Cao, greatly startled.

"He has killed my friend! I will go and avenge him," said Wei Xu, another of Lu Bu's former officers.

Cao Cao agreed. He rode out, spear in hand, and in front of the two armies he railed at Yan Liang.

Without a word Yan Liang came forward to engage him and at the first blow Wei Xu also fell under his sword.

"Now, who again dares to face him?" asked Cao Cao to his officers.

Xu Huang took up the challenge and went out. The combat endured a score of bouts and then he had to flee, defeated. This frightened all the other officers and Cao Cao was forced to draw off his men. Yan Liang also withdrew to return to his camp.

Cao Cao was very upset at the loss of two officers in such quick succession. His advisor Cheng Yu said to him: "I can recommend a person equal to Yan Liang."

"Who?" asked Cao Cao.

"Guan Yu. Only he can defeat him."

"I am afraid he will leave if he is given this opportunity to render me a service."

"If Liu Bei is still alive he must be with Yuan Shao. Now you get Guan Yu to defeat Yuan Shao's army. He will surely suspect Liu Bei and will put him to death. With Liu Bei gone, where can Guan Yu go?"

This argument appealed to Cao Cao very much and he at once sent for Guan Yu.

Before departure, Guan Yu went to take leave of his two sisters-in-law, who urged him to try to get news of Liu Bei. Guan Yu obeyed and left.

Armed with his famous sword, the Blue Dragon, and riding on the swift steed, the Red Hare, he started toward the battlefield with a few followers. When he got there he went to see Cao Cao, who told him what had happened and said that Yan Liang was too valiant for anyone to face.

"Let me look at him," said Guan Yu.

Then wine was served in his honor. While they were drinking, it was reported that Yan Liang was once again challenging for battle. So Cao Cao and his guest went up the hill from where the enemy could be seen, followed by his other officers. The two of them sat on the hilltop while the others stood about them. Cao Cao pointed at Yan Liang's men arrayed on the plain below. The ensigns and banners waving fresh and bright amid the forest of spears and swords made a grand and imposing spectacle.

"See what fine fellows these northerners are!" said Cao Cao.

"I regard them as nothing but clay fowls and mud dogs," sneered Guan Yu.

Cao Cao then pointed out Yan Liang to him and said, "There he is, under that big banner."

Clad in an embroidered robe and a gold breastplate Yan Liang was sitting on horseback with his sword in his hand.

"He seems to me like one who has stuck his head on a pole for sale," said Guan Yu, glancing at his opponent below.

"You must not despise him," warned Cao Cao.

Guan Yu rose and said, "Unworthy as I am, I will go down and bring you his head amid his 10,000 soldiers."

"No joking is allowed in the army," interposed his friend Zhang Liao. "Be careful what you say."

Guan Yu quickly mounted, held his mighty sword downward, and galloped down the hill, his phoenix eyes rounded and his bushy eyebrows fiercely bristling. He dashed straight into the enemy's line and the northern soldiers opened before him, like waves receding to the right and left. Guan Yu made directly for the commander.

Now Yan Liang, sitting in state under the banner, saw a horseman rushing toward him and before he could ask who the rider of the red horse was, lo! Guan Yu was right there in front of him. Taken utterly by surprise, Yan Liang could make no defense. Guan Yu's arm rose and the mighty weapon fell. And with it fell Yan Liang.

Leaping down from the saddle he cut off his victim's head and hung it to his horse's neck. Then he mounted again and rode back as if there was no army around him.

The northern men, panic-stricken, made no fight. Cao Cao's army attacked with vigor and scored a great victory. A great number of their enemy were slain and many horses and weapons captured. Guan Yu rode quickly up the hill and laid the proof of his prowess at the feet of the prime minister.

"You are really a superman, General!" cried Cao Cao in admiration.

"I am nothing compared with my brother Zhang Yi-de," said Guan Yu. "He can easily cut the head of a general amid an army of a million men as if it were but taking something out of a bag."

Cao Cao was so alarmed to hear this that he turned to those about him and said, "Be very careful if you meet his brother later." And he bade them make a note of the name on the cuff of their robes so that they would remember.

The beaten army, while fleeing back homeward, met Yuan Shao on the road and told him why they had suffered defeat. "A red-faced warrior with a long beard, wielding a huge sword, broke into the army and cut off the general's head and bore it off," they said.

"Who could this one be?" asked Yuan Shao in astonishment.

Ju Shou said, "This must have been Liu Bei's brother, Guan Yu."

Yuan Shao was very angry and, pointing to Liu Bei, he said, "Your brother has slain my most cherished general. You must be in the plot, too. Why should I keep you here?"

He ordered the guards to take him away and execute him.

Morning saw him guest on high,
Evening, prisoner, doomed to die.

Would he really be killed? This will be told in the next chapter.

CHAPTER TWENTY-SIX

Yuan Shao Is Defeated and Loses His Best Officers
Guan Yu Hangs up the Seal and
Abandons Cao Cao's Gifts

As the last chapter closed Liu Bei had been condemned to die. However, he spoke up quite calmly to defend himself. "Sir, how can you listen to only one side of the story and forget our past friendship? Since my defeat in Xuzhou I have lost all news about my brother. I did not even know if he was alive or dead. Many people resemble each other. Can you say that a red-faced man with a long beard must be my brother, Guan Yu? Do you not think you should consider more carefully?"

Now Yuan Shao was a man who lacked opinions of his own. When he heard Liu Bei's words, he turned to blame his advisor Ju Shou. "I nearly killed an innocent man by listening to your false accusation."

Then he asked Liu Bei to resume his seat in the tent and consulted him on how to avenge Yan Liang.

Soon from the lower end stepped out a man who said: "Yan Liang was like a brother of mine. He has been killed by Cao Cao's man. How can I not avenge his death?"

The speaker was a tall man with a face like a unicorn. He was a famous warrior from the north, named Wen Chou.

Yuan Shao was very pleased and said, "You are the only man who can do it. I will give you 100,000 men and you can cross the Yellow River at once to smite Cao Cao."

Again the advisor objected. "No, you should not cross the Yellow River so rashly now," said Ju Shou. "If anything goes wrong none will be able to return. The proper course is to hold Yanjin and post a force at Guandu."

Yuan Shao turned a deaf ear to his wise advice. Instead he became angry and said, "You fellows always try to delay action and take the momentum from my soldiers. You want to put off today and postpone for tomorrow to upset my great plan. Have you forgotten that soldiers respect decisiveness?"

The advisor withdrew sadly and said to himself, "Superiors do not curb their ambitions—inferiors must strive to render service. Eternal is the Yellow River, how shall I cross it?"

From then on he feigned illness and would not attend his master's councils.

Liu Bei said, "I have received much kindness from you but have been unable to show my gratitude. I will accompany General Wen so as to repay you with my service and also to try to get news of my brother."

Yuan Shao gladly consented and ordered Wen Chou to share his command of the army with Liu Bei. However, Wen Chou objected that Liu Bei, who had often been defeated, would bring ill fortune to his army. He proposed giving Liu Bei command of the rear division, and this being approved, Liu Bei took charge of 30,000 men to follow the main body.

Meanwhile, Cao Cao's respect for Guan Yu redoubled after he displayed his prowess with his bold attack on Yan Liang. He presented a petition to the Emperor, who conferred the title of Lord of Hanshou to Guan Yu, and a seal bearing that title was cast for him.

Just then came the news that Yuan Shao's army was moving toward the Yellow River and had already occupied Yanjin. Cao Cao at once arranged to transfer the inhabitants to the west of the river and then led out his army to oppose Yuan Shao. He gave orders for the front and rear divisions to change places, thus putting the supply wagons in front and the army behind.

"What is this reversal for?" asked one of his officers.

Cao Cao replied, "When the supply carts are in the rear they are liable to be plundered. So I have put them in the front."

"What if they are taken by the enemy?"

"Wait till the enemy appears. I will know what to do."

The officer was much perplexed at this new move by his master. In the meantime the supply wagons were being driven along the river toward Yanjin. Presently Cao Cao, who was in the rear, heard the foremost troops raise a great shout, and he immediately sent someone to find out what it meant. The messenger came back to report that Wen Chou's army had arrived and the soldiers, who had abandoned the wagons, were scattering in all directions. The rear army was still some distance away and could not go to their rescue. But Cao Cao did not seem to be worried in the least. He pointed to the two mounds in the south and said, "We will take refuge here for the present."

All moved swiftly to the mounds. There, Cao Cao ordered them to loosen their robes, lay aside their mail, and rest a while. The horses, too, were turned loose.

Wen Chou's army soon approached. As they drew near, the officers all said to Cao Cao, "The enemy is here. We must get the horses and go back to the city."

But the advisor Xun You checked them and said, "This is a bait for the enemy—why withdraw?"

Cao Cao winked at the advisor and smiled. Xun You understood and said no more.

Now having got possession of the supply carts, the enemy came to seize the horses. By this time their ranks were quite broken and they became a disorderly lot, each going his own way. Suddenly Cao Cao gave the order to go down the mounds and smite them.

The surprise attack was very successful. Wen Chou's army was in confusion, surrounded by Cao Cao's men. Wen Chou endeavored to fight it out but his soldiers trampled each other down and he could not stop them. So he had to turn back and run.

Standing on the top of the mound Cao Cao pointed to the fleeing man and called out, "Wen Chou is one of the most famous warriors of the north. Who can capture him?"

At this call Zhang Liao and Xu Huang both rode out and dashed after the fugitive. "Wen Chou, do not attempt to run away!"

Turning around, Wen Chou saw two pursuers after him so he set aside his spear, took his bow and adjusted his arrow, which he shot at Zhang Liao.

"Do not shoot, you wretch!" shouted Xu Huang to warn his friend. Zhang Liao ducked and the arrow hit his helmet, slashing off its tassel. He pressed on in pursuit but the next arrow struck his horse in the head and the animal stumbled and fell, throwing its rider to the ground.

Then Wen Chou turned back. Xu Huang, whirling his battle ax, stood in his way to engage him in a fight. By then Wen Chou's men had also turned back to assist him. Knowing that they would be too much for him, Xu Huang fled. This time Wen Chou pursued along the river. Suddenly, however, he saw coming toward him, with banners fluttering in the wind, a small party of horsemen led by a warrior with a powerful sword.

It was none other than Guan Yu. "Stop!" he cried as he galloped up, raising high his sword. The two fought but at the third bout Wen Chou, seized by fright, wheeled round and fled, following the windings of the river. But Guan Yu's steed was faster and soon caught up with him. One blow, and the unfortunate Wen Chou fell.

When Cao Cao saw from the mound that the leader of the enemy had fallen, he gave the signal for a general assault and many of the northern men were driven into the river. The carts with supplies and all the horses were quickly recovered.

Now Guan Yu, at the head of a few horsemen, was thrusting here and striking there when Liu Bei, with the rear force, arrived on the scene of the battle. At once he was told that the red-faced warrior with a long beard had slain Wen Chou. He hastily pressed forward to get a good look at the warrior. He saw across the river a group of horsemen dashing about like wind and a banner bearing the name of his brother.

"Then it is my brother and he's really with Cao Cao," thought Liu Bei, secretly thanking Heaven that his brother was safe.

He wanted to call out to Guan Yu, but a great mass of Cao Cao's soldiers came rushing forward and he was forced to retreat.

Yuan Shao, bringing the reinforcements, reached Guandu and built a stockade. Two advisors went in to see him and said, "It was Guan Yu again that killed Wen Chou. Liu Bei pretends he does not know."

In wrath, Yuan Shao railed at Lui Bei. "That long-eared wretch! How dare he do such a thing?"

Again Liu Bei was brought before Yuan Shao, who ordered him to be taken out to instant execution.

"What crime have I committed?" asked Liu Bei.

"You sent your brother to slay another of my best officers. Is that no crime?"

"Please let me explain before I die. Cao Cao has always been wary of me. Now he has found out where I am and, fearing that I may help you, has got my brother to destroy your two generals, feeling sure that when you hear of it you will be angry and put me to death. You cannot fail to see this."

"That does make sense," said Yuan Shao. Turning to his two advisors he said, "And you two nearly caused me to injure a good man."

He ordered the others to leave and asked Liu Bei to come and sit by him. Liu Bei thanked him and said, "I am deeply grateful to you, sir, for your great kindness, for which I can never sufficiently repay you. Now I desire to send some confidential messenger with a secret letter to my brother to tell him where I am, and I am sure he will come without a moment's delay. He will help you to destroy Cao Cao to make up for your loss of the two officers. Do you approve of this?"

"If I gained Guan Yu he would be ten times better than the two men I have lost," replied Yuan Shao, greatly pleased.

So Liu Bei wrote a letter but there was no one to take it to his brother. Yuan Shao ordered the army to withdraw to Wuyang, where they made a large camp. For some time no further move was undertaken.

Cao Cao sent Xiahou Dun to guard the strategic point at Guandu while he led the bulk of the army back to the capital. There, he gave many banquets in honor of the remarkable services of Guan Yu. At one of these gatherings he said, "The other day I had intentionally put the supplies in the front of the army as a bait to divert the enemy's attention. Only Xun You understood me."

Every one present praised him for his ingenuity. However, even while the banquet was proceeding there arrived news of new trouble in Runan, where two former Yellow Turban rebels, Liu Pi and Gong Du, were staging an uprising. They were very strong and Cao Hong, who had been defeated in several battles, begged for help.

Guan Yu, hearing this, said, "I would like to offer my humble service by destroying these rebels."

"You have already rendered noble services for which you have not been properly rewarded. I could not trouble you again," said Cao Cao.

"If I were left idle for too long, I would get ill. I am willing to go," said Guan Yu.

Cao Cao consented and gave him 50,000 men and two of his own officers to serve under him. They were to leave the next day.

Xun Yu warned his master in private, "Guan Yu is always thinking of returning to Liu Bei. He will leave you if he hears any news. You should not let him go on expeditions so often."

"I will not let him go into battle again after this," said Cao Cao.

In due time the force led by Guan Yu reached Runan and made camp. One night, just outside his camp, two spies were caught and taken in to Guan Yu, who was surprised that one of them was Sun Qian, Liu Bei's former advisor. He dismissed the attendants and asked, "Since our city was lost I haven't heard any news about you. How come you are here?"

"After I escaped I drifted hither and thither and finally ended up in this place," said Sun Qian. "Fortunately I was given shelter by Liu Pi. But why are you with Cao Cao, General? And where are your sisters-in-law? Are they well?"

Guan Yu told him all that had happened.

Then Sun Qian said, "I've heard lately that your brother is with Yuan Shao. I'd have liked to go and join him but I haven't found a convenient opportunity. Now the two Yellow Turban leaders I'm with have submitted to Yuan Shao and will assist him in fighting against Cao Cao. When I heard you were being sent here I thought it really a good piece of luck, so I disguised myself as a scout to see you and tell you everything. Tomorrow the two leaders will feign defeat. You must accompany the two ladies to go to Yuan Shao's place without delay. You'll see your brother there."

"Since my brother is there I'll certainly go at once to join him. But it's a misfortune that I've slain two of Yuan Shao's best officers. I fear things may have changed for the worse," said Guan Yu.

"Let me go first and find out—I'll come back and tell you."

"I'll risk myriad deaths to see my brother," said Guan Yu. "When I return to the capital I'll immediately take leave of Cao Cao."

Sun Qian was secretly sent away that night and the next day Guan Yu led out his men to offer battle. His opponent, Gong Du, put on his armor and came forth.

Guan Yu said, "Why do you people rebel against the court?"

"Why do you blame us when you yourself have turned your back on your own lord?"

"How have I turned my back on my lord?" asked Guan Yu.

"Liu Bei is now with Yuan Shao and you are with Cao Cao. Why is that?"

Guan Yu said no more but whirled round his sword and rode forward. His opponent fled and Guan Yu followed. When they were out of the hearing of others, Gong Du turned and said to Guan Yu, "Do not forget how well your old master has treated you. Now attack quickly and we will yield the city to you."

Guan Yu understood and they returned to the scene of the battle, pretending to be still engaged in a flight and chase. Guan Yu urged his men on a wide offensive and his opponents feigned defeat, scattering in all directions. So the city was taken. Having pacified the people, Guan Yu at once led his army back toward the capital. Cao Cao came out of the city to welcome him back and the army was again rewarded with feasts.

After the feast, Guan Yu went to the dwelling of his sisters-in-law to pay his respects at their door.

"Have you been able to get any news of your brother in your two expeditions?" asked Lady Gan.

"No," replied Guan Yu.

After he left the two ladies wept bitterly and said to each other, "He must be dead! Our brother-in-law is hiding the truth from us lest we should be too distressed."

One of the old soldiers, who had been with Guan Yu on the expeditions, heard the sounds of their perpetual grief, took pity on them, and said outside their door: "Do not weep, ladies. Your lord is with Yuan Shao in Hebei."

"How do you know that?" they asked.

"I went with General Guan and some soldiers told me."

The two ladies summoned Guan Yu at once and reproached him. "Your brother has not done you anything wrong and yet you remain here enjoying Cao Cao's favor and forgetting the old times. You even lied to us about your brother. How can you explain that?"

Guan Yu bowed his head and said, "My brother is really in Hebei but I dared not tell you lest it should leak out. This must be done very carefully and it needs time."

"Please make haste, brother," said Lady Gan.

Guan Yu withdrew. Back in his own quarters, he racked his brains for a scheme to leave Cao Cao. The thought caused him much uneasiness.

Meanwhile Yu Jin, having learned that Liu Bei was in the north, told Cao Cao about it, who at once sent Zhang Liao to find out Guan Yu's intention. So one day, when Guan Yu was brooding over his worries at home, Zhang Liao entered jauntily and said, "They tell me that you gained news of your brother on the battlefield. I've come to congratulate you."

"My lord is there, indeed, but I haven't even seen him. I see nothing to be glad about."

"How will you compare your friendship with Liu Bei and that between you and me?" asked Zhang Liao.

Guan Yu replied, "You and I are friends while Xuan-de and I are friends as well as brothers—and on top of this, we're also master and officer. They can't be viewed in equal terms."

"Well, now that you know where your brother is, are you going to him?"

"Certainly I won't go back on my own words! Please explain this to the prime minister."

Zhang Liao went back to tell his master what Guan Yu had said but Cao Cao did not seem to be worried. "I have a plan to keep him here," he said.

After Zhang Liao left Guan Yu sat pondering over how he could get away. Soon he was told that an old friend of his had come to see him. The visitor was admitted into his room but Guan Yu did not recognize him.

"Who are you?" asked Guan Yu.

"I am Chen Zhen of Nanyang in the service of Yuan Shao," said the stranger.

Greatly startled, Guan Yu sent away the attendants in a hurry and then asked, "There must be some special reason for your visit."

In reply the visitor drew out a letter and handed it to his host, who recognized that it was from his brother Liu Bei. Briefly it read like this:

> *You and I, sir, pledged in the Peach Orchard to die together.*
> *Why, then, do you go back on your words in the middle of your life*
> *and break an old friendship? If you are determined to seek*
> *position and wealth, I am willing to offer my head to help you*

achieve your ambition. This letter cannot contain all that I want to say but I await your command in great anxiety.

After reading the letter Guan Yu was overcome with emotion. Weeping bitterly he said, "I always wanted to find my brother but I did not know where he was. I will never break my oath for comfort!"

"Your brother eagerly seeks you. If you are still bound by the old pledge you should go and see him without delay," said the messenger.

Guan Yu said seriously, "For one born into this world integrity is what marks him as a true man. Whatever he does, he must carry it to the end. I came here openly and I will not leave in any other way. I am going to write a letter for you to take to my brother and I will bring the two ladies to join him as soon as I have taken leave of Cao Cao."

"What if Cao Cao refuses to let you go?" asked the messenger.

"I would rather die than remain here for long."

"Then please write your letter quickly and relieve your brother from anxiety."

So Guan Yu wrote the following:

> *I know that a man of principles does not betray trust and a man of loyalty does not fear death. I have taken up studies since my youth and know something of the proprieties. The legendary story about the friendship between Yang Jue-ai and Zuo Bo-tao* has moved me to sighs and tears.*
>
> *I was in charge of Xiapi but the place lacked neither provision nor outside assistance. I would have fought to death if not for the responsibility of the safety of my two sisters-in-law. Therefore I dared not die for fear of betraying your trust. And so I linger on in life hoping for a reunion later. It was only when I went to Runan that I got news of your whereabouts. I will go and see Cao Cao at once to bid him farewell, and bring the two ladies with me when I come.*
>
> *If I have ever harbored any treacherous thought, may I perish at the hands of both gods and men. Paper and brush are poor substitutes for what I want to say but I look forward to seeing you soon.*

---

*   Two friends during the period of Warring States (475–221 B.C.). On a journey to the Kingdom of Chu to seek office they were caught in a heavy snowstorm. Zuo Bo-tao gave all his clothes and food to his friend and died of hunger and cold himself. Later, his friend who had become an important official in Chu, returned to find his corpse and buried it in great honor. Then he committed suicide.

After the visitor left with the letter Guan Yu went in to inform the two ladies of his plan. Then he proceeded to Cao Cao's house to say farewell. But knowing why he was coming, Cao Cao had his men hang up a "No Visitor" sign in front of the gate. Guan Yu had to return. However, he told his few followers to be ready for the journey at any moment. He also issued orders that everything given by Cao Cao was to be left in the house—nothing was to be taken.

The next day he went again to take leave of Cao Cao, but again the sign there showed him that there was no admittance. Several times more he went but still he could not see Cao Cao. Then he went to see Zhang Liao who, too, did not come out to meet him on an excuse of poor health.

Guan Yu thought to himself, "This means he won't let me go. But I've made up my mind to leave and I won't stay any longer."

So he wrote a letter to Cao Cao to inform him of his departure and to thank him for his kindness:

> As a young man I entered the service of my sworn brother and pledged myself to sharing his fortunes. Heaven and Earth witnessed this oath. When I lost the city of Xiapi and came to you I raised three conditions, which you granted. Now I hear that my brother is with Yuan Shao and I, remembering our old pledge, must go to him. Though your kindness to me is great I cannot forget the bond of the past. Therefore I write this letter of farewell, trusting that you will not take offense. For your kindness that I have not yet repaid I hope I can find another time to show my gratitude.

He sealed the letter and sent someone to deliver it at Cao Cao's house. At the same time he locked all the gold and silver he had received from Cao Cao in the storage room and hung up his seal of title in the hall. Then he asked the two ladies to get into a carriage he had prepared for them. He himself mounted the Red Hare and carried his Blue Dragon sword in his hand. With a small group of men, those formerly under his command, he escorted the carriage and left the capital by the north gate.

The wardens there would have stopped him but he frightened them by raising the sword and yelling fiercely. Once out of the gate he told his men to proceed with the carriage while he remained behind to guard against pursuit, so as not to alarm the two ladies. So they pushed the carriage toward the main road.

Back in the city, Guan Yu's letter reached Cao Cao while he was consulting his men about how to retain the great warrior. He read it and exclaimed, "He is gone!" Then the warden of the north gate came to report that Guan Yu had forced his way out with a carriage and some twenty followers. Next came the servants from his house to report that he had left, taking nothing of the gold and silver, nor any of the waiting maids. Everything was left in the house, even his seal. His only escort was the few men of his original force.

All were surprised to hear this. Suddenly from the assembly rose a man who cried out, "Give me 3,000 mailed cavalrymen and I will bring him back alive."

The speaker was General Cai Yang.

> *He had just escaped from the dragon's pool*
> *But would be chased by thousands of wolves.*

Whether Cao Cao would approve of Cai Yang's request will be told in the next chapter.

◄○►

CHAPTER TWENTY-SEVEN

Guan Yu the Beautiful Beard Travels a Thousand *Li* And Slays Six Officers at Five Passes

◄○►

Now of all the officers in Cao Cao's army, the only one friendly toward Guan Yu, with the exception of Zhang Liao, was Xu Huang. The others treated him with respect but Cai Yang was decidedly hostile. So when he heard of Guan Yu's departure he wanted to go and pursue him. But Cao Cao said, "He does not forget his old master and he has been perfectly open and honest in all his actions. He is a man true to his words. You will do well to follow his example."

So he ordered Cai Yang out and to say no more about pursuit.

"You were exceedingly good to Guan Yu," said Cheng Yu, "but he did not even bid you farewell, leaving only a few lines to state his reasons. He has affronted you and that is no light matter. Now to let him join Yuan Shao is to add wings to a tiger. You had better catch him and put him to death so as to avoid future trouble."

Cao Cao replied, "But he had my promise and can I break my word? He has his master to serve. Do not pursue." Then he said to Zhang Liao, "He has rejected all I gave him, so bribes were powerless with him in whatever shape. I have the greatest respect for someone like him. He has not yet gone far, I think, and I will try to secure his friendship and make one more appeal to his sentiment. You ride after him and beg him to wait till I can come up to bid him farewell. I will offer him a sum of money for his journey and a fighting robe so that he will remember me kindly in later days."

So Zhang Liao alone galloped out at once—Cao Cao soon followed him with an escort of a score or so of his officers.

Now the steed that Guan Yu rode was the Red Hare and it was so fast that no one could have caught up with him. But as he was traveling with the ladies' carriage he had to check his horse's movement and go slow. Suddenly he heard a shout behind him, a voice crying, "Wait a minute, Yun-chang."

Turning back he saw it was his friend Zhang Liao. Ordering the pushers of the carriage to press on along the main road he reined in his steed, held his sword ready and waited for Zhang Liao to come up.

"Have you come to take me back, Wen-yuan?" asked Guan Yu.

"No. The prime minister knows that you are going a long way and wishes to see you off. He told me to hasten forward and beg you to wait till he can come up. That's all."

"Even if he is coming with his mailed men I will fight to the very last," said Guan Yu and he took up his position on a bridge, where he kept a close watch. Soon he saw Cao Cao approaching very quickly, with several of his best fighters close behind him. Seeing Guan Yu was ready to fight, Cao Cao ordered his escort to open out on his two sides. Guan Yu was much relieved when saw that none of them carried any weapons in their hands.

"Why do you go in such haste, Yun-chang?" asked Cao Cao.

While still mounted, Guan Yu made an obeisance to him and replied, "I have told you before that I will go and join my brother if I know where he is. Now that I know he is in Hebei I have to leave at once. I went to your place time and again but was refused admittance. So I wrote a letter to bid you farewell. I have also locked up the gold and hung up my seal to return them to you. I hope you recall the promise you once made."

Cao Cao replied, "My desire is to win the trust of all men—of course I will not go back on my word. However, I think you may find the journey expensive and therefore I have here prepared a sum of money for you."

Then one of his officers passed a packet of gold to Guan Yu.

"But I have sufficient gold left from your earlier rewards—keep that as gifts for your soldiers."

"Why should you refuse this? It is but an insignificant return for your great services," said Cao Cao.

"My services have been trifling, not worth mentioning."

"Really, Yun-chang, you are the most high-principled of men. I am very sorry that I do not have the fortune to retain you at my side. I have brought an embroidered robe to show you I am not entirely ungrateful," said Cao Cao. Then one of his followers dismounted and held up a silken coat in both hands.

Fearful of what might happen, Guan Yu dared not dismount, but picked it up with the tip of his sword and threw it over his shoulders. Turning to thank the giver he said, "Thank you for the robe, sir. I trust we will meet again."

So saying, he rode over the bridge and went away toward the north.

"He is too rude," said Xu Chu. "Why not take him prisoner?"

Cao Cao replied, "He was absolutely alone facing scores of us. No wonder he was suspicious. I have given my word and he is not to be pursued."

Cao Cao returned with his men, feeling very sad that Guan Yu had left him.

Now Guan Yu galloped down the bridge to chase the carriage carrying the two ladies, but after about thirty *li* there was still no sign of it. Alarmed, he rode hither and thither looking on all sides.

Suddenly he heard someone calling him by name from the top of a hill. It was a young man wearing a yellow turban and dressed in a silk robe. He held a spear in his hand and was mounted on a horse from the neck of which dangled a bloody head. Behind him were a hundred or so men on foot and they advanced quickly.

"Who are you?" asked Guan Yu.

The young man dropped his spear, dismounted and made a low bow. Guan Yu feared there might be some trick so he only checked his horse and gripped his sword even more firmly.

"Sir, I desire you to tell me your name."

"I am Liao Hua from Xiangyang. Since these troubled times began I have been an outlaw and lived by plunder. There are about five hundred of us in all. Just now, my mate Du Yuan came down the hill and very wrongly took the two ladies prisoners and brought them to our camp. I questioned the ones who went with him and found out that the ladies are wives of the uncle of the Emperor and that you, General, are escorting them. So I wanted them to be set free to continue their journey. Du Yuan opposed this and spoke so insolently that I killed him. And I present his head to ask for your pardon."

"Where are the two ladies?"

"They are on the hill," replied Liao Hua.

"Get them down at once," said Guan Yu.

In a short time the carriage was pushed down the hill, accompanied by a hundred or so men.

Then Guan Yu dismounted, laid aside his sword, and bowed respectfully before the ladies with his arms crossed.

"Sisters, have you been alarmed?" he asked.

They replied, "We would have suffered at the hands of Du Yuan had it not been for General Liao."

"How did Liao Hua come to save the ladies?" asked Guan Yu of his men.

They said, "Du Yuan carried off the ladies and proposed to Liao Hua that each of them take one as wife. When Liao Hua found out who the ladies were, he treated them with respect. Du Yuan disagreed so Liao Hua slew him."

Hearing this Guan Yu bowed to Liao Hua and thanked him. Liao Hua suggested escorting Guan Yu with his troops, but since he was formerly a member of the Yellow Turbans, Guan Yu would have nothing to do with him. So he simply thanked him for his kindness. Liao Hua then offered some presents to him but these were also declined.

So Liao Hua took his leave and presently disappeared in a valley among the hills. Guan Yu told his sisters-in-law his meeting with Cao Cao and the gift of a robe and then he urged the carriage on its way.

Toward dusk they came to a farm where they asked for shelter. The farmer, an old greybeard, came out and asked who they were. Guan Yu told him who he was.

"Are you not the one who slew Yan Liang and Wen Chou?" inquired the venerable host.

"Yes, I am," replied Guan Yu.

"Come in," said the old man, joyfully.

"My two sisters-in-law are waiting in the carriage," said Guan Yu.

The old man called out his wife and daughter to welcome the ladies in. When the two ladies came into the hall, Guan Yu stood respectfully beside them. The host asked him to take a seat but he said that he could not sit while his sisters-in-law were present. Then the old man told his wife to entertain the ladies in the inner quarters while he treated Guan Yu in the hall. Guan Yu asked him his name.

He replied, "I am Hu Hua. In the days of Emperor Huan I was an official of the court but I resigned and retired here to lead a private life. I have a son who is with the prefect of Yingyang and if you should be going that way, General, I would like you to take a letter to him."

Guan Yu said he would take the letter. The next day after breakfast the ladies got into their carriage, the host handed his letter to Guan Yu, and the little party once more took the road. They went toward Luoyang.

Presently they approached a pass known as East Peak Pass, guarded by Kong Xiu and five hundred soldiers. When he was informed of Guan Yu's arrival Kong Xiu came out to greet him. Guan Yu dismounted and returned the officer's salute.

Kong Xiu asked, "Where are you going, General?'

"I have taken leave of the prime minister and am going to Hebei to find my brother."

"But Yuan Shao is the prime minister's rival. You have authority from him to go there?"

"I left in a hurry and did not get it," said Guan Yu.

"If you have no authority you must wait while I send someone to confirm it with the prime minister."

"That will delay my journey greatly," said Guan Yu.

"I must stand by my orders: that is the only thing to do," said Kong Xiu.

"Then you refuse to let me pass?"

"If you want to go through leave the family as a pledge."

At this Guan Yu got very angry and made to strike at the officer on the spot, but he withdrew into the pass. Then he put on his mail, mounted his horse, and led his men to attack, accompanied by the beating of the drums. "You dare to go through, eh?"

The carriage retreated to a safe distance and then Guan Yu rode directly at Kong Xiu, who set his spear and came to meet him. The two steeds met and the men engaged, but at the first stroke of Guan Yu's mighty sword the commander of the pass fell dead. His men fled.

"Don't flee!" cried Guan Yu. "I killed him because I had no choice but I have nothing against you. I want you to tell the prime minister that I slew him in self-defense, for he wished to kill me."

The men bowed before him and Guan Yu, with the carriage, passed through the gates and then continued the journey to Luoyang. The guards there went quickly in to tell their master about his approach. Han Fu, prefect of the city, assembled his officers for counsel. One of them, whose name was Meng Tan, said, "This Guan Yu must be a fugitive or he would have a safe conduct. Our only course is to stop him or we will be blamed for neglecting our duty."

"The man is fierce and brave. Remember the fate of Yan Liang and Wen Chou. It is futile to oppose him by force and so we must think up some trap for him," said the prefect.

"I have a plan," said the same officer. "First, we should guard the gate with a rampart of felled trees. When he comes I will go to fight with him. I will feign defeat and flee to induce him to follow me, and you can shoot him from an ambush along the road. If we can capture him and his party, and send them as prisoners to the capital, we should be well rewarded."

This plan was adopted. Soon they heard that Guan Yu had arrived. Han Fu got ready his bow and arrows and rode out with a thousand men to take up positions in front of the pass. Then as the party approached Han Fu asked, "Who is that?"

Guan Yu bowed low and said, "I am Guan Yu and I wish to go through the pass."

"Do you have a written permission from the prime minister?"

"In my hurry to depart I failed to get this."

"My special orders from him are to hold this pass and guard against all spies that may come by. Any person without a written permission must be a fugitive."

Then Guan Yu began to be angry, and he told them what had happened to Kong Xiu. "Do you also seek death?" he asked.

"Who will capture him for me?" cried Han Fu, and Meng Tan offered himself. He rode out, whirling his double swords and made straight for Guan Yu.

Guan Yu sent the carriage out of danger and then rode toward Meng Tan. They engaged, but very soon Meng Tan turned his steed and fled. Guan Yu pursued. Meng Tan, intent only on leading his enemy toward where the prefect was waiting in ambush, knew little about the speed of the Red Hare. Very soon he was caught and a stroke of the mighty sword cut him into two pieces. Then Guan Yu turned back. The prefect hid himself behind the gate and mustered all his strength to shoot an arrow which lodged in the left arm of Guan Yu. He pulled it out with his teeth but the blood streamed down as he rode at the prefect, Han Fu, scattering the soldiers in front of him. Before he could escape Guan Yu raised his sword and made an oblique cut which sliced off the head and shoulder of his opponent.

Then he drove off the soldiers and returned to escort the carriage. He bound up his wound, and, fearing lest anyone might take advantage of his weakness, dared not make long halts on the road, but hurried toward Sishui Pass.

The warden of this pass was Bian Xi, a warrior whose weapon was a flying hammer. He had been a member of the Yellow Turbans but had gone over to Cao Cao, who had given him this post. As soon as he heard of the coming of the redoubtable Guan Yu he cudgeled his brains for a scheme to use against him. Finally, he decided upon an ambush. In a temple in front of the pass he placed two hundred men armed with axes and swords. He planned to entice Guan Yu to enter the temple for refreshments and when he let fall a wine cup as signal the hidden men would rush out.

All being thus arranged and ready, he went out to welcome Guan Yu, who dismounted at his coming. Bian Xi began very amiably.

"Your name, General, makes the very earth tremble and everyone looks up to you. Your return to the emperor's uncle, Liu Bei, proves you to be noble and true."

Guan Yu in reply told him about why he had slain the three men. Bian Xi replied, "You were right to slay them. When I see the prime minister I will explain to him that you had done so against your will."

Guan Yu thought he had found a friend and so rode with him through the pass to the temple, where they were met by a number of monks and the chiming of the bell.

This temple, named Guardian of the State, had been in the private use of Emperor Ming (A.D. 57–75). In the temple were some thirty monks and among these there happened to be one who came from the same village as Guan Yu. His religious name was Pujing. Hearing who the visitor was, he came forward to speak with him.

"General," he said, "How long is it since you left your home village?"

"Nearly twenty years," replied Guan Yu.

"Do you recognize me?"

"I am afraid not. I have been away from the village too long."

"My house and yours were only separated by a stream," said the monk.

Now Bian Xi, seeing the monk holding forth about village matters, feared lest he should blab about the ambush, so he told him to be silent.

"I want to invite General Guan to a feast. You priest fellows seem to have a lot to say," said Bian Xi.

Guan Yu said, "Well, when fellow villagers meet they naturally want to talk of old times."

Pujing invited the visitor to the guest room to take tea, but Guan Yu said, "The two ladies are out there in the carriage—they ought to have some refreshments first."

So the monk asked the attendants to take some tea to the ladies. Then he led Guan Yu inside, at the same time lifting the monk's knife which he wore at his side and looking meaningfully at him. Guan Yu understood and brought along his weapon to keep close at his side.

When Bian Xi invited Guan Yu to go into the main hall for some refreshments, Guan Yu turned to him and said, "Is this invitation good or evil?"

Before his host could make any reply Guan Yu saw that many armed men were concealed behind the partition. He shouted loudly at Bian Xi: "I thought you were an honorable man. How dare you plot this?"

The man saw that his plot had been exposed so he called the assassins to come out and attack, but Guan Yu had a short sword in his hand and slashed at anyone who came near. The rest of them scattered. Their commander ran down the hall and tried to escape through the corridor, but Guan Yu threw aside the short sword, took up his weighty Blue Dragon, and went after Bian Xi. Taking out his flying hammer, Bian Xi swung it at Guan Yu, who, knocking it aside with his sword, soon caught up with him. Then with one blow he cut him in halves.

The fight over, he went out to see the two ladies, who were surrounded by soldiers—but at the sight of the terrible warrior all of them fled. Seeking out the monk, his fellow villager, he thanked him for the timely warning that had saved him from death.

"I cannot remain here after this," said Pujing. "I will pack up my few belongings and my alms bowl and take to the road, uncertain in my wanderings as the clouds in the sky. But we will meet again—till then take care of yourself."

Then Guan Yu continued his journey on the road to Yingyang. The prefect of this city was named Wang Zhi, and he was related by marriage to Han Fu, who had already been killed by Guan Yu. Hearing of the death of his relative, he schemed to kill Guan Yu. He sent men to guard the city gates and, when Guan Yu approached, he himself went out to greet him, smiling agreeably. Guan Yu related to him the purpose of his journey.

"General, you must be quite exhausted riding such a long way, and the ladies in their carriage must be cramped and fatigued. Please come into the city and rest yourselves for the night in the guesthouse. You can set forth again tomorrow."

The offer was tempting and his host seemed sincere enough, so Guan Yu asked the two ladies to go into the city, where they found everything very comfortably prepared for them. And, though Guan Yu declined the prefect's invitation to a banquet, refreshments for the travelers were sent to their lodging. As all of them were fatigued from the trials of the journey, Guan Yu asked the ladies to rest in the main room and told the attendants to feed the horses and get some sleep when they could as soon as the evening meal was over. He, too, took off his armor and enjoyed some relaxation.

While the travelers were resting in their residence the prefect secretly called in one of his subordinates, named Hu Ban, with whom he shared the plot for the destruction of his guest. He said, "This Guan Yu is a fugitive, running away without the prime minister's permission. What is more, he has slain prefects of cities and commanders of passes on the road, and is guilty of serious crimes. But he is too strong and valiant for us to overcome. I want you to take a thousand soldiers this evening to surround his lodging, each one armed with a torch, and we will burn him. Start the fire about midnight and burn everyone in there to death, no matter who. I will come with a force to assist you."

After receiving the order, Hu Ban got ready the men and told them to prepare in secret a lot of firewood and other combustibles and pile them up at the gate of the guesthouse. Hu Ban thought to himself, "I have long heard the name of this Guan Yu but I don't know what manner of man he is. Let me go and have a peep at him." So he went into the guesthouse and inquired where General Guan was.

"The general is the man reading in the main hall," was the reply.

Hu Ban noiselessly made his way to the outside of the hall and peeped in. There he saw the famous warrior holding his long beard in his left hand while he read by the light of a lamp placed on a low table. An involuntary exclamation of admiration escaped him at the sight of the majesty of the figure.

"A real god indeed!" he ejaculated.

"Who is there?" asked Guan Yu.

Hu Ban entered and told him who he was.

"Are you the son of Hu Hua, who lives outside the capital?" asked Guan Yu.

"Yes, I am," replied Hu Ban.

Then Guan Yu called up his followers and told them to take out the letter from the old man. Guan Yu handed it to Hu Ban, who read it and then sighed deeply. "I very nearly caused the death of a good man," he said.

Then he betrayed the whole plot. "Wang Zhi wants to kill you. At this moment you are surrounded on all sides. At the third watch they will set fire to this place. Now I will go and open the city gates while you hasten in your preparation for flight."

Guan Yu was greatly startled, but he quickly buckled up his armor, got his steed ready, roused the two ladies and put them into their carriage. Then they left the guesthouse. As they came out they saw the soldiers all about them, each with a torch. They hastened to the outskirts of the city and found the gate already open and they lost no time in getting clear of the city. Hu Ban returned to give orders to burn down the guesthouse.

The fugitives pressed on but before long they saw lights coming up behind them and Wang Zhi called out to them to stop. Guan Yu reined in his horse and began to abuse him.

"Wicked fellow! What had you against me that you wished to burn me to death?"

Wang Zhi whipped up his steed and set his spear, but Guan Yu felled him with one mighty blow of his sword and scattered his followers.

Then the carriage pushed on. On the way Guan Yu thought of the kindness of Hu Ban and his heart was filled with gratitude to him. Then they drew near Huazhou and the prefect, Liu Yan, rode out to welcome him with a few score of riders. Seated on horseback, Guan Yu bowed to him and greeted him politely.

"Where are you going, sir?" asked Liu Yan.

"I have bidden farewell to the prime minister and am on my way to find my brother."

"Liu Bei is with Yuan Shao, who is at enmity with the prime minister. How can you be allowed to go to him?" asked Liu Yan.

"That matter was settled long ago."

"The Yellow River ferry is an important position and is guarded by an officer under Xiahou Dun. I don't think he will let you cross."

"Could you provide boats for me, then?"

"Though there are boats I dare not give them to you."

"Well, formerly I slew Yan Liang and Wen Chou and saved you from a grave danger. Now you refuse me a ferry boat!"

"I am afraid Xiahou Dun will know of it and hold it against me."

Guan Yu perceived that no help was to be expected from this useless man, so he pushed on and presently reached the ferry. There the commander of the force, Qin Qi, came out with his army to question who he was, and Guan Yu told him.

"Where are you bound?" asked Qin Qi.

"I am going to Hebei to seek my brother, Liu Bei, and I entreat you to grant me a passage over the river."

"Where is the prime minister's permission?"

"I am not serving under him so why should I have his permission?"

"I have orders from General Xiahou Dun to guard the ferry—even if you grew wings you could not fly over."

Guan Yu's anger rose. "Do you know that I have been the death of all those who have hitherto tried to hinder me?" he said.

"You have only been able to slay officers of no rank or reputation, but you dare not kill me."

"Where would you stand beside Yan Liang and Wen Chou?" asked Guan Yu.

Qin Qi grew angry and, sword in hand, he came toward Guan Yu at a gallop. The two met, but in the first encounter Qin Qi's head was swept off by his opponent's terrible weapon.

"He who opposed me is dead—you others need not be afraid," cried Guan Yu. "Be quick and prepare me a boat."

The boat was soon ready and the two women stepped on board, followed by Guan Yu and the others. They crossed, and were then in the country of Yuan Shao. In the course of his journey up to this point Guan Yu had forced his way through five passes and slain six people.

> He hung up his seal, locked the gifts, his courtly mansion left,
> He journeyed to join his brother dear, too long from his side reft.
> The horse he rode was famed for speed as for endurance great,
> His mighty sword made a way for him and opened every gate.
> His loyalty and truth stand a model for all,
> His valor is known across rivers and hills.

Alone he faced his opponents, t'was death to meet his blade,
His glory has been praised by scholars and ne'er will fade.

"I have killed all these people on my way against my will," mused Guan Yu as he rode along.

"When Cao Cao hears of it he will surely regard me as an ungrateful person."

Before long he saw a rider coming from the north, who called him by name and asked him to halt. He recognized him to be Sun Qian, whom he had not seen since they parted in Runan.

"Have you heard any news of my brother since we separated in Runan?" asked Guan Yu.

"After your departure the city fell back into the hands of its former leaders, Liu Pi and Gong Du, who sent me to the north to seek peace with Yuan Shao and to invite your brother to go and help them in planning against Cao Cao. But to my disappointment Yuan Shao's men are jealous of each other. Of the four chief advisors, one of them is in jail; another is disfavored; and the other two vie for power. Yuan Shao himself is suspicious by nature and hesitates in taking any action. So I advised your brother to seek an opportunity to get away from them all. Now he's gone to Runan to join Liu Pi and I've come specially to inform you of this. It's really fortunate for me to meet you here. Otherwise you' d go to Yuan Shao and might be harmed by him. Now we must hasten to Runan to join your brother."

Then Sun Qian paid his respects to the two ladies, who asked him for news—he told them of the risks Liu Bei had suffered because of Yuan Shao's sudden bursts of anger and that he was at present safe in Runan, where they would meet him.

The two ladies covered their faces and wept as they listened to him. Now the party no longer traveled northward but took the road toward Runan. Not long after, however, a great cloud of dust rose behind them and presently an armed force appeared, led by Xiahou Dun, who shouted out to Guan Yu and demanded him to stop.

One by one the pass commanders stopped his progress and
were slain,
Another army comes to block the way and he must fight again.

How Guan Yu managed to escape will be told in the next chapter.

CHAPTER TWENTY-EIGHT

Guan Yu Kills Cai Yang to Clear Zhang Fei's Doubt
Liu Bei Is Reunited with His Followers at Old City

The previous chapter ended with Sun Qian joining Guan Yu in escorting the two ladies on the road to Runan. Suddenly they were pursued by Xiahou Dun with three hundred followers. Sun Qian went ahead with the carriage while Guan Yu remained to deal with the pursuers. When his opponent drew near, Guan Yu said, "The prime minister is magnanimous enough to allow me to leave but your coming after me like this simply damages his name."

Xiahou Dun replied, "The prime minister has sent no instructions to the pass commanders to allow you free passage and yet you have caused the death of all these officers, including one of my men. Your behavior is unpardonable. I have come to capture you and take you back to the prime minister. Let him decide what to do with you."

Then he dashed forward with his spear ready to thrust but at that moment a rider galloped up behind him at full speed, crying, "You must not fight with Yun-chang!"

Guan Yu reined in his steed at once and waited. The messenger came up, drew from his bosom an official document and said to Xiahou Dun: "The prime minister admired General Guan for his loyalty and honor, and fearing that he might be stopped at the various passes, he sent me over to show this document at every pass on the road."

"But this Guan Yu has slain several commanders of the passes. Does the prime minister know that?" asked Xiahou Dun.

The messenger said that he did not know.

"Then," said Xiahou Dun, "I will arrest him and take him to the prime minister, who can set him free or not as he wishes."

"Do you think I am afraid of you?" said Guan Yu getting angry.

And he rode forward. His rival, too, set his spear and pushed forth for battle. They met and had reached the tenth encounter when a second horseman came up at full speed, crying, "Generals, wait a moment!"

Xiahou Dun stopped and asked the messenger, "Does the prime minister want me to arrest him?"

"No," replied the second messenger. "For fear that General Guan should have difficulties at the passes the prime minister has sent me with a dispatch to say he is to be allowed to leave."

"Did the prime minister know that he had slain several men on the way?"

"No, he did not."

"In that case, I must not let him go," and he signalled for his men to close in around Guan Yu.

But Guan Yu flourished his mighty sword and a battle was again imminent. At that moment a third rider appeared, who called the two combatants by their names and cried, "Don't fight!"

The speaker was Zhang Liao. Both combatants made no further move and waited.

Zhang Liao said, "I have brought the prime minister's strict orders. He has heard that Yun-chang has slain several men on the way and he fears that someone else may hinder his passage again, so he has sent me to deliver his command at each pass—Yun-chang is to be allowed to leave freely."

Xiahou Dun said, "Qin Qi was Cai Yang's nephew and he was left in my special care. Now this Guan Yu has killed him—how can I let him go?"

"When I see his uncle I'll explain. But now the main point is that you have the prime minister's order to let him pass and you mustn't act against his wish."

So the only thing for Xiahou Dun to do was to obey and he did.

"Where are you going now?" asked Zhang Liao to Guan Yu.

"I hear my brother is no longer with Yuan Shao and now I'm going to roam the land to look for him."

"Since you don't know where he is, why don't you return to the prime minister?"

"What's the sense of that?" said Guan Yu with a smile. "But, Wen-yuan, please apologize to the prime minister for my faults when you return."

With this he bade farewell to Zhang Liao and departed. Zhang Liao and the others returned to the capital.

Guan Yu quickly overtook the carriage and the group resumed their journey. He rode side by side with Sun Qian and told him what had happened. Several days later they were caught in a heavy rain and their luggage was all wet. Looking about for protection, they noticed a farm by the side of a hill and they went there to seek shelter. An old man came out to greet them, to whom Guan Yu told their story. When he had finished, the old man said, "My name is Guo Chang and my family has always lived here. I am very pleased to meet you, General, for I have long known your name by reputation."

So he killed a sheep and brought out wine to treat the travelers. The two ladies were ushered into the inner quarters to take a rest. While they refreshed themselves their baggage was put out to dry and their horses were fed.

As the day closed in they saw a young man leading several people into the house and their host said to him, "Come here and pay your respects to the general."

"This is my son," he said to Guan Yu, pointing to the young man.

"What has he been doing?" asked Guan Yu.

"He has just come in from hunting."

The young fellow saluted Guan Yu and went out. The old man continued, "All my family have been farmers or scholars. He is my only son and instead of following in the footsteps of his ancestors he cares for nothing but gadding about and hunting. It is a misfortune for our family."

"Why is it a misfortune?" asked Guan Yu. "In these days of disorder a good soldier can make a name for himself as well."

"If he would only learn the military arts that would be something of a career, but he is nothing but a vagabond and does everything he should not do. He is a grief to me."

Guan Yu sighed in sympathy. The old man stayed till a late hour and when he took his leave his two guests began to prepare for rest.

Suddenly there arose a great hubbub in the backyard, men shouting and horses neighing. Guan Yu called his people but as no one answered he and his companion drew their swords and went into the stable yard to investigate. There they found their host's son on the ground while their men were struggling with the farm people. Guan Yu asked what had happened and his men told him that the young fellow had tried to steal the Red Hare but had been badly kicked by the horse. They had heard shouting and had gone to see what it meant when the farm people set upon them.

Guan Yu was very angry. "You mean thieves! How dare you steal my horse?" he cried.

But before he could do anything his host came running up and implored, "It was not with my consent that my son did this evil thing. I know he deserves death but his mother loves him tenderly and I beg you to be merciful and pardon him."

"He is indeed unworthy of his father," said Guan Yu. "What you told me shows he is a degenerate. For your sake I pardon him."

Then he told his own people to keep a better lookout, sent the farm people away, and went back with Sun Qian to get some rest.

The next morning the old man and his wife came up to bow to him and to thank him for forgiving their son. "My unworthy son has offended you greatly and I am deeply grateful to you for your kindness in not punishing him," said the old man.

"Bring him here and I will teach him to reason," said Guan Yu.

"He went out before daylight with several of his fellow rogues and I do not know where he is."

So they took leave and continued their journey, picking up paths among the hills. Before they had gone far they saw a large party of men led by two riders. One of the riders wore a yellow turban and battledress. The other was the old man's son. The wearer of the yellow turban called out: "I am one of the officers of the General of Heaven, Zhang Jue. Whoever you may be, leave that horse you are riding and you may go free."

Guan Yu greeted the speech with a hearty laugh.

"You ignorant rebel! If you have been with Zhang Jue, you should have known the names of Liu, Guan, and Zhang, the three brothers."

"I have heard that the ruddy-faced man with a long beard is called Guan Yu, but I have never seen him. Who are you?"

Guan Yu laid aside his sword, reined in his horse and drew off the bag that covered his beard thus showing its magnificence.

The turban wearer immediately slipped out of the saddle, laid an angry hand on his companion and they both bowed low in front of Guan Yu's steed.

"Who are you?" asked Guan Yu.

"I am Pei Yuan-shao. After the death of Zhang Jue I was left without a leader and I gathered together people like myself and we took refuge in the forests. Early in the morning this fellow came to tell me that a guest at his father's farm had a valuable horse and asked me to steal it with him. I did not expect to meet you, General."

The wretched son of the old man entreated that his life be spared and Guan Yu pardoned him for his father's sake. He crept away in a hurry.

"You did not recognize me. How then did you know my name?" asked Guan Yu.

Pei Yuan-shao replied, "Not far from here is a mountain called the Sleeping Bull, where lives a man whose name is Zhou Cang. He is a very powerful man from the west, with a stiff curly mustache and a majestic look. He was also with the Yellow Turbans and when his leader perished he took to the forest as well. He has often mentioned your name to me but I have never had the honor of seeing you."

Guan Yu said, "The greenwood is no place for a true hero. You had better abandon this depraved way of life and return to the path of virtue. Do not prepare your own destruction."

As they were talking a troop of horsemen appeared in the distance. "This must be Zhou Cang," said Pei Yuan-shao. And Guan Yu waited for them to approach.

The leader of the group was a tall man of very dark complexion, carrying a spear in his hand. As soon as he drew near enough to see he exclaimed joyfully, "This is General Guan!"

In a moment he had slipped out of the saddle and was on his knees by the roadside.

"Zhou Cang renders obeisance to you, General," he said.

"Where could you have known me?" asked Guan Yu of the warrior.

"I was with the Yellow Turbans and saw you then. As I was a rebel at that time I could not join you, which has been one of my deepest regrets. Now that my good fortune has brought me here I hope you will not reject me. Let me be one of your foot soldiers so that I can always be near you to carry your whip and run by your stirrup. Then I will die with no regrets."

As he seemed thoroughly sincere Guan Yu said, "But if you follow me, what about your companions?"

"They may do as they please—follow me or go their own ways."

Then they all shouted, "We will follow."

Guan Yu dismounted and went to ask the ladies what they thought of this. Lady Gan said, "Brother, you have traveled thus far all alone without any fighting men to support you. You have encountered many dangers but you never wanted any assistance. Earlier you refused the service of Liao Hua, why then accept this crowd? But this is only a woman's view and you must decide."

"You are right, sister," answered Guan Yu.

Returning to Zhou Cang he said, "It is not that I am lacking in feeling but my sisters-in-law do not care for a big following. Please go back to the mountains for the time being till I have found my brother and I will surely call you."

Zhou Cang answered, "I am only a rough, uncouth fellow, wasting my life as a brigand. Meeting you, General, is like seeing the light of day and I can never bear to miss you again. As it is inconvenient for all my men to follow you I will ask my friend here to lead them away, but let me come and follow you on foot wherever you go."

Guan Yu again asked his sisters-in-law what they thought of this. Lady Gan said that one or two men made no difference and so Guan Yu consented. But Pei Yuan-shao was not satisfied with this arrangement and said that he also wished to follow.

Zhou Cang said, "If you don't stay with the band they'll disperse and be lost. You must take command for the moment and let me accompany General Guan. As soon as he has a fixed abode I'll come to fetch you."

Somewhat discontented, Pei Yuan-shao accepted the situation and marched off while his friend joined Guan Yu's party and they went toward Runan. They traveled quickly for some days and then they saw a city on the hills. From the natives they learned that the place was called Gucheng, or Old City, and that a few months before a warrior had suddenly appeared, driven out the magistrate and taken possession. Then he had begun to recruit men, buy horses, and store grain. His name was Zhang Fei. Now he had a large force and no one in the neighborhood dared to face him.

"To think that I should find my younger brother like this!" exclaimed Guan Yu in delight. "I've lost all news about him since the fall of Xuzhou."

So he dispatched Sun Qian into the city to tell its new commander to come out and greet his sisters-in-law.

Now, after being separated from his brothers, Zhang Fei had gone to the Mangdang Hills where he had remained a month or so. One day while searching for tidings of Liu Bei, he happened to pass this city. He had sent his men to borrow some grain from the magistrate but had been refused. In revenge, he had driven away the magistrate and taken possession of the city. Since then he had made this place his temporary abode.

Following Guan Yu's order, Sun Qian entered the city and, after the usual greetings, told Zhang Fei the news of his two brothers, saying that Liu Bei had left Yuan Shao and gone to Runan and that Guan Yu, with their sisters-in-law, was at his gates. Then he asked him to go and welcome them in. Zhang Fei said not a word after he heard all this but called for his armor and spear, mounted, and rode out with a thousand or so men. Sun Qian was astonished but dared not ask him what this meant and simply followed.

Guan Yu was very glad when he saw his brother coming. Handing his sword to Zhou Cang, he rode toward him at full speed. But when he approached he saw all the signs of fierce anger on the face of his brother, who roared as he attacked with his spear.

Guan Yu was entirely taken aback. Ducking hastily to evade the blow, he called out anxiously, "Brother, what does this mean? Is the Peach Orchard Oath quite forgotten?"

"You faithless fellow! What impudence is this that you come to see me after your disgraceful behavior?" shouted Zhang Fei.

"What disgraceful behavior?"

"You have betrayed our brother and surrendered to Cao Cao. You have received title and office at his hands. And now you have come to cheat me. I will fight you to death!"

"So you don't know and it's hard for me to explain. But ask our sisters-in-law, worthy brother, and they'll tell you."

At this the ladies lifted the curtain of the carriage and called out, "Brother, why is this?"

Zhang Fei said, "Wait a while, sisters, and see me slay this traitor. After that I will conduct you into the city."

Lady Gan said, "Since he did not know where you were he took temporary shelter with Cao Cao. And when he knew that your eldest brother was in Runan he braved every danger to escort us thus far on the road. Please do not misunderstand him."

Lady Mi also chimed in: "When he went to the capital there was no other course open to him."

"Sisters, do not let him blind you to the truth. Real loyalty prefers death to dishonor. No good man will serve two masters."

Guan Yu said, "Brother, don't wrong me, I beg you."

Sun Qian said, "Yun-chang has come especially to seek you."

"You are talking nonsense, too," roared Zhang Fei. "How can he be sincere? He only came to capture me, I say."

"Had I come to capture you, I should have come with men and horses," said Guan Yu.

"And aren't there men and horses coming?" said Zhang Fei pointing at something behind Guan Yu.

Guan Yu turned, and there indeed he saw a cloud of dust rising, indicating the approach of an army—and from the banners they showed themselves to be Cao Cao's men.

"Now can you try to cajole me any further?" cried Zhang Fei in a rage.

He set his long spear and was just coming on when Guan Yu said, "Brother, wait a minute—see me slay the leader of these to prove that I'm no traitor."

"Well, if you are really true, prove it by slaying that leader, whoever he may be, before I have finished three rolls of the drum."

Guan Yu agreed. Soon the army was near enough to make out the leader to be Cai Yang. Sword in hand he rode at full speed, crying, "So I have found you, killer of my nephew! I have the prime minister's command to capture you."

Guan Yu made no reply. Raising his sword he struck at once. Zhang Fei himself beat the drum. Before one roll was completed Cai Yang's head had rolled on the ground. His men scattered and fled. Guan Yu, however, captured the ensign-bearer and questioned him. The youth said that Cai Yang was incensed at the loss of his nephew and wished to pursue and attack Guan Yu, but the prime minister would not permit him to do so. To appease him he had sent Cai Yang to attack Runan and the meeting at this place was entirely an accident.

Guan Yu made him repeat this story to his brother. Zhang Fei also questioned him concerning all that had happened in the capital, and the details the soldier gave him finally convinced him of the fidelity of Guan Yu.

Just then a messenger came from the city to tell Zhang Fei that some scores of horsemen had arrived at the south gate. They seemed in a great hurry but no one knew them. Zhang Fei, with some lingering doubt in his heart, went to look at the newcomers and truly enough there were a score or two of mounted archers with light bows and short arrows. Seeing him they hastily dismounted and he discovered them to be Lady Mi's two brothers. Zhang Fei also dismounted and greeted them.

Mi Zhu said, "After the fall of Xuzhou we returned to our own village, where we sent out people all around for news of you. We heard that Yun-chang had surrendered to Cao Cao and our lord was in Hebei with Yuan Shao, but we could hear nothing about you. Yesterday, however, we fell in with some travelers, who told us a certain General Zhang of such and such an appearance had occupied the Old City. We felt it must be you so we came to inquire. How happy we are to find you here!"

Zhang Fei replied, "Yun-chang and Sun Qian have just come with my sisters-in-law. They have news of where my eldest brother is."

This added to the joy of the two newcomers, who at once went to see Guan Yu and the ladies. Then they all entered the city. When all were seated the two ladies related the whole story of Guan Yu's experience since the destruction of the city of Xiapi, at which Zhang Fei was overcome with remorse and bowed before his brother, weeping bitterly. The Mi brothers were also greatly affected. Then Zhang Fei, in his turn, related what had happened to him.

A day was spent in banquets and the next day Zhang Fei wished to join his newfound brother on his journey to Runan to see their eldest brother Liu Bei. But Guan Yu did not consent.

"You stay here and take care of the ladies while Sun Qian and I go to get news," he said.

So the two of them set out again with a few soldiers. When they reached Runan they were received by the commander Liu Pi, who told them that Liu Bei was no longer in the city. He had only spent a few days there and had gone back to consult Yuan Shao, because he found there were too few soldiers in the city.

Guan Yu was greatly disappointed and his companion did his best to console him. "Don't be so sad. It only means the trouble of another journey into Hebei to tell your brother and then we can all meet in the Old City."

Sun Qian's words comforted him so they took leave of Liu Pi and returned to the Old City, where they told the others what they had heard. Zhang Fei at once wanted to go with them to Hebei but Guan Yu again opposed this.

"This city you have here means we have a place to settle down and we must not abandon it lightly. I'll go again with Sun Qian to find our eldest brother. You must keep the city safe while we're away."

"You've killed their two generals, Yan Liang and Wen Chou. It won't be safe for you to go, Brother," said Zhang Fei.

"That won't stop me. I'll act according to changing circumstances," said Guan Yu to assure him.

Then Guan Yu summoned Zhou Cang and asked him, "How many men are there with Pei Yuan-shao at the Sleeping Bull Mountain?"

"Four or five hundred, I should think."

"Now, I'm going to take the short cut to find my brother," said Guan Yu. "You go and summon your men and lead them here along the main road."

Zhou Cang obeyed the order and left for the mountain, while Guan Yu and Sun Qian started toward the north with a score or so followers. When they drew near the boundary Sun Qian said, "You mustn't enter the city right now. Let me go in first to see our lord and we'll decide what to do. You can take a rest here."

Seeing the wisdom of this Guan Yu remained outside the city but sent his companion alone to continue the journey. He and his followers went up to a nearby farm to seek lodging.

When they got to the farm a venerable man leaning on a stick came out to greet them. After exchanging greetings with the old man Guan Yu told him about himself.

"My surname is also Guan and my given name is Ding," said the old man. "I know you by your reputation and I am very pleased to meet you."

He then sent for his two sons, who came and bowed to Guan Yu. He put up Guan Yu in his house and entertained him. All his followers were also provided shelter on the farm.

In the meantime, Sun Qian had made his way to the city and met Liu Bei who said, "Jian Yong is also here. We can send for him secretly to talk over this matter."

Soon, his former advisor Jian Yong came and after saluting Sun Qian the three began to consider the means of getting away.

Jian Yong said to Liu Bei, "You must go and see Yuan Shao tomorrow, sir, and say that you wish to go to Jingzhou to see Liu Biao. Tell him that you will persuade Liu Biao to join him in the destruction of Cao Cao. That will give you an excuse to leave here."

"Excellent!" said Liu Bei. "But can you come with me?"

"I have another plan to free myself," said Jian Yong.

Having designed their plan, Liu Bei soon went to see his protector Yuan Shao, and suggested that as Liu Biao was strong and well posted in the nine cities around Jingzhou and Xiangyang, his help should be sought against their enemy.

"I have sent messengers repeatedly to ask him for an alliance," replied Yuan Shao, "but he is unwilling."

"As he and I are of the same Liu family he will not refuse me if I go and ask him," said Liu Bei.

"He is certainly worth much more than Liu Pi in Runan." And he agreed to let Liu Bei go. Then he continued, "I hear Guan Yu has just left Cao Cao and wants to come here. If he does I will put him to death to avenge my two best officers."

"Sir, you wished to employ him and so I sent for him. Why do you now want to destroy him? The two men he slew were but deer compared with such a tiger as he is. When you exchange two deer for a tiger, what do you lose in the bargain?"

"I do like him," said Yuan Shao. "I was only joking. You can send another messenger to call him and tell him to come soon."

"I will send Sun Qian to bring him here at once," said Liu Bei to please his protector.

After Liu Bei had gone, Jian Yong also went in to see Yuan Shao to whom he said, "If Liu Bei goes he will not come back. I will go with him to speak to Liu Biao and at the same time I can keep a watch on Liu Bei."

Yuan Shao agreed and gave orders for Jian Yong to accompany Liu Bei on the mission. One of his advisors objected to this mission and argued, "Last time Liu Bei went to speak to Liu Pi but accomplished nothing. Now you are sending Jian Yong to go with him and I am sure neither will ever return."

"Do not be so suspicious," said Yuan Shao. "Jian Yong knows how to deal with him."

That was the end of the interview and the advisor left in distress.

Meanwhile, Liu Bei sent Sun Qian back to inform Guan Yu about this arrangement. Then, along with Jian Yong, he took leave of Yuan Shao and rode out of the city. As soon as they reached the boundary they were met by Sun Qian and all three rode forth to the old man's farm to see Guan Yu, who came out to welcome them. It was an emotional meeting. Guan Yu bowed to his brother at the gate and the two held each other's hands, while tears streamed down their faces.

Presently the two sons of their host came to pay their respects to the visitors. Liu Bei asked them their names.

"These are of the same surname as myself," said Guan Yu. "The elder one is Guan Ning, who is a student and the younger one is Guan Ping, who is to be a soldier."

"I have been thinking of leaving my second son in your care, General Guan," said the father. "Would you take him?"

"How old is he?" asked Liu Bei.

"Eighteen," answered the host.

Liu Bei continued, "Since you are so kind, sir, I venture to suggest that your son be adopted by my brother, who has no son of his own. What do you think of this?"

Their host was perfectly willing so he called the lad to make a son's obeisance to Guan Yu and to call Liu Bei "Uncle."

Afraid that Yuan Shao might change his mind and pursue them, they hastened to get on their way and with them went Guan Ping, who was placed in the train of his adopted father. The lad's real father accompanied them for some time and then returned.

The group took the road toward the Sleeping Bull Mountain, but before they had gone very far they met Zhou Cang with a small band. He was wounded. Guan Yu introduced him to Liu Bei and asked him how he got his wounds.

Zhou Cang replied, "Before I reached the hill a certain warrior, all alone, had fought with my friend Pei Yuan-shao and killed him. All our men surrendered to him and he occupied our camp. When I got there I tried to entice my men back to my side but only succeeded with a few. The others were too afraid to leave him. I got angry and went to fight with him but he defeated me time after time and I suffered three wounds."

"Who is the warrior? What does he look like?" asked Liu Bei.

"He is powerfully built but I do not know who he is," answered Zhou Cang.

Then they advanced toward the hill, with Guan Yu in front and Liu Bei in the rear. When they drew near Zhou Cang began to abuse his enemy who soon appeared, fully mailed and armed, galloping down the hill with his followers.

Suddenly Liu Bei rode out waving his whip and shouting, "Is that Zi-long?"

The rider, for it was Zhao Zi-long (Zhao Yun), instantly slipped out of the saddle and knelt by the roadside. The two brothers dismounted to meet him and to inquire how he came to be there.

Zhao Yun said, "Not long after we separated, Gongsun Zan was defeated and perished tragically in flames because he would not listen to good advice. Yuan Shao invited me to go to him several times but I thought too little of him to go. Then I wanted to go to you in Xuzhou but news came that you had lost that place and Yun-chang had gone over to Cao Cao and you had joined Yuan Shao. Several times I thought of coming to you, but I feared Yuan Shao might take offense. So I drifted from one place to another with nowhere to rest till I happened to come this way and that man, Pei Yuan-shao, tried to seize my horse. I slew him and took possession of his camp. I recently heard Yi-de was in the Old City and I wanted to join him but thought it might be only a rumor. How fortunate it is that I should see you today!"

Liu Bei was overjoyed and told him all that had happened to him since they parted. Guan Yu also related his story.

Liu Bei said, "The first time I saw you I felt drawn to you and did not want to part with you. I am very happy to see you again."

"In all my wanderings trying to find a lord worth serving I have seen no one quite like you. Now that I can enter your service all my life's wish is fulfilled. No matter what may happen to me I will have no regrets."

Next they burned the camp and the whole group went with Liu Bei to the Old City, where they were welcomed by Zhang Fei and the Mi brothers. They exchanged the stories of their respective adventures and the two ladies related the heroic deeds of Guan Yu, which moved Liu Bei to deep sighs.

Then they administered a great sacrifice to Heaven and Earth with the slaughter of an ox and a horse. All the soldiers were also rewarded for their toils. Liu Bei thought on their situation and found much to rejoice at. His two brothers were restored to his side and none of his advisors or officers were missing. Moreover, he had gained Zhao Yun and his brother Guan Yu had acquired Guan Ping and Zhou Cang. There was every reason for feasting and celebration.

> *Scattered apart were the brothers, none knew another's retreat,*
> *Joyfully now they reunite, dragon and tigers meet.*

At this time the force under the command of the three brothers and their adherents numbered four to five hundred men. Liu Bei was in favor of leaving the Old City for Runan and just then Liu Pi sent a messenger to invite him to go there. So they went and settled in Runan, where they devoted themselves to strengthening their army, recruiting soldiers, and buying horses.

However, Yuan Shao was much annoyed when Liu Bei did not return and at first he wanted to send an army to destroy him. But the advisor Guo Tu dissuaded him.

"Liu Bei is nothing to worry about but Cao Cao is your major enemy and must be destroyed. Even Liu Biao, though strongly deployed in Jingzhou, poses no threat to you. There is, however, Sun Ce in the east, who is very strong and much feared, with a wide territory, a large army, and many able advisors and officers. You should make an alliance with him against Cao Cao."

This advice appealed to Yuan Shao, who then sent Chen Zhen to deliver his letter to Sun Ce.

The journey by a warrior from the north
Brought forth heroes in the east.

The outcome of this journey will be told in the next chapter.

CHAPTER TWENTY-NINE

The Formidable Little Lord Sun Ce
Slays Yu Jie in Wrath
The Blue-eyed Sun Quan Takes Control of the East

While Cao Cao and Yuan Shao were opposing each other in the north, Sun Ce had become the confirmed leader in the vast region east of the Yangtze with a strong army and ample supplies. In the fourth year of the period Jian An (A.D. 199) he defeated Prefect Liu Xun and so seized the city of Lujiang. This was followed by the seizure of the city of Yuzhang, when its prefect surrendered after receiving Sun Ce's letter of challenge. Then his renown increased even further and he boldly sent Zhang Hong as his messenger to present a tribute to the Emperor to report his military successes.

Cao Cao saw in him a powerful rival and said that he was a lion, difficult to contend with. So he proposed marriage between his niece and Sun Ce's younger brother and the two families became thus connected. Sun Ce's messenger, Zhang Hong, was retained in the capital in the service of Cao Cao.

Then Sun Ce sought the title of Da Si Ma, or Minister of War—one of the highest offices of state—but Cao Cao prevented his attainment of this ambition and Sun Ce keenly resented it. Henceforward his thoughts often turned toward an attack on Cao Cao.

About this time Xu Gong, Prefect of Wujun, sent a secret letter to Cao Cao in which he wrote that Sun Ce was a fierce fellow and the government ought, under the appearance of bestowing favor to him, to recall him to the capital rather than let him grow stronger in the provinces. But the bearer of the letter was captured on the Yangtze River and sent to Sun Ce, who immediately put him to death. Then he sent someone to ask the writer of the letter to come, pretending that he had to consult with him over some affair. The unsuspecting man came.

Sun Ce produced the letter and said, "So you want to send me to my death, eh?" Then the executioners came and strangled him. The family of the victim ran away but three of his trusted servants were determined to avenge him—if only they could find some means of attacking Sun Ce.

One day Sun Ce went hunting in the hills. A stag was spotted and Sun Ce pressed after it at the topmost speed and followed it deep into the forest, where he came upon three armed men standing among the trees. Surprised to see them there, he reined in his horse and asked them who they were.

"We are Han Dang's men, shooting deer here," was the reply.

So Sun Ce shook his bridle to proceed with his pursuit of the deer. But just as he was starting one of the men suddenly struck him in the left thigh with his spear. He at once drew the sword he wore at his side to fight back, but as he did so the blade of his sword fell to the ground, leaving only the hilt in his hand. At this moment another assassin, drawing his bow and an arrow, wounded Sun Ce in the cheek. He plucked out the arrow and with it shot back at the man, who fell; but the other two men attacked him furiously with their spears, shouting, "We are Prefect Xu's men and his avengers!"

Sun Ce then understood. He had no weapons save his bow so he tried to draw off, keeping them at bay by striking with his bow. But the fight was getting too much for him and both he and his steed were wounded in several places. However, just at the critical moment some of his own men came up and they made short work of the two remaining avengers.

But their lord was in a sorry condition. His face was streaming with blood and some of the wounds were very serious. They tore up a robe to bind up his wounds and carried him home.

A poem was written in praise of the three avengers:

> In all the east the bold Sun Ce was a man to fear
> But he was attacked in the hills while hunting a deer.
> Three loyal servants went to avenge a murdered lord,
> Like the faithful Yu Rang they dreaded not the sword.

Being badly wounded Sun Ce sent for the famous doctor Hua Tuo, but he was away in the north and could not be reached. However, his assistant came to treat his wounds.

"The arrowheads were poisoned," said the doctor, "and the poison has penetrated deep. It will take a hundred days of perfect repose before danger is over. But if you give way to passion or anger the wounds will not heal."

Sun Ce was an extremely impatient man and the prospect of such a slow recovery was very distasteful. However, he managed to remain quiet for some twenty of the hundred days. Then he heard that Zhang Hong, who had been retained in the capital by Cao Cao, had sent back a messenger, and he insisted on seeing and questioning him.

"Cao Cao fears you greatly, my lord," said the messenger, "and his advisors have immense respect for you too—all except Guo Jia."

"What did he say?" asked the sick man.

The messenger was afraid to tell him and kept silent, which only irritated his master, who forced him to speak the truth. So the messenger said, "Guo Jia told Cao Cao that he did not have to fear you, that you were rash and unprepared, impulsive and shallow, just a foolhardy soldier but no strategist, who would one day come to his death at the hands of some petty persons."

This provoked the sick man beyond endurance.

"How dare he say this of me, the impudent fool!" cried Sun Ce. "I will take the capital from Cao Cao, I swear!"

He forgot all about repose. Ill as he was he wanted to begin preparations for an expedition at once. His subordinates remonstrated with him, reminding him of the doctor's words, and urged him to rest.

"You are endangering your priceless life for a moment's anger," said his chief advisor Zhang Zhao.

Just then Chen Zhen, the messenger from Yuan Shao, was announced. Sun Ce had him brought in. Chen Zhen said, "My master hopes to form an alliance with you in an attack on Cao Cao."

Such a proposal was just after Sun Ce's heart. That very day he assembled his officers in the wall tower and prepared a banquet in honor of the messenger. While this was in progress he noticed many of his officers whispering to each other and leaving the banquet table. He was surprised and asked the attendants near him what it meant. They told him that the holy man Yu Ji had just gone by and the officers had gone down to pay their respects to him. Sun Ce rose from his seat and leaned over the railing to look at the man. He saw standing in the middle of the road a Taoist priest dressed in a cape of feathers and carrying a stick, while the crowd about him burnt incense and offered obeisance.

"What wizard fellow is this? Bring him here!" said Sun Ce angrily.

"This is Yu Ji," said the attendants. "He lives in the east and goes about distributing charms and draughts. He can cure every disease and is regarded as a holy man. He must not be profaned."

This only angered Sun Ce the more, and he told them to arrest the man at once or suffer death themselves if they dared to disobey. There being no alternative they had to go down into the road and hustle the priest up the steps.

"You madman! How dare you incite men to evil?" shouted Sun Ce.

"I am but a poor priest of Langye Temple. More than half a century ago, when gathering herbs in the woods, I found near the Yangqu Spring a book called *The Way of Tranquility*. It contains a hundred and more chapters describing various ways to cure the diseases of men. Since it came into my possession I have devoted myself to spreading its teachings and saving mankind. I have never taken anything from the people. Can you say I incite men to evil deeds?"

"You say you take nothing—where do you get your clothes and your food? You are exactly like Zhang Jue, the Yellow Turban chief, and you will work mischief if you are left alive."

"Take him away and put him to death," he said to his attendants.

Zhang Zhao interceded, "This priest has been here these many years. He has never done any harm and does not deserve death or punishment."

"I tell you I will kill these wizard fellows just as I would cattle."

All the officials interceded, even the guest of honor Chen Zhen, but Sun Ce still refused to be placated. He ordered the priest to be imprisoned.

The banquet came to an end and Yuan Shao's messenger retired to his lodging. Sun Ce also returned to his place.

His treatment of the Taoist holy man soon reached the ears of his mother. She sent for her son and said to him, "They tell me you've put the holy man Yu Ji in prison. He's cured many sick people and helped soldiers and the common folk hold him in great reverence. Don't harm him."

"He's simply a wizard who upsets the multitude with his spells and craft. He must be put to death," replied Sun Ce.

She tried her best to bring him to reason but he was obstinate. "Don't heed the gossip of the street, mother," he said. "I know how to deal with this."

However, he sent his men to bring the priest over for interrogation. Now the jailers had a great respect for Yu Ji and faith in his powers so they were very kind to him and had taken off his chains and collar. But when Sun Ce sent for him, he went in fetters.

When Sun Ce learned about this he punished the jailers severely. Yu Ji was sent back to prison in fetters. Zhang Zhao and many others signed a petition that they humbly presented to their chief, offering themselves to stand surety for the prisoner.

Sun Ce said to them, "Gentlemen, you are great scholars, but why don't you understand reason? Formerly the Governor of Jiaozhou was deluded by these heretical doctrines into doing all sorts of absurd things, like beating drums, twanging lyres, and burning incense. He constantly wore a red turban and declared that it would ensure victory to an army. But he was slain by the enemy. There is nothing in all this, only none of you will see it. I am going to put this fellow to death in order to stop the spread of this pernicious doctrine."

Lu Fan interposed: "I know very well this Yu Ji is able to summon the wind and command the rain. It is very dry just now, why not make him pray for rain as a punishment?"

"We will see what sort of witchcraft he is equal to," said Sun Ce.

So he had the prisoner brought in, loosened his fetters, and sent him up to an altar to pray for rain.

The docile Taoist priest prepared to do as he was bidden. He first bathed himself, then dressed himself in clean garments. After that he bound his limbs with a cord and sat down in the fierce heat of the sun. People came in crowds to look on.

He said, "I will pray for three feet of refreshing rain for the benefit of the people. Nevertheless I will not escape death."

"But if your prayer is efficacious our lord must believe in your powers," said the people.

"The day of doom has come for me and there is no escape."

Presently, Sun Ce came near the altar and announced that if rain had not fallen by noon he would burn the priest. And to confirm this he ordered his men to prepare the pyre.

As noon drew near a strong wind sprang up and clouds gathered from all directions. But there was no rain.

"It is near noon," said Sun Ce. "Clouds are of no account without rain. He is only an impostor."

He told his attendants to put the priest on the pile of wood and light the fire on all sides. Fanned by the wind the flames rose rapidly. Suddenly from the ground emerged a wreath of black vapor that flew up to the sky, followed by roaring thunder and vivid lightning, peal after peal and flash after flash. And then came the pouring rain. In a short time the streets became rivers and it was, indeed, three feet tall.

Yu Ji, who was still lying upon the pile of firewood, uttered a loud cry and instantly the clouds dispersed, the rain stopped, and the glorious sun reappeared.

Then officials and people helped the priest down, loosened the cord that bound him, and bowed before him in gratitude for the rain.

But Sun Ce boiled with rage at seeing his officers and the people kneeling in the water regardless of the damage to their clothing.

"Rain or shine is the work of nature and the wizard has happened to hit upon the right moment. What are you making all this fuss about?" he cried.

Then he drew his sword and told the attendants to kill the priest with it. They all entreated him to spare his life.

"You want to follow Yu Ji in rebellion, I suppose," cried Sun Ce.

The officers, now thoroughly cowed by the rage of their lord, fell silent and dared not show opposition when the executioners seized the unfortunate man and beheaded him.

They saw a wreath of black smoke rise and drift away to the northeast.

The corpse was exposed in the market place as a warning to enchanters and wizards and similar people. That night there came a very violent storm and when it cleared up at daylight there was no trace of the body. The guards reported this to Sun Ce and in his wrath he wanted to sentence them to death. But at that moment he saw Yu Ji calmly walking toward him as if he were still alive. He was so furious that he drew his sword to strike at the wraith, but he fainted and fell to the ground.

They carried him to his chamber and after quite some time he recovered consciousness.

His mother, Lady Wu, came to visit him and said, "My son, you've done wrong to slay the holy man and this is your retribution."

"Mother, when I was a boy I went with my father to the wars, where men were cut down as one cuts hemp stalks. There has never been any retribution. I've put this fellow to death and so eliminated a great evil. Where does retribution come in?"

"Your illness comes from want of faith," she replied. "Now you must avert the evil by meritorious deeds."

"My fate rests with Heaven—wizards can do me no harm, so why avert anything?'

His mother saw that it was useless to try persuasion with him, but she told his attendants to do some good deeds secretly so that the evil could be turned aside.

That night, about the second watch, as Sun Ce lay in his chamber, he suddenly felt a chill breeze, which extinguished the light for a moment (although it soon brightened again), and he saw in the light the form of Yu Ji standing near his bed.

Sun Ce said, "I am the sworn foe of witchcraft and I will purge the world of all those that deal in magic. You are a ghost—how dare you approach me?"

Reaching down for a sword that hung at the head of his bed he hurled it at the phantom, which then disappeared. When his mother heard this story her grief redoubled. Sun Ce, ill as he was, did his utmost to reassure his mother.

She said, "An ancient saint once said, 'How abundantly do spiritual beings display the powers that belong to them!' Also, 'Prayers be made to the spirits of the upper and lower worlds.' Even saints believed in spirits and gods. You must have faith. You sinned in putting the Taoist priest to death and retribution is sure. I've already arranged to have sacrifices performed at the monastery and you should go in person to pray. May it all come right!"

Sun Ce dared not withstand such a mandate from his mother so, against his wish, he got into a sedan chair and went to the monastery, where the Taoist priests received him respectfully and asked him to light the incense. He did so, but he did not pray. To the surprise of all, the smoke from the burner, instead of floating upwards and dissipating, collected in a mass that gradually shaped itself into an umbrella—and there on the top sat Yu Ji.

Sun Ce simply spat abuse and started to leave the hall. But as he was going out he saw standing right at the door Yu Ji gazing at him with angry eyes.

"Do you see that wizard fellow?" he asked those about him.

They all said they saw nothing. Growing more angry than ever he flung his sword at the figure by the door but the sword struck one of his soldiers, who fell. When they turned him over they found it was the executioner who had actually slain the Taoist priest. The sword had penetrated his brain and his life drained out through the seven channels of perception. Sun Ce told them to bury the man. But as he went out of the monastery he saw Yu Ji walking in.

"This temple is nothing more than a lurking place for sorcerers and wizards and such people," he said.

Therefore he took a seat in front of the building and sent for five hundred soldiers to pull the place down. When they climbed up the roof to strip off the tiles he saw Yu Ji standing above the building and tossing tiles to the ground. In a rage he told them to drive the priests out of the monastery and burn the place. They did so and when the flames rose high he saw the dead Taoist, Yu Ji, standing in the midst of the fire.

Sun Ce returned home in a very bad humor, which turned into fury when he saw the form of Yu Ji standing at his gate. He would not enter but mustered his army and went to camp outside the city. And there he summoned his officers to talk over joining Yuan Shao in an attack on Cao Cao.

They assembled, but they remonstrated with him and begged him to consider his precious health. That night he slept in the camp and again saw Yu Ji, this time with his hair hanging loose. He raged at the vision without cessation.

The next day his mother called him into the city and he went. She was shocked at the change in his appearance—he looked so utterly miserable. Her tears fell.

"My son," she said, "how changed you are!"

He had a mirror brought forth and looked at himself—he was indeed so gaunt and thin that he was frightened and exclaimed, "How did I come to look so haggard?"

While he spoke, Yu Ji appeared again in the mirror. He struck it and shrieked. Then his half healed wounds reopened and he fainted.

He was carried into his bed. When he recovered consciousness he said, "This is the end—I'm going to die."

He sent for Zhang Zhao and his other chief officials as well as his brother, Sun Quan, who all gathered in his chamber. He exhorted: "With our vast population and the strong defense of the three rivers we have a brilliant future in this chaotic time." Then, turning to Zhang Zhao and the others, he said, "You must all assist my brother."

So saying he handed his seal to Sun Quan and said, "We both have our own merits. In leading the people to fight opposing forces and so contend with the world, you're not so suited as I am. But in encouraging the wise and confiding in the able and getting the best out of every one for the preservation of his district, I can't succeed as you will. Remember with what toil and labor your father and I have won what we possess and take good care of it."

Sun Quan wept as he knelt to receive the seal and the dying chief turned to his mother, "Mother, the days allotted by Heaven have run out and I can no longer wait upon you. I've given over the seal to my brother and trust that you'll advise him day and night, and see that he lives in a way worthy of his predecessors."

"But I fear your brother is too young for such a task," said his mother weeping. "If anything should happen, what then?"

"He's far more capable than me and fully equal to the task of ruling. Should he have doubts upon internal affairs, he can seek advice from Zhang Zhao; for external affairs he can consult Zhou Yu. It's a pity Zhou Yu is absent so that I can't tell him in person."

To his other brothers he said, "When I'm gone you must all help Zhong-mou (Sun Quan). Should anyone in the clan dare to betray, let the others punish the wrong-doer; should a brother dare to rebel, do not let him be buried among his ancestors in the family vaults."

The young men wept as they took these orders. Then he called for his wife, the famous beauty of the Qiao family, and said, "Unhappily we have to part in the middle of our married life. You must care for my mother.

When your sister comes to see you, ask her to tell her husband Zhou Yu to help my brother in all things so as not to fail my friendship and trust in him."

Then he closed his eyes and soon after passed away. He was only twenty-six.

> *Men called him Formidable Little Lord,*
> *The east had felt his might,*
> *He schemed like a tiger in wait,*
> *Struck as a hawk in flight.*
> *There was peace in the land he ruled,*
> *His fame ran with the wind,*
> *But he died and left to his brother,*
> *The great scheme in his mind.*

As he breathed his last his brother, Sun Quan, sank by his bed and wept.

"This is no time for weeping," said Zhang Zhao. "You must see to the funeral and at the same time attend to the military and civil affairs."

So the new ruler dried his tears. The supervision of the funeral was entrusted to Sun Jing and then the young master was escorted to the main hall to receive the felicitations of his subordinates.

Sun Quan was endowed with a square jaw and a large mouth and had blue eyes and a dark brown beard. Formerly, an envoy from the Han court had gone to Wu district to visit the Suns. He said of the family of brothers: "I have looked well at them all and they are all clever and perspicacious but none of them will excel in fortune and longevity. Only the second one is different. His face is remarkable, and his build unusual, and he has the look of one who will come to great honor. But none of the others will attain to the blessing of a great age."

Sun Quan succeeded his brother as ruler of the east and began to attend to daily affairs. Soon it was reported that Zhou Yu had arrived. The young ruler was very pleased and said, "I need have no anxiety now that he has come back."

It must be stated here that Zhou Yu had been sent to hold Baqiu. When he heard that Sun Ce had been wounded by arrows he decided to return to see how he was. At Wujun he was told that Sun Ce had already died so he hurried back for the funeral.

When he went to wail over the coffin of his late chief and close friend, the dead man's mother came out to deliver her son's last demands of him. Zhou Yu bowed to the ground and said, "I will exert the puny powers I have in the service of Wu as long as I live."

Shortly after, Sun Quan came in and, after receiving Zhou Yu's obeisance, said: "I trust you will not forget my brother's deathbed appeal to you."

Zhou Yu said, "I will defy any form of death to show my gratitude for the trust your brother placed in me."

"How best can I maintain this district which I have inherited from my father and brother?"

"He who wins men, prospers; he who loses them, fails. This is a truth we have learned from old days. At present you should seek men of high aims and foresight to support you and you can establish yourself firmly in the east."

"My brother told me to consult Zhang Zhao for internal affairs, and yourself on external matters," said Sun Quan.

"Zhang Zhao is a man of wisdom and understanding, equal to such a task, while I am devoid of talent and I fear I might fail to undertake such a responsibility. I would like to recommend to you a helper."

Sun Quan asked him who that person was. Zhou Yu continued, "He is called Lu Su, or Lu Zi-jing, a man of Dongchuan. This man harbors strategies and tactics in his bosom. He lost his father in early life and has been a perfectly filial son to his mother. His family is very rich and renowned for giving charity to the needy. When I was stationed at Juchao I led some hundreds of men across Linhuai. We were short of grain. Hearing that the Lu family had two granaries there, each holding 3,000 measures, I went to ask for help. Lu Su pointed to one granary and said, 'Take that as a gift.' Such was his generosity!

"He is now living in Qua and has always been fond of fencing, racing, and shooting. His grandmother died recently and he went to bury her in Dongchuan and then a friend of his asked him to go to Chaohu Lake and join Zheng Bao. However, he hesitated and has not gone yet. You should invite him without loss of time."

Sun Quan at once sent Zhou Yu to engage the service of this man and he set out. When the host and the visitor had exchanged polite greetings Zhou Yu mentioned the great respect his master had in him. Lu Su replied that he had been asked by his friend to go to Chaohu Lake and would set out soon.

Zhou Yu said, "Of old, Ma Yuan said to Emperor Guangwu, 'This is an age when not only do princes select their ministers, but ministers choose their princes as well.' Now our General Sun calls to him the wise and treats them well. He engages the help of the wonderful and gets the services of the extraordinary in a way that few others do. You do not have to seek elsewhere, just come with me to Wu. This is the best thing to do."

Lu Su returned with him to see Sun Quan, who treated him with the greatest deference and consulted him on various affairs. The discussions proved so interesting that they went on all day and neither felt tired.

One day at the close of an assembly, Sun Quan asked Lu Su to dine with him. They sat up late and by and by slept on the same couch, like the closest of friends. In the dead of the night Sun Quan said to him: "The Hans are at the end of their rule and upheavals occur on all sides. I have inherited this district from my father and brother and I am thinking of imitating what Duke Huan and Duke Wen* did to recover the dignity of the Emperor. I hope you can enlighten me."

Lu Su replied, "In the old days the founder of Han Dynasty wished to honor and serve Emperor Yi, but could not do so because of Xiang Yu's evil doings. Now Cao Cao can be compared to Xiang Yu; how can you be Huan and Wen? My humble opinion is that the Hans have fallen beyond hope of recovery and Cao Cao cannot be destroyed very quickly, so that the best scheme for you is to secure your present position while keeping a close watch on the conflicts among the others. Now you can take advantage of the turmoil in the north to smite Huang Zu and attack Liu Biao, so that you will command the whole area of the Yangtze. Then you can establish your own kingdom and gradually aspire to rule the whole of the country. This is how you can achieve the great design like that of the founder of Han."

Hearing this, Sun Quan was greatly pleased. He threw on some clothing, got up, and thanked his newfound advisor. The next day Sun Quan gave him handsome rewards and sent gifts to his mother.

Lu Su then brought a friend of his to the young master's notice, a man of wide reading and great ability. He was also a filial son. His double surname was Zhuge and his given name, Jing, and he came from Nanyang. Sun Quan invited him to his service and treated him as a superior guest. This man dissuaded Sun Quan from forming an alliance with Yuan Shao, and advised him not to antagonize Cao Cao for the moment but wait until an opportunity arose. Sun Quan therefore sent back the messenger Chen Zhen with a letter that broke off with Yuan Shao.

Hearing of Sun Ce's death, Cao Cao wanted to start an expedition to the east but Zhang Hong dissuaded him, saying that it would be mean to take advantage of the period of mourning.

"And if you should not overcome him you will make him an enemy instead of being a friend. It would be preferable to treat him generously."

---

*   Two feudal lords in the period of Spring and Autumn, who tried to establish their own power by supporting the emperor of the Zhou Dynasty.

Cao Cao accepted the advice and obtained from the Emperor the title of general and the post of Prefect of Guiji for Sun Quan. A seal of office was brought to him by Zhang Hong, who was also given a post to serve under Sun Quan. The new appointment pleased Sun Quan and he was also glad to get Zhang Hong back again. He was asked to run the administration with Zhang Zhao.

Zhang Hong helped get another into Sun Quan's service. His friend was Gu Yong, a disciple of the historian Cai Yong. A man of few words and an abstainer from wine, he was upright and strict in all his doings. Sun Quan employed him in his administration.

Henceforward Sun Quan's rule in the east became very secure and he soon won the love of all the people.

Meanwhile, Chen Zhen returned and told Yuan Shao the events in Wu, and also of the honors that Cao Cao had obtained for Sun Quan in return for his support. Yuan Shao was very angry and he set about preparing for an attack on the capital with a force of 700,000 northern men.

> *Although in the east they rest a while from war,*
> *Battle drums sound again 'neath the northern star.*

Whether Yuan Shao would be able to overcome Cao Cao will be told in the next chapter.

CHAPTER THIRTY

Yuan Shao Is Defeated at Guandu
Cao Cao Burns the Wuchao Granary

earing that Yuan Shao was advancing to attack at Guandu, Xiahou Dun wrote to the capital urgently asking for reinforcements, and Cao Cao led 70,000 soldiers to oppose his enemy. Xun Yu was left to guard the capital.

Just as Yuan Shao's army was starting out, Tian Feng sent up an objection from his prison cell denouncing the attack and advising him to wait upon favorable opportunities as Heaven should bestow.

His rival Feng Ji said to Yuan Shao, "You, sir, are sending forth an army for the cause of humanity and justice yet this Tian Feng utters such ill-omened words."

Easily moved to anger Yuan Shao was going to execute Tian Feng, but he relented at the earnest entreaties of many of his officials. However, he was not appeased, for he said, "I will punish him when I return from conquering Cao Cao."

Meanwhile the army hastened to start. Their banners filled the horizon and their swords were like trees in the forest. They marched to Yangwu and there made a strong camp.

Here the advisor Ju Shou once more warned his master of making any hasty movement. He said, "Though our soldiers are many they are not so bold as the enemy—however, old campaigners like them do not have ample supplies as we do. Therefore they will wish to bring on a speedy battle, while our policy should be to hold them off and delay. If we can keep from a decisive battle long enough the victory will be ours without fighting."

This advice, nevertheless, did not appeal to Yuan Shao, who said furiously, "Tian Feng spoke discouraging words to dishearten my army and I will assuredly put him to death on my return. How dare you follow suit?"

He summoned the guards and sent away the advisor in chains. "When I have overcome Cao Cao I will deal with you and Tian Feng together," he said.

The huge army was camped in four divisions, one facing in each direction. Camps were linked to other camps, stretching for about a hundred *li* around. The formidable build-up of Yuan Shao's army was quickly reported by scouts to Cao Cao's headquarters at Guandu. Cao Cao's army arrived and were smitten with fear when they heard of the strength of their enemy. Cao Cao called a general council. The advisor Xun You said, "The enemy are many but not terrible. Ours is an army of veterans, each man worth ten, but our advantage lies in a speedy battle, for our stores are insufficient for a protracted war."

"That is exactly what I think," said Cao Cao.

Therefore he issued orders to press forward and force a battle. Yuan Shao's men took up the challenge and then each army formed its own battle array. On Yuan Shao's side, based on a recommendation from the advisor Shen Pei, 10,000 crossbowmen were placed in ambush on the two wings, while 5,000 archers hid themselves in the center. A bomb exploding would be the signal for attack.

After three rolls of the drum Yuan Shao rode out to the front. He wore a gold helmet and breastplate and an embroidered robe held together by a jeweled belt. He took up his position in the center with his numerous warriors ranged right and left. His banners and ensigns made a magnificent show.

When the center of his army opened and the banners moved aside, Cao Cao appeared on horseback with his retinue of doughty officers, all fully armed. Pointing with his whip at Yuan Shao he cried, "I obtained for you the title of commanding general from the Emperor. Why do you now instigate a rebellion?"

Yuan Shao replied, "You take the title of a minister of Han, but you are really a rebel against the state. Your crimes and evil deeds reach to the heavens, and you are worse than the usurper Wang Mang and the rebel Dong Zhuo. And you dare to address me with such slanderous language?"

"I have the Emperor's command to capture you."

"I am commanded by His Majesty's girdle decree to arrest you," retorted Yuan Shao.

Then Cao Cao became infuriated and ordered Zhang Liao out. From the other side rode Zhang He on a bounding steed. The two fought forty to fifty bouts with no advantage to either. In his heart Cao Cao was quite impressed by Zhang He's valor. Then Xu Chu whirled up his sword and went to help. To match him rode out Gao Lan with his spear, and the contestants were now four, battling two and two. Then Cao Cao ordered two other officers, each with 3,000 men, to destroy the opponents' battle line. With this, on Yuan Shao's side the signal for the ambushers to attack was given and the crossbowmen and the archers moved to the front and let fly their arrows. Hundreds of thousands of arrows flew all over the field and Cao Cao's men could not advance. They hastened away toward the south. Yuan Shao threw his soldiers at the retreating enemy, defeating them completely. They ran away toward Guandu and Yuan Shao advanced another stage. He camped near them.

Shen Pei offered further advice to Yuan Shao. "Now send a force to guard Guandu and then throw up observation mounds in front of Cao Cao's camp to shoot arrows into its midst. If we can force him to evacuate this place we will have gained a strategic advantage. It will not be long before the capital itself can be captured."

Yuan Shao adopted this advice. From each of the camps they picked out the strongest veterans to dig with iron spades and carry earth to raise mounds opposite Cao Cao's camp.

Cao Cao's men saw what their enemies were doing and were anxious to make a sortie to drive them off. But the archers and crossbowmen guarded the narrow passage and blocked their escape. At the end of ten days they had thrown up more than fifty mounds and on top of each was built a high tower, from where the archers shot their arrows at their opponents' camp. Cao Cao's men were greatly frightened and held up their small shields to keep off the numerous arrows. At the sound of the clapper, bang! bang! arrows flew down from the mounds like a fierce rain. The men of Yuan Shao's army laughed and jeered when they saw their enemies crouching under their shields and crawling on the ground to avoid being hit.

Cao Cao saw that his soldiers were losing discipline under this attack so he called a council. Liu Ye said, "Let us make machines to hurl stones to destroy them."

Cao Cao at once had him bring forth a model and workmen were ordered to make these machines that very night. They soon constructed some hundreds and placed them along the walls of the camp inside, just opposite the high ladders on the enemy's mounds.

Then they waited for the archers to ascend the towers. As soon as they began to shoot all the machines heaved their stone balls into the sky, creating great havoc. There was no shelter from them and enormous numbers of the archers were killed. Yuan Shao's men called these machines "rumblers" and after their appearance the archers dared not ascend the mounds to shoot.

Then Shen Pei, the strategist, thought out another plan. He set men to dig a tunnel to get into the midst of the enemy's camp and called this corps "the Sappers." Cao Cao's men saw the enemy digging out pits be-

hind the mounds and reported it to him. He immediately consulted Liu
Ye for a counter plan.

"As Yuan Shao can no longer attack openly he intends to attack secretly and is digging an underground tunnel to penetrate into the midst
of our camp," he said.

"But how to meet it?"

"We can surround the camp with a deep moat that will render their
tunnel useless."

So a deep moat was dug as quickly as possible and when the enemy
arrived through the secret passage, they found to their dismay that their
labor had been in vain and the trench was useless.

The confrontation between the two armies continued all through the
eighth and ninth months. In Cao Cao's camp, as men were worn out and
provisions running short, he began to think of giving up and returning to
the capital. As he could not make up his mind he referred his difficulties
by dispatch to Xun Yu, whom he had left to guard the capital.

The reply he got was as follows: "I have received your command to
decide whether to continue the campaign or retreat. It appears to me
that by assembling such a large force at Guandu, Yuan Shao expects to
fight a decisive battle with you. Compared to his your army is very small,
and if you cannot get the better of him he will be able to dominate you.
The victor of this battle will determine who is to rule the land. Your opponents are indeed numerous, but their leader does not know how to use
them. With your excellent military acumen you are sure to succeed everywhere. Although the number of men you have is small, it is not so small
as when the founder of Han was facing his antagonist at Xingyang and
Chenggao. You are now securely positioned at a key strategic point, the
very throat of his advance. That state of things cannot endure forever but
must change. This is the time to make some surprise move and you must
not miss it. Pray consider this."

This letter greatly pleased Cao Cao and he urged his men to use every
effort to maintain the position.

With Yuan Shao having retreated some thirty *li*, Cao Cao sent out
scouts to ascertain his real strength. One of Xu Huang's officers captured
an enemy spy and sent him to his chief, who interrogated him and found
out that a convoy of supplies was expected and that this spy and others
had been sent to explore the risks of the route. Xu Huang went at once to
tell Cao Cao. When the advisor Xun You heard that the commander of
the convoy was Han Meng he said, "That fellow is valiant but foolish. An
officer with several thousand light horsemen sent to intercept him can
destroy his supplies and cause much trouble in the enemy's camp."

"Who should I send?" asked Cao Cao.

"You can send Xu Huang—he is capable of such a task."

So Xu Huang set out with Shi Huan and his soldiers, who had captured the spy. He was further supported by Zhang Liao and Xu Chu.

It was night when Han Meng escorted thousands of carts of food supplies toward Yuan Shao's camp. As they were going through a narrow pass, Xu Huang's men came out to bar their way. Han Meng galloped up to engage with Xu Huang but while they were fighting, Shi Huan went to scatter his men and burn the supplies of food. Han Meng was overcome and had to get away.

The glow of the flames seen from Yuan Shao's camp caused great anxiety, which turned to fear when the fleeing soldiers rode in and told their tale.

Yuan Shao sent out Zhang He and Gao Lan to try to intercept the raiders and they came upon Xu Huang and his men, returning after burning the supply carts. Just as they were about to fight Cao Cao's reinforcement army came up and Yuan Shao's men were trapped between two forces. They were soon driven off and Cao Cao's men rode back successfully to Guandu, where they were richly rewarded. As an additional safeguard Cao Cao established supporting outposts in front of the main camp to set up a triangle of defense.

When Han Meng returned with his woeful tidings, Yuan Shao was angry and threatened to put him to death. His colleagues begged him not to.

Shen Pei said, "Food is very important for an army in the battlefield and must be defended with the greatest diligence. Wuchao is our main depot and must be carefully guarded."

"I have made my plans," said Yuan Shao. "You may return to the capital to undertake the control of the supplies. Let there be no shortage." So Shen Pei took the order and left the army.

Then a force of 20,000 men under six officers was given orders to defend the depot. The commander, Chunyu Qiong, was a harsh fellow and a heavy drinker, who was a terror to the men. Amidst the idle life of guarding the supply depot he gave himself up to indulgence and drank heavily with his colleagues every day.

In Cao Cao's army food was also getting scarce and a message was sent to the capital to send grain quickly. The messenger, however, had not gone far when he fell into the hands of Yuan Shao's men, who took him to be questioned by the advisor Xu You. This man had been a friend of Cao Cao's in his youth but was now in Yuan Shao's service. Seeing from the letter that Cao Cao was short of supplies, he went to his master and said, "Cao Cao has been grappling with us here for a long time and the capital must be undefended. An army sent quickly there can capture it and an attack here will deliver him into our hands. Now is the moment to strike, for his supplies are short."

Yuan Shao replied, "Cao Cao is full of tricks and this letter is artfully designed to bring about a battle to suit himself."

"If you do not take this chance he will harm you by and by."

Just at this juncture in came a dispatch from the advisor Shen Pei. After giving some details regarding the forwarding of grain, he wrote that Xu You had been in the habit of receiving bribes while in Jizhou and had allowed his son and nephew to collect excess taxes to make more money for himself, so he had put them in prison.

At this Yuan Shao turned on Xu You angrily and said, "How can you have the face to stand before me and propose plans, you degenerate fellow? You and Cao Cao have been friends and he must have bribed you to do his dirty work for him. So now you want to betray my army. I ought to have you beheaded, but temporarily I will let it remain on your neck. Get out and never let me see you again."

The discredited advisor went out and looking up toward the sky, sighed: "Faithful words offend his ear. He is too mean to be worthy of advice from me. And now that Shen Pei has injured my son and nephew, how can I look my fellow men in the face again?"

So saying he drew his sword to end his life. But his followers prevented him. They said, "If Yuan Shao rejects your honest words then assuredly he will be taken by Cao Cao. You are an old friend of his—why not abandon the shade for the sunlight?"

These few words awakened him to the reality of his position and he decided to leave Yuan Shao and go over to Cao Cao.

> *Vainly now for chances lost*
> *Yuan sighs; once he was great.*
> *Had he taken Xu's advice,*
> *Cao would not set up a state.*

Xu You stealthily left and set out for Cao Cao's camp. He was captured on the way. He told his captors that he was an old friend of the prime minister's and asked them to tell him that Xu You of Nanyang wished to see him.

They did so. Cao Cao was just about to go to bed when he heard of his arrival in secret. He was so glad that he hastily went forth to greet him, without even waiting to put on his shoes. Seeing him in the distance, Cao Cao clapped his hands in joy and bowed to the ground when his visitor was invited into his tent. Xu You hastened to help him rise and said, "Sir, you are a great minister and should not thus salute a commoner like me."

"But you are my old friend and no fame or office makes any difference to us," replied Cao Cao.

"Having been unable to choose the right lord to serve I had to bow my head before Yuan Shao. But he was deaf to my words and disregarded my advice. Therefore I have left him and come now to see my old friend. I hope you will give me shelter."

"Since you are willing to come I have indeed a great helper," said Cao Cao. "Please teach me a scheme for the destruction of Yuan Shao."

"I advised Yuan Shao to send a light force to take the capital so that your head and tail will be attacked simultaneously."

Cao Cao was alarmed. "If he does so, I'm lost."

"How much grain have you in store?" inquired the new advisor.

"Enough for a year."

"Not that much, I'm afraid," said Xu You smiling.

"Well, half a year."

The visitor rose angrily to leave the tent. "I offer you good counsel and you repay me with deceit. Is this what I can expect?"

Cao Cao held him back. "Don't be angry," he said. "I will tell you the truth. Really I have only grain for three months."

"Everybody says you are a marvel of trickery and indeed it is true," said Xu You.

"But who fails to understand that in war no one objects to deceits?" replied Cao Cao. Then whispering in the other's ear he said, "Actually I have only supplies for this month's use."

"Oh, do not throw dust in my eyes any more. Your grain is exhausted and I know it."

Cao Cao was startled, for he thought no one knew of the straits he was in.

"How did you find that out?" he asked.

Xu You produced the letter and said, "Who wrote that?"

"Where did you get it?"

Then he told Cao Cao the story of the captured messenger. Cao Cao seized him by the hand and said, "Since our old friendship has brought you here I hope you have some plan to suggest to me."

Xu You said, "To oppose a great army with a small one is to walk to destruction unless you resort to a quick victory. I can propose a plan which will defeat the immense army of Yuan Shao in three days without fighting a battle. But will you follow my advice?"

"I'd like to know your good plan," answered Cao Cao with great joy.

"Your enemy's stores of all kinds are at Wuchao, where the commander is Chunyu Qiong, a very heavy drinker. You can send some of your trusted veterans there, pretending to be his men sent to help guard the depot. Once inside these men can find an opportunity to burn the supplies. In three days Yuan Shao's army will be thrown into chaos."

Cao Cao approved. He treated Xu You very liberally and kept him in his camp. Consequently he chose 5,000 horse and foot soldiers ready for the raid.

Zhang Liao was opposed to this scheme and said, "Yuan Shao's grain depot is certainly well guarded. You should not act in such haste. What if Xu You is treacherous?"

"Xu You is no traitor," said Cao Cao. "He has been sent by Heaven to defeat Yuan Shao. If we do not get grain it will be hard to hold out and I have either to follow his advice or sit still and be hemmed in. If he was a traitor he would hardly remain in my camp. Moreover, this raid has been my desire for a long time. Have no doubts, the raid will certainly succeed."

"Well then, you must look out for an attack here while the camp is undefended."

"That is already taken care of," said Cao Cao smiling.

The defenders of the camp were then deployed. The main camp was to be guarded by Cao Hong and several others, including the new advisor, while two forces under the command of four officers were placed in ambush on both sides.

The plans for the raid on the grain depot were made with extreme care to ensure success. When all was ready they set out, Cao Cao himself in the center. The army showed the ensigns of their opponents. The men carried bundles of grass and twigs to make a blaze. The men were gagged and the horses tied round the muzzles so as to prevent any noise.

They set out at dusk. The night was fine and the stars shone brightly. Ju Shou, still a prisoner in Yuan Shao's camp, saw that the stars were brilliant and told his jailers to escort him out to the courtyard where he could study them. While watching he saw the planet Venus invade the quarters of the Bear and Lyra, which startled him greatly.

"Some misfortune is near," he said.

So although it was already night he went to see his master. But Yuan Shao was sleeping after indulging in too much wine and was in a bad humor. However, when they had roused him saying that the prisoner had a secret message to deliver, he ordered him to be brought in.

"While I happened to be studying the aspect of the heavens," said the night visitor, "I saw Venus suddenly deviated from its usual course and its reflections shoot into the neighborhood of Bear and Lyra. I fear there is danger of a night raid and special precautions must be taken at the grain depot. Lose no time in sending good soldiers and vigorous officers there and keep a lookout on the byways among the hills so that you may escape the wiles of Cao Cao."

"You are a criminal," said Yuan Shao. "How dare you come with such wild nonsense to upset my army."

Then he issued orders to put the jailers to death and appointed others to keep the prisoner in close custody.

Ju Shou left, wiping his falling tears and sighing deeply. "Our army's destruction is imminent and I don't know where my poor corpse may find a resting place."

> *Blunt truth offended Yuan Shao,*
> *Too stupid any plan to make,*
> *His stores destroyed 'tis evident*
> *That Jizhou also is at stake.*

Cao Cao's raiding party carried on through the night. Passing one of Yuan Shao's outposts, they were challenged. Cao Cao sent forward a man to say, "Jiang Qi has orders to go to Wuchao to guard the grain stores."

Seeing that the raiders marched under the ensigns of Yuan Shao the guards had no suspicions and let them pass. At every post this trick was effective and they got safely through.

They reached their objective at the end of the fourth watch. The straw and wood were placed in position without loss of time and the blaze started. Then the officers attacked amid the beating of the drum and loud shouting.

At the time of the attack the commander of the grain depot was asleep after a heavy drinking bout with his fellow officers. The hubbub, however, awoke him and he sprang up and asked what the matter was. Before he could finish speaking he was caught by hooks and hauled out of his tent.

Two other officers were just returning from transporting grain to the camp and seeing the flames arise, they hastened to the rescue. Some of his soldiers ran to tell Cao Cao that some enemy forces were coming up in the rear and asked him to send reinforcements, but he only replied by ordering his men to press forward and ignore the forces behind unless they were actually close at hand. So the attackers all hastened forward.

Very soon the fire gained strength and thick smoke hung all around, filling the sky. When the two officers drew near, Cao Cao turned around and faced them. They could not stand the onslaught and after a while both were killed. Finally the stores of grain and forage were utterly destroyed.

The commander, Chunyu Qiong, was made prisoner and taken to Cao Cao, who ordered that he be deprived of ears, nose, and hands. Thus horribly mutilated, he was bound on a horse and sent to his master to humiliate him.

From Yuan Shao's camp the flames of the burning depot were seen away in the north and he knew what they meant. Hastily he summoned his officers to a council about sending a rescue party. Zhang He offered to go with Gao Lan but the advisor Guo Tu said, "They should not go. It is certain that Cao Cao is there in person, therefore his camp is undefended. Attack the camp and Cao Cao will speedily come back. This is what the ancient military strategist Sun Bin meant by 'Besieging Wei to Rescue Zhao.'"

But Zhang He said, "Not so—Cao Cao is too crafty not to have fully prepared against such an attack. If we raid his camp and fail, and Chunyu Qiong should be caught, then all of us would be caught, too."

Guo Tu said, "Cao Cao is too intent on the destruction of the grain to think of leaving a guarding force. I entreat you to attack his camp."

So Yuan Shao sent 5,000 men under Zhang He and Gao Lan to attack Cao Cao's camp and Jiang Qi was sent to try to recover the grain store.

Now after overcoming the remaining forces in the grain depot, Cao Cao's men dressed themselves in the armor and clothing of the defeated soldiers and put out their emblems, thus posing as defeated men running back to their own headquarters. On the way they came upon Jiang Qi's rescue force, who they told that they had been beaten at Wuchao and were retreating. So they passed on without raising any suspicions, while Jiang Qi hastened on. But soon he encountered Zhang Liao and Xu Chu, who cried out to him to stop. And before he could make any opposition Zhang Liao had cut him down. Soon his men were killed or dispersed and the victors sent false messengers to Yuan Shao's camp to say that Jiang Qi had succeeded in driving away the invaders of the granary. So no more reinforcement forces were sent that way, but only to Guandu.

In due course the two officers sent to raid Cao Cao's camp were attacked from three sides by the ambushers at Guandu, so that they were worsted. By the time reinforcements arrived Cao Cao's army, returning from the granary, had also come and Yuan Shao's men were further pressed in the rear. So they were quite surrounded. However, Zhang He and Gao Lan managed to force their way out and escape.

When Yuan Shao finally collected together the defeated men of the grain depot he saw the mutilated state of their leader. Yuan Shao asked how he had come to betray his trust and to suffer thus and the soldiers told their lord that their commander had been intoxicated at the time of the attack. Yuan Shao was enraged and ordered him to be executed at once.

Guo Tu, fearing lest Zhang He and Gao Lan would return and testify how wrong he had been, began to intrigue against them. First he went to his lord and said, "These two, Zhang He and Gao Lan, were certainly very glad when your armies were defeated."

"Why do you say this?" asked Yuan Shao.

"They have long cherished a desire to go over to Cao Cao, so when you sent them to destroy his camp they did not do their best and so brought about this disaster."

Yuan Shao was again furious and accordingly sent someone to recall them to be interrogated. But Guo Tu, the cunning intriguer, was quicker. He sent a messenger in advance to warn them of the adverse fate that awaited them. So when Yuan Shao's messenger reached them and asked them to return, Gao Lan asked him why they were recalled. The messenger disclaimed all knowledge of the reasons, so Gao Lan drew his sword and killed him.

Zhang He was dumbfounded at this act but his friend said, "Yuan Shao listens to slanderous tongues around him. I think he's doomed to be captured by Cao Cao. What's the sense in our sitting still and awaiting destruction? Rather let's surrender to Cao Cao."

"I've been wanting to do this for some time," replied Zhang He.

Therefore both of them, with their men, made their way to Cao Cao's camp to surrender.

When they arrived, Xiahou Dun said to his master, "These two have come to surrender but I have doubts about them."

Cao Cao replied, "I will treat them generously and win them over, even if they have treachery in their hearts."

The camp gates were opened to the two officers and they were invited to enter. They laid down their weapons, removed their armor and bowed to the ground before Cao Cao. The prime minister said, "If Yuan Shao had listened to you he would not have suffered defeat. Now your coming to me is like Wei Zi leaving the tyrant king of Shang Dynasty and Han Xin going over to the House of Han."

He gave both men the rank of general and the title of a nobleman, which pleased them very much.

And so Yuan Shao had driven away his wise advisor, Xu You, lost two of his most able officers and was deprived of his food supply at Wuchao. The army was depressed and downhearted.

At Cao Cao's camp the new advisor Xu You persuaded him to attack as promptly as he could and the two newly surrendered men volunteered to lead the way. So these two were sent to make a first attack on Yuan Shao's camp, and they left in the night in three divisions. The fighting went on confusedly all night but ceased at dawn. Yuan Shao again lost heavily.

Then the advisor Xun You also came up with a plan. "We can spread a false report of our new deployments. Say that an army will go to take Suanzao and attack Yejun, and another will take Liyang and intercept his route of retreat. Yuan Shao, when he hears of this, will be alarmed and set out his men to meet this new turn of affairs, and while he is making these new moves we can have him at great disadvantage."

The suggestion was adopted and care was taken that the report was spread far around. It came to the ears of Yuan Shao's soldiers and they repeated it in camp. Yuan Shao believed it and ordered his eldest son with a big force to rescue Yejun, and another force to seize Liyang. They marched away at once. Hearing that these armies had set forth, Cao Cao dispatched eight divisions to make a simultaneous attack on his enemy's main camp. Yuan Shao's men were too dispirited to fight and gave way on all sides.

Yuan Shao, without even the time to don his armor, mounted and escaped with only a thin coat and an ordinary cap upon his head. His younger son Yuan Shang followed him. Four of Cao Cao's officers with their men pressed in their rear and Yuan Shao hastened across the river, abandoning all his documents and papers, his carriages and his store of gold and silk. Only eight hundred men followed him over the stream. Cao Cao's men pursued hard but could not catch up with him; however, they captured all his baggage and equipment. Many thousands of innocent soldiers were killed and their blood filled up gutters and ditches. Many more were drowned, their number too numerous to count. It was a complete victory for Cao Cao and he rewarded his army with the money and silk he had got from his enemy.

Among the papers of Yuan Shao was found a bundle of letters showing secret correspondence between him and many of Cao Cao's men in the capital and in his army. Cao Cao's personal staff suggested that the names of those concerned should be traced and the persons executed, but he said, "Yuan Shao was so strong at that time that even I could not be sure of safety—how much less would the others feel?"

So he ordered the papers to be burned and nothing more was said.

Now when Yuan Shao's men ran away Ju Shou, being a prisoner, could not get away and was captured. Taken before Cao Cao, who knew him, he cried aloud, "I will not surrender."

Cao Cao said, "Yuan Shao was foolish and neglected your advice—why still cling to this delusion? If I'd had you to help me I would have been sure to win the empire."

The prisoner was well treated in the camp but he stole a horse and tried to get away to Yuan Shao. This angered Cao Cao, who put him to death, which he met with brave composure.

"I have slain a faithful and righteous man," said Cao Cao sadly. And the victim was honorably buried at Guandu. His tomb bore the inscription: THIS IS THE TOMB OF JU THE LOYAL AND VIRTUOUS.

> *Honest and virtuous Ju was,*
> *The best in Yuan's train,*
> *From him the stars no secrets held,*
> *In tactics all was plain.*
> *For him no terrors had grim death,*
> *Too lofty was his spirit,*
> *His captor slew him, but his tomb*
> *Bears witness to his merit.*

Cao Cao then gave orders to attack Jizhou.

> *A strong army lost a war for lack of good schemes;*
> *A weak force won the day by better strategies.*

Which side would win the next campaign will be told in the next chapter.

CHAPTER THIRTY-ONE

Cao Cao Overcomes Yuan Shao at Changting
Liu Bei Seeks Shelter with Liu Biao

Cao Cao lost no time in taking advantage of Yuan Shao's flight and pressed hard on the retreating men. Yuan Shao, without helmet or proper dress and with only eight hundred followers, hastily crossed the Yellow River to the north bank at Liyang. He was met by one of his generals, who welcomed him into his camp and listened to his tale of misfortunes. The general then called in the scattered remnants of the army. When the soldiers heard that their old lord was alive they swarmed back to him like ants, so that he quickly became strong enough to consider the march back to Jizhou. Soon the army set out. That night they camped among some barren hills.

That evening, sitting in his tent, Yuan Shao heard lamentations in the distance. He crept out quietly to listen and found it was his own defeated soldiers telling each other tales of woe. This one lamented over an elder brother lost; that one grieved for his younger brother slain; a third mourned a companion missing; a fourth, a relative killed. Each beat his breast and wept. And all said, "Had he but listened to Tian Feng, we would not have met this disaster."

And Yuan Shao, very remorseful, said to himself, "I did not listen to Tian Feng and now my men are lost and I am defeated. How can I return and look him in the face?"

The next day the march was resumed and on the way Feng Ji came to meet him. Yuan Shao said to him, "I disregarded Tian Feng's advice and have brought defeat to myself. Now I will be ashamed to look him in the face."

Feng Ji, being an enemy of Tian Feng, took this opportunity to slander him. "When he heard the news of your defeat in prison," said Feng Ji falsely, "he clapped his hands for joy and said, 'Indeed, just as I have predicted!'"

"How dare he laugh at me, the blockhead? I will surely kill him," said Yuan Shao angrily.

Then he sent a messenger with a sword to slay the prisoner in advance.

Meanwhile, Tian Feng's jailer had come to him one day and said: "Congratulations, sir."

"What is the joyful occasion?" asked Tian Feng.

The jailer replied, "General Yuan has been defeated and is on his way back—he will treat you with redoubled respect."

"Now my end has come," said Tian Feng with a smile.

"Why do you say that, sir, when all men feel glad for you?"

"General Yuan appears to be liberal but he is jealous and forgetful of honest advice. Had he been victorious he might have pardoned me; now that he has been defeated and put to shame I have no hope of living."

But the jailer did not believe him. Before long, the messenger came with the sword and the fatal order. The jailer was dismayed, but the victim said, "I knew all too well that I should have to die."

The jailers all wept. Tian Feng said, "He is ignorant who was born into this world but does not recognize a true lord to serve. Today I die, but I do not deserve pity."

> *Ju Shou but yesterday was killed,*
> *Tian ends his life, his fate fulfilled;*
> *Hebei's main beams break one by one,*
> *Mourn ye that house! its day is done.*

Thus Tian Feng died and all who heard of his fate sighed with grief.

When Yuan Shao came home he was troubled in mind and could not attend to the business of administration. His wife, Lady Liu, beseeched him to nominate an heir.

Now three sons had been born to him: Tan, the eldest, was commander at Qingzhou; Xian, the second son, ruled over Yuzhou; and Shang, borne to him by his second wife, Lady Liu, still lived at his father's side. This youngest son, a very handsome and noble-looking young man, was his father's favorite, so he was kept at home. After the defeat at Guandu the lad's mother was constantly urging that her son should be named as successor and Yuan Shao called together four of his counselors to consider this matter. These four happened to be divided in their sympathies, Shen Pei and Feng Ji being in favor of the youngest son, while Xin Ping and Guo Tu supporters of the eldest.

When they came Yuan Shao said, "As there is nothing but war and trouble outside our border it is necessary to settle internal affairs as soon as possible. So I wish to appoint my successor. My eldest son is stubborn and cruel while my second, mild and unfit. The youngest has the outward form of a hero, appreciates the wise, and is courteous to his subordinates.

I want him to be my heir but I would like to hear your opinions."

Guo Tu said, "Tan is your first born and he is posted away from Jizhou, beyond your control. If you disregard the eldest in favor of the youngest you sow the seeds of turbulence. The prestige of the army has been somewhat lowered recently and enemies are on our border. Should you add to our weakness by stirring up strife between father and son, elder and younger brothers? It is better to consider how the enemy can be repulsed first and turn to the question of the heir later."

Then the natural hesitation of Yuan Shao asserted itself and he could not make up his mind. Soon came news that his sons, Tan and Xi, and his nephew, Gao Gan, were coming with large armies to help him and he turned his attention to preparations for fighting with Cao Cao.

When Cao Cao drew up his victorious army on the banks of the Yellow River, some aged locals brought offerings of food and wine to bid him welcome. Their venerable and hoary appearances inspired respect from Cao Cao, who invited them to be seated in his tent.

"Venerable sirs, may I know your age?" he asked them.

"We are all nearly a hundred," replied one of the ancients.

"I'm very sorry that my men have disturbed your village," said Cao Cao.

"In the days of Emperor Huan a yellow star was seen in the southwest. A certain astrologer from the north, named Yin Kui, happened to be spending the night here and he told us that the star, shining directly over this area, foretold the arrival of the true Lord in these parts fifty years hence. That was exactly fifty years ago. Now Yuan Shao is very hard on the people and we hate him. You, sir, have raised this army in the cause of humanity and righteousness to save the people and punish the criminal lords. Your victory at Guandu that destroyed the hordes of Yuan Shao fulfills the prophecy of Yin Kui, and millions may look now for tranquillity."

"How dare I presume that I am he?" said Cao Cao with a smile.

Wine and refreshments were brought in and the old gentlemen were sent away with presents of these as well as silk and cloth. An order was issued to the army that if anyone killed so much as a fowl or a dog belonging to the villagers, he would be punished as if for murder. The soldiers obeyed it out of fear but the people admired him for his kindness. In his heart Cao Cao secretly rejoiced for the fine image he had cut among the people.

Soon, scouts came with the report that the total army from the four prefectures under the Yuan family amounted to 200–300,000 soldiers and they were camped at Changting. Cao Cao then advanced and made a strong camp near them.

The two armies set up their own battle orders against each other. On one side Cao Cao rode to the front surrounded by his officers, and on the other appeared Yuan Shao supported by his three sons, his nephew, and his officers.

Cao Cao spoke first: "Yuan Shao, you are at the end of your schemes and strength, why still refuse to consider surrender? Are you waiting till the sword is upon your neck? Then it will be too late."

Yuan Shao was beside himself with rage. He turned to those about him and said, "Who dares go out?"

His son, Yuan Shang, was anxious to exhibit his prowess in the presence of his father, so he flourished a pair of swords and rode to and fro in front of the two armies. Cao Cao pointed at him and asked who he was and they told him. Before they had finished speaking, from their own side rode out Shi Huan, armed with a spear. The two fought a few bouts and suddenly Yuan Shang turned to flee. His opponent followed. Yuan Shang took his bow, fitted an arrow, turned round and shot at Shi Huan, wounding him in the left eye. He fell from the saddle and died on the spot.

Yuan Shao, taking advantage of his son's victory, gave the signal for attack and the whole army thundered forward. A tremendous battle ensued and it was only after much slaughter that the gongs on both sides sounded the retreat and the fight ceased.

When he returned to camp Cao Cao sought counsel from his men for a plan to overcome Yuan Shao. Cheng Yu proposed the tactic of "Ten Ambushes." He advised Cao Cao to let the army retreat to the riverside and set up ten ambushes on the way to induce Yuan Shao to pursue as far as the river. "Our men will be placed in a desperate situation as they must either fight for their lives or be driven into the river. They will surely exert themselves and Yuan Shao can be defeated," he concluded.

Cao Cao accepted this scheme and he dispatched five troops to lie in ambush on one side of the road of retreat and another five on the other, while Xu Chu commanded the vanguard of the central force.

The next day the ten companies started first and hid themselves right and left, as ordered. Deep in the night Cao Cao ordered Xu Chu to lead his force forward and feign an attack on Yuan Shao's camps, which aroused all the men in his five camps. This done, Xu Chu retreated and the enemy army pursued. The roar of battle went on without cessation and at dawn Cao Cao's army was chased to the riverside and could retreat no further. Then Cao Cao shouted, "There is no road in front, so all must fight to the death."

The retreating army turned about and advanced vigorously. Xu Chu flew to the very front and killed more than ten enemy officers, throwing Yuan Shao's army into great confusion. They hastened to turn back, but

Cao Cao was close behind. As they marched quickly, suddenly drums of the enemy were heard and from right and left there appeared the first pair of the ambushing forces. Yuan Shao collected about him his three sons and his nephew and they struggled desperately to cut their way out and flee. Ten *li* further on, they fell into another ambush and here many more men were lost so that their corpses lay over the open fields and their blood filled the water courses.

A further ten *li* and they met the third pair of companies barring their road of retreat. Here they lost heart and bolted for an old camp that was near, and bade their men prepare a meal. But just as the food was ready to eat, down came Zhang Liao and Zhang He to attack the camp.

Yuan Shao mounted and fled as far as Changting, where he was exhausted and his steed spent. But there was still no rest, for Cao Cao's men came in close pursuit. Yuan Shao now raced for life. But presently he found his onward course again blocked and he groaned aloud.

"If we don't make most desperate efforts we are all captives," he shouted, and they plunged forward and finally managed to get through. His second son and his nephew were wounded by arrows and almost all of his men were dead or had disappeared. He gathered his sons into his arms and wept bitterly. Then he fell unconscious. The others hurried to help him up.

When he came to, blood gushed out of his mouth. He sighed, "Many battles have I fought and little did I think to be driven to this embarrassing state. Heaven is afflicting me. Each of you had better return to your own place. I swear to fight Cao Cao to the end."

Then he told the two advisors, Xin Ping and Guo Tu, to follow his eldest son to his district at once and get prepared for any possible attack from the enemy. His second son and his nephew were to go back to their own prefectures to muster men and horses for repulsing Cao Cao. Yuan Shao returned to Jizhou to nurse his health, together with his youngest son and the remnant of his officers. All military affairs were entrusted to his youngest son and the two advisors Shen Pei and Feng Ji.

Meanwhile, Cao Cao was distributing liberal rewards to his army for the victory and at the same time sending out scouts to find out the situation in Jizhou. He soon learned that Yuan Shao was ill and that his youngest son and Shen Pei were maintaining strong defenses in the city, while his two other sons and nephew had each returned to their own districts. Cao Cao's advisors were all in favor of a speedy attack, but he objected.

"Jizhou is large and well supplied. Shen Pei is an able strategist and it is necessary to be careful. I would rather wait till autumn, when the crops have been gathered in, so that the people will not suffer."

While the attack was being discussed there came a letter from Xun Yu in which he said that Liu Bei had strengthened himself in Runan and was taking advantage of the prime minister's expedition to invade the capital. He advised Cao Cao to hasten homeward to defend it. This news disturbed Cao Cao greatly and, with orders for Cao Hong to maintain an appearance of strength on the river, he led the main part of his army back to meet the threatened attack from Runan.

Now Liu Bei, together with his brothers and supporters, had led his army out on a march with the intention of attacking the capital. As they approached the Rang Hills Cao Cao's men came upon them. So Liu Bei camped by the hills and divided his army into three forces, sending his two brothers with one section each to entrench themselves at the southeast and southwest angles respectively, while he himself and Zhao Yun commanded the main body.

When Cao Cao came close, Liu Bei's army beat the drums and went out. Cao Cao arrayed his men and called Liu Bei to speak with him, and when the latter appeared under his great standard, Cao Cao pointed at him with his whip and reproached him.

"I treated you as a guest of high honor—why do you turn your back on righteousness and forget my kindness?"

Liu Bei replied, "Under the name of prime minister you are really a rebel. I am a direct descendant of the Emperor's family and I have a secret decree from the throne to defeat you."

Then, seated on his steed, he recited the secret decree that the Emperor had given to Dong Cheng, hidden in the girdle.

Cao Cao grew very angry and ordered Xu Chu to go out to give battle. On Liu Bei's side, out rode Zhao Yun with his spear ready to thrust. The two warriors exchanged thirty bouts but neither could prevail over the other. Then there arose an earth-rending shout and up came the two brothers, Guan Yu from the southeast and Zhang Fei from the southwest. The three armies then began a great attack. Fatigued by the long march, Cao Cao's men were worsted and fled. Having scored this victory, Liu Bei returned to camp.

On the following day he sent out Zhao Yun again to challenge but no response came from his enemy. For ten days Cao Cao's army remained inside. Then Zhang Fei went out to offer battle but again the offer went unanswered. Liu Bei began to grow more and more anxious. Suddenly, news came that the enemy had intercepted their supplies and at once Zhang Fei went to the rescue. Worse still was the news that followed—an army led by Xiahou Dun had outflanked them to attack Runan.

Extremely alarmed, Liu Bei said, "If this is true I'll have enemies in front and behind and there'll be no place for me to go."

He then sent Guan Yu to try to recover the city and thus both his brothers were absent from his side. Very soon a messenger rode up to report that Runan had fallen, but Liu Pi had escaped, and Guan Yu was surrounded by enemies. To make matters worse another disheartening piece of news came to say that Zhang Fei, who had gone to protect the supplies, was also trapped.

Liu Bei wanted to withdraw but was afraid of being attacked from behind by Cao Cao. He was thus undecided what step to take when the sentinels came in to say that Xu Chu was challenging outside the camp. Liu Bei was too scared to lead his men out. He waited till dawn, and then the soldiers were told to eat a good meal and be ready to start. When ready, the infantry went out first followed by the cavalry, leaving only a few nightwatchmen to beat the gongs to mark time and maintain an appearance of habitation.

After traveling a short distance they passed some low hills but all of a sudden torches blazed out and from the top of a hill came loud shouting: "Don't let Liu Bei get away! The prime minister is waiting for him here!"

Liu Bei hastened to look for a way of escape.

Zhao Yun said, "Have no fear, my lord, just follow me." And setting his spear, he galloped in front opening a lane as he went. Liu Bei gripped his double swords and followed close behind. As they fought their way ahead, Xu Chu came in pursuit and engaged Zhao Yun in a fierce combat, but soon two other of Cao Cao's officers came up. Seeing the situation so desperate Liu Bei plunged into the wilderness and fled. Gradually the sounds of battle died down and he picked his way among the most secluded parts of the hills, a single horseman fleeing for his life. He kept on thus till daybreak, when a troop suddenly appeared beside the road. Liu Bei was terrified at first but was relieved to find that it was the friendly Liu Pi with about a thousand of his defeated men from Runan, escorting his family. With them also were Sun Qian, Jian Yong, and Mi Fang.

They told him that the attack on their city had been too strong to resist so they had been compelled to abandon it and flee, but then they had been chased and only Guan Yu's timely arrival had rescued them.

Liu Bei said, "I wonder where Yun-chang is now."

"Let's push ahead first and try to find out later," said Liu Pi.

They pushed on. Before they had gone far the beating of drums was heard and in front of them appeared Zhang He and his troops. He cried, "Liu Bei, quickly dismount and surrender."

Liu Bei was about to turn back when he saw red banners waving at the top of a hill and down rushed forth another body of men under Gao Lan.

Caught between two enemy forces, there was no escape for Liu Bei. He looked up to Heaven and cried, "Oh, Heaven, why render me into this state of misery? Nothing is left to me but death." And he drew his sword to slay himself.

Liu Pi hastily stayed his hand and said, "Let me try to fight a way out to save you."

So saying, he went forth to engage Gao Lan, but unfortunately the bold man was cut down in the third bout. Liu Bei, now panic-stricken, was on the verge of fighting himself when there was sudden confusion among the rear ranks of his opponents and a warrior dashed up and knocked Gao Lan down from his horse with one powerful thrust. The newcomer was Zhao Yun.

His arrival was most opportune. With his spear set, he plunged into the enemy's rank and scattered the soldiers in all directions. Then he turned back all by himself to fight the enemy in front. Zhang He came into the combat and fought with Zhao Yun for about thirty bouts before he had to turn away defeated. Zhao Yun and the others followed vigorously but were presently trapped in a narrow passage in the hill, strongly defended by their opponents. While trying to find an outlet they saw Guan Yu coming up with Guan Ping, Zhou Cang, and three hundred men. Together they attacked Zhang He and soon drove him off. Then they came out of the narrow defile and occupied a strong position on the hill, where they made a camp. Liu Bei at once asked Guan Yu to go and look for their brother Zhang Fei.

Now Zhang Fei had been sent to rescue Gong Du and the grain supplies, but when he reached there Gong Du had already been slain by the enemy. Zhang Fei beat the enemy off and gave chase. Then another of Cao Cao's forces came along and surrounded him. Guan Yu found him in this plight, after having met some of his scattered men and learned about his situation. They drove off the enemy and returned to their eldest brother. Soon they were informed of the approach of a large body of Cao Cao's army. Liu Bei asked Sun Qian and some others to guard his family and sent them on ahead, while he and his brothers and Zhao Yun followed behind, sometimes fighting and sometimes marching. Seeing that Liu Bei had gone very far, Cao Cao decided to call off the chase and withdrew his army.

When Liu Bei collected his men he found they numbered only a thousand. This scattered and broken force marched as fast as possible to the west. Coming to a river they asked the natives its name, and were told it was the Han. Nearby Liu Bei made a temporary camp. When the local people found out who he was they presented him with wine.

By the sandy bank of the Han River, they drank the wine. After they had been drinking awhile, Liu Bei addressed his faithful followers with a deep sigh: "All of you have talents to be major advisors to a monarch, but your destiny has led you to follow my poor self. My fate is bitter and full of misery. Today I do not even have an inch of land to call my own and I fear I am leading you astray. I think you should abandon me and go to some illustrious lords, where you may be able to make a career."

At these words they all covered their faces and wept. Guan Yu said, "Brother, you are wrong to speak like this. When the great founder of Han contended with Xiang Yu he was defeated many times, but he won at Nine Mile Hill and that victory was the foundation of a dynasty that endured for four centuries. Victory and defeat are but ordinary events in a soldier's career—why should you give up?"

"Success and failure both have their seasons," said Sun Qian, "but we are not to lose heart. This place is not too far from Jingzhou, where Liu Biao is positioned. He commands nine prefectures and has a powerful army and affluent supplies. Besides, he is also of the House of Han. Why not go to him?"

"But he may not receive me," said Liu Bei.

"Let me go and prepare the way. I will make Liu Biao come out of his border to welcome you."

Liu Bei was very pleased. So with his lord's approval Sun Qian set off immediately for Jingzhou. When he reached there he was taken to see Liu Biao. After exchanging greetings, Liu Biao asked him of the purpose of his visit.

Sun Qian said, "My lord Liu Bei is one of the heroes of the day. Although at the moment he does not have many soldiers and officers, his mind is set upon restoring the Han House to its former glory. While at Runan the two commanders, Liu Pi and Gong Du, though bound to him by no ties, were willing to die for the sake of this ideal. You, illustrious sir, like Liu Bei, are a scion of the imperial family. Now my lord has recently suffered a defeat and he thinks of seeking a home in the east with Sun Quan. I have ventured to dissuade him, saying that he should not turn from a relative and go to a mere acquaintance. I told him that you, sir, are well known to be courteous to the wise and polite to scholars, so that they flock to you as the waters flow to the east, and I assured him that you would certainly show kindness to one of your kinsmen. Therefore he has sent me to explain matters and request your commands."

"He is like my own brother," said Liu Biao in great joy, "and I have long desired to see him, but so far no opportunity has occurred. I should be very happy if he would come."

Here Cai Mao broke in. "No, no!" he objected. "Liu Bei first followed Lu Bu, then he served Cao Cao, and next he joined himself to Yuan Shao. But he stayed with none of these, so you can see what manner of man he is. If he comes here Cao Cao will assuredly move against us. Better cut off this messenger's head and send it as an offering to Cao Cao, who will reward you well for that."

Sun Qian sat unmoved by this hostile speech. Then he said solemnly, "I am not afraid of death. My lord is true and loyal to the state and cannot be mentioned in the same breath with Lu Bu, Cao Cao, or Yuan Shao. It is true he once followed these three, but only because he had no choice. Now he knows your lord is a descendant of the Han House and so of the same ancestry as himself. That is why he has come thus far to join you. How can you slander a good man like that?"

Liu Biao ordered Cai Mao to be silent and said, "I have decided and you need say no more."

Cai Mao sulkily left the audience chamber. Then Sun Qian was told to return with the news that Liu Bei would be welcome and Liu Biao went thirty *li* beyond his city wall to meet his guest. Liu Bei greeted his host with the utmost politeness and was warmly welcomed in return. Then Liu Bei introduced his two sworn brothers and friends to his host and together they entered Jingzhou. Liu Bei and his followers were properly accommodated in separate quarters.

As soon as Cao Cao knew where his enemy had gone he wished to attack Liu Biao, but Cheng Yu argued against such a move because Yuan Shao, the dangerous enemy, was still left with potential power to inflict damage. He advised him to return to the capital to refresh the men so that they might be ready for a campaign in the mild spring weather. Cao Cao accepted his advice and set out for the capital.

In the first month of the seventh year of the period Jian An, Cao Cao once again prepared for war. He sent two officers to guard Runan as a precaution against Liu Biao. Then, leaving Xun Yu and one of his cousins to be responsible for the safety of the capital, he marched a large army to Guandu, the scene of the battle against Yuan Shao the year before.

As for Yuan Shao, who had been spitting blood but was then in better health, he, too, began to think of moving against the capital. Shen Pei tried to dissuade him. "The army is not yet fully recovered from last year's setbacks," he said. "It would be better to make your position impregnable and set to improving the army."

Just then came the news of Cao Cao's arrival in Guandu for an invasion of their city. Yuan Shao said, "If we allow our enemy to get close to the city we will have missed our opportunity. I must go out to repel this army."

Here his youngest son interposed: "Father, you are not well enough for a campaign and should not go so far. Let me lead the army to challenge the enemy."

Yuan Shao consented and he sent messengers to call upon his other two sons and his nephew to launch a joint attack against Cao Cao.

Against Runan they beat the drum,
And from Jizhou the armies come.

Who would win the victory will be related in the next chapter.

CHAPTER THIRTY-TWO

Yuan Shang Strives for the Rule of Jizhou
Xu You Schemes to Flood the Zhang River

Yuan Shang was puffed up with pride after his last victory over one of Cao Cao's minor officers and, without deigning to wait for the arrival of his brothers, he marched out to Liyang to meet the enemy. Zhang Liao came out to challenge him and Yuan Shang rode out with spear set. But he only managed to fight three bouts before he had to give way. Zhang Liao smote with full force and Yuan Shang, quite broken, fled pell-mell back to Jizhou. His defeat was a heavy blow to his father, who suffered a severe fit at the news and collapsed.

Lady Liu, mother of Yuan Shang, got him to his bed in a hurry, but he did not rally and she soon saw it was necessary to prepare for the end. So she at once sent for the two advisors loyal to her son to determine the matter of succession. They came and stood by the sick man's bed, but by this time he could no longer speak and only made gestures with his hands. When his wife asked him whether Yuan Shang was to succeed he nodded. Shen Pei, the advisor, wrote out the dying man's testament at the bedside. Presently Yuan Shao turned in his bed, uttered a loud moan and, after another violent fit of vomiting blood, he passed away.

> Born of a line of nobles famous for generations,
> He himself in his youth was vigorous and daring.
> Vainly he called to his side warriors skilled and courageous,
> Gathered beneath his banner countless legions of soldiers.
> He was, however, timid at heart, a lambskin dressed as a tiger,
> Merely a cowardly chicken, phoenix-feathered but spurless.
> Pitiful was the fate of his house, for when he departed
> Brothers strove and quarrels arose in the household.

Shen Pei and the others set about the mourning ceremonies for their dead leader. His wife, Lady Liu, put to death all five of his favorite concubines, and such was the bitterness of her jealousy that she even shaved the hair and slashed the faces of the corpses lest their spirits should meet and rejoin her late husband in the other world. Her son followed up this piece of cruelty by slaying all the relatives of the five victims in case they should avenge their death.

Shen Pei and Feng Ji declared Yuan Shang successor and governor of the four prefectures of Jizhou, Qingzhou, Youzhou, and Bingzhou and sent out reports of the death of the late governor.

At this time, Yuan Tan, the eldest son, had already marched out his army to oppose Cao Cao but hearing of his father's death he called in his two advisors to discuss what course of action he should take.

"In your absence, sir," said Guo Tu, "the two advisors of your youngest brother will certainly have set him up as ruler. Therefore you must act quickly."

"But those two will have already laid their plans," warned Xin Ping. "If you go you will be harmed."

"Then what should I do?" asked Yuan Tan.

Guo Tu replied, "Go and camp near the city and watch what is taking place, while I enter and inquire."

Accordingly, Guo Tu went into the city and sought an interview with the new governor.

Saluting them, Yuan Shang asked, "Why didn't my brother come?"

Guo Tu said, "He is not feeling well so he cannot come."

"By the command of my late father I have taken the governorship. Now I confer upon my brother the rank of General of Cavalry and I want him to go at once to attack Cao Cao, who is pressing on our border. I will follow as soon as my army is in order."

"There is no one in our camp to consult for good advice," said Guo Tu. "We wish to have the services of Shen Pei and Feng Ji."

"I also rely on these two to work out schemes for me now and then," said Yuan Shang. "I don't see how I can do without them."

"Then let one of them come," replied Guo Tu.

Yuan Shang could not but accede to this request, so he told the two men to cast lots to determine who should go to his brother. The task fell to Feng Ji, who then accompanied Guo Tu to his camp, taking with him the seal of the new office for Yuan Tan. When he arrived, however, he found Yuan Tan in perfect health. Full of apprehension, he presented the seal. Yuan Tan felt humiliated at this appointment and he was inclined to put the advisor to death, but Guo Tu dissuaded him in private.

"Cao Cao is pressing down on our border at present. It is better to keep him here to allay your brother's suspicion. After we have beaten Cao Cao we can make an attempt on Jizhou."

Yuan Tan agreed and at once broke up his camp to march toward Li-yang. When he reached there he lost no time in offering battle. But the first encounter between the two armies ended in a severe defeat on his side and he hastily retreated back into Liyang, from where he dispatched a messenger to his brother for reinforcements.

Yuan Shang discussed the matter with Shen Pei and only sent 5,000 men. Cao Cao, hearing of the arrival of the rescue force, sent two of his officers to waylay them, and the meager force was soon destroyed. When Yuan Tan heard of the inadequate force sent and its destruction he was very angry and severely abused Feng Ji.

"Let me write to my lord and beg him to come himself," said Feng Ji.

So the letter was written and sent. When it arrived Yuan Shang again consulted Shen Pei who said, "Guo Tu, your eldest brother's advisor, is full of guile. Last time your brother did not contend with you for governorship because Cao Cao's army was on the border. If he should overpower Cao Cao he will surely aim at this city. Better to withhold assistance and use Cao Cao's hand to destroy your rival."

Yuan Shang took his advice and no reinforcements were sent. When the messenger returned without success Yuan Tan was very angry and showed it by putting Feng Ji to death. He also began to consider surrendering to Cao Cao. Soon, spies brought news of this to Yuan Shang and again Shen Pei was called in.

"If he goes over to Cao Cao they will both attack Jizhou and we will be in great danger," said the advisor.

Finally it was decided that Shen Pei and a general were to take care of the defense of the city while Yuan Shang marched his army to the rescue of his brother.

"Who dares to lead the van?" asked Yuan Shang to his men.

Two brothers named Lu volunteered and they were given 30,000 men under their command. They were the first to reach Liyang.

Yuan Tan was pleased that his brother had come to his aid himself so he abandoned the thought of going over to the enemy. Soon, Yuan Shang arrived and camped outside the city to occupy a strategic position. Before long the second brother, Yuan Xi, and their cousin, Gao Gan, arrived with their troops and they also camped outside the city.

Skirmishes occurred daily. Yuan Shang suffered many defeats and Cao Cao was victorious. In the second month of the eighth year of Jian An, Cao Cao launched separate attacks on all four armies and claimed victory against each. Then they abandoned Liyang and Cao Cao pursued them to Jizhou, where Yuan Tan and Yuan Shang fortified the city, while their brother and cousin camped about thirty *li* away to put up a show of strength. For days Cao Cao attempted to take the city, but without success. At this point Guo Jia suggested the following plan.

He said, "There is dissension among the Yuan brothers because the elder one has been superseded in the succession. Each of them is as strong as the other and each has his own party of followers. If we press them hard they will unite to assist each other but if we loosen our grip they will split and compete for power among themselves. I think we will do better to march southward to attack Liu Biao first and let the fraternal quarrels develop. When the brothers are more weakened by family strife we can smite them and settle the matter in one battle."

Cao Cao approved of the plan. So after arrangement was made to ensure the defense of the newly-acquired cities of Liyang and Guandu, he led the army to move toward Jingzhou.

The two brothers, Yuan Tan and Yuan Shang, congratulated each other on the withdrawal of their enemy, and their brother Yuan Xi and cousin returned to their own districts.

Then the quarrels began. Yuan Tan said to his two trusted advisors, "I am the eldest and yet I have been deprived of the right to succeed my father while the youngest son, born of a second wife, received the governorship. I feel bitter at this."

Guo Tu said, "Camp your men outside, then invite your brother and Shen Pei to a banquet and assassinate them. The whole matter can be easily solved."

Yuan Tan agreed. It so happened that one of his subordinates arrived just then from his own city and Yuan Tan confided to him the plot. But the official opposed this plan and said, "Brothers are as one's own limbs. How can you possibly succeed if at a moment of conflict with an enemy you cut off one of your hands? If you abandon your own brother and sever the relationship, whom can you call a relation in all the world? That fellow Guo Tu is a dangerous mischief maker, who is ready to sow dissension between brothers for a temporary advantage—I beg you to shut your ears to his vile words."

This was displeasing to Yuan Tan and he angrily dismissed the official. In the meantime, the treacherous invitation was sent to his brother.

Yuan Shang talked over the matter with his advisor who said, "This must be a trick of Guo Tu's. If you go you will be the victim of their plot. Rather strike at them first."

So Yuan Shang put on his mail and rode out to give battle. Seeing that he had come with a big army, Yuan Tan knew that his plot had been discovered, so he also took the field. When the two forces were close enough, Yuan Shang let out a volley of abuse on his eldest brother, who returned the curses. "You poisoned our father and usurped power—and now you have come to slay your elder brother!" shouted Yuan Tan.

The two brothers fought with each other but the elder one was soon defeated. Yuan Shang himself took part in the battle, risking arrows and stones. He urged on his men and drove his elder brother from the field. Yuan Tan took refuge in Pingyuan and Yuan Shang drew off his men to his won city.

Yuan Tan and his advisor decided upon a new attack and this time they chose Cen Bi to lead the army. Yuan Shang went to meet him. When both sides had been arrayed and the banners were flying and the drums beating, Cen Bi rode out to challenge and railed at his opponent. Yuan Shang was going to answer the challenge himself, when one of his officers went out before him. The two of them fought but a few bouts when Cen Bi fell. Yuan Tan's men were once more defeated and fled to Pingyuan again. Shen Pei urged his master to follow it up with pursuit and Yuan Tan was driven into the city, where he fortified himself and would not go forth. So the city was besieged on three sides.

Yuan Tan consulted his strategist on what should be done next and the latter said, "The city is short of food and our enemy is too flushed with victory for us to withstand. My idea is to send someone to offer surrender to Cao Cao and thus get him to attack Jizhou. Your brother will be forced to return there, which will leave you free to join the attack. And he can be captured. If Cao Cao gets the better of your brother's army we will collect his force to fight against Cao Cao, and as Cao Cao's army comes from a long way away, he will be short of supply and he will soon withdraw. Then we can seize Jizhou and plan our own great cause."

Yuan Tan accepted his advice and asked him who could be sent as a messenger.

"I think Xin Bi is the right person to send. He is the younger brother of your advisor Xin Ping, and magistrate of this very place. He is a fluent speaker and well-suited to your purpose."

So Xin Bi was summoned and he accepted the mission readily enough. A letter was given to him and an escort of 3,000 soldiers took him beyond the border. He traveled as quickly as possible to see Cao Cao.

At that time Cao Cao's camp was at Xiping and he was attacking Liu Biao, who had sent Liu Bei out as the pioneer force to resist the enemy. No battle had yet taken place.

Soon after his arrival Xin Bi was admitted to Cao Cao's presence and, after exchanging friendly salutations, was asked about the object of his visit. Xin Bi explained that Yuan Tan wanted assistance and presented his letter. Cao Cao read it and told the messenger to wait in his camp while he called his advisors and officers to a council.

The council met. Cheng Yu said, "Yuan Tan has been forced into making this offer because of the pressure from his brother's attack. You cannot trust him."

Lu Qian and Man Chong said, "You have led your armies here for a special purpose; how can you abandon that and go to assist Yuan Tan?"

"Gentlemen, I'm afraid none of your advice is good enough," interposed Xun You. "This is how I regard it. As we know, there is universal strife in the country, yet in the midst of this Liu Biao remains quietly content with his position between the Yangtze and the Han rivers. It is evident that he has no ambition to enlarge his borders. The Yuans hold four prefectures and have many legions of soldiers. Harmony between the two brothers means success for the family and none can foresee who will rule the land in the future. Now the fraternal conflict has forced one of them to yield to our lord. We can take advantage of this to remove Yuan Shang, and then wait until suitable opportunities arise so that Yuan Tan can be destroyed in his turn. Thus the empire will be ours. These present circumstances should be taken advantage of in full."

Cao Cao realized the truth of this and treated the messenger well. At a banquet he asked, "But is Yuan Tan's surrender real or false? Do you really think that Yuan Shang's army is sure to overcome him?"

Xin Bi replied, "Do not inquire the degree of his sincerity, sir—rather, consider if the situation is favorable to you. The Yuans have been suffering military losses for years. They are exhausted by wars abroad and weakened by conflicts among advisors within. The brothers are alienated from each other because they listen to slanders around them and their land is thus divided. In addition to all this there is famine, supplemented by calamities and general exhaustion. Therefore, everybody, wise or simple, can see that the catastrophe is near—that the time ordained by Heaven for the destruction of the Yuans is at hand. Now, when you go and attack Jizhou, Yuan Shang will be put in a dilemma. If he does not return to rescue the city, he will lose his place of refuge; but if he does, he will be pursued from behind by his brother. With your military power to counter his exhausted army it will be as easy as an autumn gale sweeping away the fallen leaves.

"If you do not give up this opportunity to attack Liu Biao in Jingzhou, you will be making a serious mistake. Now Jingzhou is a land of prosperity, the government is peaceful, the people submissive and it cannot be shaken. Moreover, Hebei is the very place that nourishes trouble. If Hebei is conquered, then your supremacy will be established. I pray you, sir, think of all this."

"How I regret that I had not met you earlier!" said Cao Cao, much gratified with this speech.

So orders were given to return and attack Jizhou. Liu Bei, fearing this retreat was only a trick, allowed it to proceed without interference, and he himself returned to Jingzhou.

When Yuan Shang heard that Cao Cao had crossed the river he hastily led his army back to his own place, ordering the two Lus to guard the rear. Seeing this, his brother Yuan Tan started from Pingyuan with a force in pursuit. He had not proceeded far when he heard an explosion and two bodies of men came out in front of him and checked his progress. Their leaders were the Lu brothers.

Yuan Tan reined in and addressed them. "While my father lived I never treated you badly—why do you support my brother and try to injure me?"

The two men had no reply, so they dismounted and yielded to him.

Yuan Tan said, "Don't surrender to me but to Prime Minister Cao." And he led them back to camp, where he waited the arrival of Cao Cao and then presented the two of them. Cao Cao was very happy and promised to give his daughter in marriage to Yuan Tan, with the two Lu brothers as matchmakers.

Yuan Tan asked Cao Cao to attack Jizhou but his new patron said, "Supplies are short and difficult to transport. I must first dredge the rivers so that grain can be conveyed here, and afterwards I can advance."

Ordering Yuan Tan to remain in Pingyuan, Cao Cao withdrew into camp at Liyang. The two Lu brothers, who were renegades from Yuan Shang, now raised to the ranks of nobles, followed the army to render their service whenever necessary.

Guo Tu noted their advancement and said to Yuan Tan, "Cao Cao has promised you a daughter as wife. I fear he is not being true. Now he has given titles of nobility to the two Lus and taken them with him. This is a trick to win the hearts of the northern people, which will ultimately ruin us. You, my lord, should confer the title of general on the two Lus and have the seals engraved. Then send them secretly to the brothers and ask them to be your men in his camp, ready for the day when Cao Cao has destroyed your brother and we can begin to work against him."

The seals were engraved and sent. However, as soon as the Lu brothers received them they went to show them to Cao Cao, who laughed and said: "He wants your support so he sends you seals as his officers. He is waiting for his chance after I have dealt with Yuan Shang. You may keep the seals for the time being. I know what to do." After this Cao Cao began to think of killing Yuan Tan.

In Jizhou Yuan Shang was also discussing the situation with his advisor Shen Pei.

"Cao Cao is getting grain into Baigou, which means he will attack Jizhou. What is to be done?" asked Yuan Shang.

Shen Pei replied, "Send a letter to Yin Kai, bidding him to camp at Maocheng to secure the road of transportation for grain, and direct Ju Gu to maintain Handan as a distant support. Then you can unleash a swift assault on Pingyuan and attack your brother. First destroy him and then deal with Cao Cao."

The plan seemed good. Yuan Shang left Shen Pei and Chen Lin in charge of Jizhou, appointed two officers as van leaders, and set out hastily for Pingyuan.

When Yuan Tan heard of the approach of his brother's army, he sent urgent messages to Cao Cao for help. Cao Cao said, "I am going to get Jizhou this time."

Just at this time, Xu You came down from the capital. When he heard that Yuan Shang was attacking his brother, Yuan Tan he went in to see Cao Cao and said, "Sir, you sit here idle—are you waiting for thunder from Heaven to strike down the two Yuans?"

"I have thought it all out," smiled Cao Cao.

Then he ordered Cao Hong to go and attack Jizhou, while he led another force to smite Yin Kai. When Cao Cao's army arrived, Yin Kai led his men out to oppose him. However, he was soon killed by Xu Chu and his men ran away and presently joined Cao Cao's army. Next he led the army to Handan and Ju Gu came out to fight him. Zhang Liao advanced to engage him in combat and after the third encounter Ju Gu was defeated and fled. Zhang Liao went after him and when their two horses were not far apart, he took his bow and shot. The fleeing officer fell as the bowstring twanged. Cao Cao himself commanded the onslaught that completed the rout and Ju Hu's force was dispersed.

Now Cao Cao led his army for an attack on Jizhou. Cao Hong was close to the city and a regular siege began. The invading army surrounded the city by throwing up mounds all around. They also secretly dug tunnels in order to enter the city through the underground passage.

Within the city Shen Pei turned his whole care to the defense and issued the severest commands. The officer of the east gate, Feng Li, was drunk and failed to maintain his watch, for which he was severely punished. In resentment he sneaked out of the city to surrender to the besiegers and told them how the city could be entered. The traitor told that the earth within one of the gates was solid enough to be tunneled and entrance could be effected there. So Feng Li was sent with three hundred men to carry out his plan under cover of darkness.

After Feng Li had deserted to the enemy, Shen Pei went every night to the wall to inspect the men on duty. That night he went to that gate and saw that there were no lights outside the city. All was perfectly quiet. He said to himself, "Feng Li is certain to guide the enemy into the city by an underground passage." So he ordered his men to carry stones and pile them outside the opening of the tunnel. The opening was stopped up and Feng Li and the three hundred men perished in the tunnel. Cao Cao, having failed in this attempt, abandoned the scheme of underground attack. He drew off the army to a place by the Huan River to wait till Yuan Shang should return to relieve the city.

As soon as Yuan Shang heard of the defeat of his two supporters by Cao Cao and the siege of his own city, he withdrew from Pingyuan to return to Jizhou. One of his officers said: "The high road will surely be ambushed—we must find some other way. We can take a byroad from the West Hills and get through to the Fu River, from where we can fall upon Cao Cao's camp."

The plan was accepted and Yuan Shang started off with the main body while two of his officers brought up the rear.

Cao Cao's spies soon found out this move and reported it to him. Cao Cao said, "If he comes by the high road I will have to keep out of the way but if he comes by the byroad I can decisively defeat him. And I think he will light a blaze as a signal to the besieged so that they will make a sortie. I will prepare to attack both." So he made his arrangements.

Now Yuan Shang went out by the Fu River Pass and turned east to Yangping near where he camped. The place was seventeen *li* to his own city and the Fu River ran beside the camp. He ordered his men to collect firewood and grass ready for the blaze he intended to make at night as a signal. He also sent Li Fu, a civil official, disguised as an officer of Cao Cao's army, to inform Shen Pei of his intentions.

Li Fu reached the city wall safely and called out to the guards to open the gates for him. Shen Pei recognized his voice and let him in. Thus Shen Pei knew of his master's arrangements and it was agreed that a blaze should be raised within the city so that the sortie could be simultaneous with Yuan Shang's attack. Orders were given to collect inflammables.

Then Li Fu said, "As your food supply is short it would be well for the old, the feeble, and the women to surrender. The enemy will have no suspicion and so will not be prepared. And we can send the soldiers out behind the people."

Shen Pei agreed to do all this and the next day they hoisted on the wall a white flag with the words "The populace of Jizhou surrenders" written on it.

"This means no food," said Cao Cao. "They are sending the non-combatants out and the soldiers will follow behind them."

So on both sides he laid an ambush of 3,000 soldiers while he went up to the wall in full state regalia. At the open gates he saw the people coming out supporting their aged folk and leading their little ones by the hand. Each carried a white flag. As soon as the people had passed the gate, the soldiers followed with a rush.

Then Cao Cao showed a red flag and the ambushing soldiers sortied forth. The Jizhou men had to fall back to the city and Cao Cao himself dashed forth to pursue them to the drawbridge, but there a tremendous shower of arrows and crossbow bolts came down from the wall tower. Cao Cao's helmet was hit and his head was nearly injured. His men hastily came to the rescue and brought him back to camp.

As soon as Cao Cao had changed his robe and mounted a fresh horse he set out at the head of the army to attack Yuan Shang's camp.

Yuan Shang led the defense. As the attack came simultaneously from many directions, the defenders were quite disorganized and presently defeated. Yuan Shang led his men back to the hills and made a camp under their shelter. Then he sent messengers to urge the two officers at the rear to bring up the supporters but he did not know that these two had been persuaded by the Lu brothers into joining Cao Cao's banner and had been given high ranks.

Just before attacking the West Hills, Cao Cao sent the two Lus to seize Yuan Shang's supplies. Yuan Shang realized he could not hold the hills so he went by night to Lankou. Before he could get properly camped he saw flaring lights spring up all around him and soon an attack began. He was caught by surprise and had to oppose the enemy with his men half armed, their mail hardly put on and their steeds unsaddled. His army suffered a tremendous loss and he had to retreat another fifty *li*.

By that time his force was too enfeebled to show any resistance. As no other course was possible, he sent an envoy to ask that he might surrender. Cao Cao feigned consent, but that very night he instigated a raid on Yuan Shang's camp. Then came the hasty flight. Yuan Shang made for the Zhongshan Hills, abandoning everything—seals, emblems of office, mail and baggage—as he went.

Cao Cao resumed his attack on Jizhou. Xu You suggested drowning the city by turning the course of the River Zhang. Cao Cao adopted the advice and at once sent a small number of men to dig a channel of forty *li* in circumference to lead the water into the city.

Shen Pei saw the diggers from the city wall and knew immediately what his enemies were trying to do. However, he noticed that they made only a shallow channel. Chuckling to himself, he thought, "What is the use of such a shallow channel if they want to drown out the city?"

But as soon as night came on Cao Cao increased his army of diggers tenfold and by daylight the channel was deepened to twenty feet. The water gushed in a great stream into the city, where it stood some feet deep. So this misfortune was added to the lack of food.

Xin Bi now displayed Yuan Shang's seal and garments hung out on spears, to the great shame of their late owner, and called upon the people of the city to surrender. This angered Shen Pei, who avenged the insult by putting to death on the city wall the whole of the Xin family who were still within the city. There were nearly a hundred of them and their severed heads were cast down from the walls. Xin Bi wailed incessantly.

Shen Pei's nephew was a close friend of Xin Bi's and the execution of Xin's family greatly distressed him. He wrote a secret letter offering to betray the city, tied it to an arrow, and fired it out to the besiegers. The soldiers found it and gave it to Xin Bi, who took it to his chief.

Cao Cao issued an order that the family of the Yuans should be spared when the city is taken and that no one who surrendered should be put to death. The next day the soldiers entered by the west gate, opened for them by Shen Pei's nephew. Xin Bi was the first to prance in on horseback and the men followed.

When Shen Pei, who was in the southeast of the city, saw the enemy within the gates he placed himself at the head of some horsemen to put up a last-ditch struggle. He was met and captured by Xu Huang, who bound him and took him outside the city. On the road they met Xin Bi who, grinding his teeth with rage at the killer of his family, struck the prisoner over the head with his whip and cursed him. Shen Pei railed in response: "You shameless traitor! How I regretted I had not slain you!"

The captive was taken before Cao Cao. "Do you know who opened the gate to let me in?" he asked.

"No."

"It was your nephew Shen Rong who gave up the gate," said Cao Cao.

"That brat! He has even sunk to this!" said the indignant Shen Pei.

"Before, when I approached the city, why were there so many arrows?"

"Too few! Too few!"

"As a faithful supporter of the Yuans you could do nothing else, I presume. Now will you come over to me?"

"Never! I will never surrender," shouted the loyal Shen Pei.

Xin Bi threw himself to the ground with lamentations, saying, "Eighty of my people were murdered by this ruffian. I beg you to slay him, my lord!"

"Alive, I have served the Yuans," said Shen Pei. "Dead, I will be their ghost. I am no flattering time-server as you are. Kill me quickly!"

Cao Cao gave the order and he was led out to be slain. On the execution ground he reproached the executioners: "My lord is in the north, how can you make me die facing the south?" So he knelt facing the north and extended his neck for the fatal blow.

> *Who of all the men of fame*
> *In Hebei was true like Shen Pei?*
> *Sad his fate! he served a fool,*
> *But faithful as the ancient sage.*
> *Straight and true was his word,*
> *Never from the road he swerved.*
> *Faithful unto death, he died*
> *Gazing toward the lord he'd served.*

Thus Shen Pei died. From respect for his character Cao Cao ordered that he be buried honorably on the north of the city.

Then he was ready to enter the city. Just as he was starting he saw the executioners hurrying forward a prisoner, who proved to be Chen Lin.

"You wrote that manifesto for Yuan Shao. If you had only directed your vitriol against me, it would not have mattered. But why did you shame my forefathers?" said Cao Cao.

"When the arrow is on the string, it must fly," replied Chen Lin.

The others urged Cao Cao to put him to death but he was spared on account of his talents and given a minor civil post.

Now Cao Cao's eldest son was named Pi. At the seizure of the city he was eighteen years of age. When he was born a dark purplish halo hung over the house for a whole day. At the time someone who understood the meaning of such manifestations had secretly told Cao Cao that the halo belonged to the imperial family and portended greatest honors to his son.

At eight the lad could compose very skillfully and his talents far exceeded others. He was well-read in ancient history. Now he was adept at all military arts and very fond of fencing. He had accompanied his father on this campaign. After the fall of Jizhou, he led his escort in the direction of Yuan Shao's family dwelling and when he reached it he strode in sword in hand. The officer at the gate tried to stop him, saying that by order of the prime minister no one was to enter the house, but was told to step back. The guards fell back as he made his way into the interior, where he saw two women weeping in each other's arms. He went forward to slay them.

> *Four generations of honors, gone like a dream,*
> *Now misfortune has fallen to the family it seems.*

The fate of the two women will be told in the next chapter.

CHAPTER THIRTY-THREE

Cao Pi Takes Advantage of Confusion to Find a Wife
Guo Jia Leaves a Plan After Death for Settling Liaodong

As was said, Cao Pi, having made his way into the Yuan house, saw two women there, whom he was about to kill. Suddenly a red light shone in his eyes and he paused. Lowering his sword he asked, "Who are you?"

"I am the widow of the late General Yuan," said the elder of the two, "and this is the wife of Xi, his second son. She was of the Zheng family. When Xi was sent to command in Youzhou, she did not want to go so far from home and so she stayed behind."

Cao Pi drew her toward him and looked at her closely. Her hair hung disordered, her face was dusty and tear-stained; but when, with the sleeve of his inner garment, he had wiped away these blemishes, he saw a woman of exquisite loveliness, with a complexion clear as jade touched with the tenderness of a flower, a woman indeed beautiful enough to ruin a kingdom.

"I am the son of Prime Minister Cao," he said turning to the elder woman. "I will guarantee your safety, so you need not fear anything."

He then put his hand on his sword and sat down in the hall.

As Cao Cao was entering the gate of the conquered city Xu You rode up to him very quickly and, pointing with his whip at the gate, he called him by his familiar name and said, "You would not be able to enter this gate without my help."

Cao Cao laughed but his officers were much annoyed. When he reached the Yuan residence he stopped at the gate and asked if anyone had gone in. The guard at the gate said, "The young master is inside." Cao Cao called him out and scolded him but Lady Liu interposed, saying, "But for your son we would not have been saved. I want to offer to you this lady of the Zheng family to wait upon your son."

The girl was brought before him and she curtsied to him. After looking at her intently he said, "Just the wife for my son!" And he told Cao Pi to take her as a wife.

As the conquest of Jizhou had been made secure, Cao Cao made a ceremonial visit to the Yuan family cemetery, where he offered a sacrifice at the tomb of his late rival Yuan Shao, bowed several times, and lamented bitterly.

Turning to those around him he said, "Not long ago when Ben-chu and I worked together against Dong Zhuo he asked me, 'If we fail this time what districts can be held?' and I replied to by asking him what he thought. He said, 'To the south I would hold the Yellow River and in the north, guard against Yan and Dai and the hordes from the desert areas. Then I will try to extend my influence southward—don't you think I might succeed?' I replied, 'If the wisdom and force of the world be directed by righteous doctrines, then everything would be possible.' These words seem as if spoken only yesterday, and now he is gone. Recalling all this I cannot refrain from tears."

His men all sighed with sympathy. Cao Cao treated the widow generously, giving her gold and silks and food.

He also issued a further order that taxes in Hebei be exempted that year in consideration of the sufferings of the people during the military operations. Then he sent up a memorial to the Emperor and nominated himself Governor of Jizhou.

One day Xu Chu, riding in at the east gate, met Xu You, who called out to him: "Would you fellows be riding through this gate if it had not been for me?"

Xu Chu replied, "We risked our lives in bloody battles to capture this city. How dare you brag so!"

"You are a mere bunch of blockheads, not worth talking about," said Xu You.

Xu Chu in his anger drew his sword and ran him through. Then, carrying the dead man's head, he went to tell Cao Cao that he had killed Xu You for his insolence.

Cao Cao said, "He and I were old friends so he would joke with you. Why did you kill him?"

He chastised Xu Chu very severely and gave orders that the corpse should be buried honorably.

He then inquired if there were any wise and reputable men living in the district and was told of a certain cavalry officer named Cui Yan who had on many occasions given valuable advice to Yuan Shao. As his advice had not been followed, he had pleaded indisposition and retired to his home.

Cao Cao sent for this man, gave him a post and said to him, "According to the former registers there are 300,000 households in the district, so it may be called a major district."

Cui Yan replied, "The empire is divided and the country is torn; the Yuan brothers are at war and the people have suffered. Yet, sir, you do not hasten to inquire after the local conditions and how to rescue the people from misery, but first compute the possibilities of taxation. Can you expect to gain the support of our people?"

Cao Cao was impressed by the righteousness of the rebuke. He earnestly thanked him and treated him as an honored guest.

As soon as Jizhou was occupied, Cao Cao sent out scouts to discover the movements of Yuan Tan. Reports soon came to say that Yuan Tan was ravaging Ganling and the places near it in the south and west. When he heard that his brother Yuan Shang had fled to the Zhongshan hills he had rushed there to fight with him, but Yuan Shang had no heart to face a battle so he had gone to Youzhou to his second brother Yuan Xi. Yuan Tan, having collected all his brother's army, was preparing for another attempt on Jizhou.

After hearing the reports, Cao Cao summoned him. However, Yuan Tan refused to come and Cao Cao sent a letter to break off the marriage with his daughter. Soon after, Cao Cao led an expedition to Pingyuan to deal with him and Yuan Tan turned to Liu Biao for assistance.

Liu Biao sent for Liu Bei to consult with him on this. Liu Bei said, "Cao Cao is very strong now that he has overcome Jizhou and the Yuans will be unable to hold out for long. Nothing is to be gained by helping this man and it may give Cao Cao the excuse he is seeking to attack this place. My advice is to keep the army in a state of readiness and devote all our energies to defense."

"But what shall I say to refuse him?" asked Liu Biao.

"Write to both brothers in gracious terms as their peacemaker."

Accordingly, Liu Biao wrote to Yuan Tan: "When the superior man wants to escape from danger he does not go to an enemy's state. I heard recently that you had bowed your knee to Cao Cao, which was ignoring the enmity between him and your father, rejecting the duties of brotherhood, and leaving behind you the shame of an alliance with the enemy. If your brother, the successor to Jizhou, has acted unfraternally, you should try to overlook that now and wait until the present trouble be settled."

And to Yuan Shang he wrote: "Your brother, the ruler of Qingzhou, is of an impulsive temperament and confuses right with wrong. You ought first to have destroyed Cao Cao in order to vent the hatred which your father bore him and to redress the wrongs when the situation had become settled. Would it not be well? If you persist in following this mistaken course, then only your enemy will benefit. Remember the story of the fastest hound and the hare, both so wearied that the peasant caught them?"

From this letter Yuan Tan saw that Liu Biao had no intention of helping him, and feeling he alone could not withstand Cao Cao, he abandoned Pingyuan and fled to Nanpi.

Cao Cao pursued him. As the weather was very cold, his grain boats could not move in the frozen river. Therefore Cao Cao ordered the inhabitants to break the ice and tow the boats. When the peasants were given the order they ran away. Cao Cao was angry and wanted to punish them with beheading. When they heard this they went to his camp in a body to surrender themselves.

"If I do not kill you, my orders will not be obeyed," said Cao Cao. "Yet I cannot bear to cut off your heads. Quickly flee to the hills and hide so that my soldiers do not capture you."

The peasants left weeping.

Then Yuan Tan led out his army to oppose Cao Cao. When both sides were arrayed Cao Cao rode to the front, pointed with his whip at his opponent, and railed at him: "I treated you well—why, then, have you turned against me?"

Yuan Tan replied, "You have invaded my land, captured my cities, and broken off my marriage—yet you accuse me of turning against you?"

Cao Cao ordered Xu Huang to go out and give battle. Yuan Tan bade Peng An accept the challenge. After a few bouts Peng An was slain and Yuan Tan, having lost, fled and went into Nanpi, where he was besieged. Yuan Tan, panic-stricken, sent Xin Ping to see Cao Cao to arrange surrender.

"He is capricious and unreliable," said Cao Cao, "and I cannot depend upon what he says. Now your brother Xin Pi is in my employment and has a post of importance—you had better remain here as well."

"Sir, you are mistaken," said Xin Ping. "It is said that the lord's honor is the servant's glory, the lord's sadness is the servant's shame. How can I turn my back on the family I have so long served?"

Feeling that he could not be persuaded, Cao Cao sent him back. Xin Ping returned and told Yuan Tan the surrender could not be arranged and Yuan Tan turned on him angrily, accusing him of disloyalty. At this unmerited reproach such a huge wave of anger welled up in the man's breast that he collapsed in a swoon. They carried him out, but the shock had been too severe and soon after he died. Yuan Tan regretted his actions, but it was too late.

Then Guo Tu said, "Tomorrow when we go out to battle we will drive the common people out in front as a screen for the soldiers—we must fight a winning battle."

That night they assembled all the common people of that place and forced into their hands swords and spears. At daylight they opened the four gates and, with much shouting, a huge party came out at each gate, peasantry carrying arms in front, with soldiers behind them. They pushed on toward Cao Cao's camps and a melee began that lasted till near midday. But the result of the battle was still not clear, although heaps of dead lay everywhere.

Seeing that success was at best only partial Cao Cao abandoned his horse and climbed to the top of a hill, where he himself beat the drum. Encouraged by this, his officers and men exerted themselves to the utmost and Yuan Tan's army was severely defeated. Of the peasantry driven into the battlefield, multitudes were slain.

Cao Hong, who displayed great valor, burst into the heart of the battle and met Yuan Tan face to face. The two slashed and hammered at each other. Yuan Tan, unable to withstand Cao Hong's fierce thrusts, was slain. Thus ended the life of this eldest of Yuan Shao, whose ambition alienated him from his own brothers, making himself an easy prey to Cao Cao.

Guo Tu saw that his side was wholly disorganized and tried to gain the shelter of the city. Seeing this, Yu Jin let fly an arrow which hit the advisor, sending him and his horse down into the moat.

The city was overwhelmed. Cao Cao entered it and set about restoring peace and order. Suddenly, there appeared a new army under two of Yuan Xi's officers. Cao Cao led out his men to meet them, but the two commanders laid down their arms and yielded. They were duly rewarded with high ranks.

Soon, another force came to surrender to Cao Cao. Zhang Yan, leader of the Black Hills brigands, came with 100,000 men and offered his submission. For this he was made a general.

By an order of Cao Cao's the head of Yuan Tan was exposed and death was threatened to anyone who should lament for him. Nevertheless, a man dressed in mourning attire was arrested for weeping below the exposed head at the north gate. Taken into Cao Cao's presence, he said he was Wang Xiu and had been an officer in Qingzhou, where Yuan Tan used to rule. He had been expelled because he had remonstrated with his master, but at the news of his death had come to weep for him.

"Did you know of my command?"

"Yes, I did."

"Yet you were not afraid?"

"When one has received favors from a man in life it would be wrong not to mourn him at his death. How can one live in the world if one forgets duty because of fear? If I could bury his body I would not mind death."

Cao Cao said, "How many men of loyalty there are in his district! What a pity that the Yuan family could not make the best of them! If they had done so I should never have dared to turn my eyes toward this place."

The intrepid mourner was not put to death. The remains of Yuan Tan were properly interred and Wang Xiu was well treated and even given an appointment.

In his new position he was asked for advice about the best way to proceed against Yuan Shang, who had fled to his brother, but he held his peace, thereby winning from Cao Cao renewed admiration for his constancy. "He is indeed loyal!" said Cao Cao.

Then he questioned Guo Jia, who suggested sending the newly- surrendered officers to bring about the capitulation of the Yuans. So five of the former Yuan officers went to attack Youzhou along three routes, and another army was sent to take Bingzhou.

The two Yuan brothers heard of Cao Cao's advance with dismay for they had no hope of successful resistance. Therefore, they left the city of Youzhou and hastily escaped to Liaoxi* to seek refuge with Wu Huanchu, chief of the Wuhuan† tribesmen. After the brothers were gone the governor of Youzhou did not want to incur the enmity of the powerful Cao Cao, so he called his subordinates together and said, "I understand that Cao Cao is the most powerful man of the day and I am going to surrender to him; those who do not go with me will be put to death."

Each in turn smeared his lips with the blood of sacrifice and took the oath till it came to Han Heng. Instead, he dashed his sword to the ground and cried out, "I have received great benefits from the Yuans. Now my lord has been vanquished. I could not save him with my wisdom nor could I die for him with my bravery. I have therefore failed in my duty. But I refuse to commit the crowning act of treachery and ally myself with Cao Cao."

This speech made the others turn pale. The governor said, "For a great undertaking there must be strict principles. However, success does not necessarily depend upon universal support and since Han Heng is im-

---

* In modern Liaoning Province in northeast China.

† An ancient nomadic tribe in northeast China.

peled by such sentiments then let him follow his conscience." So he ordered Han Heng to be taken out and executed.

He then went out of the city to welcome Cao Cao's army and render his submission. He was well received and given the rank of a general.

Then scouts came to say that the three officers who had gone to attack Bingzhou were not successful because Gao Gan, nephew of Yuan Shao, had occupied Wu Pass and could not be dislodged. So Cao Cao marched there himself and a general council was convened to discuss ways to destroy Gao Gan. The advisor Xun You proposed the ruse of false surrender. Cao Cao assented and then summoned the two Lu brothers, to whom he gave whispered orders. They left with several score of soldiers.

Soon they came near the pass and called out, "We are old officers of the Yuans forced into surrendering to Cao Cao. We find him so false and he treats us so meanly that we want to return to help our old master. Please open your gates quickly to us."

Gao Gan was suspicious, but he agreed to let the two officers come up to the pass and when they had stripped off their armor and left their horses they were permitted to enter. They said to Gao Gan, "Cao Cao's men are new to the country and not settled. You ought to fall upon their camp this very evening. If you approve we will lead the battle."

Gao Gan decided to trust them and prepared to attack, taking the two brothers with him as van leaders. But as he and his army drew near Cao Cao's camp a great noise arose behind them and they found themselves in an ambush, assailed on all sides. Realizing too late that he had been the victim of a trick, Gao Gan retreated to the pass but found it already occupied by the enemy. Gao Gan then made his way to seek refuge with the Huan chieftain. Cao Cao gave orders to hold the pass and sent a troop in pursuit.

When Gao Gan reached the boundary of the Huan territory he met the chieftain. Gao Gan dismounted and made a low obeisance, saying, "Cao Cao is conquering and absorbing all the territories and your turn, Your Highness, will come quickly. I beg you to help me and let us fight together for the safety of the northern regions."

The chieftain replied, "I have no quarrel with Cao Cao. Why, then, should he invade my land? Do you desire to embroil me with him?"

He would have nothing to do with Gao Gan and sent him away. At his wits' end, Gao Gan decided to try to join Liu Biao, and got so far on his journey as Shangluo when he was slain by one of his subordinates. His head was sent to Cao Cao and the killer was rewarded with a high rank for his service.

Thus Bingzhou was conquered. Then Cao Cao began to think of going to the west to crush Wuhuan, who had provided shelter to the two Yuan brothers. Cao Hong and the others all objected. They argued, "The two Yuan brothers are nearly done for and too weak to be feared. They have fled far into the desert and if we pursue them there it may encourage Liu Biao and Liu Bei to attack the capital. Should we fail to rescue it, the misfortune would be immense. We beg you to return to the capital."

But Guo Jia was of different opinion.

"You are wrong," he said. "Though the prestige of our minister fills the empire, yet the men of the desert, relying on their inaccessibility, will not be prepared against us. A surprise attack will conquer them. Besides, Yuan Shao used to be kind to the nomads, so they will support the two brothers. We cannot allow them to live. As for Liu Biao, he knows he is not talented enough to command Liu Bei. If he delegates a heavy responsibility to Liu Bei he will be afraid of losing control of him, but if he entrusts him with a light task then Liu Bei will be dissatisfied. So even though you make a long expedition, leaving the capital almost unguarded, you do not have to worry about him. Nothing will happen."

Cao Cao was inclined to agree with Guo Jia and he led his whole army to move ahead, followed by thousands of wagons.

The army marched into the desert. What greeted them was rolling waves of yellow sand and howling winds all around. The road was rugged and rough, making progress extremely difficult for both men and horses. Cao Cao began to think of returning and he consulted Guo Jia. The advisor had by then fallen victim to the effects of the climate and lay in his cart, very ill.

Cao Cao's tears fell as he said, "My friend, you are suffering for my ambition to subdue the desert. I cannot bear to think you should be ill."

"You have always been very good to me," said the sick man, "and I can never repay what I owe you."

"The country is exceedingly precipitous and I am thinking of going back. What do you say?"

Guo Jia replied, "The success of an expedition of this kind depends upon speed. To strike a sudden blow on a distant spot with a heavy baggage train is difficult. To ensure triumph you need light troops and a good road to strike quickly before an enemy has time to prepare. Now you must find guides who know the road well."

Then the sick advisor was left at Yizhou for treatment and Cao Cao sought among the natives for someone to serve as guide. They recommended a former officer of Yuan Shao's, who knew those parts well. Cao Cao called him in and questioned him.

The officer, named Tian Chou, said, "Between summer and autumn this route is under water, the shallow parts too deep for vehicles and horses, but the deep parts too shallow for boats. It is always difficult. Therefore you would do better to return and cross the dangerous zone of Baitan at Lulong Pass to get out of the desert. You will not be too far from the Willow City and attack before there is time for your opponents to prepare. One sudden onslaught will settle them."

For this valuable information Tian Chou was made a general and went in front as guide. In the center came Zhang Liao and Cao Cao brought up the rear. They advanced swiflty by double marches.

Tian Chou led Zhang Liao to White Wolf Hill, where they came upon the two Yuans and Ta Dun, chief of the Wuhuan tribesmen, followed by a large mass of riders. Zhang Liao at once informed Cao Cao, who rode up to the top of a promontory to survey his foe. He saw the enemy force advancing in a disorderly mass without any military formation.

He said, "They have no formation. We can easily rout them."

Then he handed over his ensign of command to Zhang Liao who, with three other officers, made a vigorous attack from four different points, with the result that the enemy was thrown into great confusion. Zhang Liao rode forward and slew Ta Dun and the others gave in. The two Yuan brothers, with a few thousand followers, got away to the east.

Cao Cao then led his army into the Willow City. To reward his service, Cao Cao conferred on Tian Chou the title of Lord of the Willow City and put him in charge of its defense. But Tian Chou declined the title. With tears in his eyes he said, "I am a renegade and a fugitive. It is my good fortune that you spared my life. How can I accept a reward for betraying the Lulong camp? I would rather die than receive the title of a lord."

Cao Cao recognized the truth of his words and conferred upon him another post. He then pacified the tribesmen, collected a large number of horses from them, and at once set out on the homeward march.

The season was winter, cold and dry. For two hundred *li* there was no water and grain was also scanty. The troops could only feed on horse flesh. They had to dig very deep to find water.

When Cao Cao reached Yizhou he rewarded those who had tried to dissuade him from undertaking the expedition. He said, "I took some risk in going so far and by good fortune I have succeeded. But I owe the victory to the help of Heaven and it should not be viewed as the right course of action. Your counsels were for safety and therefore I reward you to show my appreciation of your advice so that you will not fear to speak your mind in future."

The advisor Guo Jia did not live to see the return of his lord. His coffin was placed on the bier in a hall of the government offices and Cao Cao went there to mourn over his loyal advisor. He wept.

"Alas! Heaven has smitten me! Feng-xiao* is no more."

Turning to his men, he said, "You gentlemen are of the same age as myself but he was the youngest. I intended to entrust my future plans to him. What a misfortune it is that he should be snatched from me in the prime of his life. How my heart is torn with grief!"

The servant of the late advisor presented his last letter written on his deathbed and delivered his last words, "If the prime minister follows the advice given in it then Liaodong will be secure."

Cao Cao opened the envelop and read the letter, nodding in agreement and uttering deep sighs. But the others did not know what was written.

Shortly after, Xiahou Dun came up to speak for a group of officers. "For a long time Gongsun Kang, Prefect of Liaodong, has been disobedient and now the Yuan brothers have fled to his protection. Would it not be well to attack before they move against you?"

"I need not trouble you, gentlemen," said Cao Cao smiling. "Wait a few days and you will see the heads of our two enemies sent to me."

They did not believe him.

As has been related, the two Yuan brothers had escaped to the east with a few thousand followers. When the prefect of Liaodong heard that the Yuans were on their way to his territory he called a council to decide what to do. At the council one of his advisors said, "When Yuan Shao was alive he often harbored the plan to annex our district. Now his sons, homeless, with a broken army and no officers, are coming here. It seems to me like the trick of the turtledove stealing the magpie's nest. If we offer them shelter they will assuredly intrigue against us. I advise you to lure them into the city and then put them to death. Then send their heads to Cao Cao, who will be most grateful to us."

"But I fear Cao Cao will come down to attack us," said the prefect. "If so, it would be better to have the help of the Yuans against him."

"Then you can send spies out to ascertain whether his army is preparing to attack us," said the advisor. "If it is, then spare their lives; if not, then follow my advice."

It was decided to wait till the spies came back. In the meantime, the two Yuan brothers had also been discussing their next move as they approached Liaodong. They said to each other, "Liaodong has a large army strong enough to oppose Cao Cao. We will go there and submit ourselves temporarily. Later, we will slay the prefect and take possession. Then

---

* Familiar name of Guo Jia, used here by Cao Cao to show his affection for the dead advisor.

when we have mustered enough strength, we will attack and recover our own land."

With these intentions they went into the city. They were received and accommodated in the guesthouse, but when they wished to see the prefect he put them off with an excuse of indisposition. However, before many days the spies returned with the news that Cao Cao's army was camped in Yizhou and there was no hint of any attack against Liaodong.

Then the prefect called the Yuans into his presence—but before they came, he hid swordsmen and axmen behind the arras in the hall. When the visitors had arrived and made their salutations, he told them to be seated.

Now it was bitterly cold and on the couch where Yuan Shang was sitting there were no coverings. So he asked for a cushion. The host said sullenly, "When your heads take that long, long journey, will there be any cushion?"

Before Yuan Shang could recover from the shock, the prefect shouted to the hidden assassins, "Why don't you begin?"

At this, out rushed the assassins and the heads of the two brothers were cut off, even as they sat. Then they were placed in wooden boxes and sent to Cao Cao at Yizhou.

All this time Cao Cao had been calmly waiting and when his impatient officers petitioned again that he should return to the capital if he intended no attack on the east, he told them what he was waiting for. He would go as soon as the heads arrived.

In their hearts they doubted and secretly laughed at him. But then, surely enough, a messenger came from Liaodong bringing the heads. Then they were greatly surprised and when the messenger presented the prefect's letter, Cao Cao cried, "Just as Feng-xiao had predicted!"

He amply rewarded the messenger and the prefect of Liaodong was created a nobleman and general. The officers asked him what his remark about Guo Jia meant and he told them what the late advisor had predicted. He read to them the last letter of the deceased advisor:

"Yuan Shang and his brother are going to Liaodong. You are on no account to attack Gongsun Kang, for he has long lived in fear lest the Yuans should annex his region. When the brothers arrive he will hesitate. If you attack, he will keep them to help him—if you wait, they will work against each other. This is evident."

The officers all jumped with admiration when they saw how perfectly events had been foreseen.

Then Cao Cao at the head of all his men performed a grand sacrifice before the coffin of the wise Guo Jia. He had died at the age of thirty-eight, after eleven years of meritorious and wonderful service in the wars.

> *When Heaven permitted Guo Jia's birth,*
> *It made him ablest man on earth.*
> *He knew by rote all histories,*
> *From him war kept no mysteries.*
> *Like Fan Li, his plans were quite decisive,*
> *As Chen Ping, his strokes were most incisive.*
> *Too soon he ran his earthly race,*
> *Too soon the great beam fell from place.*

When Cao Cao returned to Jizhou, he sent people to escort the coffin of his late advisor to the capital, where it was interred.

Then several of his officers said that as the north had been overcome it was time to settle the area south of the Yangtze. Cao Cao was pleased and said that it had long occupied his thoughts.

That night he went to stay in the east corner tower, where he leaned over the railing and studied the sky. His only companion was Xun You. Cao Cao said, "That is a very brilliant glow there in the south. It seems too strong for me to do anything there."

"Who can oppose your heaven-sent prestige?" said Xun You.

Suddenly a beam of golden light shot up out of the earth. "Surely a treasure is buried there," remarked Xun You.

They went down from the tower and ordered some men to dig at the point where the light had dazzled.

> *The southern skies with portents glow,*
> *The northern lands their treasures show.*

What treasure would be found will be told in the next chapter.

CHAPTER THIRTY-FOUR

Lady Cai Overhears a Secret
Liu Bei Leaps Over a Stream

As it happens the diggers unearthed a bronze bird at the point where the golden light had shot up. Turning to his companion, Cao Cao asked, "What is the portent?"

"You must remember that Emperor Shun's mother dreamed of a jade bird before his birth, so certainly it is a felicitous omen," replied Xun You.

Cao Cao was very pleased and he at once ordered the building of a lofty tower to celebrate the find. So they began to dig foundations and cut timber, to burn tiles and smooth bricks for the Bronze Bird Tower on the banks of the Zhang River. Cao Cao set a year for the building.

His youngest son, Cao Zhi, said to him, "If you build a terraced tower, father, you should add two others, one on each side. The center tower will be the tallest and should be named The Bronze Bird Tower—the side ones can be named Jade Dragon and Golden Phoenix. Then connect these by flying bridges and the effect will be superb."

"You're quite right, my boy. By and by when the towers are complete I can solace my old age there."

Cao Cao had five sons but this one was the most clever and his essays were particularly elegant. His father was very fond of him and seeing that the young man took an interest in the building, Cao Cao left him with his eldest brother, Cao Pi, at Jizhou to superintend the work. Meanwhile, Cao Cao led the army, which was greatly strengthened by the addition of Yuan Shao's men and amounted to about half a million men, back to the capital. When he arrived there he distributed rewards liberally and presented a memorial to the Emperor, obtaining the title of "Lord of Purity" for the late advisor Guo Jia. And he took his son to be brought up in his own house.

Next he began to consider an expedition southward to destroy Liu Biao. His advisor Xun Yu objected: "The army has only just returned from the north and needs a good rest. Wait six months so that the men may recover from the fatigue of their last campaign and then both Liu Biao and Sun Quan will fall at one battle." Cao Cao approved of this and he distributed pieces of land to his various troops so that they could work the land while they rested.

Away in Jingzhou, Liu Biao had been very generous to Liu Bei ever since he had arrived, a fugitive seeking shelter. One day while they were drinking together, there came the news that two officers who had recently surrendered to him had suddenly begun plundering the people in Jiangxia and fomenting rebellion.

Liu Biao was greatly alarmed. "This rebellion will cause a lot of trouble," he said.

"Don't let that upset you. Let me go and deal with them," said Liu Bei.

Pleased with this offer, Liu Biao gave him 30,000 men to command and the army marched as soon as the orders were issued. In a short time it reached the scene and the two malcontents came out to fight. Liu Bei, his two brothers, and Zhao Yun took their stand beneath the great banner and looked over at the enemy. They saw that one of the rebels was riding a handsome prancing steed and Liu Bei said, "That must be a one thousand *li* a day horse."

As he spoke Zhao Yun galloped out with his spear set and dashed toward the enemy. Zhang Wu, rider of the fine horse, came out to meet him but the combat was very brief, for he was soon killed. Then Zhao Yun laid his hand upon the bridle of the fallen man's horse to lead it back. The other rebel leader at once rode out to retrieve the horse, but Zhang Fei uttered a loud shout and dashed out with his spear ready to strike. With one thrust he slew the rebel. Their followers now scattered and Liu Bei speedily restored order and returned.

Liu Biao, grateful for this service, went out of the city to welcome the victors back. A grand banquet was held at which they emptied great goblets of wine in celebration of the victory. In the middle of the banquet, Liu Biao said to Liu Bei, "Brother, with such heroism as you have shown, Jingzhou has someone to rely upon. But I'm still worried by the constant assaults from South Yue. Zhang Lu and Sun Quan also pose threats."

"I have three officers," said Liu Bei, "equal to any task you may set them. You can send Zhang Fei to patrol the country of South Yue, Guan Yu to guard the city of Guzi against Zhang Lu, and Zhao Yun to hold the three rivers against Sun Quan. That will relieve you of any worries."

The plan appealed strongly to the prefect but his brother-in-law, Cai Mao, did not approve. He went to see his sister and told her that it would be dangerous for Liu Bei to stay in Jingzhou while his three officers were to be sent to hold different positions.

Influenced by her brother, Lady Cai said to her husband that night, "They say that many Jingzhou men are on very good terms with Liu Bei. You ought to take precautions. I don't think you should let him stay in the city. Why not send him to some other place?"

"Xuan-de is a good man," replied Liu Biao.

"I'm afraid other people may not be as open-minded as you are," said the lady.

Liu Biao fell into thinking but said nothing.

The next day he went out of the city with Liu Bei and noticed that he was riding an exceptionally fine horse. When he learned that it was a prize taken from the recently suppressed rebels, and as he praised it very warmly, Liu Bei gave the horse to him as a gift. The prefect was delighted and rode it back to the city. His advisor Kuai Yue saw it and asked his master where he had got it. The prefect told him.

"My brother knows horses very well and I am not a bad judge," said Kuai Yue. "This horse has tear tracks under its eyes and a white blaze on its forehead. It belongs to the breed of Dilu and is a danger to its master. The rebel leader rode the horse and for that he was killed. I advise you not to ride it."

The prefect was persuaded and he invited Liu Bei to a banquet the following day. In the course of it he said, "You kindly presented me the horse yesterday and I'm most grateful but then I remembered you probably would need it more with your frequent expeditions. So I think I should return it to you."

Liu Bei rose and thanked him. The prefect continued, "You've been here for a long time and I fear I'm spoiling your career as a warrior. Now the town of Xinye in Xiangyang is quite a prosperous place. How do you feel about going there with your own troops?"

Liu Bei naturally accepted the offer as a command. After taking leave of the prefect, he set out the next day for his new post. Outside the gate of Jingzhou, however, a man came up to salute to him and said, "You should not ride that horse."

The speaker turned to be one of the prefect's secretaries named Yi Ji. Liu Bei hastily dismounted and asked him why. Yi Ji replied, "Yesterday I heard Kuai Yue telling the prefect that this horse was a Dilu and that it would bring disaster to its master. That was why it was returned to you. How can you ride it again?"

"Thank you very much for your kindness," replied Liu Bei, "but I think a man's life is governed by fate. How can any horse interfere with that?"

Yi Ji was quite impressed by this superior view, so from then on he kept contact with Liu Bei.

The arrival of Liu Bei in Xinye was a matter of rejoicing to all its inhabitants and the whole administration was reformed.

In the spring of the twelfth year of the reign Jian An (A.D. 207), Lady Gan gave birth to a son, who was named Liu Shan. The night he was born a white crane settled on the roof of the house, screeched some forty times, and then flew away westward.* At the time of his birth a miraculous fragrance filled the chamber. As Lady Gan had conceived of the child soon after she had dreamed of looking up at the sky and feeling the constellation of the Great Bear falling down her throat, the child was also given the milk name A Dou.†

At the time Cao Cao was away from the capital on his northern expedition. Liu Bei went to see the prefect and said to him, "The capital is unguarded at the moment. Why don't you take this opportunity to attack it? You will be able to accomplish the greatest design."

"I'm well contented with my nine districts of Jingzhou," replied Liu Biao. "How can I hope for other things?"

Liu Bei said no more. Then the prefect invited him inside for a drink. While they were so engaged he suddenly began to sigh despondently.

"Why do you sigh like this, brother?" asked Liu Bei.

"I have something on my mind that is difficult to tell you about," said the prefect.

Liu Bei was on the point of asking him what it was when Lady Cai came and stood behind the screen. The prefect hung his head and fell silent. Before long they took leave of each other and Liu Bei went back to his own place. That winter they heard that Cao Cao had returned from the Willow City and Liu Bei sighed when he reflected how the prefect would not heed his advice.

One day the prefect sent a messenger to ask Liu Bei to see him in Jingzhou. So he started out at once with the messenger. He was given a cordial welcome and when the salutations were over the two men went into the private quarters at the rear to dine.

Presently the prefect said, "Cao Cao has returned and he is stronger than ever. I'm afraid he means to absorb this district as well. I'm sorry I didn't follow your advice and have therefore missed a good opportunity."

Liu Bei said, "In this period of disruption, with strife on every side, there are bound to be other opportunities. If you will only seize them you will have nothing to regret."

---

* An allusion to the fact that Liu Shan would later rule in western regions for forty years.
† The constellation is known in Chinese as the Northern Dou or the Northern Dipper. Hence the child was affectionately called A Dou.

"You're right, brother," replied the prefect.

They drank on for some time. Suddenly the prefect began to weep. When asked why, he said, "There is something on my mind. I wanted to tell you last time but there was no opportunity that day."

"What's troubling you, brother? If I can be of any assistance to you I will not hesitate, even though I have to face a thousand deaths."

"I have two sons," said the prefect. "The elder one, Qi, was born to me by my first wife from the Chen family. He grew up virtuous but weakly and unfitted to succeed me in my office. The younger one Zong, from my second wife of the Cai family, was fairly intelligent. If I pass over the elder in favor of the younger I will be violating conventional law; and if I follow the law and set up the elder as my heir then there are the intrigues of the Cai family to be reckoned with. As members of that family are all in the army, there will be trouble in the future. That's why I can't decide what to do."

Liu Bei said, "History has proven that to set aside the elder for the younger is to stir up trouble. If you fear the power of the Cai clan, you can gradually reduce it, but don't let doting affection lead you into making the younger son your heir."

The prefect fell silent. However, they did not know that they had been overheard by Lady Cai. She always had a sneaking suspicion of Liu Bei. So wherever her husband talked to Liu Bei she would come and listen secretly to their conversation. At that very moment she was standing behind the screen and listening with great resentment against Liu Bei for his words.

Liu Bei felt that he had made a mistake to speak so bluntly. Making an excuse, he rose and went to the toilet, where he noticed that he was getting heavy and stiff from lack of exercise and he, too, shed tears. When he returned and sat down his host found there were traces of weeping on his face. Surprised, he asked Liu Bei about the cause of his sorrow.

"In the past I was always in the saddle and I was slender and lithe. Now it has been so long since I rode that I'm getting stout and flabby. My days and months are slipping by, wasted, and in no time old age will come upon me—and yet I haven't accomplished anything. So I'm sad."

The prefect tried to comfort him. "I was told that when you were in the capital you and Cao Cao had discussed heroes while drinking wine and eating green plums. To every name you mentioned as having the merit of a hero, he wouldn't give consent. Finally he said you and he were the only two men of real worth in the whole country. If Cao Cao, with all his power, didn't dare to place himself before you, I don't think you have to grieve about having accomplishing nothing."

Partly due to this flattering speech and partly due to too much wine, Liu Bei forgot his usual prudence and said rather boastfully, "If only I had a starting base I wouldn't really have to worry about all the mediocre men of the world!"

His host became silent and Liu Bei, realizing that he had blundered in speech, pretended to be drunk and rose to leave for his lodging at the guesthouse.

Though Liu Biao kept silent when he heard Liu Bei's words he felt rather hurt in his heart. After his departure, the prefect retired into the inner quarters, where he met his wife.

Lady Cai said, "Just now I happened to be behind the screen and so heard what Liu Bei said to you. He was so arrogant. It clearly reveals his intention to take your district, if he can. He'll harm you in the future unless you remove him now."

Her husband made no reply but only shook his head. Then Lady Cai secretly took counsel with her brother Cai Mao who said, "Let me go to the guesthouse and slay him tonight. We can report what we've done later."

His sister consented and the brother went out to assemble the army for the night raid.

Now Liu Bei sat in his lodging with candles lit till about the third watch, when he prepared to retire to bed. Just then there was a knock on his door and in came Yi Ji, who had heard of the plot against him and had come in the dark to warn him. He related to Liu Bei the details of the plot and urged him to escape at once.

"I haven't taken leave of my host. How can I slip away?" said Liu Bei.

"If you go to bid him farewell you will fall a victim to Cai Mao," said Yi Ji.

So with a hasty word of thanks to his friend, Liu Bei called up his escort and they all rode back to Xinye without waiting for daylight. By the time Cai Mao arrived with the soldiers, his intended victim was far away.

The failure of the plot annoyed Cai Mao very much but he took the occasion to scribble some lines of verse on the wall. Then he went to see Liu Biao and said, "Liu Bei does have treacherous intentions. He has written a malicious poem on the wall and left without bidding you farewell."

Liu Biao did not believe him so he went to the guesthouse to find out. True enough, there on the wall he read the following four lines:

> *Too long, far too long I have been trapped here,*
> *Gazing idly at the rivers and hills.*
> *A dragon can never be kept in a pond,*
> *He should ride on the thunder to heaven and beyond.*

Greatly angered by what he read, Liu Biao drew his sword and swore to slay the writer. But before he had gone many paces his anger died down as he suddenly remembered that during all the time they had been together he had never known Liu Bei to write verses. He thought to himself, "This must be the work of someone who wishes to sow discord between us." So thinking, he turned back and with the point of his sword scraped away the poem. Throwing away his sword, he mounted to leave.

"The army is ready," said Cai Mao. "Let us go and capture him."

"There is no hurry," replied Liu Biao.

Cai Mao saw his brother-in-law's hesitation and again sought his sister for secret counsel. He said to her, "We can call a great gathering in Xiangyang and do something there."

The next day he went to the prefect: "We have good harvests these past few years. I think we should assemble all the officials in Xiangyang to celebrate the Harvest Festival. I pray you, sir, will attend the celebration. It will be an encouragement to the people."

"I have been suffering from my old ailment again—I certainly cannot go," said the prefect. "Let my two sons represent me and receive the guests."

"They are too young," replied Cai Mao, "and may make mistakes in etiquette."

"Then go to Xinye and ask Liu Bei to go and receive the guests," said the prefect.

Nothing could have pleased Cai Mao more, for this would bring Liu Bei within reach of his plot. Without loss of time he sent a messenger to invite Liu Bei over to preside at the festival.

Now Liu Bei had made his way home to Xinye. He knew that the present trouble was caused by his slip in speech, so he did not mention it to the others. Then the messenger came with the prefect's request, asking him to preside at the festival in Xiangyang.

Sun Qian said, "I saw you look preoccupied when you hurried back yesterday and I thought something must have happened in Jingzhou. Now suddenly comes this invitation. You should consider well before you accept it."

Then Liu Bei told them the whole story.

Guan Yu said, "All this may be your own conjecture, brother. You thought you had offended the prefect by your speech but he did not say anything that showed displeasure. You mustn't pay attention to the babble of outsiders. Xiangyang is quite near and if you don't go the prefect will begin to suspect something really is wrong."

"You're right, Yun-chang," said Liu Bei.

Zhang Fei objected, "Banquets are no good and gatherings are no better. It's best not to go."

"Let me take three hundred horse and foot soldiers to accompany you," said Zhao Yun. "That will guarantee your safety."

"Very good," said Liu Bei.

They soon set out for the gathering place. When they reached the city boundary Cai Mao was there to welcome them most courteously. Soon they were met by the prefect's two sons at the head of a great company of civil and military officials. Their appearance put Liu Bei more at ease. He was conducted to the guesthouse and Zhao Yun posted his three hundred men all around to guard it completely, while he himself, fully armed, remained by the side of his chief.

Liu Qi, the prefect's elder son, said to Liu Bei, "My father is feeling unwell and could not come so he begs you, Uncle Liu, to entertain the guests and urge the officials in charge of agriculture and husbandry to make greater contributions."

"I'm really unfit for such responsibilities," said Liu Bei modestly, "but your father's command must be obeyed."

By the following day all the officials from the forty-two counties of the nine districts had arrived.

Then Cai Mao said to his colleague Kuai Yue: "This Liu Bei is the villain of the age. If he were to stay here for long he would certainly bring harm to us. We must get rid of him today."

"You might not get popular support if you harm him," said Kuai Yue.

"I have already secretly spoken in these terms to the prefect," said Cai Mao. "I have his word here."

"If so, we must first make preparations."

Cai Mao told him that he had sent three of his brothers to guard the east, south, and north gates. "No guard is needed at the west gate as the stream in front of it provides a natural safeguard," he added.

Kuai Yue said, "I notice that Zhao Yun never leaves him. It might be difficult to approach him."

"I have placed five hundred men in ambush in the city."

Kuai Yue said, "You can tell Wen Ping and Wang Wei to invite all the military officers to a banquet in the outer hall so as to separate Zhao Yun from his master. Then our opportunity will come."

Cai Mao thought this a good scheme to get Zhao Yun out of the way.

Meanwhile, oxen and horses were slaughtered and an enormous feast was prepared. Liu Bei rode to the banquet hall on his newly-acquired horse and when he arrived the steed was led into the back part of the enclosure and tethered there. Soon the guests also came, and Liu Bei took his place as the host between the two sons of the prefect. The guests were seated in order of rank. Zhao Yun stood near his lord, sword in hand.

Presently Wen Ping and Wang Wei came to invite Zhao Yun to the banquet they had prepared for the military officers, but he declined. However, Liu Bei told him to go and Zhao Yun reluctantly agreed.

Outside the banquet hall, Cai Mao had made every possible arrangement and the whole place was as tight as an iron barrel. Liu Bei's three hundred guards were all sent back to the guesthouse. Everything was ready and Cai Mao was only waiting for the wine to go a few more rounds before he would give the signal for action.

At the third course, Yi Ji took a goblet of wine in his hand and approached Liu Bei. With a meaningful look in his eyes, Yi Ji whispered to him, "Make an excuse to get away."

Liu Bei understood and presently rose as if he needed to relieve himself and went outside. There he found Yi Ji, who had gone out to wait for him after pouring wine for the guests. Yi Ji then told him about Cai Mao's plot to kill him and that all the gates were guarded except the west gate. And he advised him to lose no time to escape.

Liu Bei was quite taken aback. However, he hastened to get hold of his Dilu horse, opened the door of the garden, and led it out. Then he took a flying leap into the saddle and galloped off, without waiting for his escort. He made straight for the west gate. At the gate the wardens wanted to question him, but he only whipped up his steed and rode through. The guards at the gate ran to report to Cai Mao, who quickly went in pursuit with five hundred soldiers.

After he burst out of the west gate, Liu Bei was soon face to face with a big stream barring his way of escape. It was the Tan River, many score of feet in width, which pours its water into the Xiang River. Its current was very swift.

Liu Bei reached the bank and saw the river was unfordable. So he turned his horse and rode back. Then, not far off, he saw a cloud of dust and knew that his pursuers were coming. He thought that it was all over. In despair he turned again toward the swift river and, seeing the soldiers now quite near, plunged into the stream. After a few paces, he felt the horse's forelegs floundering, while the water rose over the skirt of his robe. Then he plied his whip furiously, crying, "Dilu, Dilu, don't harm me today!"

Whereupon the good steed suddenly reared up out of the water and, with one tremendous leap, was on the western bank. Liu Bei felt as if he had come out of the clouds.

In later years the famous poet, Su Dongpo,* wrote a poem on this leap over the Tan River:

> *I'm growing old, the leaves are bare,*
> *The sun sloping westward, soon will sink,*
> *And I recall that yester year*
> *I wandered by Tan River brink.*
> *Irresolute, anon I paused,*
> *Anon advanced, and gazed around,*
> *I marked the autumn's reddened leaves,*
> *And watched them eddying to the ground.*
> *I thought of all the mighty deeds*
> *Of him who set the House of Han*
> *On high, and all the struggles since,*
> *The battlefields, the blood that ran.*
> *I saw the nobles gather round*
> *The board, set in the banquet hall;*
> *Amid them, one, above whose head*
> *There hung a sword about to fall.*
> *I saw him quit that festive throng*
> *And westward ride, a lonely way;*
> *I saw a squadron follow swift,*
> *Intent the fugitive to slay.*
> *I saw him reach the River Tan*
> *Whose swirling current rushes by;*
> *Toward the bank he galloped fast,*
> *"Now leap, my steed!" I heard him cry.*
> *His steed's hoofs churn the swollen stream;*
> *What wrecks he that the waves run high?*
> *He hears the sound of clashing steel,*
> *Of thundering squadrons coming nigh.*
> *And upward from the foaming waves*
> *I saw two peerless beings soar;*
> *One was a destined western king,*
> *And him another dragon bore.*
> *The Tan still rolls from east to west,*
> *Its roaring torrent ne'er dry.*
> *Those dragons twain, Ah! where are they?*
> *Yes, where? But there is no reply.*

---

* (A.D. 1037–1101), one of the most important poets of Song Dynasty.

The setting sun, in dark relief
Against the glowing western sky,
Throws out the everlasting hills
While, saddened, here I stand and sigh.
Men died to found the kingdoms three
Which now as misty dreams remain.
Of greatest deeds the traces oft
Are faint that fleeting years retain.

Thus Liu Bei crossed the rolling stream. Then he turned and looked back at the other bank that his pursuers had just gained.

"Why did you run away from the feast, sir?" cried Cai Mao.

"Why do you wish to harm one who has done you no injury?" replied Liu Bei.

"I have never thought of such a thing—do not listen to what people say to you."

But Liu Bei saw that his enemy was fitting an arrow to his bowstring, so he whipped up his steed and rode away toward the southwest.

"What god aided him?" said Cai Mao to his followers.

Then he turned to go back to the city, but then he saw Zhao Yun coming out of the west gate at the head of his company of guards.

By wondrous leap the dragon steed his rider's life could save,
Now follows him, on vengeance bent, his master's warrior brave.

The fate of Cai Mao will be told in the next chapter.

CHAPTER THIRTY-FIVE

Liu Bei Meets a Recluse at Nanyang
Shan Fu Finds a Noble Lord at Xinye

Just as Cai Mao was going into the city he met Zhao Yun and his three hundred soldiers. Now Zhao Yun, who was drinking with the other military officers, had noticed some movements of men and horses and had at once gone into the banquet hall to see if all was well with his lord. To his great shock he found Liu Bei missing from his seat. He had become extremely anxious and rushed back to the guesthouse to look for him. There, he heard that Cai Mao had gone off to the west gate with troops. So he quickly took his spear, mounted his horse, and went with the escort in hot haste along the same road. Seeing Cai Mao near the gate he asked, "Where is my lord?"

"He left the banquet hall quite suddenly and I do not know where he has gone," was the reply.

Now Zhao Yun was a man of prudence and had no desire to act hastily, so he urged his horse forward till he came to the river. There he was checked by a wide stream, without ford or bridge. At once he turned back and questioned Cai Mao sternly: "You invited my lord to a feast—what do you mean by going after him with armed troops?"

Cai Mao replied, "All the officials of the nine districts have assembled here. As chief officer I am responsible for their safety."

"Where have you driven my lord?" asked Zhao Yun.

"They told me he rode quite alone out through the west gate but when I came here I did not see him."

Zhao Yun was anxious and doubtful. Again he rode to the river and looked around. This time he noticed a wet track on the other side of the stream. He thought to himself, "Could it be that both my lord and his horse have leaped across the river...?" And he ordered his men to scatter and search, but they could find no trace of Liu Bei.

Zhao Yun turned again toward the city. By that time, however, Cai Mao had gone within. He then questioned the gate wardens and they all said that Liu Bei had ridden out at full gallop. That was all they knew. He would like to re-enter the city but was afraid lest he should fall into an ambush, so he started for home.

After that marvelous life-saving leap over the surging waves, Liu Bei felt elated but rather dazed. He could not help feeling that his safety was due to a special intervention of providence. Following a tortuous path, he urged his steed toward Nanzhang. Dusk was falling and the sun was waning in the west, but his destination seemed yet a long way off. As he was riding along he saw a young cowherd seated on the back of a buffalo, playing on a short flute.

"If I were only as happy!" sighed Liu Bei.

He reined in his steed and looked at the lad who stopped his beast, ceased playing on the instrument, and stared back at the stranger.

"You must be General Liu Xuan-de, who overcame the Yellow Turbans," said the boy presently.

Liu Bei could not believe his ears.

"How can you know my name, a mere lad like you living in such a secluded place?" he asked incredulously.

"Of course I do not know you but my master often has visitors and they all mention Liu Bei, a man of medium height whose hands hang down below his knees and whose eyes are able to see his own ears. They say that he is the real hero of the day. Now you, General, look exactly the same as the man they talk about and so I think you must be he."

"Well, who is your master?"

"My master's surname is Sima, a compound surname, and his given name is Hui. He is a native of Yingchuan and his Taoist title is Shui Jing, or Water Mirror."

"Who are your master's friends, then?"

"They are Pang De-gong and Pang Tong of Xiangyang."

"And what is the relationship between these two?" asked Liu Bei.

"Uncle and nephew. Pang De-gong is ten years older than my master and the other is five years younger. One day my master was up in a mulberry tree plucking the leaves, when Pang Tong arrived. He seated himself under the tree and they began to talk. All through the day they talked just like that, with one up in the tree and the other underneath, without betraying any sign of fatigue. My master is very fond of Pang Tong and calls him 'younger brother.'"

"And where does your master live?"

"His farm house is right there in the wood ahead," said the cowherd, pointing to it.

"I am Liu Bei. Take me to your master so that I can pay my respects to him."

The lad led the way for about two *li* to a farm house. Liu Bei dismounted and went to the gate in the center. There he was greeted by the melodious sound of a lute played most skillfully and the music was extremely beautiful. He told his guide not to announce him then and stood there rapt by the melody.

Suddenly the music ceased. He heard laughter inside and a man soon appeared.

"Amidst the clear and subtle notes of the lute there suddenly rang out a high note and I know some noble man must have come," said the man.

"That is my master," said the lad, pointing to the man.

Liu Bei saw before him a very superior figure, slender and straight as a pine tree. Hastening forward, he bowed to him. The skirt of his robe was still wet from the leap over the river.

"You have escaped from a grave danger today, sir," said Sima Hui.

Liu Bei was startled. The lad said to his master, "This is Liu Bei."

Sima Hui asked him to enter and when they took their seats respectively as host and guest, Liu Bei glanced around the room. Piled on the shelves were many volumes of books and upon a stone couch lay a lute. From the window emerged a fine picture of pines and bamboo. The whole room breathed of refinement to its last degree.

"Where did you come from, sir?" asked the host.

"I happened to be passing this area and the lad guided me here so I was able to pay my respects to you, sir. I cannot tell what great pleasure it gives me."

His host laughed. "You do not have to conceal the truth from me, sir. I know you must have just escaped from a grave danger."

Then Liu Bei could no longer hold back the truth and so the story of the banquet and the flight was told.

"I knew it all from your appearance," said his host. "Your name has long been familiar. But why is it that up to the present you are still unsettled?"

"I have suffered many setbacks in my life," replied Liu Bei, "and so I am still down in the mire."

"It should not be so—but the reason is that you lack the right person to aid you."

"I am common enough myself, I know. But I have Sun Qian, Mi Zhu, and Jian Yong on the civil side, and for warriors I have Guan Yu, Zhang Fei, and Zhao Yun. These are all most loyal helpers and I depend upon them greatly."

"Your fighting men are good, each able to oppose 10,000 men. The pity is you have no really able advisor to bring the best out of them. Your civilians are but pallid students of books, not men fitted to weave and control destiny."

"I have also yearned to find one of those wise recluses who live among the hills. So far I have sought in vain."

"You know what the great master Confucius said: 'In a hamlet of ten households there must be one true man.' Can you say that there is none?"

"I am foolish and uninstructed—I pray you enlighten me."

"You have heard what the street boys sing:

> *In eight and nine begins decay,*
> *Four years, then comes the fateful day,*
> *When destiny will show the way,*
> *And the dragon flies out of the mire straight!*

"This song was first heard when the new reigning title Jian An was adopted. The first line refers to the eighth year of Jian An, when Liu Biao lost his first wife and his family troubles began. The next line relates to the approaching death of Liu Biao and the dispersing of his crowd of officers. The last two lines will be fulfilled by you, General."

Liu Bei was surprised, yet pleased. He thanked him and said, "How dare I attempt to be that?"

Sima Hui continued, "At this moment the most remarkable talents of the land are all here and you, sir, ought to seek them."

"Where can I find them? And who are they?" asked Liu Bei eagerly.

"If you could get either Fulong (Sleeping Dragon) or Fengchu (Phoenix Fledgling) to aid you, the empire will be yours."

"But who are these men?"

His host clapped his hands, laughed and said, "Good, very good."

When Liu Bei asked again, his host said, "It is getting late. You can spend the night here, General, and we will talk over these things tomorrow."

He called the lad to bring wine and food for his guest and take his horse to the stable to be fed. After Liu Bei had eaten he was shown to a chamber beside the hall. He went to bed but he could hardly get to sleep, for the words of his host would not be banished. Suddenly he became fully awake at the sound of a knock at the door and a person entering. And he heard his host say, "Where are you from, Yuan-zhi?"

Liu Bei rose from his couch and listened secretly. He heard the man reply, "It has long been said that Liu Biao liked good men and despised bad men. So I went to see for myself. But that reputation is undeserved. He does like good men but he can't use them, and indeed he hates wicked men, but he doesn't dismiss them. So I left a letter for him and came away—and here I am."

Sima Hui replied, "You are capable enough to be the advisor of a king and you ought to be able to find someone fit to serve. Why did you demean yourself by going to Liu Biao? Besides, there is a real hero right under your eyes and you don't know him."

"You're absolutely right," replied the stranger.

Liu Bei listened with great joy, for he thought this visitor was certainly one of the two geniuses he was advised to look for. He would have shown himself then and there but he feared he might be intruding. So he waited till daylight, when he sought out his host and asked, "Who was it that came last night?"

"A friend of mine," was the reply.

Liu Bei begged for an introduction. His host said, "He wants to find an enlightened master to serve and so he has gone elsewhere."

When he asked him about the visitor's name the host only replied, "Good, good." And when he tried to find out who Fulong and Fengchu were, all he could get from his host was the same mysterious reply.

Then, bowing low before his host, Liu Bei begged him to leave the hills and help him restore the House of Han. Sima Hui replied, "Men of the hills are unequal to such a task. However, there must be men far abler than me who will help you if you seek them."

While they were talking they heard outside the farm men shouting and horses neighing, and a servant came in to say that a general with a large company of men had arrived. Liu Bei went out hastily to see who it was and found it was Zhao Yun and his men. He was much relieved and pleased. Zhao Yun dismounted and entered the house.

"Last night when I returned to our city," said Zhao Yun, "I could not find you, my lord, so I followed at once and traced you here. Please return quickly as I fear there might be an attack on the city."

So Liu Bei took leave of his host and the whole company returned to Xinye. Before they had gone far another troop appeared and, when they had come nearer, they saw it was Guan Yu and Zhang Fei. They met each other with great joy and Liu Bei told them of the wonderful leap his horse had made over the river. All marveled at the miracle.

As soon as they reached the city a council was called and Sun Qian said, "You ought first of all to send a letter to Liu Biao explaining what happened."

The letter was prepared and Sun Qian bore it to Jingzhou, where he was received by Liu Biao, who asked him the reason for Liu Bei's hasty flight from the festival. Then the letter was presented and Sun Qian related the intrigue of Cai Mao and his master's miraculous escape. The furious prefect sent for Cai Mao at once and berated him soundly.

"How dare you try to hurt my brother?" and he ordered him out to be executed.

Liu Biao's wife, Cai Mao's sister, prayed with tears for a remission of the death penalty, but Liu Biao refused to be appeased. At this moment Sun Qian interposed. "If you put Cai Mao to death I fear my master will be unable to remain here."

Cai Mao was reprieved but dismissed with a severe reprimand.

Liu Biao sent his elder son back with Sun Qian to apologize. When he reached Xinye, Liu Bei welcomed him and gave a banquet in his honor. After they had been drinking for some time, Liu Qi, the elder son of the prefect, suddenly began to weep. Liu Bei asked him why and he said, "My stepmother is always attempting to put me out of the way, and I don't know how to avoid the danger. Could you advise me, uncle?"

Liu Bei exhorted him to be perfectly filial and nothing would happen.

The next day the young man took his leave and wept at parting. Liu Bei escorted him outside the city and, pointing to his steed, said, "I owe my life to this horse—had it not been for it I would have been a dead man."

"It wasn't the strength of the horse but your extraordinary good fortune, Uncle."

They parted, the young man weeping heartbrokenly. On re-entering the city, Liu Bei met a person in the street wearing a hemp turban, a cotton robe held by a black sash, and black shoes. He was singing a song.

> *The universe is riven, alas! now nears the end of all,*
> *The noble mansion quakes, alas! what beam can stay the fall?*
> *A wise one waits his lord, alas! but hidden in the glen,*
> *The seeker knows not him, alas! nor me, of common men.*

Liu Bei listened. "Surely this is one of the men Sima Hui spoke of," he thought.

He dismounted to greet the singer and invited him into his residence. Then, when they were seated, he asked the stranger's name.

"I am from Yingchuan and my name is Shan Fu. I have known you by reputation for a long time and they say you appreciate men of ability. I wanted to come to you but I hesitated lest I was intruding. So I thought of attracting your notice by singing that song in the market place."

Liu Bei thought he had found a treasure and treated the newcomer with the greatest respect. Then Shan Fu spoke of the horse that he had seen Liu Bei riding and asked to look at it again. So the animal was brought round.

"Is this not a Dilu?' said Shan Fu. "But though it is a good steed it will bring danger to its master. You must not ride it."

"He has already fulfilled the omen," said Liu Bei and he related the story of that miraculous leap across the wide stream.

"But this was saving its master, not harming him—he will surely harm someone in the end. But I can tell you how to avert the omen."

"I should be glad to hear it," said Liu Bei.

"If you have an enemy against whom you bear a grudge, give him the horse and wait till the evil omen is fulfilled on this man. Then you can ride it in safety."

Liu Bei changed color. "What, sir! You are but a newcomer and yet, instead of leading me to the road of virtue, you advise me to take an evil course and to harm another for my own advantage? No, sir! I do not want to hear your advice."

His guest smiled. "People said you were virtuous but I was still dubious, so I put it that way to test you."

Liu Bei became polite again. He rose and returned the compliment. "But how can I be virtuous while I lack your teaching?" he said modestly.

"When I came here, I heard people singing: 'Since Liu came, oh blessed is the day! We've had good luck—long may he stay!' So you see, your virtue has benefited the ordinary people."

Then Shan Fu was made chief military advisor of the army.

After his sweeping victory in the north Cao Cao had often nursed the thought of capturing Jingzhou. He sent Cao Ren and Li Dian, with the two Lu brothers, to camp at Fancheng with 30,000 men so as to pose a threat against Liu Biao's region and to spy on his actual strength.

The two Lus said to Cao Ren: "Liu Bei is strengthening his position at Xinye and bringing in large supplies. He is ambitious and should be dealt with as soon as possible. Since our surrender we have not performed any noteworthy service—if you will give us 5,000 men, we promise to bring you the head of Liu Bei."

Cao Ren was only too glad and the expedition set out. The scouts reported this to Liu Bei, who turned to Shan Fu for advice.

Shan Fu said, "We must not let the enemy get into our city. Send your two brothers to lay an ambush on the right and the left, one to attack the enemy in the middle of their march, and the other to cut off the retreat. You and Zhao Yun will make a front attack."

The two brothers started out, while Liu Bei went out of the gate with 2,000 men to oppose the enemy. Before they had gone far they saw a great cloud of dust behind the hills. This marked the approach of the Lu brothers. When both sides had formed a battle array, Liu Bei rode out and stood by his standard. He called out, "Who are you that dare to encroach on my territory?"

"I am the great general Lu Kuang, and I have the prime minister's order to capture you," said the leader.

Liu Bei ordered Zhao Yun to go out and the two engaged. Very soon Zhao Yun had disposed of his opponent and Liu Bei gave the signal to advance. Lu Xiang could not maintain his position and fell back. Soon, his men found themselves attacked from the side by a force led by Guan Yu. The losses were very heavy and the remainder fled for safety.

About ten *li* farther on they found their retreat barred by an army under Zhang Fei, who stood in the way with a long spear ready to thrust. Crying out who he was, he bore down upon Lu Xiang, who was slain without a chance of striking a blow. His men again fled in disorder. They were pursued by Liu Bei and most of them were captured.

Then Liu Bei returned to his own city, where he rewarded Shan Fu very handsomely and entertained his victorious soldiers with feasts.

Some of the defeated men took the news of the deaths of the two Lus and the capture of their comrades to Cao Ren. Much distressed, Cao Ren consulted his colleague, Li Dian, who advised him to stay where they were and hold on until reinforcements from the capital could arrive.

"No," objected Cao Ren. "We cannot sit idly at the death of our two officers and the loss of so many men. We must avenge them quickly. Xinye is a poor place and not worth disturbing the prime minister for."

"Liu Bei is an extraordinary figure," said Li Dian. "Don't take him lightly."

"What are you afraid of?" sneered Cao Ren.

"The *Art of War* says, 'To know your enemy and yourself is the secret of victory.'" replied Li Dian. "I'm not afraid of fighting the battle but I'm not sure if we can win."

"You want to rebel?" cried Cao Ren angrily. "Then I will capture Liu Bei myself."

"If you go I will guard this city," said Li Dian.

"If you don't go with me, then you really are rebelling," retorted Cao Ren.

At this reproach, Li Dian felt compelled to join the expedition. So they led all their men to cross the river and marched toward Xinye.

> *Feeling keenly the shame of his officers and men slain,*
> *Their chief determines on revenge and marches out again.*

The result of the expedition will be told in the next chapter.

Continued in Volume Two of *The Three Kingdoms.*

About the Authors

Ron Iverson first visited China in 1984 as the personal representative of the Mayor of Chicago as part of a Sister Cities program. For the past 30 years he has continued to regularly visit China and has founded joint business ventures with Chinese partners and taught Business Strategy at Tongji University in Shanghai. He also personally arranged the first ever exhibition of Forbidden City artifacts from the palace Museum in Beijing to tour the US.

Early in his visits to China, Iverson discovered *The Three Kingdoms* and came to realize the enormous cultural significance the Chinese people place in the book. Believing that one needed to be familiar with the principles revealed in the book in order to find business or political success in China, and being dissatisfied with existing translations, Iverson decided to fund and edit a new translation aimed towards delivering the thrill of a contemporary novel while imparting understanding of a key aspect of Chinese culture.

Yu Sumei is a professor of English at East China Normal University. She has translated several English language books into Chinese and is the first native Chinese speaker to translate *The Three Kingdoms* into English. She invested a total of two years into working on this new translation of *The Three Kingdoms*, spending the time on sabbatical in New York with her daughter, who typed the translation out as she completed it.

"Books to Span the East and West"

Tuttle Publishing was founded in 1832 in the small New England town of Rutland, Vermont [USA]. Our core values remain as strong today as they were then—to publish best-in-class books which bring people together one page at a time. In 1948, we established a publishing office in Japan—and Tuttle is now a leader in publishing English-language books about the arts, languages and cultures of Asia. The world has become a much smaller place today and Asia's economic and cultural influence has grown. Yet the need for meaningful dialogue and information about this diverse region has never been greater. Over the past seven decades, Tuttle has published thousands of books on subjects ranging from martial arts and paper crafts to language learning and literature—and our talented authors, illustrators, designers and photographers have won many prestigious awards. We welcome you to explore the wealth of information available on Asia at **www.tuttlepublishing.com**.